EPIC

Book

Epic Zero 7: Tales of a Long Lost Leader

Epic Zero 8: Tales of a Colossal Boy Blunder

Epic Zero 9: Tales of a Souled-Out Superhero

By

R.L. Ullman

Cover designs and character illustrations by Yusup Mediyan

Published by But That's Another Story… Press
Ridgefield, CT

Printed in the United States of America.

First Printing, 2021.

ISBN: 978-1-953713-10-0
Library of Congress Control Number: 2021918620

For Matthew,
my Meta 4

BOOKS BY R.L. ULLMAN

EPIC ZERO SERIES

Epic Zero: Tales of a Not-So-Super 6th Grader
Epic Zero Extra (free at rlullman.com)
Epic Zero 2: Tales of a Pathetic Power Failure
Epic Zero 3: Tales of a Super Lame Last Hope
Epic Zero 4: Tales of a Total Waste of Time
Epic Zero 5: Tales of an Unlikely Kid Outlaw
Epic Zero 6: Tales of a Major Meta Disaster
Epic Zero 7: Tales of a Long Lost Leader
Epic Zero 8: Tales of a Colossal Boy Blunder
Epic Zero 9: Tales of a Souled-Out Superhero
Epic Zero 10: Tales of a Seriously Sore Loser
Epic Zero 11: Tales of a Mere Meta Mortal
Epic Zero 12: Tales of a Cosmic Catastrophe
Epic Zero: The Epic Character Guide

MONSTER PROBLEMS SERIES

Monster Problems: Vampire Misfire
Monster Problems 2: Down for the Count
Monster Problems 3: Prince of Dorkness

UNLEGENDARY DRAGON SERIES

Unlegendary Dragon: The Magical Kids of Lore
Unlegendary Dragon 2: The Fall of Camelot
Unlegendary Dragon 3: The Battle for Avalon

TABLE OF CONTENTS

Epic Zero 7: Tales of a Long Lost Leader

ONE

I DISPLAY MY MAD SKILLS

If things go according to plan this should be awesome.

Ten minutes ago, I got an alert from the Meta Monitor about a break-in at the Keystone City Museum. That gives us approximately seven minutes to beat the Freedom Force to the scene of the crime. They won't be expecting us, but I guess that's the advantage of being a member of two superhero teams. When evil flares up, I now have twice the chance of snuffing it out first.

Fortunately, we were already in the neighborhood eating ice cream a few blocks away. And since the Freedom Force will be dropping in from outer space, we'll easily get the jump on them. Boy, I can't wait to see Grace's face when she realizes we've already put the bad guy in handcuffs. I just hope someone gets it on camera.

But what'll be even better is if Dad is with them. Because if he is, then it will be the first time the leader of the Freedom Force and the leader of Next Gen showed up for the very same mission. And who is that brave, devilishly handsome new leader of Next Gen?

Oh yeah, that's me.

Truthfully, I still can't believe I've got my very own superhero team. I take in the faces of my teammates running beside me. All of them are focused. Determined. Ready to show the world what we can do. I can just see Dad looking at me with pride and saying something profound like—

"I've gotta go wee-wee."

Um, what?

"Seriously, Pinball?" Skunk Girl says. "Like, now?"

"I can't hold it," Pinball says, bouncing to a stop behind us. "I drank a whole milkshake before that alert came in. Can you guys just wait a sec? I don't know this area of town very well." Then, he bounds off into the nearest alley.

"But the bad guy will get away!" I call out, but it's no use. I run my hands through my hair. Well, there goes our time advantage. Now we'll never beat the Freedom Force to the scene. Sometimes I wonder why I bother getting out of bed.

"I knew we shouldn't have stopped for ice cream," Selfie says. "His bladder is even smaller than his brain."

Just then, I hear a tinkling sound to my left, and when I look down Dog-Gone is relieving himself on an unfortunate fire hydrant.

"You too, huh?" I say. "What a surprise."

This couldn't have happened at a worse time because this was our big chance to establish ourselves. I mean, if the Meta community is going to take us seriously we'll have to prove ourselves on the battlefield, not in the bathroom.

And so far our track record is less than stellar.

To date, our first and only real mission as a formal team was against Erase Face and that was almost a complete disaster. Erase Face is a Meta 1 villain who can erase things for good with his nose. I warned the team not to approach him head-on, but that didn't stop Skunk Girl from nearly losing her fingers, or Pinball from nearly losing his backside. Thank goodness for Selfie who blinded Erase Face with her magic phone while I neutralized his powers.

And Erase Face is only a Meta 1!

Since this mission will be far more dangerous maybe Pinball's bladder issue is a sign. Maybe we should pack up and go home before things get out of hand. After all, the Meta Monitor identified the perpetrator as a Meta 2.

"So, boss-man," Skunk Girl says, tapping her foot impatiently, "while we're waiting for pin-head can you run through this creep's background again?"

"Sure," I say, picturing his Meta profile in my mind.

"His name is Lunatick, and he's a Meta 2 Energy Manipulator with a toxic bite. He once was an archaeologist specializing in Egyptian ruins, but during one of his excavations, he was bitten by a strange, radioactive tick. The tick's venom took over his system, turning him into a Meta 2 bad guy with eight legs and a radioactive bite. Over time, the venom also messed with his mind, making him certifiably nuts. Hence, the name Luna-tick, as in 'Lunatic.' He's unpredictable, so let's try to be more careful this time."

"Understood," Skunk Girl says, flexing her fingers.

"Okay," Pinball says, bouncing out of the alley. "Sorry about that. You know, I really need to put a zipper in this costume."

"TMI," Selfie says. "Now let's go. We've lost a lot of time."

We take off again, but in my mind, we've 'lost' way more than time, because I'm betting the Freedom Force is already on the scene.

As we round the corner onto Main Street, I spot the Keystone City Museum in the distance. It's a large building that sort of looks like a giant seashell, with a domed roof and smooth, curved sides. But the impressive exterior isn't what has my attention, because I'm focused on the huge hole near the entrance where dozens of museumgoers are streaming outside.

"I think we're the first ones here," Selfie says. "I don't even see the police."

I scan the area and realize she's right. There aren't any cops, and more importantly, there aren't any heroes either. So, that means we still have a chance! But we've got to act fast.

"Follow me!" I yell. "And no more stopping!"

We race past the panicked crowd and through the large hole into the museum's cavernous entrance hall. That's when we see two security guards lying on the ground—and they're not moving.

"They're still breathing," Selfie says, checking on them. "They're just unconscious."

That's great news but I'm not surprised they're down for the count. I mean, Lunatick is a dangerous character. But when I scan the place there's no one around except for us and a giant Woolly Mammoth statue. Where did Lunatick go?

"What now?" Pinball asks, looking around. "Last year my class took a field trip here and this museum is ginormous. There's like a hall for everything."

I grab a map off the front desk and study it. It's been a while since I've been to the museum, but I know Pinball is right. There's a Hall of Meteorites, a Hall of Ocean Life, a Hall of American Mammals, and so much more. Where do we start? And why is Lunatick even here?

"Hey, look up," Selfie says, pointing to a large banner hanging from the ceiling. "This museum has a temporary exhibit of King Totenhotem's Tomb! And according to the banner, it opened today."

King Totenhotem's Tomb? King Tot? I remember studying King Tot in social studies class. He was an Egyptian kid pharaoh who died under mysterious circumstances. I stare at the giant image of King Tot's face and then look down at my map.

Then, everything clicks.

"This way!" I say, taking off to our right.

"Where are you going?" Skunk Girl calls out.

"To the Hall of Ancient Egypt," I say. "That's where King Tot's exhibit is located. Lunatick was an archaeologist, remember? I bet he's after something there. Now let's, um, squash that bug!"

Note to self: One thing I desperately need to do is come up with a good battle cry for our team. Before a fight, Dad always yells: "Freedom Force—It's Fight Time!" I tried using it for us, but it just didn't seem right. We need our own battle cry, but at the moment I've got nothing even close to that good.

To get to the Hall of Ancient Egypt, we first have to pass through the Hall of Biodiversity and its garden of rare plants, the Hall of Jurassic Dinosaurs and its giant T-Rex statue (which nearly gives me PTSD by the way), and the Hall of Meteorites with its giant map of the solar system. Then, we book down a flight of steps, swing around a corner, and find ourselves standing in front of the Hall of Ancient Egypt.

Over the door is a banner that reads: *King Tot Exhibit: Treasure of the Golden Kid Pharaoh. Ticket Holders Only.*

"He must be in there," I whisper. "Let's go inside."

"But we can't," Pinball whispers back, pointing to the sign. "We don't have tickets."

"Skunk Girl," I say, "feel free to slap him silly."

"Noted," she says.

"Now follow me," I say, "and remember, he's dangerous." I tiptoe through the entrance into a large chamber filled with hundreds of solid gold artifacts displayed inside glass cases. There are gold animal statues, gold musical instruments, gold dishware, and loads of other gold objects. As I pass through I realize this exhibit must be worth an absolute fortune.

But surprisingly, none of it looks disturbed. For some reason, Lunatick didn't want any of this stuff.

GRRRR.

I turn to find Dog-Gone staring at the statue of a life-sized, gold cat.

"Quiet," I whisper, clamping his muzzle shut. It's times like these I wish dogs came with a mute button.

Then, I notice there's another doorway on the far side of the room. A plaque above the entrance reads: *King Tot's Royal Sarcophagus.* Lunatick has to be in there.

I signal to the rest of the team and they nod. This is a time for maximum stealth. We got lucky he didn't hear Dog-Gone the first time, so now we've got to—

CRASH!

What was that? I spin around to find Pinball standing next to a tipped garbage can.

"Sorry," he whispers. "It didn't see me coming."

Just. Freaking. Wonderful.

Well, so much for the element of surprise.

"Okay, Next Gen," I say. "There's no hiding us now. Let's rock!"

"Let's *rock*?" Skunk Girl repeats dryly. "Can't you be more original than that?"

"I'll work on it later," I say. "Right now, we've got to focus on the task at—"

THOOM!

But before we can reach the next room, a bizarre insect-man bursts through the entranceway and lands directly in front of us! It's Lunatick, and he's way bigger than I expected! His round, insect body is wider than a refrigerator, and his swollen, human face stares at us with surprise. Then, I notice he's holding a golden staff in one of his eight legs, and the staff ends in the shape of an Egyptian ankh. That's King Tot's staff!

"Drop the artifact!" I command. "You're under arrest!"

"Well, what do we have here?" Lunatick says, seemingly amused by our presence. "Is the museum holding a preschool costume party?"

"Not funny," I reply, "and, well, actually rather insulting. No, we're Next Gen, and we're taking you down."

"I really don't have time for this," Lunatick says, jumping up and sticking to the ceiling. "So, if you'll excuse me, I'll just be crawling on my way now."

"Okay, team," I say, "here's the plan." But before I can utter another word, Pinball blurts out—

"I've got him!" And then he inflates his body into a giant ball and bounces up towards Lunatick.

"Pinball!" I yell. "Look—"

But Lunatick rears back and swats Pinball with the staff like he was backhanding a tennis ball.

"—out!" I finish.

"Duck!" Selfie yells as Pinball careens all over the room, shattering exhibit after exhibit until he finally wedges face-first into a display case!

"Help!" his muffled voice calls out. "I'm stuck!"

Something tells me this little outing just got more expensive than my piggy bank can afford.

"My turn!" Skunk Girl says, aiming her hands at Lunatick. But as her obnoxious scent hits Lunatick's nostrils it has the opposite effect of what was intended.

"My, that is delightful," Lunatick says, dropping to the ground and inhaling deep. "Perhaps you can bottle that fragrance for me and I can take it to go?" Then, he smashes through a display case, pulls out a gold vase, and flings it at Skunk Girl, hitting her hard on the shoulder.

Skunk Girl collapses in a heap.

"Skunk Girl!" Selfie cries, rushing to her side.

Well, this mission has quickly spiraled out of control, just like the last one. If I don't put an end to it now someone could get seriously hurt.

But when I turn to face Lunatick, he's gone! And so is Dog-Gone! I just catch the tip of his tail before he bolts out of the room after Lunatick.

"Dog-Gone, wait!"

But not surprisingly, he doesn't listen either.

"Selfie, help the others!" I say. "I'll get Lunatick!"

I race out of the room but Lunatick and Dog-Gone are long gone. Fortunately, they left a clear trail to follow! I climb back up the stairs and race through a huge hole in the Hall of Meteorites where Mars used to be, past a pile of T-Rex bones in the Hall of Jurassic Dinosaurs, and over several trampled rare plant species in the Hall of Biodiversity. Seconds later, I'm back in the entrance hall where I find Dog-Gone playing tug-of-war with Lunatick over the golden staff!

"Let go!" Lunatick yells, pulling at the staff with four legs. "I've spent my life searching for King Tot's tomb and this staff is worth a fortune on the black market! I'm not going to let some stupid mutt take it from me!"

But Dog-Gone doesn't yield and drops lower to the ground to gain more leverage.

"I warned you!" Lunatick says. "Now come closer and I'll show you what a real bite feels like!" Then, he opens his mouth, which is glowing with green energy, and reaches for Dog-Gone with two of his other legs!

"Dog-Gone!" I yell, but I'm too far away!

Lunatick is going to sink his toxic teeth into Dog-Gone! I'm about to negate his radioactive toxins when—

"Did someone call for an exterminator?" comes a familiar girl's voice.

Suddenly, a crimson streak flashes through the museum entrance and CRASHES into Lunatick, sending him flying. Lunatick SLAMS into the wall hard and sticks to the surface. Then, Grace lands next to me.

"Needed some help, huh?" she says, putting her arm around my shoulder.

That's when I notice Lunatick isn't holding the staff anymore. Dog-Gone has it!

"Fools!" Lunatick yells. "That artifact is mine!"

"I don't think so," comes a booming voice.

I turn to see Dad standing in the entranceway, flanked by the Freedom Force! "That staff belongs to the King Tot Foundation."

Great. We ran out of time before we could get the job done. Some leader I am.

"Now, you can either make this easy and surrender," Dad says, "or things could get ugly."

Just then, the rest of my team shows up.

"Wow, it's the Freedom Force!" Selfie says.

"Um, are you really Glory Girl?" Pinball asks Grace, staring at her wide-eyed with his jaw hanging open.

"Yeah," I say. "It's her. Why are you flipping out?"

"Never!" Lunatick responds to Dad.

"I was hoping you'd say that," Dad says, cracking his knuckles. "Freedom Force—It's Fight Time!"

"Now that's what a cool battle cry sounds like,"

Skunk Girl says, jabbing me in the arm.

***

Less than a minute later, the Freedom Force has wrapped everything up. Master Mime has Lunatick in four pairs of energy handcuffs, TechnocRat is tending to Skunk Girl's shoulder, and I'm sitting on the floor with the rest of my team wondering what went wrong. At least Dog-Gone was a hero today, although we can't even take credit for that because he hasn't officially joined our team.

So, I'd say this was pretty much an epic failure.

"Epic Zero," Dad calls from across the room. "Can we talk to you for a minute?"

And now I suspect it's about to get even worse.

"First of all, are you okay?" Dad asks as I approach.

"Yeah," I say. "I'm fine."

"Great," Dad says. "Lunatick is a Meta 2 villain, but I'm guessing you knew that, right?"

"Well, yeah," I say, looking at my feet.

"And your team has very little combat experience," Mom says. "Didn't you think this was more than you could handle? You're lucky Skunk Girl's injury wasn't more serious."

"I… I…," I stammer.

"Not to mention half the museum is destroyed," Dad adds. "Most of these things are irreplaceable."

"Yeah, I know," I say. "But Lunatick was—"

"—a dangerous villain," Dad says. "Too dangerous for your team to handle alone."

"Well, I… I mean, we…," I mutter.

Then, Mom and Dad exchange one of those looks that tells me they're having a private, telepathic conversation. And more often than not, those conversations end badly for me.

"Captain?" Blue Bolt calls out from across the room. "Can you look at this?"

"Coming," Dad says.

"We'll continue this later," Mom says.

"Yeah, fine," I say, slinking back over to my friends.

"What was that about?" Selfie asks.

"Oh, nothing good," I say. "Nothing good at all."

Meta Profile
Next Gen
Epic Zero
Class: Meta Manipulator
Meta :
Skunk Girl
Class: Energy Manipulator
Meta :
Selfie
Class: Magic
Meta :
Pinball
Class: Meta-Morph
Meta :

TWO

I RECEIVE SOME VERY BAD NEWS

There's nothing worse than waiting for the ax to fall.

I mean, it's been hours since my debacle at the Keystone City Museum. Of course, I offered to help with the cleanup but they said it would be best if my team and I went home. So, we said our goodbyes and now here I am, pacing anxiously on the Waystation 2.0 waiting for my parents to get back so we can finish our conversation.

The good news is Dad just got home after putting Lunatick in Lockdown. And Mom is on her way after working with the museum curators to assess all the damage we caused. Which means I know where my allowance will be going for the next hundred years.

I have so much on my mind I'd love to be alone.

But unfortunately, I'm not.

"So, wa' argh you gettin' merf for mye berfday?" Grace asks, talking with a mouth full of jelly doughnut.

"Um, what?" I say, barely catching a word.

"Holf on," she says, downing a glass of milk and wiping her chin with her sleeve. "I said, what are you getting me for my birthday? I'm turning fifteen in just a few days, remember? I'm expecting a big gift from you. Just a birthday card isn't going to cut it anymore."

"What?" I say, shocked we're even talking about this right now. "I don't know. Look, I'm a little preoccupied at the moment."

"Still thinking about your huge museum disaster, huh?" she says with a wry smile. "You screwed up. It happens."

"Gee, thanks," I say. "I know I screwed up, but I'm worried Mom and Dad aren't going to let this go. I think they might try to break up my team."

"For sure," Grace says, getting ready to take another bite of jelly doughnut. "You're all in over your heads."

"We are not!" I snap back.

"Seriously?" Grace says, looking at me like I have three heads. "Don't be a dufus and face the facts. You led an inexperienced team against a dangerous Meta 2 villain. What did you think would happen?"

"I… well, I…," I stammer. But truthfully, I don't have a great answer. I mean, she's right, what did I think would happen? Maybe I was being irresponsible.

"Now, let's get back to something more important," she says. "Like, what are you getting me for my birthday?"

"Elliott," comes Dad's voice over the intercom system, "please meet your mother and me in the Mission Room."

"Great," I say. "Well, I guess you can have my room for your birthday because apparently, I won't be needing it anymore."

"Awesome," she says. "I'll use it as a walk-in closet."

"Go for it," I say, heading into the hallway toward the Mission Room. As I walk, I feel like a prisoner heading for death row. I mean, based on Dad's stern tone, there's no way I'll escape without some kind of punishment. But I'll serve any sentence as long as they don't ask me to disband Next Gen.

Suddenly, something cold and wet nuzzles into my palm. "Hey, Dog-Gone," I say. "It's been nice knowing you. I hope you find a new master who isn't such a screw-up. Maybe try Shadow Hawk. He's got his act together."

Dog-Gone whimpers as I reach the Mission Room and see Mom and Dad sitting inside. "Stay out here, old boy," I say to Dog-Gone. "You don't want to see this."

Then, I go inside to face the music.

"Have a seat, son," Dad says, his expression serious.

As I plop into one of the chairs around the circular conference table, I glance at Mom to judge her demeanor but she looks just as serious as Dad. So, this is gonna be bad. As Dad opens his mouth, I brace myself for what's to come.

"Elliott," Dad says, "we want to have a conversation with you about leadership."

What? Did he just say they want to have a conversation with me about leadership? Seriously? That's it? "Um, sure," I say, sitting up straighter. "Great. Let's converse then. I love conversing."

"Being a leader is a big job," Dad says. "And at its core are two fundamental responsibilities. The first, of course, is accomplishing the mission at hand. But the second is less obvious but equally important, and that's looking out for the welfare of your team. In our business, we deal with life and death situations, and a leader must quickly assess if his or her team is even capable of handling the mission. And if the answer is 'no,' the leader must protect the team from unnecessary harm. Do you understand what I'm saying?"

"Yeah," I say, nodding. "You're saying we bit off more than we could chew. But the Freedom Force takes on every mission. It's easy for you because you don't have to worry about the capabilities of your team."

"I'll let you in on a little secret," Dad says. "I'm always worried about our team. Even though we're all capable heroes who have worked together for years, we're constantly learning how to be a better team. We encounter new threats every day, and I never stop thinking about how we'll handle certain situations. It's part of being a leader. Feeling too comfortable can be your undoing."

"Okay, I get it," I say, crossing my arms. "So, is that it? Is that all you wanted to tell me?"

Mom and Dad look at one another.

"No," Mom says. "Elliott, we don't think Next Gen is ready for action. We think it's great that you have Meta friends, and we think it would be good for you to get together to practice every once in a while, maybe even here in the Combat Room, but it's just not safe for you to be out in the real world taking on real Meta criminals."

"That's not fair!" I shoot back. "You just told me the Freedom Force is constantly learning how to be a better team. That's no different than us."

"That's true," Mom says, "but we are all established heroes in our own right. Your friends are just kids who are still learning how to use their powers."

"Well, this kid has already saved the universe a few times," I say, pointing to myself. "You know, in case it slipped your minds."

"Elliott," Mom says, "we know that. And that's why you're a member of the Freedom Force. But being a part of *our* team and leading a team of inexperienced heroes is not the same thing."

"So, just to be clear," I say, "you're saying you don't think I'm a good enough leader?"

"We're saying that you're still an inexperienced

leader," Dad says. "Leadership is a skill that takes time to develop, and until you get more experience it's simply not safe for you and your friends to be developing your skills on the fly and in public. What if Lunatick had hit Skunk Girl in the head with that vase instead of her shoulder?"

"Well...," I mutter.

"Or what if the museum was filled with people when you confronted Lunatick?" Dad continues.

"Well, I guess, um," I sputter.

"Leaders need to think these scenarios through," Dad says, "often before they even happen. Elliott, you have all the potential in the world to be a great leader, but you and your friends are still kids. You need to practice in a safe environment."

I open my mouth to respond, but nothing comes out. Deep down I know he's probably right, but I don't want to tell him that.

"Are we done?" I ask.

"Almost," Mom says. "We would like you to officially disband Next Gen."

"What?" I say. "Really?"

"Really," Dad says. "We know this isn't what you wanted to hear, but it's the right thing to do for the safety of everyone involved. Then, when you guys are older, you can get the band back together again."

"Are we finished conversing?" I say, standing up.

"Elliott—," Mom starts.

"No, I got the message loud and clear," I say.

"Thanks for the pep talk."

"Elliott, please understand," Dad says.

But I'm so upset I can't respond. As I walk out of the Mission Room I find Dog-Gone still standing there. He looks at me with sad eyes and whimpers. "Not now," I say, brushing past him. My blood is boiling and I just want to get as far away from my parents as possible.

I mean, I can't believe they want me to disband Next Gen! How overprotective can you get? They're not even giving us a chance to show what we can do. It's not fair.

As I wander through the halls I can just picture the reaction of the team when I tell them the news. I can see them staring at me with disappointment on their faces. And who's to say they won't just continue without me? I mean, they were already a team before they asked me to join them. They'll probably just say goodbye to me and keep on fighting.

Not that I'm a big help anyway.

Grace was right, the mission was a disaster. And I hate to admit it, but if Grace didn't get there when she did, I could have lost Dog-Gone. Breaking up Next Gen is the last thing I want, but maybe it's for the best.

Just then, I nearly crash into a huge object blocking my path. What the—?

I look up to find a giant, yellow brain suspended in clear goo inside a glass tube. It's spongy and absolutely disgusting. For a second, I'm totally confused. Did I just get transported to an alien planet? But when I look around I realize what happened.

I wandered into the Trophy Room.

The Trophy Room is a section on the Waystation that collects all sorts of interesting—and sometimes dangerous—mementos from the Freedom Force's various missions. Ironically, I guess it's sort of like a museum itself, with hundreds of items on display. The Trophy Room used to be even larger, but what's here now is everything we were able to recover from space after the first Waystation was blown to smithereens thanks to me and the Meta-Busters.

I guess it's just another reminder of my failures as a Meta hero.

I look at the large brain floating in front of me and read the plaque beneath it: *Hive Mind of the Bee-lug Race (Alien)*. Interesting. I saunter through the chamber, looking at other fascinating artifacts like the *Battle Armor of Nikademis*, the *Sphere of Dark Matter*, the *4-D Ray Gun of Doom*, and the *Statue of Medusa IV*.

Then, something shiny catches my eye that I've never noticed before.

On a stand in the corner is a bronze signet ring beneath a glass cover. It's only when I get closer that I notice the symbol of a lightning bolt carved into its face. The plaque on the stand reads: *The Three Rings of Suffering. Extremely Dangerous. Do not remove from glass. DO NOT WEAR UNDER ANY CIRCUMSTANCES.*

The Three Rings of Suffering? What does that mean?

And what happened to the other two rings? Hopefully, they're not floating in outer space.

I stretch my arms and yawn. I should probably just go to bed. And based on what my parents want me to do, I'll need all the rest I can get. Not that I'm going to get any sleep anyway. After all, I have no idea how I'll break the news to my team without looking like a total loser.

Which, I'm guessing, will be impossible.

As I wander to my room I can't stop thinking about how I could prove my parents wrong. I mean, how can I show them that Next Gen is a great superhero team too? Unfortunately, nothing comes to mind. I just wish they would give us some space. And speaking of space, when I reach my door an unexpected visitor is waiting for me with his tail wagging.

"Okay, Dog-Gone," I say, opening the door. "You can sleep with me, but no hogging the covers."

I brush my teeth, put my mask and cape on my desk, and crawl into bed with my uniform still on. Dog-Gone hops onto the bed, circles around, and settles down on my legs, crushing them. Note to self: start a doggie diet plan tomorrow.

And as I drift off to sleep, there's only one thought floating through my brain:

Why do grown-ups get to make all the rules?

Meta Profile
The Freedom Force
Captain Justice
Class: Super-Strength
Meta :
Ms. Understood
Class: Psychic
Meta :
Glory Girl
Class: Flight
Meta :
Shadow Hawk
Class: None
Meta :
Epic Zero
Class: Meta Manipulator
Meta :
TechnocRat
Class: Super-Intellect
Meta :
Blue Bolt
Class: Super-Speed
Meta :
Master Mime
Class: Magic
Meta :
Makeshift
Class: Energy Manipulator
Meta :

THREE

I WISH I STAYED IN BED

I wake up shivering.

I reach down to pull up my covers but they aren't there. What happened? But it's not until I roll over that I find my answer, because Dog-Gone is snoring blissfully by my side with his head on my pillow and his body wrapped snugly inside my blankets. Yep, I should have known better.

I rub my eyes and look at the clock. It's 6:01 a.m. which is way earlier than I wanted to get up. It would have been great to sleep in, but thanks to my slobbering bunkmate that's not going to happen. But I can't blame him for everything. After all, there's so much on my mind I was bound to have a restless sleep anyway.

I mean, I still don't know what I'm going to say to Next Gen. I must have woken up ten times sweating about it, and I still don't have a clue. The team is relying on me to lead them, and now I get to tell them we need to disband.

I can just see their reactions now. Pinball will be shocked, Selfie will be disappointed, and Skunk Girl will ask me some really tough questions—like if I'm also quitting the Freedom Force. And what's worse is I can already see her laughing at me when I tell her I'm not. So, this is pretty much a lose-lose situation.

Thanks, Mom and Dad.

But maybe if I'm just straightforward with them they'll understand. Maybe they'll get it if I tell them it's for our safety and the safety of those around us.

Then again, maybe I'm delusional.

I get out of bed, walk into the bathroom, and check myself in the mirror. My hair is messy, my eyes are puffy, and my skin is paler than a zombie. Well, I look far from confident, so they'll probably eat me alive.

And I'm pretty sure this will be the last time I see Selfie. I mean, I get this weird feeling in my stomach whenever I'm around her. But after she hears what I'm going to say she'll probably hate me forever.

I breathe in and exhale. This just might be the worst day of my life. And believe me, that's saying something. Well, I'd better fuel up with a good breakfast because it's going to be a long day. I exit the bathroom to find Dog-

Gone yawning by the door.

"Oh, did I disturb you?" I ask. "Gee, I'm so sorry."

But he just scratches his ear with his hind leg.

"C'mon," I say, grabbing my mask and cape. "I'll put you in the Evacuation Chamber and then we'll get something to eat."

I have to say, TechnocRat thought of almost everything when he designed the Waystation 2.0. Now, when Dog-Gone has to go to the bathroom, we put him in the Evacuation Chamber and push a button to eject his business into outer space where it'll burn up before it hits Earth's atmosphere. Sadly, based on what I need to tell Next Gen, I'm tempted to eject myself with it.

Anyway, once he's done we head to the Galley to find a distressed-looking Grace in her Glory Girl uniform frantically reading all the post-it notes on the refrigerator.

"You're up early," I say.

"Have you seen Mom or Dad?" she asks, ripping the notes down one by one.

"No," I say. "Are they in the Mission Room? Usually, they're up at five to catch the early news."

"Duh," Grace says. "I know what they usually do but they're not there. In fact, I can't find them anywhere and they didn't leave a note."

"Did you ask Blue Bolt or Shadow Hawk?" I ask, opening the cupboard to grab Dog-Gone's food.

"They're not here either," Grace says. "And neither are Master Mime, Makeshift, or TechnocRat."

"Really?" I say. Come to think of it, I haven't seen any of them either. "And there's no note?"

"No," Grace says. "I've checked everywhere. Dad was supposed to meet me in the Combat Room at six for a workout, but he never showed up."

"Well, that is weird," I say. Mom and Dad always leave a note if they go on a mission while we're sleeping. Suddenly, I get an uneasy feeling in my stomach.

I put down Dog-Gone's food and he starts crunching away. Where could they be? Just then, I remember that time when Leo kidnapped me and I wasn't able to leave a note. I wonder if they were adult-napped?

"I even had the Meta Monitor scan the Waystation for Meta readings," Grace says. "But there's nothing."

"Okay," I say. "That's not good. Did you see if there was anything big happening on the news?"

"No," Grace says. "Hand me the remote."

I pass her the remote control and she flicks on the big television near the table, but there's just static.

"Did you mess up the remote again?" she asks.

"No," I say. "I didn't touch it."

But as Grace clicks through, there's static on every channel. "This is ridiculous," she says. "Turn on the radio."

I flip on the radio, which is usually tuned into the news, but all we hear is a high-pitched beep. I change the station but it's the same thing. Every station has the same high-pitched beep.

"Something is wrong," Grace says, grabbing her phone off the counter. "There's no text messages either."

Okay, now I'm starting to worry. This is totally unlike Mom and Dad. Where did they go?

"Elliott!" Grace blurts out wide-eyed as she scrolls through her phone. "Look at this!"

"What?" I say, running over. "What is it?"

"Look!" she says. "Look at all these kids posting on social media. Their parents are missing too!"

As Grace scrolls through her newsfeed, I see all of these posts and videos from kids whose parents are missing. But it's not just the parents, but their older brothers and sisters too! And these posts are coming from all over the world!

"This is nuts!" Grace says. "According to these kids, anyone over the age of fifteen is gone!"

Gone? But gone where?

"Follow me," Grace says. "Let's see if we can figure out what's happening in the Mission Room."

As Dog-Gone and I chase her through the hallway I think back to last night when I was in the Mission Room with Mom and Dad. At the time I was so mad I just wanted to get away from them. But I didn't really mean it! I would never want anything bad to happen to them.

By the time we reach the Mission Room, Grace is already putting on a headset at the control panel.

"Freedom Force to White House," she says into the microphone. "White House, do you read me?"

But all we hear is static.

"Freedom Force to Keystone City Police," she tries next. "Anyone there? Hello? Hello?"

But there's nothing.

"No one is responding," Grace says.

"Are the vehicles still in the Hangar?" I ask. "Did they take a Freedom Flyer?"

"Good question," Grace says, and then she pushes a few buttons and a visual of the Hangar pops up on the main screen. "Nope," she says. "All of the vehicles are parked in their spots. Holy smokes!"

"What?" I ask. "Holy smokes what?"

"If anyone over fifteen just up and vanished," she says, typing into the keyboard, "then what about all of the vehicles that adults drive? Like cars, buses, and—"

"—planes!" I finish for her. "Do a scan!"

"Scanning," Grace says, typing away, and then up pops a list of flights in the air. Luckily, there are only three flights in service across the United States. "I'm on it," she says, hopping off her chair. "I'll take a Freedom Ferry and land them one by one. Do another scan and see what else you can turn up. And don't do anything stupid!"

But before I can respond she's gone. I hop into her chair and start punching into the keyboard. Based on the limited number of planes in the air, whatever happened must have taken place between midnight and six o'clock in the morning when most people are asleep. At least that might limit some of the damage.

Okay, let's take a look at the highway. I push some buttons and an image of the interstate appears. The good news is that no vehicles are moving. The bad news is that the ones I do see are crashed all over the place. Then, I remember the subway system. I press a few keys and a visual of the subway routing system appears. Fortunately, there aren't any cars on the tracks, which pretty much confirms this happened before the subway opened at six.

Now, what else do adults drive? Suddenly, I hear crunching and look over to find Dog-Gone still chewing his food. Wait, chewing? Chew. Choo Choo! Trains!

I punch in a few more commands and a map of the railroad system pops up. It's all clear, except for a massive freight train running along a stretch of track heading straight for Keystone City! And there's another train already parked at the terminal! They're gonna collide!

I've got to stop that train! But before I do I'm going to need help managing anything else that pops up. So, I type into the new transmitter watch I asked TechnocRat to develop for me and my team.

<Epic Zero: Team I need help! Everyone over 15 is gone! Go see if any kids need help on streets & highways!>

Five seconds later I get:

<Selfie: On it! My parents r gone too!>

<Skunk Girl: Roger and same! 🙁 >

<Pinball: Just need a sec 2 eat breakfast.>

Okay, great. While Pinball finishes his pancakes, I've

got a runaway train to catch! But before I go I've got one last thing to handle.

"Dog-Gone, stay," I order. "I'll be back in a bit."

But Dog-Gone growls in disagreement. Honestly, I don't have time to argue, and now that I think of it, maybe he should come along anyway. After all, who knows what kinds of trouble he'll get into if he stays here all by himself.

"Okay, okay," I say. "You can come, but you have to listen to everything I say. Is that a deal?"

Dog-Gone barks and we race for the Hangar.

***

Five minutes later, our Freedom Ferry touches down at the Keystone City Railroad Terminal. We hop out and make our way onto the tracks. Here's the parked train, but where's the—

CHUGACHUGACHUGA!

I spin around to see a massive train heading our way! Smoke is pouring out of the chimney and it doesn't seem like it's going to stop on its own. I've probably got a minute before it's here.

The only problem is that I didn't think this through. My powers don't work on inanimate objects, and other than Dog-Gone, there's no Metas around to duplicate.

So, now what?

Think, Elliott, think!

I look over at the Freedom Ferry. I guess we could get back inside and shoot it with a missile, but what if someone is on board? I mean, kids stowaway on trains all the time in the movies.

But as I look back at the train, I realize there's no time! In fact, that train is coming in way faster than I expected! It's nearly on top of us! I grab Dog-Gone's collar, but before we can move—

"Look out, kid!" comes a girl's voice.

Suddenly, a masked girl riding a black slide generated from her fingertips flies towards us. Then, she raises her other hand and shifts a shadow from the ground to right in front of us! The next thing I know, the shadow solidifies and arcs over our heads just as the train reaches us! But instead of crushing us, the train rides up the solid shadow and goes right over us!

THOOM!

I spin around as the runaway train drops on top of the parked train! I can't believe it. We're okay. The train didn't touch us at all!

Then, the girl rides her strange slide over to us.

"Are you okay?" she asks.

"Um, yeah," I say, kind of embarrassed. I mean, she probably just saved our lives. "Thanks for that."

"No problem," she says, with a slight smile.

She looks like she's about my age, with long, black hair and bright, brown eyes. Her costume is all black, except for the insignia on her top that looks like a small, gray owl.

"Um, why are you wearing that costume?" she asks. "I mean, you're dressed like a Meta but you sure didn't act like one."

"Oh," I say, my face feeling flush. "Well, I am a Meta but my powers didn't quite fit the situation. I'm Epic Zero."

Dog-Gone barks.

"And that's Dog-Gone," I add. "My dog."

Dog-Gone claws my leg.

"Ow!" I say, and when I look down at him he looks none too pleased with me. "And apparently he'd like you to know that he's a Meta too."

"I see," she says. "Nice to meet you. Well, you'd better be careful. All of the adults are missing which is why that train wasn't going to stop."

"Yeah, I know," I say. "And actually, it's anyone over fifteen."

"Really?" she says. "I didn't know that. I've been trying to help wherever I can but everything is nuts."

"Clearly," I say. "Are you new around here?"

"Yeah," she says. "You can say that. Well, I've got to go but here's a tip for you, don't stand in front of a runaway train. See ya."

Then, she generates another dark slide and takes off!

"Wait!" I call after her. "I never got your—"

But then she disappears over the terminal.

"—name."

Meta Profile

Lunatick

Name: Carter Jones	Height: 6'0"
Race: Humanoid	Weight: 390 lbs
Status: Villain/Active	Eyes/Hair: Brown/Brown

META 2: Energy Manipulator

- Considerable Radioactive Bite
- Possesses the reflexes and wall-climbing abilities of a tick

Observed Characteristics

Combat 62	
Durability 44	Leadership 16
Strategy 23	Willpower 64

FOUR

I GATHER THE TROOPS

I couldn't get away from there fast enough.

I mean, after thoroughly embarrassing myself with the mysterious masked girl at the train station, I was feeling pretty low. So, I grabbed Dog-Gone and jetted over to the Hangout to meet up with Next Gen. The Hangout is the name we gave our treehouse headquarters in Selfie's backyard. It's not as decked out as the Waystation 2.0, or even the Waystation 1.0 for that matter, but it's got all the basics for effective crime-fighting, including a police monitor, maps of the city, and plenty of snacks.

Since there's no one left on the planet with a driver's license, I park the Freedom Ferry in Selfie's driveway and head around back. Unfortunately, Dog-Gone is still afraid to climb the treehouse ladder, so I spend the next few minutes chasing him around the yard until I bribe him with cheese puffs. After pushing his rump up the ladder, we finally make it to the top where I find the rest of Next Gen watching us from above.

"Here," Selfie says, handing me the bag of cheese puffs. "I think he has you trained by now."

"Probably," I say, fishing out a few. Dog-Gone gobbles them up and looks at me with his orange-covered snout. "That's it. No more."

"That's what you said last time," Skunk Girl says. "And yet, here we are again."

"Anyway," I say, ignoring her. "What did you guys run into?"

"Craziness," Selfie says. "It's complete and utter craziness out there. Kids are running around town in packs. The older ones have collected the younger ones and are trying to feed them and keep them calm, but they're just kids themselves. Everyone is scared and everyone is looking for their parents. And the babies are the ones suffering the most. They're crying non-stop for food and no one is volunteering for diaper duty, if you catch my drift."

"I do," Skunk Girl says, raising her right arm. "But for some of us, being odoriferous is a good thing."

"Funny," Selfie says. "But we've got serious problems here. I mean, no one knows what happened to our parents or older siblings. There's panic out there and most of the kids are way too young to take care of themselves. And I'm not just talking about Keystone City. This is happening across the country, let alone the world!"

"It's nuts," Pinball says, leaning his round body against the squared-off corner. "I never realized how much we relied on adults. A toddler I was helping thought I was a watermelon and tried to bite me! Can you believe it? What were you up to, Epic Zero?"

Great question. I could tell them I was nearly run over by a freight train until a masked Meta-girl saved my bacon, but I'm not sure that would instill confidence in my leadership abilities. So, instead, I settle on—

"I, um, tried to prevent an accident at the railroad station."

"Speaking of accidents," Skunk Girl says. "There are, like, thousands of bashed up, stranded cars on the roads. It's like the aftermath of a giant demolition derby. Who's going to fix this mess?"

"We are," I say boldly.

"You've got that right, squirt," comes a familiar voice.

"Glory Girl?" Pinball says, his jaw hanging open. "W-What are you doing here?"

"He called me," Grace says, nodding at me as she floats through the entrance and touches down next to me. "So, is this really your headquarters?"

"Don't start," I say.

"H-Hey," Pinball says, sitting up straighter. "I'm Binpall, I mean, Pinbowl. I-I mean, Pinball. I'm a big fan of yours."

"Nice to meet you," Grace says.

"I'm Selfie," Selfie says, shaking Grace's hand. "We didn't introduce ourselves last time but it's a real honor to meet you."

"An honor?" I say, crossing my arms. "So, what am I? Chopped liver?"

"I'm Skunk Girl," Skunk Girl says, waving awkwardly.

"Yes, you are," Grace says, her nose twitching. Then, she looks at me and whispers, "So, did you tell them the bad news?"

"Shut it," I whisper back.

"You mean, you didn't tell them?" she asks.

"I said shut it," I reply.

"Tell us what?" Selfie asks.

"Absolutely nothing," I say quickly. Then, I give Grace a death stare and say, "It's just that now that there are no adults around, the things that some adults may have wanted before this situation happened are no longer valid because the adults aren't here. So, we're operating in an adult-free environment right now and everyone—and I mean everyone—needs to adapt accordingly."

"Okay, okay, relax," Grace says. "Under the 'adult-free' situation that's fine. But once we fix this we'll talk."

"Are people on the Freedom Force always this weird?" Skunk Girl asks Pinball.

"I hope so," Pinball says, staring at Grace with goo-goo eyes.

"What's his problem?" Grace asks, looking at Pinball.

"No one really knows," Selfie answers. "Anyway, you said we were the ones who were going to fix this. How are we going to do that?"

"Well, we've got three problems to solve," Grace says, grabbing the bag of cheese puffs from me. "One, we're out of jelly doughnuts on the Waystation. Two, we've got to find out what's happening. I mean, it's not every day that people over the age of fifteen disappear off the face of the Earth. Someone is responsible for this. The question is who? And why?"

Well, she's right about that. But as I think through all of the evil profiles in the Meta Monitor's database, I can't think of anyone powerful enough to pull off something like this.

"So," Grace continues, shoving a cheese puff into her mouth, "after I safely landed all three airplanes I went back to the Waystation and asked the Meta Monitor to identify any strange Meta readings."

"And?" I ask.

"Bupkus," she says, eating another cheese puff.

"Great," I say.

"The third problem," Grace says, "is how are we

going to govern society until we can get the adults back? I mean, think about it. Who's in charge of the country right now? No one. There's no president, vice president, or Congress. There's no army, no air force, and no police protecting us. No one is producing or selling food. There aren't any doctors, nurses, or even dentists. Well, maybe that last one is a blessing, but you get the point. It's a kids' world now."

"That's a great summary," Skunk Girl says, "but what are we going to do about it? I mean, we're just kids ourselves."

"True," Grace says, gobbling the last cheese puff. "We're kids but we're not ordinary kids. We're Meta kids and we've got to step up."

"Exactly," I say. "That's what I was trying to tell them when you showed—"

"So, here's the plan," Grace says, cutting me off and handing me the empty bag. "It's up to us to run the nation. So, effective immediately, I'll be taking the role of President of the United States of America."

"Wait, what?" I say.

"Yep," she says, "we need someone to lead the country. And as a Meta and member of the Freedom Force, I'm the only logical choice."

"Um, sorry to remind you," I say, "but I'm also a Meta and member of the Freedom Force."

"True," Grace says, "but I'm the senior-ranking member of the Freedom Force. And besides, the people need a face they can trust. Plus, I'm more popular."

"That's great for you," I say, "but running the country isn't about getting brand sponsorship deals. It's about making smart decisions for the people. Besides, you can't just claim the presidency. Normally there's, like, a whole election process, remember?"

"These aren't normal times," Grace says matter-of-factly. "This is a time for swift action."

"Well, I'd vote for her," Pinball says.

"See, there you go," Grace says, heading for the exit. "I've just been elected. Now, I'm heading to the White House to get our government up and running. In the meantime, I need you guys to help guide and protect my citizens while I search for the culprit."

"*My* citizens?" I say. "Look, you can't be serious."

"As you said, we're operating in an 'adult-free environment,'" Grace says, looking me dead in the eyes. "And *everyone* needs to adapt accordingly. Otherwise, someone's beans may be spilled. Capeesh?"

We stare at each other for a few seconds.

"Capeesh," I say reluctantly. "But, um, aren't you forgetting something?"

"What's that?" she says, stopping at the ladder.

"Well, you turn fifteen in a few days," I say. "So, if we don't figure this out fast, you'll be the shortest tenured president in American history."

Grace's smile fades and I see the concern in her eyes.

"Then we'd better get to work as soon as possible,"

she says, and then she steps off the platform and flies away.

"Goodbye, Madame President!" Pinball calls out.

"Well, this should be interesting," Selfie says.

"Oh, you have no idea," I answer.

Honestly, the thought of a 'President Grace' doesn't leave me feeling warm and fuzzy. I mean, this is the girl who spends more time in front of a mirror than a newspaper. But she's right, someone needs to get the government running. And even though she's my annoying big sister, I trust her to do the right thing. Plus, there's so much to do right now it's not productive to squabble over who does what.

But what's worse than President Grace is no Grace at all. So, we've got to solve this mystery before her birthday. I can't have her disappearing on me too.

"What now, boss?" Skunk Girl asks.

I turn to find the team looking at me like I've actually got an answer. I smile as my mind goes into overdrive. Truthfully, I have no idea what to do next. According to our self-elected new president, it's up to us to guide and protect the public.

But if we're going to do that, we're gonna need a lot of help because it's a big country out there. If only there were more of us. Then, we could all join forces and become the next Freedom F—

Wait a second. That's it!

My parents wanted me to disband Next Gen, but

desperate times call for desperate measures!

"Um, are you okay?" Selfie asks. "You've got a strange look on your face."

"What?" I say. "Oh, sorry. Didn't you tell me that you guys met in a chat room or something like that?"

"Yeah," Pinball says. "It's called the Freedom Force Kids Forum. There are lots of kids in there who are fans of the Freedom Force. But once the three of us found each other, we sort of started chatting on our own. That's when we realized we all had Meta powers."

"Interesting," I say. "So, if you guys were in that chat room, then maybe there are other Meta kids in there too."

"Um, sorry but I'm totally confused," Skunk Girl says. "Why are we talking about chat rooms right now? Where are you going with this?"

"I'm thinking big," I say, "because if we're going to guide and protect the country, we're going to need a larger squad."

"Wait," Selfie says. "Are you saying we need a bigger team?"

"Yep," I say. "That's why we're going to hold our first-open audition to recruit new members for Next Gen!"

DG

FIVE

I HOLD AN AUDITION

The turnout is way bigger than I expected.

I mean, Pinball posted our superhero tryout in the Freedom Force Kids Forum only a few hours ago, but apparently, word got around quick because every seat in the Keystone Middle School auditorium is taken. I'm standing on the stage with the rest of the team marveling at the large crowd. There must be a hundred kids here who want to try out for Next Gen!

I haven't felt this pumped in a while. This is, without a doubt, the best call I've made as team leader so far. I glance over at Selfie who smiles at me. Yep, Grace can be president for all I care, I'm happy right where I am.

Now, I don't like to toot my own horn, but I'm pretty sure most of these kids are here because of me.

After all, I asked Pinball to include in his post that Next Gen isn't led by just any Meta hero, but by a bona fide member of the Freedom Force. I thought it might be a draw, but maybe it worked too well. The place is so packed it'll take hours to get through the auditions.

"Excuse me," calls a little girl with her hand in the air. She's sitting in the front row and can't be older than nine. I wonder what her powers are.

"Yes," I say, kneeling. She probably wants my autograph but that'll have to wait. In fact, maybe I'll do an autograph signing for everyone at the end of the audition. I just hope my hand doesn't cramp.

"Is Glory Girl late?" the little girl asks.

"Glory Girl?" I say, confused. "Um, no, she's not part of our team."

"Oh," the little girl says, her face falling with disappointment. "The post said Glory Girl was in charge of Next Gen."

"It said what?" I say, looking over at Pinball.

"Well," Pinball says, turning bright red, "you weren't very specific. You told me to say the team was led by a member of the Freedom Force. So, I, um, kinda said Glory Girl was in charge. But it's sort of true, right? I mean, she is the president and all."

"Glory Girl may be the president," I say, "but I'm the leader of Next Gen. Not Glory Girl."

"Where are the chips and salsa?" a boy calls out from the back of the auditorium. "The post said there would be chips and salsa."

Chips and salsa?

I glare at Pinball again.

"Well," Pinball says, his rotund stature somehow shrinking. "I, um, sort of said we'd be serving free chips and salsa too."

"You said what?" Skunk Girl says, slapping her palm against her forehead. "We're not serving chips and salsa! We don't even have chips and salsa! Why would you say something like that?"

"Because I, um, didn't think anyone would show up otherwise," Pinball says, shuffling uncomfortably on his feet. "I didn't want it to be just us."

"Holy smokes," Selfie says, running her hands through her hair. "So, that means none of these kids have Meta powers."

"I'm hungry!" a boy calls out.

"Me too!" another boy says.

Suddenly, the whole crowd starts complaining and the volume level rises until I can't even think straight anymore. This has gotten out of control!

"Everyone, please stay calm!" I shout out to the crowd. "Can I get your attention please?"

It takes a few seconds for the auditorium to quiet down, but when it does I say, "I'm sorry to make this announcement, but despite what the post said, Glory Girl is not in charge of Next Gen and we are not serving chips and salsa. I repeat we are not serving chips and salsa. The only people who should be here are those kids who have Meta powers and want to try out for Next Gen, our superhero team. If you are not one of those people then please exit the auditorium in a calm and orderly manner."

There, that should do it.

But then the complaining starts all over again.

"There's no chips and salsa?"

"Glory Girl isn't here?"

"You stink, Epic Zebra!"

Well, so much for my autograph session. As the crowd stands up and files out of the auditorium, I bury my face in my hands and try to take calming breaths. Note to self: fire Pinball as head of our public relations department.

"Epic Zero," Selfie whispers, elbowing me in the ribs. "Look!"

What now? But when I look up I'm shocked, because three kids are still sitting in their seats. And they're all wearing costumes! They must be real Metas!

"See," I say to the team, perking up again. "I told you it would work out." Then, I look at our three candidates and say, "Welcome! Thank you so much for coming. Why don't we get off the stage and we'll hand it over to you so you can show us what you can do."

We take our seats in the front row as the three kids make their way up to the stage. There are two boys and a girl who all look about our age. This is exciting. I just hope they're good enough to make the cut.

"This should be entertaining," Pinball says. "Boy, I sure wish we brought chips and salsa."

"Shut it," Skunk Girl says.

"Okay," I say. "Who would like to go first?"

"I'll go," one of the boys offers, moving to center stage. He's tall and thin, with red hair and freckles on his nose and cheeks. His blue eyes shift nervously in his red mask and he's wearing a red costume with a blue-and-orange 'T' on the front.

"Thanks for volunteering," I say, wishing I had something to take notes with. "What's your name?"

"I call myself Thermo," he says.

"Nice to meet you, Thermo," I say. "And thanks for coming down to audition for Next Gen. As of, well, this morning, we became the premier superhero team on the planet. So, to join us you'll really need to knock our capes off. Are you ready to show us what you can do?"

"Oh, I already have," he says, furrowing his brow.

"Um, is something happening I'm not seeing?" Skunk Girl whispers after a few seconds. "Because I'm not seeing him do anything."

Just then, Selfie shudders and crosses her arms. "W-Why is it so c-cold in here all of a s-sudden?"

One second later, my skin starts feeling numb and my teeth begin to chatter! Selfie is right, it's absolutely freezing in here. And when I exhale I can see my breath rise in front of my face as wispy puffs of vapor! "A-A-Are y-y-you d-d-doing th-th-this?" I stammer.

"Too cold in here for you?" Thermo asks, raising his eyebrows. "Don't worry, I can change that."

Suddenly, the frigid chill fades, only to be replaced by thick, oppressive humidity! In fact, it's so unbearably warm I just want to tear off my costume and jump in a swimming pool! I look over at Dog-Gone who is lying on the floor with his tongue hanging out, panting like crazy.

"This is… getting ridiculous," Skunk Girls says, breathing hard and pulling down the fur neckline of her costume.

"C-Can't breathe," Pinball says. His cheeks are red and sweat is pouring down his face.

"O-Okay," I say. "Please, stop!"

"Certainly," Thermo says, relaxing his expression.

Just then, the temperature returns to normal.

"Thank goodness," Selfie says, wiping her brow.

"Well, I'm impressed," I say. And I really am. I mean, my body literally felt like it was put through the wringer. This kid has unique powers that could be useful. "So, how long have you had the ability to control the temperature?"

"For a year or so," Thermo says. "I realized I could do it at school when I was trying to get out of a math test. I shut the whole air conditioning system down."

"Well, that might be the best use of a power I've ever heard of," I say. "But have you ever used it in battle?"

"No," Thermo says. "I can only do it indoors where there's a thermostat system to connect to. My powers don't work outside."

"Wait, did you just say your powers don't work outside?" Pinball repeats. "Like, not at all?"

"No," Thermo says. "But I'm an orange belt in karate so I can chop some people if you need me to."

"Riiight," I say. Suddenly, I'm feeling much less enthusiastic about Thermo. I mean, I can't think of too many battles I've fought in the comfort of air conditioning. "Thank you. We'll, um, make our decisions at the end of all of the auditions. For now, let's move on to the next person."

"I-I'll go," the other boy says nervously. He's much shorter than Thermo and his stringy hair nearly covers his eyes. He's wearing flippers and snorkeling gear and carrying a bucket.

"What's your name?" I ask.

"I-I call myself Monsoon," he says.

"Oh, thank goodness," Pinball whispers. "Because if he said his name was 'Puke-in-the-Bucket Boy' I'd be bouncing out of the auditorium right now."

"Shhh!" Skunk Girl whispers back.

"Welcome, Monsoon," I say. "Well, with a name like that I'm expecting big things. Please, don't be nervous. Just show us what you can do."

"O-Okay," he says, putting the bucket on the floor. "I-I practiced but I apologize in advance if I splash you."

"Splash us?" Pinball says, grabbing his armrests. "I was just kidding. He's not really going to puke, is he?"

But before we can react, his body suddenly transforms into water and fills the bucket at his feet! I have to admit, it was impressive, but as I lean forward, waiting for the next demonstration of his power, there's nothing. Like, nothing at all for several minutes.

"Well, this is awkward," Skunk Girl whispers.

"You know," Pinball whispers. "Maybe he should call himself 'Trickle' instead of Monsoon."

"Should we check if he's okay?" Selfie asks. "He's been in that bucket a long time."

"Um, Monsoon?" I call out. "Are you okay? Do you need help?"

Suddenly, water flies up from the bucket and the next thing we know, Monsoon is back to human form!

"Sorry," he says, cleaning out his ears. "I can't hear a thing when I'm in water form. I'm so glad that worked out. Last time I missed the bucket and ended up in the toilet."

"Oh, wow," I say. "Well, thanks for that little tidbit, but can you, um, do anything else? You know, like form into a giant water torpedo or mentally control fish or anything like that?"

"Oh, no," he says. "That's it."

"I see," I say. "Well, thank you for auditioning."

"No problem," he says, picking up his bucket.

"Well, I guess that leaves me," the girl says, moving to the front of the stage. She has wild, dark hair, purple goggles, and a purple costume with the symbol of a messy spiral on her top.

"Based on the last two auditions," Pinball whispers, "I can't wait to see this one."

"I can," Skunk Girl says, covering her eyes.

"So, tell us your name and what you do," I say.

"Sure," she says. "I call myself Haywire, and my powers are, well, a little unusual."

"How so?" I ask.

Just then, a giant spotlight over the stage shoots out white, electric sparks.

"YIP!" Dog-Gone cries, jumping into my lap.

"Ow!" I yell. "Get off me you scaredy-cat!"

Then, the whole auditorium goes pitch-dark.

"Hey!" Selfie says. "Dog-Gone is biting my phone!"

"Ow!" Skunk Girl says. "Pinball, you idiot! You just elbowed me in the nose!"

"Sorry," Pinball says. "I'm stuck in my seat and can't get out!"

"Yuck!" Selfie says. "What's that smell?"

"I-I think it's me," Skunk Girl says. "For some reason, I can't control my powers!"

As I pinch my nose and try to push Dog-Gone to the floor, I wonder what happened. I mean, a second ago everything was fine, but now everything has gone completely hay… wire.

"Hold on," I say, calling up to the stage. "You're doing this, aren't you?"

"Yeah," Haywire says. "That's kind of my thing.

When I use my powers, things get out of control."

"Well, do you mind turning your powers off?" Pinball asks. "Otherwise, we'll all die from this skunk bomb."

"Very funny," Skunk Girl says.

"Sure," Haywire says. "I can stop my power but if something has already started, it'll just keep going. Like, once I was hiking with my parents in the mountains and I accidentally triggered an avalanche. Once gravity started going, I couldn't stop the rocks from falling. Fortunately, I got my parents out of the way before anyone got hurt. It was always just the three of us, but now they're gone and I'll do whatever it takes to find them."

Everyone is silent as her words hit us all.

She's right and we all feel the same way. I'll do anything to get my parents back. Even if it means breaking up Next Gen later on.

Just then, the lights come back on and I'm staring at the three eager candidates. I feel terrible because I know what it's like to be in their shoes. I mean, all I ever wanted was to join the Freedom Force. But ironically, now it's my turn to decide if they'll be joining us.

"Can you just give us a minute to discuss?" I ask.

The candidates nod and we huddle up.

"So, what do you think?" I ask the team.

"Unfortunately, it's a no for me," Selfie says.

"Hard no," Skunk Girl says.

"Big thumbs down," Pinball says.

Even Dog-Gone shakes his head 'no.'

And I can't argue. As much as I'd want to let them in, they're simply not ready. But now comes the hard part. Now I've got to deliver the bad news.

"So, here's what we think," I start.

But then—BEEP! BEEP! BEEP!

"What's that?" Selfie asks.

"My Freedom Force transmitter," I say. Following my misadventures with Krule and the Skelton Emperor, Mom made TechnocRat put a transmitter into my utility belt. She said it was to stay in closer communication, but I'm pretty sure it was for her to keep tabs on me. I press the button on the front of my belt and say, "Hello?"

"Get your squad over to the Keystone City Zoo pronto!" comes Grace's voice. "Someone is letting all of the animals loose! Kids could get hurt!"

"What?" I say. "Who would do something like that?"

"Do you think I have time to figure that out?" she barks. "That's why I called you. I'm trying to run the country here!"

CLICK!

Well, I guess that was an executive order. The zoo is filled with all sorts of dangerous animals. We're going to need help to get them back in their cages, let alone find the bad guy. Lots of help.

I look up at the hopeful faces on the stage and announce, "Congratulations, candidates. You've all made it to phase two of the audition!"

Meta Profile

Thermo

▯ Name: Lyle McGann	▯ Height: 5'5"
▯ Race: Human	▯ Weight: 127 lbs
▯ Status: Hero/Active	▯ Eyes/Hair: Blue/Red

META 1: Energy Manipulator
▯ Limited Temperature Control
▯ Can only use his powers indoors with a thermostat

Observed Characteristics	
Combat 12	
Durability 15	Leadership 18
Strategy 11	Willpower 38

SIX

I STEW AT THE ZOO

"What were you thinking?" Selfie whispers firmly as we run through the gates of the Keystone City Zoo.

I glance over my shoulder at the three candidates trailing behind us and wonder the same thing. I mean, none of us thought these kids had what it takes to join Next Gen, but I brought them along anyway. Maybe it wasn't a great idea, but I figured we'll need all the help we can get to capture the freed animals and find the perpetrator.

The rest of the team, however, clearly doesn't agree. In fact, up until Selfie asked me that question, they've been giving me the cold shoulder. Not that I can blame them. I pretty much ignored what they had to say.

So much for being a great leader.

But I really believe that bringing these rookies along was the right decision. There's no better way for them to prove themselves. I look back again to find Haywire looking determined, Thermo looking winded, and Monsoon looking like he wants to barf into his bucket.

Okay, maybe this wasn't such a good idea after all.

Especially after I spot the lion.

"Everybody stop!" I call out, skidding to a halt.

We all slam into each other as the giant feline stares us down with his calculating pupils. He's perched on top of the ticket booth counter, licking his lips like he's found his next meal, otherwise known as us!

"Th-That's a lion!" Pinball stammers. "Um, wh-what's up, my mane man? Get it? 'Main' man?"

"You're hilarious," Skunk Girl says, rolling her eyes. "But bad jokes aren't going to get him back in his cage."

"I can try," Thermo says, assuming a karate pose.

"Um, no," I say. "Why don't you stand back."

Suddenly, the lion GROWLS and leaps gracefully to the ground with surprising speed. I can't say I've ever been this close to a lion before—or its super-sharp, boy-eating teeth! No wonder he's called the King of the Jungle! Why couldn't we have run into a koala first?

Okay, think. We're going to have to capture him, but unfortunately, lions don't have Meta powers. So, unless Dog-Gone can lure this beast over to his cage using his invisibility, we're pretty useless. But when I look around, Dog-Gone is gone! What a surprise. Not.

"Okay, move over," Selfie says, stepping forward and holding up her phone. "Look over here, Mr. Kitty Cat, and you'll start to feel very, very sleepy."

But just as she's about to push the button—

"I'll help!" Haywire says, running over to Selfie.

"No!" I call out, but it's too late because just as Selfie presses the button, a streetlamp CRASHES down in front of us and the flash from Selfie's phone reflects off the metal light fixture! I shield my eyes just in time, but when I look back up, Selfie, Skunk Girl, and Pinball are all standing stock-still with dazed expressions on their faces!

They've been hypnotized by Selfie's magic phone!

"Sorry," Haywire says. "I-I didn't know that would happen. Will they be okay?"

"Don't worry," I say, "it'll go away eventually." And speaking of 'going away,' where's the lion? I look around but he's gone. I guess the streetlamp scared him away.

"What now?" Thermo asks. "I'm ready for action."

But as I look at the three candidates I realize how *not* ready for action they actually are. I should have listened to the team. I was wrong and they were right. And my foolish decision nearly got them killed.

Suddenly, I realize how my parents must have felt when I would beg them to take me on missions when I was a Zero. And even though these kids have powers, they either can't control them or they're just not useful in a crisis. It's simply too dangerous for them to use their powers in public.

Suddenly, I flashback to my conversation with Mom and Dad. I can still hear Dad telling me what it takes to be a leader. He said a leader must assess if the team can handle the mission. And if not, the leader must protect the team from harm. Now I see how right he was, and no matter how painful it is I know what I need to do.

"Look, guys," I say, "thank you for auditioning for Next Gen, but I'm afraid we can't add any of you to the team right now."

I pause for a second to gauge their reaction. Haywire looks disappointed, Thermo looks confused, and Monsoon actually looks relieved.

"You guys have some cool powers," I continue, "but until you have better control over them and can use them in a variety of situations, it's just too dangerous for you, us, and, well, everyone else for you to operate in public. I'm really sorry but I hope you understand."

"So, wait," Thermo says, "are you saying it's over?"

"Yeah," I say. "I'm really sorry. But I'm hoping you'd be willing to do me a favor. I still have a lot of superhero stuff to do, so would you mind helping my colleagues here into one of the buildings where they'll be safe until Selfie's hypnosis power wears off?"

"Sure," Monsoon says. "Do you need my bucket?"

"Um, no," I say. "I'm good. But thanks."

"I appreciate the opportunity," Haywire says, her face looking sad. "But given my luck, I'm not surprised by your decision. Thanks for letting me try out."

"Hey, don't be down," I say. "You did your best and with more practice, you'll learn how to control your powers. Then, maybe you can try out again in the future."

"Yeah," she says, "if there even is a future. I'll help your friends get to safety, and don't worry, I'll keep my powers 'off.' But just so you know, I'm not going to stop looking for my parents. Whatever it takes, whatever I have to do, I'll find them. I'm going to be a great hero one day, even without Next Gen."

As I look into her determined eyes I'm torn. I mean, I really like her fighting spirit but I know in my gut it would be a mistake to keep her around. Her powers are just too unpredictable. Yet, she's clearly going to keep going, even without Next Gen.

"Look, I get it," I say. "I'm sure you'll be great too, but please, just practice a lot first. And be careful."

"You too," she says.

As I watch Haywire, Thermo, and Monsoon guide the others, I realize I'm all on my own. Well, all on my own except for a criminal on the premises and a billion wild animals who'd love nothing more than to eat me. Then, it dawns on me that I've got my own wild animal.

"Dog-Gone?" I call out. "Where are you, you coward? Are you really going to let a big cat scare you?"

Just then, Dog-Gone appears on the other side of the pathway. He's just sitting there, trying to look innocent but I know he feels guilty for abandoning me.

"I forgive you," I say. "Just don't disappear on me

again, got it?"

Dog-Gone barks when suddenly we hear a chorus of SCREECHING coming from our right. That sounded like a tribe of monkeys, or rather, a tribe of agitated monkeys. Maybe we'll find something there!

We run down a pathway marked PRIMATES and round the corner to find a group of capuchin monkeys swarming out of their cage. Whoever is responsible for this was just here! If I'm fast enough maybe I can catch him!

"Dog-Gone," I say. "Get these monkeys back in their cage. I'm going ahead."

As I continue, I hear Dog-Gone BARKING followed by even more SCREECHING. I don't know what's going on back there, but either he's succeeding in wrangling those monkeys or they've just tied him to the nearest tree. But I can't stop to look because I've got my own job to do.

I run past more empty cages, a lemur looting a trash can, and an emu just looking ugly before I stumble across my target standing in front of the elephant pen.

Except, he's not a 'he' at all.

Because it's… a robot?

Why is a robot letting animals out of their cages?

"Stop right there!" I order.

But as the seven-foot-tall giant turns and takes me in with its cold, red eyes, I realize I'm in big, big trouble.

"L-Let go of that gate!" I say meekly.

The robot's eyes flicker, and I get the sense that it really doesn't care what I have to say. And then I notice the strange, yellow glow coming off of its body.

What is that?

And come to think of it, why does that robot look so darn familiar? Like I've seen it somewhere before?

Suddenly, it raises an arm and its metal hand retracts into its socket only to be replaced by a gun.

Uh oh.

THOOM!

I leap into the bushes just as the laser wipes out the ground I was standing on. Okay, this bucket of bolts means business! Somehow I've got to stop it, but my powers don't work on robots. And I still can't shake why it looks so familiar? Then, its eyes flicker again.

THOOM! THOOM!

I spring from the bushes and roll behind a tree as the robot continues to track me. This isn't good. As long as I'm visible I've got no chance! So, I concentrate hard and reach out far and wide until I connect with Dog-Gone. Then, I pull in his powers and make myself invisible. At least that fleabag is good for something!

I peer around the trunk to see the robot scanning the area. Thankfully, he doesn't have infrared vision because he clearly doesn't see me. I wait for him to finish and when he turns around I step lightly into the clearing.

That's when I get another shock, because on the back of its right shoulder is a giant 'on/off' switch.

Suddenly, I realize where I've seen this guy before because that's no ordinary robot, that's a—

"Light's out, buddy!" comes a girl's voice, and the next thing I know the robot is encased in a cone of darkness!

Just then, that mysterious masked girl in black comes sailing over the elephant house on one of her shadow slides and practically lands on top of me.

"Hey!" I call out, turning visible again. "Watch where you're going!"

"You again?" she says, clearly surprised to see me. "How come you keep showing up wherever I find trouble?"

"I was going to ask you the same thing," I say.

"Really?" she says. "Well, don't worry. I've got this in hand." Then, she closes her fist and the cone of darkness solidifies and squeezes the robot, crushing it into a gazillion pieces.

"There," she says. "Crisis averted."

"Nice job," I say. "Now what are you doing here?"

"There was a gorilla loose on Main Street," she says. "And when I brought him back to the zoo I ran into other loose animals too. I figured someone was responsible for this. I just wasn't expecting it to be you."

"I'm not responsible," I say. "I'm a hero, remember? We already had this conversation."

"Yeah," she says. "I remember, I just may not believe you. Maybe you created this robot."

"It's not a robot," I say, walking over to pick up one of its pieces. But that's when I get another surprise. All of the scattered body parts have shrunken in size.

"What happened to it?" the girl asks.

"I'm not sure," I say, picking up a tiny arm. "But this 'robot' is actually called a Powerbot. It's a toy. I had a bunch of them when I was younger. You must have seen the commercials. Powerbots—weapons in disguise? They're toy robots that turn into weapons."

"Wait," she says. "So, you're saying that gigantic robot was once a toy?"

"Yeah," I say. "It's like someone made it huge and sent it to the zoo to free all the animals. But who would do that?"

"No clue," she says.

"Well, I'm going to collect all the parts and bring them to the Waystation for analysis."

"The Waystation?" she says. "Isn't that, like, the Freedom Force's headquarters?"

"Yeah," I say. "I'm a member of the Freedom Force."

"Seriously?" she says, looking at me funny. "Have they lowered their standards?"

"No," I say, staying calm. "By the way, I never caught your name."

"I'm Night Owl," she says. "I can control shadows by shifting them around and making them solid."

"That's cool," I say.

And as I look into her eyes I realize her powers and control would be perfect for Next Gen.

"Hey, listen, I know we got off on the wrong foot, well, twice, but I'm also leading a new superhero team called Next Gen. We're a bunch of Meta kids who fight for truth and justice. Funny enough, we just had a tryout for new members, and I think you would be great—"

"Whoa," she says. "Hang on there, sparky. I'm not much of a joiner. I prefer working alone."

"Okay," I say, taken aback by her strong reaction. "I get it, but given the current state of the world maybe you'd reconsider and—"

"Look, it's been fun saving you—again—but I've really got to go," she says, generating another shadow slide. "So, while you and your friends pretend to play superhero, I'm going to round up the rest of these animals. Oh, and one last thing before I go, I'm warning you, I've got my eyes on you."

And before I can respond, she takes off.

Well, that didn't go well. And as I watch her disappear over the treetops, I realize another challenge has been added to my list. I need to prove to her that I'm not a villain.

Meta Profile

Monsoon

Name: Mikey Waterson	Height: 4'10"
Race: Human	Weight: 101 lbs
Status: Hero/Active	Eyes/Hair: Blue/Brown

META 1: Meta-morph
Limited Water Morphing
Can only move a few inches while in water form

Observed Characteristics	
Combat 8	
Durability 10	Leadership 11
Strategy 9	Willpower 26

SEVEN

I GET A CLUE

Time is clearly of the essence.

I mean, not only are all of the grown-ups missing, but Grace will turn fifteen in just a few days. So, it's not like there's time to sit around twiddling my thumbs. As Grace said, this is a time for swift action, which is why I did something that would normally get me in heaps of trouble.

I brought Next Gen up to the Waystation.

You see, we have a sacred rule that no outsiders can visit the Waystation. And the rule exists for good reason because there are all sorts of top-secret and dangerous things up here. But right now, I have to throw rules out the window. Besides, it's not like there's anyone around to argue with me.

I put the team in the Medi-wing so they could recover from Selfie's hypnosis power. Then, I left Dog-Gone behind to keep an eye on them, which was probably a mistake since he has the attention span of a fruit fly. But I can't worry about that now because I need to analyze that Powerbot toy to figure out how it came alive.

Luckily, I managed to collect all of its parts except for a leg, and I'm hoping that strange, yellow energy coming from its body will provide the clue I need. But as I navigate through the halls I can't stop thinking about what Night Owl said. She has some nerve accusing me of being responsible for this. She doesn't know me at all.

Yet, I still feel bad for wanting space from my parents. But I'm sure I'm not the only kid who ever wanted that. I mean, there's no way this could be my fault. Could it?

I hang a left and then a right and find myself standing in front of a sliding double door with a sign that reads: TECHNOCRAT'S LABORATORY. DANGER. DO NOT ENTER. ELLIOTT, THAT MEANS YOU!

Well, I have to admit, that rat has quite the sense of humor. But funny guy or not, I need to get inside his lab to properly analyze these toy parts.

The problem is, he told me he changed his passcode when he built the Waystation 2.0. I stare at the keypad and do some deep thinking. There are nine entry fields so I need a code with nine letters. There's no way he would use CAMEMBERT again, would he? I mean, he knows I figured it out last time.

So, what else has nine letters? I try hard to get inside the mind of a rat, but it's not easy. What does he love? Hmm, maybe? I punch C-O-M-P-U-T-E-R-S into the keypad and the console spits back:

ERROR: TWO ATTEMPTS REMAINING.

Great. Why does this seem like déjà vu all over again? For some reason, I can't think of anything else and that's when I realize he's probably playing mind games with me. Knowing him, I bet he never changed his password at all! That would be just like him to use reverse psychology on me. Well, I'm no fool.

I type in C-A-M-E-M-B-E-R-T and wait for the doors to slide open, but instead, I get:

ERROR: ONE ATTEMPT REMAINING.

Aaaaaaah!

He got me! I'm such a fool! And now I've wasted an attempt! I need to get inside so I can analyze these parts. I just need the freaking passcode! In my mind's eye, I can just picture TechnocRat standing there all smug with his little arms crossed and saying, "Holy guacamole, you *are* clueless aren't you?" And I would say…

Wait a minute! Could it be?

But if I screw this up, I'll kiss my chance of getting inside goodbye. But it's my only shot, so I take a deep breath and type: G-U-A-C-A-M-O-L-E.

Suddenly, the console turns green and the doors slide

open! I did it! I'm in!

As soon as I step inside I realize cracking the code was probably the easy part because TechnocRat's refurbished lab is twice the size of his previous one, which only means it's twice as messy. Clutter is piled high as far as my eyes can see—on the floor, on the desks, and even climbing the walls! This is going to be tough because I'm looking for one piece of equipment in particular.

The Meta Spectrometer.

The Meta Spectrometer is a device TechnocRat invented to identify hard to read Meta powers—including my own. When my powers finally showed up, there was no way to figure out what they actually were. In fact, at the time there wasn't even a classification for Meta Manipulation! But by using the Meta Spectrometer, Technocrat was able to analyze my unique Meta signature to determine that my powers were unlike anyone else's on the planet, except for Meta-Taker.

So, I figure if I feed these toy parts into the Meta Spectrometer then maybe it can identify what that weird yellow energy was. The problem is, I need to find the device first. Now where could it be?

I dig through papers, instruments, and random thingamajigs before I finally find what I'm looking for beneath a stack of blueprints. The Meta Spectrometer looks exactly how I remember it, which is sort of like a mini slot machine. You can either set the Meta Spectrometer on 'scan' or put an object directly inside.

So, I dust it off and place the toy parts into the compartment.

Then, I pull the lever.

A tiny hourglass icon appears on the monitor along with the words: *CURRENTLY ANALYZING. THIS MAY TAKE SEVERAL MINUTES SO NOW IS A GOOD TIME TO GET SOME CHEESE.*

Boy, that rat never misses an opportunity for cheese.

Well, there's no use hanging around while the Meta Spectrometer is doing its thing, so I decide to head back to the Medi-wing to check on the others. As my footsteps echo through the halls I realize how strange it feels to be up here without the Freedom Force. I used to be here alone all the time when I didn't have powers, but now we're usually together. And every time I turn a corner I expect to run into Blue Bolt or Shadow Hawk or my parents.

But they're not here.

Suddenly, I feel tears welling up in my eyes. I mean, so much has happened since they disappeared that I haven't had time for it to sink in. I want to stay hopeful, but I don't know where they are or even if they're still alive. I shudder at the thought but as much as I don't want to think it, I can't rule it out. I guess deep down I need to prepare myself for anything.

As I reach the Medi-wing I pause, wipe my eyes, and go through the door. I need to be strong for the team. If I break down they might lose hope. After all, we're the ones who need to find out what happened. Luckily, they're all sitting up and looking much more like themselves. "How do you feel?" I ask.

"Fine," Selfie says, rubbing her cheeks, "embarrassed but fine."

"It's not your fault," I say. "You got caught in Haywire's bad luck. It could've happened to any of us."

"That girl is a walking disaster," Skunk Girl says. "Her costume should be a big, yellow warning sign."

"You've got that right," Pinball says. "The next time I see her coming I'm going the other way."

"Hey, take it easy on her," I say. "She meant well. She's just inexperienced, that's all."

"Speaking of inexperienced," comes a familiar voice from behind me, "what are these kids doing here? You know we're not allowed to bring outsiders to the Waystation."

I turn to find Grace scowling in the doorway.

"They're not 'outsiders,' they're my team and… forget it," I say. "The real question is what are *you* doing here? I thought you were busy running the country?"

"I am," she says, "but I need to broadcast a State of the Union Address so I thought I'd do it from here. But since your 'team' is around they can help."

"A State of the Union?" Pinball says. "What's that?"

"It's when the president addresses the nation, dumbo," Skunk Girl says.

"Exactly," Grace says. "So, get your rumps in gear,

and let's go."

"Is she always this bossy?" Selfie asks.

"Yep," I answer. "But it's always worse when we're out of jelly doughnuts."

We follow Grace to the Media Room, which is another one of the snazzy new additions TechnocRat added to the Waystation 2.0. The Media Room is basically a studio space where we can film communications or conduct interviews with the media back on Earth. Grace stands behind the podium in front of the American flag and whips out her compact mirror.

"Wow," Pinball says, looking around. "This headquarters sure beats the Hangout. By like, a lot."

"Epic Zero," Grace barks while picking food out of her teeth, "you manage the camera. Selfie, you make sure he stays on my good side—slightly left at a fifteen-degree angle. Skunk Lass, you make sure my lighting is perfect. I don't want shadows under my eyes."

"It's 'Girl'," Skunk Girl says. "Skunk 'Girl.'"

"And what about me, Madame President?" Pinball asks. "What can I do?"

"You?" Grace says, looking him up and down. "You keep your eye on the dog and make sure he doesn't steal the limelight. This is my moment."

"Yes, Ma'am," Pinball says with a salute, and then steps in front of Dog-Gone who looks none too happy about it. "You sit. I've got both eyes on you."

"Great, let's get my speech filmed first, and then

we'll post it to all the social media channels," Grace says, snapping her compact mirror closed. "Hit the lights, Skunk Gal, it's showtime!"

I hear Skunk Girl groan as she flicks on the lights.

"Check the angle," Grace says, as I aim the camera.

"Relax, I've got it," I tell Selfie. "Okay, I'm hitting the record button in three, two, one…"

Grace stands up straight, flashes a big smile, and says with great gusto, "Greetings, citizens of Earth! I—"

"Whoa!" I say, stopping the camera. "Seriously? Greetings, citizens of Earth? What are you, an alien conqueror? And you're coming on way too strong. You need to be cool and collected. People are already panicking out there."

"Okay, okay," Grace says, looking annoyed. "I'll start over. And make sure to check the camera angle."

"I'm good," I say. "And three, two, one…"

"Good evening, fellow Americans," Grace says, sounding more calm and deliberate. "As you already know, I'm Glory Girl of the Freedom Force. This morning we woke up to a terrible tragedy that has left our nation reeling. The grown-ups in our world, including those aged fifteen and older, have vanished without a trace. At the moment we don't know who is behind this or what their motivations might be, but I can assure you we are on the case. However, due to the absence of anyone in authority, we are now experiencing a gap in leadership for our country."

I have to admit, she's actually doing a good job.

"Therefore," she continues, putting a hand over her heart, "despite my initial reservations, I simply could not ignore the thousands of text messages, emails, and personal pleas begging me to step into a leadership role. So, after a lot of soul searching, I have selflessly and humbly decided to assume the role of President of the United States to help our nation get back on our feet."

Um, what? That's not how it happened. Okay, now she's going a little off the rails.

"To that end," she carries on, "I have laid out a five-point plan to help our nation return to prosperity which I will share with you now. Point number one, from this day forward, all Metas will respectfully treat me as Commander and Chief and follow my orders without question. Point number two—"

"Okay, cut!" I say, turning off the camera.

"What are you doing?" Grace asks. "I have four more points to outline."

"The only point you've outlined is the one on your head," I say. "You're getting power-hungry."

"I am not!" Grace objects.

"Is she getting power-hungry?" I ask, turning to Pinball.

"Well, maybe just an eensy-weensy bit power-hungry," he says, closing his thumb and forefinger.

"See?" I say. "And he's the only one here who actually voted for you."

"Turn that camera back on!" Grace orders. "I'm your president! You have to listen to me!"

"No, I don't," I say. "You elected yourself!"

"Well, this is fun," Skunk Girl says.

"ANALYSIS COMPLETE," comes a mechanical voice over the intercom system.

"Um, what was that?" Selfie asks.

"The Meta Spectrometer!" I say, booking out of the Media Room. With all of Grace's ridiculousness, I almost forgot about it! Thank goodness TechnocRat had it hooked up to the intercom system.

"Come back!" Grace demands, but I'm already gone.

And I guess the team has had enough of her too because they're right behind me, including Pinball.

I lead the team to TechnocRat's lab and race over to the Meta Spectrometer.

"Um, what are we doing here?" Pinball asks, looking at all the mess. "Because this place doesn't seem very hygienic."

"Hang on," I say. "I put the toy parts into this device to see if we could identify its Meta classification."

Then, I look at the console which reads: PRESS BUTTON FOR RESULTS. Yes! Here we go. I push the button and my jaw drops. Because the console reads:

META CLASS: MAGIC.

META SUB-TYPE: BLACK MAGIC.

Meta Profile

Haywire

Name: Hayley Providence	Height: 5'0"
Race: Human	Weight: 87 lbs
Status: Hero/Active	Eyes/Hair: Brown/Brown

META 1: Energy Manipulator
Limited Bad Luck Generation
Power activation will cause random acts of poor luck

Observed Characteristics			
Combat 20			
Durability	11	Leadership	26
Strategy	19	Willpower	45

EIGHT

I DON'T WANT TO BELIEVE IN MAGIC

I have to say, I'm kind of shocked right now.

When I fed the toy parts into the Meta Spectrometer to analyze the strange, yellow energy they were emitting, it never crossed my mind that it would come back as Black Magic. I mean, I've never faced a Meta who used Black Magic before.

"Um, I'm guessing that's not good," Pinball says.

"Nope," I say, "probably not."

"Sorry for being dense here," Skunk Girl says, "but what exactly is Black Magic anyway?"

"Well," I say, trying to think of how best to answer her question, "Magic is one of the nine major classifications of Meta powers. Metas who use Magic, like Master Mime, and even Selfie here, typically channel their powers through an enchanted object. For example, Selfie's power comes from her phone which she uses for good. Black Magic works the same way, but the power inside the enchanted object typically comes from a dark source, like a demon, a departed soul, or a dark realm. You know, something like that."

"Well, that sounds ominous," Skunk Girl says.

"So, if that toy was giving off Black Magic," Selfie says, "do you think the toy itself was the enchanted object?"

That's another good question. But as I think about it, Night Owl shattered that Powerbot with ease. Could an enchanted object really break that easily? I mean, Master Mime's amulet is super solid, and Selfie's phone is way more durable than a normal phone.

"No," I say. "I don't think so. I think somebody else used their power on the toy robot and that's what the Meta Spectrometer picked up."

"The question is *who*?" Pinball asks.

Yep, that is the big question.

Who? Who? Who?

"Hold on!" I blurt out as a lightbulb goes on in my brain. Sometimes I'm such a dufus. "We *can* find out who did it right here. All we have to do is feed the reading from the Meta Spectrometer directly into the Meta Monitor and see if we get a Meta Profile match."

"Um, is it just me or is he speaking Meta gibberish?" Skunk Girl asks.

"Just follow me," I say, pressing a button on the Meta Spectrometer to extract the reading onto a printout.

As soon as it spits out the paper, I grab it and head for the exit. I lead the team back through the Waystation and up the twenty-three steps to the Monitor Room 2.0. TechnocRat did a great job rebuilding the Monitor Room with plenty of enhancements, including a soda machine. But the best feature of all is the improved Meta Monitor. This version is far more sensitive than the last one, so it should be able to pick up even the slightest indication of a power signature. I hop into the command chair.

"This headquarters is incredible," Pinball says, admiring the soda machine. "I bet there's even a swimming pool."

"There is," I say, typing into the keyboard. "But I can't give you a tour right now. Okay, fingers crossed."

Then, I insert the printout from the Meta Spectrometer into the Meta Monitor. As the Meta Monitor ingests the paper, I can barely contain my excitement. I mean, this could be the break we've been looking for. This could tell us who is responsible for the grown-ups disappearing.

Just then, another spinning hourglass flashes on the screen with the familiar words: *CURRENTLY ANALYZING. THIS MAY TAKE SEVERAL MINUTES SO NOW IS A GOOD TIME TO GET SOME CHEESE.*

Gotta love that rat. At least he's consistent.

"I'd love some cheese right now," Pinball says, patting his stomach. "And crackers. I'd love some crackers too."

"Can't you stop thinking about your stomach for a minute?" Skunk Girl says. "This is serious."

"I'm serious too," Pinball says. "Seriously hungry."

Suddenly, the screen flashes green and the words on the monitor read: META PROFILE IDENTIFIED.

"Yes!" I say, pumping my fist. "We're about to get our answer."

Just then, a Meta profile kicks up. It reads:

- *Beezle*
- *Race: Djinn*
- *Status: Villain/Inactive*
- *Height: Unknown*
- *Weight: Unknown*
- *Eye Color: Yellow*
- *Hair Color: Bald*
- *Meta Class: Magic*
- *Meta Level: Meta 2*
- *Considerable Wish Fulfillment Power*
- *Considerable Mind-Warping Power*
- *Considerable Shapeshifting Power*
- *Beezle is only able to use his powers if he has a human guide to steer it.*
- *Known Origin: Beezle is one of three brothers known as the Djinn Three. The other brothers of the Djinn Three*

are Rasp and Terrog. The Djinn Three are believed to be thousands of years old and have plagued mankind for centuries. Each of the Djinn Three is bound to one of three mystical rings known as the Rings of Suffering and possess varying levels of observed Meta powers. Rasp (Meta 1) is bound to the bronze ring, Beezle (Meta 2) is bound to the silver ring, and Terrog (Meta 3) is bound to the gold ring. Once a ring is placed on the finger, the Djinn Three are freed from their ring to grant their host three wishes. The Djinn Three also possess varying levels of mind-warping power that can influence their host's desires. The only way to stop the Djinn Three is to trap them back inside their respective ring. It is unknown who created the Rings of Suffering. Currently, all three rings are safely in the possession of the Freedom Force.

I swallow hard and read that last part again:

Currently, all three rings are safely in the possession of the Freedom Force.

I check the date of the last update which was over two years ago. Suddenly, I feel like I'm gonna puke.

"Well, that Beezle guy sounds like the life of the party," Skunk Girl says.

"Epic Zero, are you okay?" Selfie asks. "You look like you've seen a ghost."

"I… I…," I stammer, but the words just don't come out. I mean, it says all three Rings of Suffering are safely in the possession of the Freedom Force, but from what I remember, only one ring was in the Trophy Room.

Which means…

I take off.

"Epic Zero?" Selfie calls out. "Wait, where are you going?"

But by the time she finishes I'm already halfway down the stairs, hoping my mind was just playing tricks on me. I hear shouting and footsteps behind me and look back to see Dog-Gone and the others on my tail, but I can't stop. I need to check for myself.

Seconds later, I'm inside the Trophy Room. I hang a left at the giant brain and make my way over to the display case in question: The Three Rings of Suffering.

But as I look inside I feel like someone punched me in the gut because I was right. There's only one ring here and it's the bronze one which supposedly holds Rasp. That means the other two rings are missing—and I'm pretty sure I know what happened to them!

All three rings must have been on the Waystation 1.0 before the Meta-Busters blew it up trying to murder me. After that, the Freedom Force must have only recovered one of the rings. So, the silver one containing Beezle must have been blown to Earth! And who knows where the gold one might be!

"Epic Zero?" Selfie says, catching up to us. "Are you okay? Why did you run off like that?"

"Well, that's my exercise for the day," Pinball says, breathing heavily. "That was a full-on sprint."

"Wait, is that one of the rings?" Skunk Girl asks,

looking inside the display case. "That's the bronze one! So, there must be a djinn in there!"

"Did you say dinner is in there?" Pinball asks. "That's great because I'm starving."

"Not dinner, you dufus, a djinn," Skunk Girl says. "A djinn is like a genie, but an evil one."

"In that case," Pinball says, "I'll order room service."

"So, is that for real?" Selfie asks, looking at the ring. "But I thought the Freedom Force had all three. What happened to the other two?"

I'm about to answer but stop myself. I mean, is there really any reason to tell them my theory on what happened to the other rings? After all, I feel bad enough already. Especially because I know it's somehow tied to the toy robot and the grown-ups disappearing.

Wait, that's it!

"Epic?" Selfie says. "What's wrong?"

"Nothing," I say. "In fact, everything is starting to make sense. Because if that djinn named Beezle was responsible for turning that toy into a giant, then that means it's on Earth. Which means we may be able to pinpoint its location. Come on!"

"Seriously?" Pinball says. "We're running again?"

I lead the team back the way we came and hustle up the steps to the Monitor Room. Then, I get to work.

"What are you doing?" Skunk Girl asks.

"Plugging in Beezle's Meta signature," I answer. "The Meta Monitor is programmed to identify Meta powers. Every power has a unique signature, and now that we've matched that signature to Beezle, it's only a matter of time before the Meta Monitor finds him."

"That's cool," Pinball says, leaning against a console, "as long as we can stop rushing back and forth. You know, they say too much exercise isn't healthy. I think I heard a guy who played a doctor on TV mention it once."

"Alert! Alert! Alert!" the Meta Monitor blares. "Meta 2 disturbance. Repeat: Meta 2 disturbance. Power signature identified as Beezle. Alert! Alert! Alert! Meta 2 disturbance. Power signature identified as Beezle."

"Bingo!" I say. "We've got him!"

"Where is he?" Selfie asks.

Just then, the location pops up on the monitor and my heart starts racing because it reads:

META SIGNATURE IDENTIFIED.

LOCATION: LOCKDOWN META-MAXIMUM FEDERAL PENITENTIARY.

Meta Profile

Three Rings of Suffering

THREE RINGS OF SUFFERING

- **Gold Ring: Terrog (Meta 3) - click link for Meta Profile**
- **Silver Ring: Beezle (Meta 2) - click link for Meta Profile**
- **Bronze Ring: Rasp (Meta 1) - click link for Meta Profile**

NINE

I PLAY LET'S MAKE A DEAL

This is the last place I expected to be right now.

I mean, my history with Lockdown isn't exactly a good one. And as I think back to all of my misadventures with this place, nothing sticks out more than the death of my friend K'ami. I still have nightmares about that horrific moment in the courtyard—that moment when K'ami died in my arms.

But no matter how painful that memory is, I have to soldier on. There's just too much at stake and too many people counting on me to back out now. So, I need to focus on the task at hand, which is finding Beezle.

I touch down the Freedom Flyer inside the gates. Under normal circumstances, I wouldn't be able to get close to the facility without being barraged by security.

But clearly, these aren't normal circumstances. And once we're on the ground, there's nothing between us and the front door.

"Well, this place is creepy," Pinball says. "Maybe I'll wait inside the Freedom Flyer until you're done."

Wow, and I thought Dog-Gone was chicken. Yet, Pinball may have the right idea because this could be dangerous. I mean, I didn't really want to bring the team with me, but I couldn't just leave them on the Waystation.

Thankfully, I brought some extra muscle.

"Sorry," Grace says, cracking her knuckles, "but if you want to be a real superhero then you'll need to put your big boy pants on. This prison is massive and we need all hands on deck."

"Okay, okay," Pinball says, exiting the Freedom Flyer with the rest of us, "but I don't have a good feeling about this."

"Relax," Skunk Girl says. "The prison should be empty. Logically speaking, if all the grown-ups are gone then the prisoners should be gone too, right?"

"Let's hope so, Skunkie," Grace says.

I hear Skunk Girl mutter under her breath.

Skunk Girl's logic makes sense except for one small crack in her theory. If everyone is gone, then how did the Meta Monitor pick up Beezle's signature inside of Lockdown? Needless to say, I'm feeling far less 'relaxed' about this mission than she is.

We reach the entrance and when I grab the handle

and push, the front door swings open with ease. Well, that was suspiciously unlocked. I look back at Grace who nods and I step inside. The entryway looks the same as I remember, dark and narrow with small sconces lining the walls. And the air conditioning system is still too loud and pumping out way too much cold air.

"W-Well, this is j-just l-lovely," Pinball says, his teeth chattering.

But as we move past the unmanned control room and veer left, I'm surprised to find two doors instead of one. Well, this is different. I remember Dad saying he had to restructure the facility given the increase in Meta prisoners, but I didn't realize he split the actual prison into two wings.

A sign over the first door reads: *Meta Wing A: Energy Manipulators, Flyers, Magicians, Meta-Manipulators, Meta-morphs: Official Access Only.* The sign over the second door reads: *Meta Wing B: Psychics, Super-Intellects, Super-Speedsters, Super-Strength, Official Access Only.*

Well, as Grace said, this facility is massive and Beezle could be anywhere. And since we need to cover as much ground as quickly as possible there's only one conclusion.

"We should split up," I suggest.

"Great idea," Grace says. "You boys take Wing A and us girls will take Wing B."

"Deal," I say. "C'mon, Dog-Gone and Pinball."

"Hang on," Pinball says. "I want to go with Glory Girl. I think we'd make great partners!"

"Sorry," Grace says. "Girls rule, boys drool. Later."

As the girls head off, Pinball looks dejected, but I'm hoping he'll get over it. After all, Wing A is exactly where I want to be because it's the wing holding the Magicians. And since Beezle uses Magic maybe we'll find something.

I open the door and step inside.

"Do you think Glory Girl goes for younger men?" Pinball asks. "Because she's amazing."

"Dude, really?" I whisper. "We're trying to find an evil genie in a prison right now, so please focus."

"Right," he whispers.

Sometimes I wish I could forget things as easily as Pinball, but unfortunately, that's not going to happen. As we make our way through the Energy Manipulator cell block I see familiar names on the doors, like Taser, Heatwave, Magneton, and the Atomic Rage. But when I look through the cell windows there's no one inside.

And it's the same as we pass by the Flyers. Notorious villains like Atmo-Spear, Bicyclone, and Fly-Guy are all missing in action. I guess Skunk Girl was right. Since the prisoners were all grown-ups they disappeared too. So, did the Meta Monitor make a mistake? Maybe there's no one here but us.

But even if that's true, there's still one area I need to check out. We enter the Magician cell block when Dog-Gone suddenly bares his teeth and lets out a low growl.

"What's up with him?" Pinball whispers. "He's freaking me out."

"I don't know," I whisper back. "Dog-Gone, what is it? Do you smell something?"

But Dog-Gone doesn't answer.

In fact, he doesn't move at all!

"Dog-Gone, are you okay?" I ask, but when I touch his head he doesn't react. That's when I realize he's not blinking! It's like he's frozen solid even though he's not cold to the touch! "Pinball, quick—," I start, but when I turn around Pinball is frozen too!

What's going on?

Suddenly, a chill runs down my spine and I spin around. Did something just move? "Come out and face me, Beezle!" I call out, my voice cracking nervously as it echoes through the cell block.

But there's no response.

My eyes dart all over the place when I spot something I didn't see before. One of the cell doors in the Magician section is open. That's strange because none of the doors were open before. I blink hard and look again but I wasn't imagining things.

The door is still open.

Okay, this is weird. Now what? Do I check it out myself or go find Grace? But I can't just leave Dog-Gone and Pinball here like this. So, I guess I have my answer.

It's time to put my own big boy pants on.

But as I tiptoe over to the door I realize Beezle's Meta profile didn't say anything about him being able to freeze people like statues. So, how did that happen? You know, maybe this isn't such a good idea.

But when I try to stop myself, I can't! In fact, despite my best efforts, my feet just keep moving forward. It's like I'm trapped in my own body and I can't get out!

As I approach the cell, I realize the nameplate on the door is blank. Okay, that's unusual because I know every cell is specifically designed to resist the powers of its inhabitant. I try to stop, to slow myself down, but I can't. I'm being pulled in against my will!

And then I'm inside.

But the cell is no longer a cell, but a cave, complete with rock walls and a musty smell. I look around totally confused. I mean, how did that happen?

"Welcome, Epic Zero," comes a smooth, male voice.

Huh? But when I look back to the center of the room there's a man cloaked in shadows sitting at a table. Um, what's going on here? He wasn't there a second ago, and neither were the table and chairs.

"Please, join me," he says, beckoning me closer.

My feet start doing their own thing again, and as I get closer the shadows fall away from his face and I do a double-take, because he has long, dark hair, yellow eyes, and purple skin!

Okay, this clearly isn't Beezle, so I flip through all of the Meta profiles I can remember but come up empty. I don't know who this guy is, but I notice he's not wearing Beezle's silver ring.

"It's an honor to finally meet the all-powerful Epic

Zero," he says. His tone is strangely warm, like how honey would sound if it could talk. "Or would you rather be called Elliott Harkness?" Then, he offers me the chair on the other side of the table. "Please, have a seat."

But before I can object my body starts moving and plops me in the seat across from him.

"Yes, and now that you're here I can sense I was right," he says, closing his eyes and inhaling deeply. "Your aura is strong. Unusually strong."

"H-How do you know my name?" I stammer.

"Oh, I know lots of things," he says, putting his long fingers into a steeple and tapping the tips together. "You see, knowing things is my business, and I know all about you. I know what you eat for breakfast, I know who your parents are, and I even know what you're doing here. You're looking for clues like this, aren't you?"

Then, an object appears on the table and I gasp.

"That's the toy leg!" I exclaim. "That's the one piece I couldn't find at the zoo. H-How did you get it?"

"It's not important," he says, waving a hand dismissively. "But it helped get you here."

Get me here? What's he talking about? Was this a trap? "Where's Beezle?" I demand.

"Not here," the man says. "But I can help you find him if you'd like?"

"Wh-Who are you?" I ask.

"I'm known by many names," the man says. "But I prefer my true name, Tormentus."

Tormentus?

I don't know any Metas by that name.

"What do you want?" I ask.

"To be business partners," Tormentus says, his left eyebrow rising. "Maybe even friends. I suppose it depends on the bargain we strike."

"The bargain we strike?" I repeat. "What are you talking about?" And then I realize something. This guy is the only adult left on the entire freaking planet. But why? Unless…

"You look like you have a question," he says.

"A-Are you responsible for what happened to the grown-ups?" I ask. "What did you do to them? Where did you send them?"

"Slow down," Tormentus says, sitting back in his chair. "I knew you had questions, but I didn't expect so many at once."

"What did you do to the grown-ups?" I yell.

"*I* didn't do anything," Tormentus says. "But as I said, knowing things is my business, and that particular answer comes at a price."

"What are you even talking about?" I say, totally confused. "Why am I here?"

"It's actually quite simple," he says, picking up the toy leg. "You see, I'm willing to offer you a deal for the knowledge you seek. I'll tell you how to get your precious grown-ups back in exchange for something relatively small in comparison. Something rather meaningless in the grand scheme of things."

"Um, okay," I say. "And what's that?"

"Your soul," Tormentus says matter-of-factly.

"Excuse me?" I say.

"It's a no-brainer," Tormentus says. "I'll tell you how to get your loved ones and all of the others back, and in exchange, you'll give me your soul when you die. Think about it, you'll restore the lives of billions, and save your sister. Why, you'll be the greatest hero who ever lived. All for something you won't even need when your time comes. What do you say?"

I have to admit, what he's saying makes sense. I mean, if that's all it takes to bring the grown-ups back, then why wouldn't I do it? I'd get my parents back and keep Grace around. She'd owe me big time. Besides, do I really need my soul when I'm gone anyway?

"Just say 'yes,'" Tormentus says, "and I'll grant you your heart's desire. Imagine the fame you'll gain. Imagine the adulation. You'd be the greatest hero of all time."

The greatest hero of all time?

I'd like that. But wait a second. I don't care about fame and adulation—whatever that means. What's happening here? I feel like he's inside my head. Like he's brainwashing me. But that's not gonna happen. I'm not giving my soul to this nutjob!

"Sorry," I say, digging down and pushing my negation powers out, "but the answer is no! This soul can't be bought!"

Suddenly, the table and chairs disappear and I land hard on my rump. And when I look up, Tormentus is standing over me, shaking his head from side to side.

"Foolish child," he says. "You just turned down the deal of a lifetime. But don't sweat it, because someone else took me up on my generous offer. And while her soul may not be as powerful as yours, it's not as naïve. But have no fear, Elliott Harkness, I'm sure you'll get another bite at the apple real soon. And who knows? You might change your mind when your own life is on the line."

And then he snaps his fingers and he's gone!

Just then, something rattles by my feet and I pick it up. It's the toy leg! But as I squeeze it tight Tormentus' words sink in.

He said someone else took him up on his offer.

Who could that be?

But then, I look at the toy leg in my hand and have my answer.

Meta Profile

Rasp

Name: Rasp	Height: Variable
Race: Djinn	Weight: Variable
Status: Villain/Inactive	Eyes/Hair: Gray/Bald

META 1: Magic
Limited Wish Fulfillment
Limited Mind-Warping
Limited Shapeshifting

Observed Characteristics			
Combat 33			
Durability	36	Leadership	24
Strategy	53	Willpower	49

TEN

I FIND OUT HOO DID IT

Thankfully, Dog-Gone and Pinball are back to normal.

Well, I guess they were never really 'normal' to begin with so let's just say they're back to their usual annoying selves. But what's strange is that Pinball doesn't even remember being frozen. And when we caught up with Grace, Selfie, and Skunk Girl they said they didn't see another soul in their entire wing.

Another soul.

What an interesting choice of words.

So, that makes me the only one who actually saw Tormentus. Lucky me. I still don't know why he wanted my soul but he certainly was pushy about getting it. Unfortunately for him, it's not for sale at the moment.

Yet, I do feel kind of guilty for not taking him up on

his deal. But the thing is, I don't know if that's how I really feel or if he's somehow still influencing my thinking. But even if I took his offer and got my parents back, I know they wouldn't approve of what I had to do to get it done. Besides, the fact that Tormentus revealed it was even possible to get them back tells me it can still be done.

I just need to figure out how.

The good news is that he left some pretty big clues. He said someone else agreed to his bargain already, and that someone is a 'she' whose soul is less naïve than mine. Funny, I don't think anyone has insulted my soul before but I guess there's a first time for everything. But while that was interesting, it's the toy leg he left behind that'll help me crack this case wide open.

After recapping my run-in with Tormentus, we race to the Freedom Flyer to confirm my suspicions. And I'm pretty sure I'm right because there was only one other person at the zoo who helped me fight that giant Powerbot. And that person also happens to be a girl. She's the only one who could have delivered that toy leg to Tormentus. So, I think I know exactly who took him up on his offer.

Night Owl.

"Never heard of her," Grace says, looking over my shoulder as I type into the dashboard console.

"I hadn't either," I say. "But now I've run into her twice and she actually thinks I'm responsible for this mess. Can you believe it?"

"No," Grace says. "Unless, of course, you are?"

"What?" I say, turning to look her dead in the eyes. "Are you kidding me? I'm not!"

"Okay, relax," Grace says. "I'm just double-checking. I mean, even you have to admit that strange stuff always happens to you. Stuff that never happens to, like, ninety-nine percent of other Meta heroes. Bad luck follows you around like a black cloud."

"Yeah," I say fuming, "but not this time."

Even though I'm annoyed with her I get what she's saying. It's true I've had some weird things happen to me, but they mostly weren't my fault. And in this case, Night Owl is the missing link. That's why I'm having the Meta Monitor triangulate her Meta signatures over the last few days. Then we'll be able to pinpoint her location.

"So, are you really sure this Night Owl kid knows what's going on?" Grace asks.

"Positive," I say. "I'm sure she's the one who made a deal with Tormentus, so you can stop watching me like a hawk."

"Are they fighting again?" I hear Skunk Girl whisper from the back of the Freedom Flyer.

"Like cats and dogs," Pinball whispers back.

"Alert! Alert! Alert!" the Meta Monitor blares. "Meta 2 disturbance. Repeat: Meta 2 disturbance. Power signature identified as Night Owl. Alert! Alert! Alert! Meta 2 disturbance. Power signature identified as Night Owl."

"Bingo!" I say. "Now we just need the location."

Then, the cursor spits out:

META SIGNATURE IDENTIFIED.

LOCATION: 224 SHADOW LAKE LANE, KEYSTONE CITY USA.

"That's it!" I say. "We've got her! And based on the map I think that's her home address."

"Okay," Selfie says. "So, now what?"

"Now?" I say. "Now we make a house call."

***

"I didn't know superheroes made house calls," Pinball says as we crowd onto the doorstep of 224 Shadow Lake Lane.

"You wouldn't believe some of the things we do," I say. But as I reach to press the doorbell I hesitate. I mean, the house is a lovely blue-and-white colonial in a nice family neighborhood with neatly trimmed hedges and gnome statues in the garden. There's nothing here that screams "sketchy character on the premises."

Maybe I've got this all wrong.

"Can you just ring the doorbell so we can get this over with already?" Grace asks from the back.

"Hold on," Skunk Girl says from behind me. "If this girl is home, do you really think she's gonna open the door for five costumed kids and a masked dog? I say we break the door down and take her by surprise."

"Break the door down?" Pinball says. "But that'll be impossible to repair. I mean, there aren't any handymen around."

"Well, then I'll smoke her out," Skunk Girl offers, wiggling her fingers. "I'll stink up the whole joint and she'll come running."

"Can someone please ring the stupid doorbell?" Grace barks. "This is getting ridiculous."

Ugh! With all of this commotion, I can't think straight. Note to self: next time we agree on the plan before deboarding the Freedom Flyer. "Can we all just calm—"

DING-DONG!

"—down?"

Huh? Who rang the doorbell?

Then, I turn to see Dog-Gone's nose pressed against the button.

"Thank you!" Grace says. "At least one of you idiots has some sense. I just didn't think it'd be the dog."

Everyone quiets down as we wait for Night Owl to answer the door, but she doesn't come.

"Told you she wouldn't open it," Skunk Girl huffs.

"What now, genius?" Grace asks.

Now there's a great question. What do we do now?

"Well, I guess we have no choice but to bust down the door and—"

But as I reach for the doorknob, I notice the shadow beneath the door disappear. That's weird? Did the sun shift? Or… uh-oh. "Duck!"

Just then, the door BURSTS off its hinges!

I grab Selfie and Skunk Girl and hit the ground as the door goes flying over us! The next thing I know, Night Owl comes riding out the front door on one of her shadow slides!

"There she goes!" Pinball yells, pointing to the sky as Night Owl disappears over the house across the street. "She's getting away!"

"Not on my watch!" Grace says, taking off into the air after her.

But something tells me I can't just leave this up to Grace, so I concentrate hard and duplicate her power. And then I go airborne!

"Hey!" Skunk Girl calls out. "What about us?"

"Wait here!" I yell. "We'll be back!"

I have to say, one of the coolest parts of being a Meta Manipulator is copying the powers of a Flyer like Grace. There's nothing in the world like zooming through the air at supersonic speed, especially when you're chasing a villain. Unfortunately, it always takes me a few seconds to remember how to do it right.

So, after nearly crashing through a second-story window, sideswiping a brick chimney, and avoiding a head-on collision with a flock of geese, I'm finally stable enough to join the chase. Grace is way up ahead and she's nearly caught up to Night Owl, who is shooting solid shadow blasts back at Grace to shake her off her tail!

The good news is she doesn't see me coming. The bad news is that we're flying directly over Keystone City, which means this could get messy if we don't take her down quickly. But Night Owl is going really fast, and if Grace can't catch her I'm pretty sure I won't either.

Time for plan B.

I veer left and head for downtown. If I can circle those office buildings I'll surprise Night Owl from the other side. But as I loop around it dawns on me that if we collide in mid-air we could end up going splat. So, I come up with a new idea to end this sky chase. I'll just need to act quickly so no one gets hurt.

As I clear the last building I spot Night Owl and Grace heading right for me. I hover in the air, concentrate hard, and send a wave of negation energy right at Night Owl.

"You!" she says as soon as she sees me, her brown eyes growing wide. "I should have known it was—Hey, what's happening?"

Just then, the darkness coming from her fingertips dries up and her shadow slide dissipates into nothing. She hangs there for a second, shocked and grasping at empty air, and then she falls like a rock. But before I can go after her—

"I've got her," Grace calls out, but then disaster strikes as Grace flies right through my negation zone! The next thing I know, Grace screams and starts falling too!

Holy smokes! We're hundreds of feet in the air! And

that's when I realize I'm tapping into Grace's power. If I didn't store enough to keep myself afloat we're all toast!

I've got to act fast!

I divebomb after them and reach Grace first, grabbing her tightly around the waist.

"Remember that black cloud thing?" I shout.

"If we survive this," she shouts back, "I'm gonna kill you."

That's fair. But first I've got to catch Night Owl. The only problem is that I'm running out of gas. In fact, I can actually feel my flight power waning! I've got to motor!

"Stretch out your legs!" I yell at Grace. "We need to be more aerodynamic!"

Grace kicks out her arms and legs and we pick up more speed. That's great but I've got another problem. Where will we land? Grabbing Night Owl will just add more weight and I won't have enough power left to get the three of us safely to the ground.

That's when I spot the police station below. It's just a few stories above the ground, but it might be my best target. I stretch my legs and make an extra push. But based on how Night Owl is falling I think she's passed out. That's not going to be helpful, but we're closing in on the police station.

Last chance!

I accelerate with everything I've got and grab Night Owl around the waist. She flops limply against me and I pull up with everything I've got. Suddenly, we clear the roofline of the police station and tumble over one another. My body pounds against the cement, and by the time we stop rolling it feels like I've been run over by a fleet of trucks.

"G-Grace?" I call out, lying on my back and trying to catch my breath. "A-Are you okay?"

"Y-Yeah," she says, lying face down with a bruised cheek and bloody nose. "I'm just dandy, thanks."

"I'm so sorry," I say, "I guess I didn't think that through."

"Really?" Grace says. "I couldn't tell. By the way, my birthday present from you just got a whole lot bigger. How's the girl?"

I crawl over to Night Owl relieved to see she's still breathing. And she doesn't look too beat up which probably means Grace and I broke her fall.

"Night Owl?" I say, leaning over her. "It's Epic Zero. Are you okay? Can you hear me?"

Slowly, her eyelids flutter, and when she opens her eyes she says, "W-What did you do to me?"

"I negated your powers," I say.

"B-But you saved me," she says. "Why?"

"Because I told you I'm a hero," I say. "That's what heroes do."

"Right," she says. "I thought you and your friends were villains coming to attack me. I thought you were going to kill me. That's why I ran."

"What? No," I say. "We weren't trying to kill you.

We wanted to know what you know about a guy named Tormentus."

"Tormentus?" she says. "I-I don't know anyone called Tormentus."

Um, what? That wasn't the answer I was expecting.

"Are you sure?" I ask. "Maybe he gave you a different name, but he's got yellow eyes and purple skin. He told you he would trade information on how to get our parents back in exchange for your soul."

"What?" she says. "No, I never met anyone like that."

I look into her confused eyes and I know she's telling me the truth. So, that means this was all a mistake, because if Night Owl wasn't the one who sold her soul to Tormentus then who did? I mean, we were the only two who knew about the giant Powerbot toy.

"So, wait," Grace says, limping over. "Are you telling me this was all for nothing? I almost died for nothing? Dude, you're nothing but bad luck!"

Bad. Luck?

And that's when it hits me.

We went after the wrong Meta girl.

Meta Profile

Night Owl

Name: Tamika Thomas	Height: 5'1"
Race: Human	Weight: 108 lbs
Status: Hero/Active	Eyes/Hair: Brown/Black

META 2: Energy Manipulator
Considerable Shadow Manipulation
Can transform shadows into solid objects

Observed Characteristics			
Combat 55			
Durability	20	Leadership	50
Strategy	56	Willpower	75

ELEVEN

I CAN'T REST FOR A SECOND

"Don't be so hard on yourself," Selfie says.

That's easy for her to say. After all, she didn't nearly get her sister killed chasing the wrong suspect. After that embarrassing episode, I'm surprised anyone is still willing to listen to me. But Next Gen considers me to be their leader so I've got to bounce back. And that's why we're back on the Waystation starting at square one.

"Do you think you can find her?" Selfie asks as I type into the Meta Monitor.

"I know I can," I say, and this time I'm convinced I'm after the right person.

Haywire.

The more I think about it, the more I realize how everything points back to her. Tormentus told me the person who sold him that soul was a 'she.' And Haywire was at the Keystone City Zoo with me and Night Owl. I can still see the determination in her eyes when she told me she'll do anything to find her parents and be a great hero, even without Next Gen. So, would she make a pact with Tormentus to get what she wanted?

I'm thinking yes.

And I'm kicking myself for not figuring it out sooner. We're losing time by the second. Especially if we're going to save—

"Epic Zero?" Grace says, entering the Monitor Room with an ice bag over her bruised cheek, "can I speak with you privately?"

"Oh, sure," Selfie says, shooting me a concerned look. "I'll just step out."

"Thanks," Grace says. "I suggest you go down to the Galley. Pinball and Dog-Gone were arguing over some leftover fried chicken and it was getting nasty."

"Right," Selfie says. "Will do. See you later."

As Selfie leaves, I'm pretty sure I know what Grace is doing here. She's probably going to let me have it. I mean, she has every right to be angry with me after the Night Owl incident. So, I brace myself, and as soon as Selfie's footsteps stop echoing down the stairway, we both blurt out—

"Grace, I'm sorry."

"Elliott, I'm scared."

"Wait, what?" I say, totally confused. "What did you

just say?"

"I-I said I'm scared," Grace says, her eyes welling up. "I mean, I turn fifteen tomorrow and I don't know what'll happen to me. I could vanish off the face of the Earth, never to be seen again. I don't know what to do."

As I watch tears stream down her cheeks I'm taken aback. I don't think I've ever seen Grace cry like, ever. She's always the tough one. The strong one.

"I-I miss Mom and Dad," she says, her voice cracking, "but I don't want to end up like them. We've got to find them. We've got to find out what happened to them and stop it from happening to others, including me." She pauses and wipes her tears away with her forearm. "Sorry, you know I'm not normally like this, but you're the only one I can talk to."

"N-No," I say, "it's okay. I'm glad you're telling me. Look, I'm doing everything I can to figure this out. And I'm sorry about all of those mistakes I made. I guess I am a bonehead sometimes."

"No, Elliott," she says, putting her hand on my shoulder, "you're not a bonehead. Well, not all the time. Look, if anyone is going to solve this mystery it's you. You're more patient than me, and I hate to admit it, but you're a better thinker too. Hey, you're not recording me saying this stuff, are you?"

"What?" I say, pretending to move my hand away from the dashboard. "No, but maybe I should."

"I'm counting on you, squirt," Grace says, her voice

sounding more like herself. "Got it?"

"Yeah," I say. "Look, as often as I joke about it I don't want you disappearing on me. Now Dog-Gone on the other hand…"

"Ha," she says. "He's your best friend so I don't believe that for a second. Anyway, did you find out anything about that Tormentus guy?"

"Nothing," I answer. The first thing I did when we got back to the Waystation was look him up on the Meta Monitor, but there's no profile. It's like he doesn't even exist."

"And Haywire?" she asks.

"The Meta Monitor is doing its thing," I say. "Fortunately, I was able to put in the coordinates of the places I know she used her powers but they're not active readings anymore. Night Owl was really active so she was easy to find. Hopefully, Haywire has been active recently."

"Speaking of Night Owl," Grace says, "she seems kind of reserved. She's not really saying much to anyone."

"Can you blame her?" I say. "I mean, I nearly killed her only fifteen minutes ago."

"Fair," Grace says. "But she's still an odd bird."

Well, I agree with her about that. I invited Night Owl to join us and she declined at first but then changed her mind right before we left. I've seen her in action and I know she'll be a big help. Hopefully, she'll stick around.

"Alert! Alert! Alert!" the Meta Monitor blares.

"Here it comes!" I say.

"Meta 1 disturbance. Repeat: Meta 1 disturbance. Power signature identified as Haywire. Alert! Alert! Alert! Meta 1 disturbance. Power signature identified as Haywire."

"Where's the signal coming from?" Grace asks. "What's the location?"

I look at the monitor and do a double take.

"Um, is that right?" I ask. "Because it says it's coming from Safari Park."

***

"I love Safari Park," Pinball says. "My parents took me and my brother there a few years ago. It's the largest animal park in the whole world."

"Great," Skunk Girl says, "maybe we can leave you there when we're done."

"Actually," Pinball says, "being around you is kind of like being at Safari Park, especially if you're standing downwind."

"Can you guys please stop?" Selfie says. "The constant digs are just getting annoying."

"You can say that again," Grace says. "How much longer until we're there?"

"We'll be there in one minute," I say, checking the Freedom Flyer's radar. But the thing I can't figure out is why Haywire is even at Safari Park. I mean, the last place

I saw her was at the Keystone City Zoo, which is over a thousand miles north of Safari Park. And come to think of it, what's with the animal theme? I'm guessing this is all connected, I just don't know how.

"Anyway," Pinball says, "Safari Park is so enormous you can't do the whole thing in one day. They have all of these different lands inside, like Elephant Land, Big Cat Land, and Giraffe Land. Each land has its own animal preserve you can tour, amazing animal shows, and they even let you feed some of the animals at designated times. Plus, they also have Fun Land where you can ride rollercoasters and stuff. It's super awesome. Have you been there, Night Owl?"

"Nope," Night Owl says. "Can't say I have."

"You'd like it," Pinball says. "They have owls you can hang with."

"I'll keep that in mind," Night Owl says.

Well, Grace was right. Night Owl is acting a bit reserved. She probably just needs some time to warm up. After all, we're still strangers to her. But one thing I do know is that she's as committed to this mission as we are. She told me she wants to get her parents back. And after our little case of mistaken identity, she also wants to catch Haywire.

Just then, we fly over a massive, well-manicured park that stretches for miles. Well, I've never been to Safari Park myself but that must be it. Looking down I can see large animals moving through the park but something seems off. That's when I realize the animals aren't confined to designated areas. They're roaming lose all over the park! It's just like the zoo! Someone set the animals free!

"Is that an elephant walking down Main Street?" Selfie asks.

"Guys?" Pinball says.

"And look at the white rhino," Skunk Girl says. "It's crushing that picnic table."

"Um, guys," Pinball says.

"Does anyone else see a polar bear knocking over a vending machine?" Grace asks.

"Guys!" Pinball yells.

"What?" Skunk Girl says. "What is it?"

"Th-There's a… robot behind us," Pinball says, pointing over his shoulder.

THOOM!

Suddenly, our left wing explodes and the Freedom Flyer tilts off course! I peer into the rearview mirror to see Pinball is right, there is a robot flying behind us! But it's not just any robot, it's another giant Powerbot! And it's got us dead in its sights!

"Hold on!" I yell.

I rotate sideways just as another missile shoots by, but my dashboard is lit up like a Christmas tree. We've lost a thruster and smoke is pouring out of my wing!

We're going down!

"Keep your eyes on the road!" Grace yells.

I grit my teeth and try to level us out, but the steering column isn't cooperating. If I don't land this puppy fast that bucket of bolts will blow us clear out of the sky. I look for the closest place to touch down when—

"He's aiming at us again!" Pinball yells.

"Not if I can help it," Night Owl says.

Then, she unbuckles herself, setting off the safety alarm.

"What are you doing back there?" I call out.

"Saving us," she says. And then she lifts the large shadow from beneath Pinball and projects it through the rear window, enveloping the Powerbot in darkness. And when she closes her fist the robot shatters into a gazillion pieces.

"Whoa!" Skunk Girl says. "I didn't know you could do that!"

"I think I have a new love," Pinball mutters.

"That's the best news I've heard all day," Grace says.

I knew Night Owl would come in handy, but we're not out of the woods yet because we're coming in hot. I engage the landing gear and pull back on the throttle with everything I've got to level us off.

"Should I drive?" Grace yells, gripping her armrests so tightly her knuckles are white.

"Nope," I say, "I've got it."

By now I've had more experience with emergency landings than I'd care to admit, but I've never had one that required dodging free-range animals. I spot the longest strip of roadway available, and then angle the Freedom Flyer toward it. This isn't going to be easy.

"Hold on tight!" I yell, trying to sound confident but my voice betrays me. I drop the back of the Freedom Flyer and Dog-Gone YIPS as the wheels touch the ground hard. We're halfway there! But as I lay down the front—

"Ostrich!" Grace yells.

Ostrich? Suddenly, a giant bird jumps in front of us and I swerve right, just missing it except for a few feathers that get pinned to the windshield. I quickly pull left to level off the Freedom Flyer and slam on the brakes. Selfie grabs Night Owl as everyone flies forward in their seatbelts as we SCREECH to a stop, just a few feet away from a confused pack of porcupines.

That's when I realize I'm completely covered in sweat. And that I also despise ostriches.

"Nice driving," Skunk Girl says, "now who's going to clean-up Dog-Gone's barf?"

"Not it," Pinball says, his finger on his nose.

I look back at Dog-Gone's green face and the mess on the floor and now I know who won the battle over the leftover fried chicken. Well, at least that's one mystery solved.

"We'll deal with it later," I say, unbuckling my seatbelt. "We've lost any element of surprise. We've got to get out of here and find Haywire before she takes off on us. Next Gen—Let's Get Even!"

"Um, is that your new battle cry?" Skunk Girl asks as she hops out. "Because it's super lame."

"I guess not," I say. "Let's just go."

But as soon as I step out of the Freedom Flyer I realize we won't be going far.

Because we're surrounded by Powerbots!

TWELVE

I GET QUITE THE SURPRISE

This is not good.

I mean, first, we're shot out of the air by a flying Powerbot, and now we're surrounded by dozens more. They're big, mean, and aiming their assorted weaponry right at us. I look at Night Owl who has her hands in the air like the rest of us. I guess there's too many of them even for her.

Of course, my powers don't work on robots so I'm crippled with uselessness. As I stare into the red, unblinking eyes of the Powerbot in front of me it triggers a memory. You know, I think I actually had that one as a toy. His name is Star-warp or something like that. I remember him having a heat-seeking missile-arm which, coincidentally, seems to be pointed right at me.

I still can't figure out where these giant-sized toys came from, let alone what their purpose is. But right now, I need to do something before this turns ugly. I'm about to open my mouth when Star-warp pushes his missile-arm hard into my chest!

"Ow!" I say. "Back off!"

But the Powerbot doesn't move.

"Your name is Star-warp, isn't it?" I ask. "Or is it Warp-star? Anyway, we're not looking for trouble here. We were just passing overhead when one of your guys decided to blow us out of the sky. So, let's say we skip the obligatory fight scene and go for some ice cream and motor oil?"

But Star-warp doesn't respond.

"Okay, I get it," I say. "If you're not into motor oil we could go for premium gas instead?"

Then, his eyes start pulsing.

"Epic Zero!" Selfie calls out. "He's gonna shoot!"

She's right! But before I can move, Star-warp's torso swivels and his missile-arm fires! THOOM! I shield my face as robot-parts explode everywhere. But when I look back up I realize he's blown three of his buddies to smithereens!

But why? What's going on?

Suddenly, all of the robots aim at one another.

"Everyone down!" Grace yells.

We hit the deck as a barrage of crossfire flashes overhead. THOOM! THOOM! I curl into a ball as more robot-parts shower my body, and when the onslaught finally stops I look up to find smoldering Powerbots lying all around us.

What the heck just happened? Why did they take each other out? But I don't have to wait long for an answer, because suddenly a girl says—

"So, do you think I'm Next Gen material now?"

I turn to find Haywire standing over us with her arms crossed and a scowl on her face. And as I look into her eyes I can tell that something has changed—and maybe not for the better.

"Wait, did you do this?" Skunk Girl asks. "Because I thought you couldn't control your powers."

"That was the old me," Haywire says. "But things are different now. In fact, things are so different that I don't need your little team anymore. So, now that I've shown you what you passed up on, I suggest you losers crawl back into your shuttle and leave."

"Well, that's harsh," Pinball says.

Harsh is right. This is definitely not the Haywire I remember. I mean, when she tried out for our team she was determined but sincere. Now she's got an edge, and I don't doubt for a minute where it came from.

Tormentus.

"Life is harsh, isn't it?" Haywire says. "Now I've got a job to do and I don't need you getting in my way. So, you can either leave on your own, or I can provide a little motivation to help you on your way."

"Now hang on there, missy," Grace starts.

"Wait," I say, cutting her off. "We'll go."

Grace shoots me a look but I know what I'm doing. Tormentus must have given Haywire better control of her powers in exchange for her soul, and that makes her extremely dangerous. I mean, just look at how easily she disposed of those Powerbots.

But I'm betting that's not all Tormentus gave her.

If he offered her the same deal he offered me, then I'm guessing Haywire knows who is doing all of this. Yet, my gut tells me she'll clam up if I confront her about her deal with Tormentus. She wants us to believe she got this powerful all on her own. So, this is going to take some delicate probing. I just need to get her talking. Maybe if I boost her ego she'll let something slip.

"I knew you'd be a great hero someday," I say.

"Not just a great hero," she says, "but the greatest of all time. And today I'm going to prove it."

"I bet you will," I say. "But if you don't mind me asking, how exactly will you prove you're the greatest hero ever? Maybe we can help."

"Sorry, but no," Haywire says. "I'm taking him down all on my own."

"Him?" I say. "Who exactly is 'him?'"

But instead of answering me, her eyes narrow. "You're trying to trick me, aren't you? You're trying to get me to tell you stuff. Well, that's not happening. So, here's your last warning. Leave or else."

"I pick 'or else,'" Night Owl says.

"Wait!" I call out, but it's too late.

Night Owl pulls a shadow from beneath the Freedom Flyer and launches it at Haywire when it suddenly reverses direction and wraps around Night Owl herself!

"My, how unlucky," Haywire says with an evil grin.

Night Owl screams as the shadow squeezes her like a tube of toothpaste. For a second, I debate negating Haywire's power but who knows if it will work. Plus, if I do that she'll never cooperate with us. Instead, I've got a new plan. I just need her to release Night Owl.

"Stop!" I call out. "We'll go. Just let her free first."

Haywire hesitates before relenting. "Fine," she says. Then, the shadow slips away dumping Night Owl to the ground. "Take your lame new recruit and go."

"I'm not… their new recruit," Night Owl says, breathing heavily and holding her ribs.

"Let's go," I say, helping Night Owl to her feet.

"Can the Freedom Flyer even fly?" Pinball asks. "Look at the wing. Half of it is destroyed."

Well, he's right about that. "If we stay low we should be able to clear Safari Park," I say. Then, I turn to Haywire and say, "Good luck."

"I won't need it," she says, watching us board.

I leave the hatch open and when everyone gets to their seats, I stand up and offer Grace the controls. "You take it from here."

"Me?" she says. "Why, where are you going?"

"After Haywire," I whisper. "Listen, she's too unpredictable to fight head-on and it's my responsibility as leader to keep my team safe. But I'm gonna take Dog-Gone and follow her invisibly. You fly out of here so it looks like we've all left and I'll radio you later when I find out what's happening."

"Is that a good idea?" Grace whispers back.

"Do you have a better one?" I ask.

"Hey," Skunk Girl says, "where's Night Owl?"

I look back and Night Owl is gone. She must have snuck out in the shadows!

Just. Freaking. Wonderful.

Well, I can't worry about her now because I'll lose Haywire's trail. "C'mon, boy," I say to Dog-Gone.

"Where are you going?" Selfie asks.

"You guys are in good hands with Glory Girl," I say. "Listen to everything she says. I'll catch up later."

"Hey, be careful," Grace says.

"I will," I say. "And remember to overcompensate on the steering column to account for the wing—"

"I've got it," Grace says. "Don't do anything stupid."

"You too," I say, and then smile as I borrow Dog-Gone's power and we exit the Freedom Flyer invisibly. As Grace closes the hatch behind me and takes off overhead, I watch Haywire turn satisfied and head down a pathway. Great, she didn't notice us, but I guess she didn't notice Night Owl either.

I look up as the Freedom Flyer skims the trees, leaving a trail of smoke behind it. Grace is a good pilot so they'll be okay, but now I've got to do my part. The only thing is, I can't see Dog-Gone when he turned invisible.

"Where are you?" I whisper, reaching out for him. Then, I feel a wet nose against my palm. "Okay, follow that girl. But don't make any noise because we need to see where she's going. And no growling."

Dog-Gone brushes past me and we're off. As we run, I check out Safari Park for the first time. It looks like a fun place to visit, you know, if you had a normal life and all. Suddenly, I'm dodging all sorts of exotic birds strutting across the grounds and realize we've ventured into Feather Land. That's when I have a momentary flash of panic. What if Dog-Gone is hunting peacocks right now?

But when I reach out with my powers I find him way up ahead. As long as he's hot on Haywire's trail I just need to stay connected to him. His signal leads me over a bridge with a sign that reads: *Big Cat Land.*

Well, let's hope he's around here somewhere.

"Dog-Gone?" I whisper. "Are you here?"

Suddenly, there's a low GRRROOOWWWLLLL.

"Um, Dog-Gone?"

But as I round the corner I find myself face-to-face with a four-legged creature that's definitely not my mutt. Now, I'm no zoologist, but by the muscular body and cat-like head, I'd bet my bottom dollar that's a puma. And even though I'm invisible, its nose is working overtime—which means he knows I'm here!

"Um, nice kitty cat," I say, my heart racing.

But as the puma steps towards me, newspaper headlines flash before my eyes: *Invisible Boy Presumed Eaten by Puma. Remains Never Found.* Or even: *Kid Hero Gives Puma Indigestion. Puma Recovers After Full Bottle of Antacids.*

Just then, the puma leaps, and I open my mouth to scream for my life when the cat is suddenly wrapped inside a blanket of darkness. I've been saved! And as the puma struggles in vain to get out my savior appears.

"I know you're there, Epic Zero," Night Owl says, stepping off her shadow slide behind the puma. "I've been following your footsteps since you left the Freedom Flyer. Rescuing you is becoming a habit."

"Well, you know what they say," I remark while turning visible. "Third times the charm. But enough about me, what are you doing here? Why didn't you stay on the Freedom Flyer?"

"And miss my shot at revenge on Haywire?" Night Owl says. "No chance. And what about you?"

"I want to find out what she knows to get the grown-ups back," I say.

"Well, that makes two of us," she says.

"Then I guess we're joining forces on this one," I say, offering my hand. "Deal?"

"Deal," she says, shaking it. "Now let's find Haywire. She could be anywhere by now."

"Don't worry, I've got a mole on her tail," I say.

"Then this time ride with me," Night Owl says, forming a shadow slide and offering her hand.

I climb up and realize it's super solid.

"Hold on tight," she says, "and tell me where to go."

I grab her waist and we're off! I have to say, I've never ridden a shadow before, and it kind of feels like surfing through the air. Under ordinary circumstances, I'm sure this would be a blast, but right now I need to focus on staying connected to Dog-Gone while not falling off.

Suddenly, I see all kinds of rides below and realize we must be over Fun Land, the amusement park section. There's a Ferris wheel, a water flume, and an absolutely massive roller coaster track going through the middle of a fake mountain with a sign that reads: *Expedition Danger. Ride at Your Own Risk.* And Dog-Gone's signal is coming in strong at the base of the mountain!

"Down there," I say, pointing to the spot. But then I see Haywire standing by the Expedition Danger entrance. "Wait! Pull up! She's right there!"

Night Owl raises her shadow slide just as Haywire disappears through the entrance. We hover in the air for a few seconds until the coast is clear.

"Okay, you can take us down now," I say.

Night Owl lowers the slide to ground level and I jump off. "Dog-Gone," I whisper, "where are you?"

Just then, Dog-Gone appears out of thin air with his

tongue hanging out and tail wagging.

"Good boy," I say, rubbing his muzzle. "Of course, you did leave me to die at the paws of that puma, but at least you stuck to your assignment. Now I've got to see what Haywire is up to. Night Owl, follow—"

But when I turn around, she's gone again.

Well, so much for teamwork.

Time to go, but maybe I shouldn't bring Dog-Gone with me. I mean, this will definitely be dangerous, and while he followed instructions earlier, he's not exactly the most obedient dog on the planet. "Dog-Gone, stay here," I say, "and stay out of sight."

Dog-Gone furrows his brow and cocks an ear.

Uh-oh. I feel a bribe coming on. I don't have time for this. "Fine," I say. "You listen and I'll give you all the treats you want."

Dog-Gone sticks out his tongue and disappears.

Well, I'm not proud of caving to his demands but that ought to hold him. Besides, I've got more important things to do. So, I borrow his invisibility power and head for the ride entrance, passing by a warning sign that reads:

Persons with the following conditions should not ride: (1) Heart Conditions. (2) Back, Neck, or Similar Physical Conditions. (3) Pregnant Mothers. (4) Motion Sickness. (5) Other Medical Conditions that may be Aggravated by this Ride.

Funny, for some reason I was hoping it'd say: *(6) Or any Kid Wearing a Cape.* But no such luck so I press on.

The entrance to the Expedition Danger ride is dark

and narrow, and I follow a wooden pathway lined with frayed, waist-high ropes. The walls are covered with rusty climbing equipment and yellowed newspapers warning about a man-eating Yeti. Well, this ride definitely makes you feel like you're about to go on a treacherous expedition—which in my case isn't too far from the truth. As I move through the queue I keep an eye out for Haywire and Night Owl, but I don't see them anywhere.

Then, the pathway goes up.

About a hundred feet later, I walk beneath a red, hand-painted sign that says: *Expedition Danger: Proceed at Your Own Risk*. The next thing I know, the wall decorations give way to mountain scenery as a chilly breeze whips across my face. I keep climbing up, past a pile of fake goat bones, and around a steep bend until I reach a plateau. Funny, but I do feel out of breath, like I'm standing at a crazy high altitude.

Then, voices echo through the chamber—

"I've been waiting for you," comes a voice that sounds strangely familiar.

"Bring my parents back!" Haywire yells.

Even though I'm invisible, I get down on my hands and knees and peer over the edge of the plateau. The first thing I see is a rickety, wooden staircase leading down to a row of empty roller coaster cars. Well, I guess that's where the actual ride starts. But that's not what grabs my attention because Haywire is standing on the other side of the cars with her back to me. And she's facing a rather enormous man sitting in a gold throne in front of a fake, golden temple.

That's strange, why does that guy look so familiar?

But as I take a closer look a chill runs down my spine and I gasp in disbelief.

He has white skin, white hair, and giant muscles.

B-But that's impossible. I mean, it couldn't be.

Then, his blue eyes blaze red and I feel sick to my stomach. Because that's not a man at all.

It's… Siphon!

Meta Profile

Siphon

Name: Siphon	Height: 6'5"
Race: Human	Weight: 1,050 lbs
Status: Villain/Inactive	Eyes/Hair: Blue/White

META 3: Meta Manipulator
Extreme Power Duplication
WARNING: It is not known if Siphon can reach Meta 4 power levels like his father Meta-Taker

Observed Characteristics			
Combat 100			
Durability	100	Leadership	40
Strategy	80	Willpower	90

THIRTEEN

I BREAK A DATE WITH DESTINY

My eyes must be playing tricks on me.

I mean, it's just not possible. There's no way Siphon could be sitting there. But when I blink and open my eyes again, there he is.

But how? The last time I saw Siphon was back on Arena World where he sacrificed himself to put an end to Order and Chaos. By using the opposing powers of the Orb of Oblivion and the Building Block, Siphon blew all of them, not to mention Arena World, into nothingness.

There's no way he could have survived that.

Could he?

As I think back to that horrific day, I realize I never actually saw Siphon die. Just before everything went nuts, he used Wind Walker's power to wormhole me to safety. So, all of this time I just assumed he was dead. But maybe

I was wrong. Except, it just doesn't make any sense.

"I know you did it!" Haywire yells at Siphon. "I know you're responsible for making the grown-ups disappear! Now bring them back, or else!"

"You have a unique power, don't you?" Siphon says, closing his eyes and breathing in deep. "I can sense it within you."

"Yeah?" Haywire says. "Well, if you don't tell me the truth you'll feel my power firsthand, bozo!"

Uh-oh. Haywire may be stronger than she was, but she has no idea who she's dealing with. Siphon is a Meta 3 Meta Manipulator just like his father, Meta-Taker, which means he can duplicate the powers of others, including multiple Metas at the same time.

My mind flashes back to the first time I scuffled with Siphon back at that abandoned warehouse. I was much less experienced then and he would have destroyed me if he weren't transported to Arena World by that strange orange energy. I was lucky, but I can't count on lightning striking twice.

"If you fancy a sparring partner," Siphon says, standing up from his throne and waving his left hand with a grand flourish, "I'm at your service."

But as he flicks his wrist, something reflects off his finger and I do a double take. He's wearing a silver ring! But that can't be a coincidence, can it? Because if that ring is the silver Ring of Suffering, then things have just gone from bad to much, much worse.

I need to get a closer look.

I step carefully onto the rickety staircase, which shakes under the weight of my foot. Great. The last thing I need is to give myself away. Yet, I'm going to need help because stopping Siphon alone is downright difficult. But stopping Siphon while he's wearing a Ring of Suffering is freaking impossible! I reach for my transmitter to contact the team when—

"I sense we have a guest," Siphon says.

I stop in my tracks. Um, what?

"Perhaps we should welcome him," he continues.

"What are you talking about?" Haywire asks.

"There's someone here I know all too well," Siphon says, breathing in deep with his arms extended to his sides. "Isn't that right, Epic Zero?"

What? How did he know I was here? Then, I remember he can sense Meta power, just like he did when I first met him. Well, I guess it's no use being invisible now. I just need to look more confident than I feel.

"I'm here," I say, turning visible and striking a heroic pose with my hands on my hips. "But the real question is, what are you doing here? I thought you were dead."

"So did I," Siphon says, "but fortunately, I'm not."

"But how is that possible?" I ask. "There was a massive explosion. Nobody could have survived that."

"Hold on there, buddy," Haywire interjects, pointing at me. "I'll be the one asking all the questions around here. I told you this guy was mine and mine alone."

"You're being rude to our guest," Siphon says to Haywire. "I don't think I like you."

"So what?" Haywire says. "I came here to get answers and I'm not leaving until you—"

BOOM!

Siphon socks her with unbelievable speed and Haywire flies across the room, crashing into a rock wall.

"Haywire!" I yell, running down the staircase. "What did you do that for?"

"She annoyed me," Siphon says, sitting back down on his throne. "I no longer tolerate things that annoy me."

I kneel next to Haywire and she's still breathing but out cold. I can't believe Siphon sucker punched her. I mean, he was bad when I first met him, but he was a hero in the end. What happened to him?

But as he cracks his knuckles I get a good look at the silver ring on his finger. It has a lightning bolt on its face, just like the bronze ring in the Trophy Room! I feel sick to my stomach.

And that's when I remember Beezle's Meta profile. It said the Djinn Three can control the desires of their hosts. Is that what's going on? Is Beezle mind-controlling Siphon? Is that why he's acting so strange?

"Look, we were friends, remember?" I say, standing up. "I'm glad to see you again, but you have to tell me why you're doing this."

"*Friends?*" Siphon says, staring at me oddly. "I don't

have any friends. I wasn't ever allowed to have friends."

"Well, I consider you a friend," I say. "You saved my life. You even told me to remember you as a hero."

"Yeah," Siphon says with a chuckle. "I guess I did say that, didn't I? Imagine, me, a hero? Well, it wasn't in the cards. And once I came back I decided to be true to myself. I guess the apple doesn't fall far from the tree."

I don't know what he's talking about, but he's clearly not himself.

"But how did you come back?" I ask. "I still don't understand how you're even alive?"

"Just lucky I guess," Siphon says. "You see, after I sent you away, a fraction of a second before I pulled Order and Chaos together, it was like time stood still. Except the funny thing was, I wasn't on Arena World anymore, but sitting at a table inside a dark room. And across from me was this purple-skinned guy who welcomed me to his 'office.'"

Purple-skinned guy? A chill runs down my spine.

"I'd never seen him before so I asked him if I was dead." Siphon continues. "And he said that was up to me. He said I could choose death if I wanted, or he could save me and send me back to Earth if I was willing to bargain with him. He said all he wanted in exchange for my life was—"

"—your soul?" I say, finishing his sentence.

"Yeah," Siphon says, his eyebrows raised. "How'd you know that?"

"Because he tried the same thing with me," I say. "He calls himself Tormentus. But I didn't take him up on his offer."

"Well, I did," Siphon says. "After all, what did I have to lose? I was a goner anyway. But first I asked him why he even wanted my soul. What was he going to do with it? He said he needed powerful souls for a war he was going to start. But when I asked him who he was fighting he wouldn't tell me. But what did I care? So, I agreed to his deal on the spot, and then asked him what I was supposed to do next. Do you know what he told me?"

"Um, no," I say.

"He said I should go fulfill my destiny," Siphon says. "And the next thing I knew I was back on Earth. I never learned what happened on Arena World after I was gone. I figured I was pulling Order and Chaos together so hard they had to touch, but I didn't think you or any of the others survived. Then, I saw you on the news a few weeks later and I knew you got out okay."

"But why didn't you try to contact me?" I ask. "I could have helped you."

"Nah," he says. "No one can help me. I'm a lost cause. My dad made sure of that."

"But you're not your dad," I say. "Your dad was pure evil, but you're not like him. I mean, I've seen what you're capable of. You have so much potential."

"Wasted potential," Siphon says. "So, I kind of wandered around aimlessly for a while trying to figure things out. I mean, I couldn't understand why I got a second chance? What good did I ever do to even deserve it? Was I supposed to become a hero and try to right my dad's wrongs? Was that my destiny? Or was I supposed to honor my dad by picking up the torch he left behind? I couldn't decide what to do. And then I found this."

He turns the silver ring around his finger.

"This ring was a sign," Siphon says. "I found it just sitting there in the back of an alley. Like it was waiting just for me. It had this strange lightning bolt on it and I felt like I had to put it on. And when I did, well, that's when my destiny became clear. Isn't that right, Beezle?"

Just then, the ring sparks with electricity, and the next thing I know out comes a giant, yellow spirit-like thing that looks like a cross between a human and a troll! I crane my neck as it swells to twenty feet in size and circles Siphon like a cobra protecting its young.

I-It's Beezle!

The evil genie looks down at me with yellow eyes and a sinister grin. Well, I guess I finally found him. The thing is, now that he's actually here I don't feel like sticking around. But I can't bolt because I know there's more to the story. And I have a funny feeling I'm about to find out what it is.

"So, um, if you don't mind me asking," I say, "now that you have your own evil genie and all, what exactly is your destiny?"

"To rule," Siphon says. "After all, Beezle called me

'master' and I liked the sound of that. And then he told me I could have three wishes. Isn't that right, Beezle?"

"Yes, master," Beezle says, his voice cold and gritty, like fingernails scraping a chalkboard.

"Oh," I say. "And you didn't wish for world peace?"

"No," Siphon says. "I wished for world domination, all thanks to you."

"Me?" I say. "What did I do?"

"You told me the truth about my dad," Siphon says. "You made me realize he lied to me my entire life. When he was around he said it was us against the world. But he never told me who he really was or what he was really doing. And when he disappeared, I was on my own. I couldn't even get an orphanage to take me in. When I took off my hood, the lady screamed and slammed the door in my face. I was living on the streets, scrounging for food and shelter. And the older kids, runaways themselves, wouldn't help me. They just made fun of me for the way I looked. They called me a savage. A beast. They said no one would take me in and I'd be on the streets forever like a dog. Well, I showed them. I showed them all."

He showed them? What does that mean?

And then it hits me.

"You wished the grown-ups away!" I blurt out. "You used one of Beezle's three wishes to get rid of them, didn't you?"

"Yeah," Siphon says. "I did. No adults or older kids

wanted me around so why would I want them around? My whole life feels like I've been trapped in a cage, like an animal. All of those people looking at me, laughing at me. But what makes them so special? I could crush them if I wanted to. So, now I'm choosing to be free. To be my true self. And I figure if I'm such a savage, then I'll live with animals instead of humans. That's why I came to Safari Park. Here, we can all be free."

Free?

Suddenly, the dots connect.

"You freed those animals at the zoo," I say. "You made those souped-up Powerbots too, didn't you? But why? Why would you waste a wish on that?"

"I didn't 'waste' anything," Siphon says, clearly annoyed. "When I was young my dad brought me some Powerbot toys he found in the trash, and those were the only friends I had. So, I got a whole bunch of them and made them into my army. They do all of my dirty work for me."

I-I can't believe it. Everything is coming together.

And Siphon is the one responsible!

But then I realize something.

"You said you had three wishes," I say. "What did you do with the third one?"

"That's easy," Siphon says. "I realized I can't pretend to be someone I'm not. My destiny was always right in front of my face. I'm no hero. After all, look who my father was. So, just before you and the annoying girl got here, I wished for the one thing I've always wanted the most."

"And… what's that?" I ask, afraid to hear the answer.

"To be a Meta 4," he says. "So, *friend*, if you think you're going to stop me you've got another thing coming."

Meta Profile

Beezle

Name: Beezle	Height: Variable
Race: Djinn	Weight: Variable
Status: Villain/Inactive	Eyes/Hair: Yellow/Bald

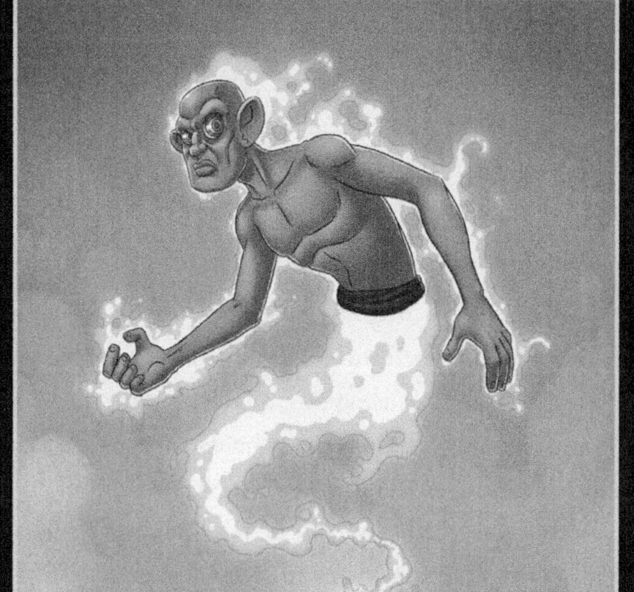

META 2: Magic
Considerable Wish Fulfillment
Considerable Mind-Warping
Considerable Shapeshifting

Observed Characteristics			
Combat 52			
Durability	55	Leadership	42
Strategy	75	Willpower	77

FOURTEEN

I FIGHT FOR MY LIFE

I'm in complete and total shock.

Not only did I just discover that Siphon is still alive, but I've also learned he's responsible for making the grown-ups disappear using one of Beezle's three wishes.

And now he's told me what he used his last wish for.

To become a META-FREAKING-4!

Which essentially means he's all-powerful. So, now I'm at a complete loss. I mean, I couldn't even stop him when he was just a Meta 3! I look down at the still unconscious Haywire and realize I'm on my own.

I'm not going to beat Siphon in battle, so I've got to find a way to get him to bring the grown-ups back without crushing me first. But then I realize something that gives me pause. Siphon said Beezle only granted him three wishes—and he's used them all already!

So, even if I somehow convince him to bring the grown-ups back, how would he do it? I mean, all the genies I've ever read about only come with three wishes. Will Beezle actually grant him a fourth wish? Something tells me I already know the answer to that one.

But no matter how impossible this situation looks, I can't just curl up into a ball. Right now, I'm the only one who knows the truth, and it's up to me to get my parents and the rest of the Freedom Force back. Not to mention the millions of other missing people.

No pressure.

Maybe I can convince him he's taken the wrong path—that he can still be a hero. I did it once before so I'll just have to do it again.

"Siphon, look," I say, "we don't have to fight. I know you think you had to follow in your father's footsteps, but it doesn't have to be that way. Let's just back up to the good versus evil fork-in-the-road and take the other path. Everyone deserves a second chance, and in your case, even a third."

"Nice try," Siphon says, cracking his very, very large knuckles, "but you're not talking me out of it this time. You see, now I know who I really am, so it's time we finished what we started the first time we met."

"The, um, first time we met?" I repeat nervously.

Suddenly, I flashback to when he nearly destroyed me in that abandoned warehouse. He borrowed all of the Ominous Eight's powers with ease and I barely escaped with my life. Then, I realize something.

Thank goodness I didn't call for help. If I did, then Siphon could use the powers of Grace and Next Gen against us! The less Metas around, the better shot I have.

"It's payback time," Siphon says. "And this time, I don't care what you say. I know you were responsible for my father's death, and now it's time for revenge. What's that saying, 'an eye for an eye?'"

"Oh, that ridiculous old saying?" I say, waving my hand dismissively. "I'm much more partial to, 'treat others how you want to be treated.'"

"Enough," Siphon says, his eyes flashing red.

This is it! I'm in for the fight of my life—literally!

How am I going to stop him!

As Siphon steps towards me, I glance up at Beezle who is smiling sinisterly overhead. And as my eyes follow Beezle's floating body, I realize he's still connected to the silver ring like a tetherball on a rope. And then a lightbulb goes off!

As long as Siphon is wearing the Ring of Suffering, he's under Beezle's influence. But what would happen if I got that ring off his finger?

"Sorry, *friend*," Siphon says. "I've enjoyed your little visit, but now it's time for you to die."

But before he takes a step, I concentrate and bathe him with negation power. The red embers in his eyes sputter for a few seconds before completely going out. But my victory is short-lived as he smiles and his eyes light right back up! Well, that didn't work. Not that I'm surprised because I couldn't negate his powers the first time we met.

Time for Plan B!

I reach out to duplicate his power, but instead of feeling the incredible, all-powerful surge of Meta 4 energy coursing through my veins, I feel absolutely nothing!

What gives?

"Is something wrong?" Siphon asks knowingly. "Perhaps you're feeling a bit powerless yourself? After all, I've just used your own negation power against you. Tell me, how does it feel to be a Zero?"

What? But the more I try to use my powers, the emptier I feel inside. I-I can't believe it. He's wiped my powers out!

"Even if I weren't a Meta 4," Siphon says, approaching me with a giant smirk across his mug, "your Meta Manipulation powers were never a match for mine. Now come take your punishment like a man."

"Well, that's the funny thing," I say, backing up quickly. "You got rid of all the men. I'm still a kid, remember?"

Just then, Siphon swings, and I duck as his fist swooshes overhead. Then, I nail him in the ribs with a roundhouse kick but he doesn't move.

"Augh!" I scream as pain shoots through my foot. Kicking him is like kicking a boulder. He's way too strong for me, powers, or no powers.

Suddenly, he grabs my collar and lifts me high into the air. As his hot breath blows in my face, I open my mouth to beg for my life but no words come out. He's squeezing my uniform so tight it's cutting off the circulation to my neck!

I feel woozy, and for a split second, instead of Siphon, I think I see Meta-Taker staring back at me. But then I blink and it's Siphon again. He's saying something but I can't really hear him. I… I'm having a… hard time breathing!

Siphon smiles as red energy crackles around his narrowing eyes. I'm… losing consciousness.

But then, a thick, black band wraps around Siphon's eyes and two more wrap around his wrists! Siphon yells something as his arms are pulled back with extreme force.

The next thing I know, I fall to the ground and land hard on my tailbone. Pain shoots up my backside as I try to catch my breath. But as much as I want to just sit here and recover, I can't because I've got to get my rescuer out of here.

"Night Owl!" I call out, my throat feeling hoarse.

"I could make a career out of saving you," she says, riding close to the hundred-foot-high ceiling.

"Get out of here!" I yell. "He'll copy your powers!"

Just then, Siphon breaks the shadows off his wrists and snaps the one covering his eyes in two. Then, he breathes in deep and spews a giant shadow tentacle out of his mouth straight toward Night Owl!

"Look out!" I yell, but it's too late because the tentacle wraps around Night Owl's shadow slide and pulls, shattering it into pieces!

Night Owl screams as she starts to plummet to the ground. I've got to do something! But Siphon negated my powers! I can't give up!

I concentrate harder than I've ever concentrated before, digging deep inside. I pull every last ember of Meta energy I can muster to the surface. And then I push, sweat trickling down my forehead, until I feel my Meta power moving, slowly at first, and then faster, until it explodes like water flowing through a dam. I-I did it!

But there's no time to celebrate. Got to be fast.

I copy Night Owl's power, grab the shadow beneath the staircase, and inflate it beneath her, breaking her fall with the biggest, fluffiest shadow marshmallow ever created. Night Owl lands in its cushiony center and bounces softly. Whew!

"Impressive," Siphon says, "but not impressive enough." Then, he creates a giant shadow whip and cracks it at me!

I pull another shadow from beneath the throne and protect myself with a flimsy shadow shield, but Siphon's strike destroys it with one blow. Boy, the way he's fighting you'd think Siphon's been using shadow weapons all his life. But then again, I guess being a Meta 4 gives him even faster mastery of the powers he duplicates.

"Thanks for the save," Night Owl says, running over

and shielding us both with a stronger shadow barrier. "I think we're even now. But if you don't mind me asking, who's the nutso, muscular guy and what's up with the ugly, yellow dude watching this all go down?"

"The yellow guy is Beezle," I say. "He's the evil genie we were looking for. The guy wearing his ring is Siphon, the most dangerous Meta in the entire universe right now. He copies Meta powers so I'm thinking you should get out of here as quickly as possible."

"What?" Night Owl says, blocking another of Siphon's blows. "Are you crazy? I'm not leaving. I've saved you too many times to just let you die. You're like my pet project now."

"Thanks," I say. "But the longer you stay here the more he'll use your powers against us. I need you to grab Haywire and get out of here."

"Haywire?" she says. "Why do we want to help her?"

"Because she's a good person," I say. "She just got herself in over her head. Now go, and make sure you get far away so he can't sense your powers. I'll come up with a plan."

"Like what?" she asks.

"Don't know yet," I answer.

"Well, that's a confidence builder," Night Owl says.

"Thanks," I say. "I'll cover you. Now go!"

Before she can respond, I jump outside her barrier, grab the shadow beneath the roller coaster cars, and push it at Siphon as hard as I can, pinning him to the rock wall.

"I'll be back for you," Night Owl says, shooting me a frustrated look as she jumps on a shadow slide and heads for Haywire.

But just as Night Owl scoops up Haywire, Siphon swipes my own shadow and turns it into a giant hammer, sending it after Night Owl!

"Look out!" I yell.

But just as Night Owl takes off with Haywire in her arms, Siphon's hammer pummels her with a massive blow. Night Owl's body goes limp and she falls to the ground, taking Haywire down with her.

"No one leaves," Siphon says, busting through my shadow barrier. "No one escapes alive. Including you."

Then, he charges at me.

I turn for the stairs and stumble, my hand hitting the podium that controls the ride. I need to protect myself, but as my eyes dart around the room I realize we've used all the shadows in the place. Then, I hear his footsteps behind me and when I turn, I gasp as his big mitt reaches for my neck!

But instead of grabbing me, his hand slows to a stop!

In fact, his entire body has frozen like a statue!

What's going on?

"Hello, Elliott Harkness," comes a familiar voice from behind me.

I turn to find Tormentus standing there with his arms crossed and a devious smile on his face!

What's he doing here?

"My, my," he says, buffing his fingernails. "I'd say you've gotten yourself into quite a bit of trouble."

"D-Did you do this?" I ask. "Did you make him freeze?"

"I did," Tormentus says. "I'm feeling generous today, so given your current circumstances, I thought I'd offer you one last chance to make a deal before you die. And I even have some new terms I think you'll find interesting."

"A-A deal?" I say, totally confused.

"Yes, a deal," Tormentus says. "It's quite a simple one actually. Would you like to hear it?"

"Um, I guess so," I say, cringing as I answer.

"I'll save your life by getting you out of here safe and sound," Tormentus says, "and when you die, I get your soul. Now, I'm rather busy, so I'll give you thirty seconds to decide before I unfreeze your friend here and things go back to being ugly."

Meta Profile

Terrog

▯ Name: Terrog	▯ Height: Variable
▯ Race: Djinn	▯ Weight: Variable
▯ Status: Villain/Inactive	▯ Eyes/Hair: Red/Black

META 3: Magic	Observed Characteristics	
▯ Extreme Wish Fulfillment	Combat 85	
▯ Extreme Mind-Warping	Durability 72	Leadership 66
▯ Extreme Shapeshifting	Strategy 79	Willpower 90

FIFTEEN

I GET MORE THAN I WISHED FOR

Time sure flies when you've got thirty seconds to make the decision of an eternal lifetime.

The way I see it, I'm in a lose-lose situation. Either I sell my soul to Tormentus in exchange for saving my skin, or I tell him to go suck an egg and let Siphon rip me to pieces. Why do I always get myself in these situations?

But as I contemplate my fate, Tormentus just stares at me with a goofy grin on his face. I bet that creep has been waiting for a moment like this. Somehow, he kept tabs on me and swooped in just when I was up against the ropes—exactly like he did to Siphon.

The thing is, Tormentus knows he's got me exactly where he wants me. I mean, Siphon is a Meta 4! The odds of me surviving a battle with him are slim to none.

What to do, what to do?

If I agree to Tormentus' deal, I can get out of here scot-free and live to fight another day. Then, I can regroup and come back with a real plan to stop Siphon. Besides, does anyone really need their soul when they're dead anyway? According to Siphon, Tormentus said he's collecting souls for some kind of war. That sounds ominous, but I guess I wouldn't be around anyway.

But then again, if I take the easy option I'll be leaving Night Owl and Haywire behind. Who knows what Siphon will do to them? Plus, what about Grace? If I can't convince Siphon to bring back the grown-ups then Grace is a goner when she turns fifteen.

Decisions. Decisions.

I look into Tormentus' yellow eyes and wonder if he's trying to influence my thinking like he did at Lockdown. It doesn't seem like he's inside my brain, but it's hard to know for sure so I throw up a little negation field.

"Time's up," Tormentus says, tapping his wrist. "What's it going to be? Will you live, or will you press your luck against this unsophisticated brute?"

Press my luck?

Holy smokes, why didn't I think of that before?

It's a risk, but it's a risk worth taking. Otherwise, I've failed everyone—including myself.

"Well?" Tormentus asks. "What's your answer?"

"Sorry to disappoint," I say, "but I'm going with 'no way Jose!'"

"What?" Tormentus exclaims. "That makes no sense!

As soon as I disappear, time will revert to normal and Siphon will rip you limb from pathetic limb."

"Probably," I say, "but I'd rather do what's right than have my soul spend eternity with a creep like you."

Tormentus' lips curl in anger but I need to act fast because he'll hit the road any second. I turn towards Haywire who is still down for the count. This probably isn't a good idea, but it's the only idea I've got.

"Then you will die a fool!" Tormentus yells, raising his hand to snap his fingers.

I send my duplication powers out and copy as much of Haywire's power as possible. As her Meta energy enters my body, I feel an itchy sensation, like ants are crawling on my skin. But I can't worry about that now, because just as Tormentus SNAPS his fingers and disappears, I spin and project Haywire's power all over Siphon.

Suddenly, Siphon is in motion again and I hit the deck as he trips over his own feet and flies over me, crashing face-first into the rock wall beneath the staircase. It worked! Haywire's bad luck is working on Siphon!

"You're lucky I tripped," Siphon says, getting to his feet. "But your luck has run out."

But then, there's a loud CREAKING noise overhead, and when I look up, the rickety staircase over Siphon collapses, crashing down on top of him! That's when I notice new shadows on the ground beneath the rubble!

Now's my chance!

I project my duplication powers at Night Owl, and as I absorb her power, I make sure I hold onto Haywire's bad luck power. Then, I use Night Owl's power to quickly grab the shadows just as Siphon punches through the debris, sending planks flying everywhere! But as I turn to shield my body I see Beezle floating calmly overhead—and that's when I realize what I need to do.

"Now I'm really annoyed," Siphon says, dusting himself off. But then, he raises his eyebrows and looks frantically from side-to-side. "Who else is here?"

Huh? I don't know what he's talking about, but I'm certainly not going to waste a good opportunity. I form a pair of shadow tongs by his hand and rip the silver ring right off his finger. There's a yellow flash as Beezle gets sucked back into the ring and then a TINGING sound as the ring hits something hard by Siphon's feet.

"The ring!" Siphon yells, dropping to his hands and knees. "Where'd it go?"

"How unlucky," I say, noticing the roller coaster cars behind him. "I don't know where the ring went, but I do know you're going for a ride!"

Then, I create a massive shadow fist and CLOCK him with everything I've got. Siphon flies backward into one of the cars, and as he tumbles inside I convert the shadow fist into an anvil and drop it on him, pinning him down. After that, I make a beeline for the control podium and flick on the ride.

As the roller coaster jolts into operation and takes

Siphon into a tunnel, I race over to grab the ring. But I can't find it! Where'd it go? I've got to find that ring!

But when I kneel, something wet hits my cheek and I'm pushed backward. The next thing I know, a furry dog materializes on top of me.

"Dog-Gone?" I exclaim. "So, that was you Siphon sensed?" As I wrap my arms around him he drops the silver ring into my hands. "And you found the ring! Good boy! For once, I'm glad you didn't listen to me. Now let me up because I've got to end this before Siphon comes back around."

I look at the silver ring in my palm. It's hard to imagine this little ring caused so much craziness. But then again, it's no ordinary ring. I take a deep breath and Dog-Gone whimpers.

"I know," I say, "but it's our only chance."

Then, I put the ring on my finger.

Suddenly, the ring sparks with yellow electricity, and out comes Beezle! He slithers around my body until reaching full size and then looks down with surprise.

"Well, I was not expecting this," he says, "but as you are now the bearer of the silver Ring of Suffering, you are my master and I am at your service."

"Master?" I say. "Don't call me master."

"As you wish, master," Beezle says. "I am here to fulfill your utmost desires. I can grant you three wishes. However, even I have limitations. I am not able to bring the dead back to life and I am not permitted to grant you unlimited wishes. You have three wishes at your disposal, so tell me, what is your desire, master? Perhaps you would like to rule this world?"

"Um, no," I say. "Listen, I'd like—"

"Pardon me, master," Beezle interjects. "But before you speak, I implore you not to be frivolous. After all, you only have three wishes. Let us use them wisely. Let us use them for your benefit, if you know what I mean."

I open my mouth to object but then stop myself. I mean, maybe he's right. Maybe I could use at least one of these wishes to help myself out a bit.

WOOF!

I look down to find Dog-Gone growling at me. Wait a minute, what am I thinking? Beezle is influencing my thinking somehow. I surround myself with negation energy and push Beezle out.

"Master, please?" Beezle pleads.

"Listen, Beezle," I say, "and listen close because I'm making my first wish. I want you to bring back every person Siphon made disappear. All of the grown-ups. All of the teenagers. I want you to put them back exactly as they were when you made them disappear. Got it?"

"Very well, master," Beezle says dryly. And then he waves his hands and two maintenance workers suddenly appear next to the roller coaster track. "Wish fulfilled."

Yes! It worked! So, that means my parents should be back on the Waystation. I'd give anything to go see them, but I'm not done here. Not by a long shot.

"Um, Doug," one of the workers says. "What was in that coffee you gave me? Because if I didn't know better, I'd say I'm looking at the Genie from Aladdin and Superman's dog."

"Same here," Doug says, dropping his tools. "Let's get out of here!"

As they take off, I hear the ROAR of the roller coaster overhead and realize I probably don't have much time until Siphon comes back around. And when he does, he's not going to be happy. There's no way I'll be able to defeat him. In fact, I'm not sure the entire Freedom Force could defeat him. He's just too powerful.

"Beezle, I'd like to make my second wish."

"I cannot wait to hear this one, master," Beezle says.

"I want you to remove Siphon's Meta energy," I say quickly. "All of it, permanently. And fast."

"You said you would like me to remove all of his energy?" Beezle asks, raising his left eyebrow.

Just then, the front of the roller coaster appears in the opposite tunnel. Oh no! Siphon is back!

"Yes!" I answer quickly. "All of it! And do it now!"

"As you wish, master," Beezle says, and then he waves both of his hands. "Wish fulfilled."

I feel an incredible sense of relief as the roller coaster SCREECHES to a halt with Siphon still inside. But while Siphon clearly managed to destroy my shadow anchor, he's slumped over in his seat, not moving. What's going on? Is he knocked out?

Just then, Tormentus appears.

"Wait, what are you doing here?" I ask. "I turned your offer down."

"*You* did," Tormentus says. But then he points to Siphon and says, "But he didn't. And now it's time to collect what is owed to me."

"Collect?" I say, totally confused. But then I realize what he's talking about. He's here for Siphon's soul. B-But that means… "You killed him!" I scream at Beezle.

"Yes, master," Beezle says. "I did as you wished."

"N-No!" I yell. "I-I told you to remove his Meta energy! That's all!"

"Oh, what a shame," Beezle says, covering his mouth with a hand. "I thought I clarified your wish and you desired that I remove his life energy. What a pity."

"You did it on purpose!" I yell. "Bring him back!"

"I cannot do that, master," Beezle says.

"Then I'm using my third wish," I say. "I want you to bring him back from the dead!"

"I am afraid that is not permitted," Beezle says. "I already explained that to you."

"N-No," I say, dropping to my knees.

"I guess there's a lesson here for you," Tormentus says, his eyes glowing white. "When you're working with your enemies the devil is always in the details."

Then, a white mist flows out of Siphon's body and gets sucked into Tormentus' eyes. Tormentus glows bright white as his body temporarily expands. And after he absorbs the last tendrils of Siphon's soul, he shrinks back down to normal size. Then, he looks at me with an evil smile and disappears with a SNAP—leaving Siphon's soulless body behind.

"Epic Zero?"

I feel a hand on my shoulder and look up to see Night Owl standing over me.

"Are you okay?" she asks.

Great question. No, I'm not okay. I never wished for Beezle to kill Siphon. He twisted my words for his own sick purposes. H-He burned me. I'm so overwhelmed with emotion I feel kind of dizzy. But I can't let him do this to anyone, ever again.

"N-Not really," I say, feeling shaky as I get to my feet. "But this ends now. Beezle, I'm making my third wish."

"Of course, master," Beezle says. "Your wish is my command. And now that your greatest enemy is out of our way, perhaps you would like to possess ultimate power? I can grant that for you. I can make you a Meta 4 if that is your desire."

"No, Beezle," I say, "that's not my desire. My desire is really clear so I want you to listen carefully."

"Yes, master," Beezle says. "Of course."

"Excellent," I say. "My wish is for you to go back inside your ring, and never, ever come out again."

"My apologies, master," Beezle says, his voice cracking, "but surely you are joking. There are so many other ways to use your remaining wish. For power. For glory. For—"

"No!" I yell. "That's my third wish and you must obey. After all, I am your master."

"I-I am forced to obey," Beezle says, gritting his teeth. But as he waves his hands, he says, "But beware, my brothers will avennngggeee meeeee…"

And then he disappears into the silver ring.

Suddenly, I hear moaning to our left, and when I turn around Haywire is rolling over slowly. Thank goodness she's okay, but I guess I'll have to tell her about Tormentus and Siphon. After all, her soul is on his collection list.

"Epic Zero!" comes an excited voice.

I look up to see Grace flying towards us with a huge smile on her face. "There you are! I've been looking all over the park for you. You were supposed to call me." Then, she looks around and says. "What the heck happened in here?"

"Long story," I say. Suddenly, I feel really woozy.

"Guess what?" she says, grabbing my shoulders and shaking me. "Mom called me from the Waystation! Mom and Dad are back! The whole team is back! And that means I'm not going to disappear on my birthday!"

"Yeah," I say, my vision fading quickly. I feel like I'm going to… pass out. "Imagine that…"

Then, she let's go of me and I feel myself falling.

And then everything goes dark…

EPILOGUE

I RECEIVE A SURPRISE GIFT

"Happy birthday to you!"

After everyone stops singing, Grace makes a wish and blows out fifteen candles on her birthday cake with one breath, proving once and for all that she's full of hot air. But all jokes aside, it's great to see her so happy, even though she had to give up the presidency. And it also feels great to be surrounded by the Freedom Force again. I mean, even Shadow Hawk is smiling!

But Grace's birthday isn't the only thing I have to celebrate, because my parents invited Next Gen and Night Owl to join the party too. I mean, this is a real first. I've never been allowed to have friends on the Waystation before.

I don't know why my parents changed their minds, but I guess they had a lot of time to think about things after Beezle transported them and the other grown-ups to some strange, misty world. My parents said they could see one another through the haze but they couldn't move a muscle. That sounds unbelievably torturous but I'm just glad they're back.

After passing out at Safari Park, I woke up in the Medi-wing and Mom was the first person I saw. We hugged long and hard and I admit I may have even shed a tear or two. Then, Dad gave me a big hug and said to rest up because my body shut down from the stress of saving everyone.

But the thing is, I didn't save everyone.

I still can't shake what happened to Siphon. I know Beezle intentionally misinterpreted my command but it doesn't hurt any less. Siphon was a good kid who was just so misguided. I wish I could have helped him more.

And speaking of wishes, TechnocRat gave his theory on why the Meta Monitor didn't pick up Beezle's signature once he banished the grown-ups. Apparently, Black Magic can only be detected on the things it leaves its trace on. Once my parents and the others were sent away, they took Beezle's power signature with them. That's why the Meta Monitor could read Beezle's signal off the Powerbots because they were still here. TechnocRat said he'll try tweaking the Meta Monitor to fix that, which would be great.

And in other great news, the team reunited Haywire with her parents at the hospital. According to Selfie, Siphon hurt Haywire pretty badly, but now that her parents are back Haywire said she didn't plan on fighting crime anymore. But we'll keep tabs on her anyway, just in case.

Especially if Tormentus pops up again.

The funny thing is, my parents hadn't heard of Tormentus either. I checked again and there's nothing on him in the Meta database. I'll never forget that creep's face. I just hope I never see it again.

"Okay," Mom says, putting a stack of gifts in front of Grace. "Time for presents!"

Presents? Oh no, I never got Grace a present.

"My favorite part!" Grace says, unwrapping the first gift and pulling out a long, white cape. "Wow, a new cape? This is cool."

"That's from me," TechnocRat says, fiddling with his whiskers. "And it's not just any cape. I invented a new polymer to make you more aerodynamic."

"Thanks, T-Rat," she says. "That's so thoughtful. Okay, I'll open this one next." She opens up a small box and pulls out a gift card. "Whoa! That's a lot of cash!"

"That's from Blue Bolt, Makeshift, Master Mime, and me," Shadow Hawk says. "We thought you could redecorate your bedroom."

"Now that you're a sophisticated young lady, of course," Blue Bolt adds with a curtsy.

"Of course," Grace says with a smile. "Gee, thanks. That's amazing. Okay, I'll do this one next." Then, she tears it open and pulls out a new phone. "Really?" she says, hugging it and looking at Mom and Dad. "You got me the latest model? How did you know I wanted one?"

"Gee, I don't know," Mom says slyly. "It's not like I could read your mind or anything."

"Happy birthday, dear," Dad says.

I look at the pile and see two presents left. One is large and neatly wrapped, while the other is small and looks like it was wrapped by a rabid raccoon.

"I'll open this one," Grace says, carefully picking up the small one. But as she unwraps it, a bone falls out and THUNKS onto the table.

"Wow," Grace says. "Dog-Gone, is this from you?"

Dog-Gone appears, picks up the bone, and then disappears.

"Um, okay," Grace says. "You play with it first."

Great. Even Dog-Gone got her a present.

Ugh! Now she's opening the last one and she'll know I got her nothing! I wish I could disappear like Dog-Gone.

"Just one more," she says, looking at me. "It's a big one too. Yum, this one smells good." And when she unwraps it her eyes light up with surprise. "It's two dozen jelly doughnuts!"

"That's from all of us in Next Gen," Selfie says, "including Epic Zero."

What? Really? I look over at Selfie and she smiles.

"Thanks, guys," she says, grabbing a doughnut and taking a huge bite. "Yah know," she says, talking with her mouth full, "you guyth aren't tho bad."

"Okay, let's eat," Mom says, using her telekinesis to start cutting the cake.

"Thanks for the save," I whisper to Selfie.

"We're a team, right?" she whispers back with a wink. "Besides, I figured you weren't exactly in a state to get her anything."

"By the way," Night Owl says, "when Selfie said that gift was from *all* of us in Next Gen, she meant *all* of us, including me."

"Wait, what?" I say. "Are you joining the team?"

"Yeah," she says. "Like Glory Girl said, you guys aren't so bad. Besides, I could get used to hanging around a place like this."

"That's awesome!" I say.

"Anyone else notice we're being taken over by girls?" Pinball asks, taking a giant bite of cake. "I kinda like it."

"Epic Zero," Dad says, "can we see you for a minute?"

"Um, sure," I say. And suddenly I have a feeling of dread. The last conversation I had with my parents was about disbanding Next Gen. Is that why they invited them? Is this our last hurrah?

"Um, what's up?" I say, meeting them in the corner.

"We just wanted to tell you we're proud of you,"

Dad says. "Really proud of you."

"Really?" I say.

"Yes," Mom says. "And we see you've taken our leadership lessons to heart."

"I-I did?" I say.

"Yes," Dad says. "Grace told us you protected your team from danger because you recognized they couldn't handle Haywire, and that's the sign of a great leader."

"Thanks," I say, totally floored.

"But that's not all," Mom says. "Your father and I agreed that you should continue leading Next Gen."

"Wait, what?" I say. "You mean we don't have to disband?"

"No," Dad says. "In fact, we'd like the Freedom Force to help mentor you—all of you. If you're going to be the next generation of heroes, then let's train you to do it the right way."

"Seriously?" I say. "That's amazing! Wait until I tell the team!"

"Absolutely," Mom says, "but let's celebrate your sister for today. After all, she's only fifteen once."

"Right," I say, turning to see Grace showing Night Owl her new cape.

Even though I'm bursting with excitement, I'm happy to wait to share the news. I still can't believe what my parents said. I mean, now we'll really have a chance to become a great superhero team. We'll be able to fight major bad guys, and who knows, we might end up collecting a few trophies of our own.

Speaking of trophies, Grace said she put the silver Ring of Suffering back in the Trophy Room next to the bronze one. But that still leaves the gold ring unaccounted for. I look out the porthole towards Earth, wondering where it could be.

"Epic Zero!" Pinball shouts, snapping me back to reality. "Come on! Makeshift is giving us a tour of the Waystation. Did you know there's an Evacuation Chamber that actually shoots dog poo into space?"

Okay, so maybe it'll take us a while to become a great superhero team, but I know one thing, I'm ready for the journey!

Meta Profile
Next Gen
Epic Zero
Dog-Gone
Night Owl
Class: Meta Manipulator
Meta :
Class: Meta-Morph
Meta :
Class: Energy Manipulator
Meta :
Skunk Girl
Selfie
Pinball
Class: Energy Manipulator
Meta :
Class: Magic
Meta :
Class: Meta-Morph
Meta :

Epic Zero 8: Tales of a Colossal Boy Blunder

ONE

I HATE CARNIVAL GAMES

This is taking way longer than I expected.

I mean, we've been weaving through crowds at the Keystone City carnival for over an hour hunting for Gigantox, a transparent Meta 2 villain filled with toxic growth chemicals. He kind of sticks out in a crowd so I figured we would've found him by now, but I'm starting to think we're looking for a needle in a haystack. Of course, it doesn't help that some of us are focused on entirely the wrong things.

"Is that guy selling corn dogs?" Pinball asks, inhaling deeply. "Yum, I love corn dogs. Can't you just smell that golden-brown, cornmeal batter deliciousness?"

"Keep your saucer-sized eyes on the prize," Night Owl says. "We're here to find Gigantox, not disgusting carnival food. So, stay alert."

"Carnival food is not disgusting," Pinball huffs. "In fact, if I were running the Department of Health I'd make carnival food one of the five major food groups. You know, right up there with bread, fruit, meat, and vegetables. Ooooh, are those deep-fried peanut butter-stuffed pickles?"

"Pinball, please," Selfie says. "Can't you focus on finding Gigantox and not the food?"

"Sure can," Pinball says, holding his stomach. "But after we catch him let's grab a few of those funnel cake cheeseburgers."

Well, Pinball may be as useless as ever, but even I have to admit that staying focused is pretty difficult right now. Between the throngs of people, flashing carnival lights, and fast-moving rides, my senses are on overload. But despite all of the distractions, I need to set a good example as the leader of Next Gen because this mission is critical for a bunch of reasons.

Gigantox is not only a major safety threat, but he's also our chance for redemption. That's because we still haven't gelled as a team, and our last outing at the Keystone City Museum was a complete disaster. If it weren't for the Freedom Force, Lunatick would have escaped scot-free. So, this is our chance to prove we've gotten our act together.

Especially since the Freedom Force is watching.

Now don't get me wrong, I'm thrilled my parents

and the rest of the gang are mentoring us, but it's also a double-edged sword. We're getting the best Meta training in the world, but we also have to show that we're applying it in the real world.

And that's the part that worries me.

"Okay, boss-man," Skunk Girl says, "where is this bad guy already? You said we couldn't miss him about ten minutes ago, which was twenty minutes after my feet started hurting."

"Don't worry," I say, mustering as much confidence as I can, "he's here somewhere." But truthfully, I'm getting nervous. I mean, where did Gigantox go? It's not like he blends easily into a crowd. After all, he's an android shaped like a man, but his skin is made of a clear, indestructible plastic containing a toxic mix of growth chemicals.

You'd think he'd stand out like a sore thumb.

"Um, guys," Pinball says, stopping suddenly.

"Keep walking, Pinball," Skunk Girl says. "I don't want to hear about your love for panini-pressed bacon doughnuts again."

"Um, this isn't about bacon doughnuts," Pinball says. "Look at that guy over there by the ring toss booth. The guy with the hat and trench coat. It's, like, ninety degrees out. Why would anybody be wearing a trench coat on a hot day like this?"

A trench coat?

Just then, the crowd in front of us parts, and I see

the back of a large man wearing a tan hat and matching trench coat. And when the man turns around, I'm staring right through his plastic face at a cluster of metal gears immersed in a bubbling, purplish liquid.

It's him! It's Gigantox!

"Next Gen—Power Up!" I yell.

"Still working on that battle cry, huh?" Skunk Girl says, patting my shoulder. "Sad."

I didn't think it was that bad but I'll work on it later. Right now, we've got a job to do! Our first order of business is to get these people to safety, and as team leader, it's my job to call the right play.

"Initiate crowd control!" I yell.

"On it!" Night Owl yells back as she jumps on a shadow slide and creates a shadow barrier to block the now confused crowd from Gigantox.

"Everyone, please look over here!" Selfie belts out, using her magic phone to amplify her voice a hundred decibels.

Then, I shield my eyes as a white flash radiates from her phone, blanketing the crowd. And when I look back over everyone has been hypnotized.

"Please leave the premises in a quick and orderly manner!" Selfie commands.

"I'll generate a bad odor to corral them towards the exit," Skunk Girl says, generating a wall of stink.

As the crowd holds their noses and starts to move, I have to say I'm feeling pretty good about our teamwork.

Now we just have to apprehend the bad guy. But apparently, Gigantox has other ideas.

"Look out!" Pinball yells.

The next thing I know, Gigantox rips through his trench coat as his body starts growing rapidly! I crane my neck as he grows twenty feet tall, and then forty feet tall, and then one hundred feet tall! And that's when I see something up high that makes my stomach sink.

There are people on the Ferris wheel!

We forgot about the people on the Ferris wheel!

Just. Freaking. Wonderful.

Then, Gigantox notices the Ferris wheel himself and the passengers scream. We have to save them!

"Epic Zero, negate his power!" Night Owl yells.

"Right!" I answer. I concentrate hard and bathe Gigantox with my negation power but nothing happens! Are you kidding me? I know my powers don't work on robots, but does it have to include androids too? And now Gigantox is extending his massive mitt towards the Ferris wheel! I might not be able to do anything, but maybe the others can!

"Pinball! Night Owl!" I yell at the top of my lungs. "Execute the slingshot maneuver!"

"Yes, sir!" Pinball says, inflating his body and bouncing over to Night Owl.

Night Owl creates a long, thin shadow and wraps it around two lampposts. Then, Pinball leans back into it, pulling the shadow taut like a slingshot.

"You know," Pinball says nervously. "The one time we tried this I missed the practice target by miles and had to take a bus back to the Hangout."

"Here's the deal," Night Owl says. "If you knock Gigantox out with one blow, I'll buy you all the funnel cake cheeseburgers you can eat."

"Seriously?" Pinball says, narrowing his eyes with determination. "Then consider me locked and loooaaaaddededddd!"

Suddenly, Pinball is hurtling through the air! I cringe as he flies over the Tilt-a-Whirl, just misses the Orbiter, and passes straight through the Loop de Loop before SMASHING into Gigantox's massive forehead.

"Ouch," Skunk Girls says, crinkling her nose. "That'll leave a mark."

Gigantox staggers over the bumper cars and falls backward, casting a large shadow over a row of Porta Potty's just as two kids step out. Holy cow! They'll be crushed! There's no time to lose!

I borrow Night Owl's power, grab a shadow off the pavement, and pull the kids to safety with a shadow fist seconds before Gigantox CRASHES down on top of the bathroom stalls.

"Are you guys okay?" I ask, opening the shadow fist.

"See," one kid says to the other. "I told you the carnival would be more exciting this year."

"Now what, boss-man?" Skunk Girl asks. "We got the bad guy."

"Yes, you did," comes a gritty, familiar voice. "But maybe not in the most efficient way possible. GISMO 2.0, end training module."

"Training module ended, Shadow Hawk," comes GISMO 2.0's warm, mechanical voice.

Just then, everything around us, including Gigantox, the carnival, and the two kids I just rescued all disappear, and we're standing in an enormous, stark white Combat Room 2.0.

"Wait, where'd the carnival go?" Pinball asks, lying flat on his back and looking confused.

"It was all part of the simulation, numbskull," Skunk Girl says. "None of it was real."

"So, does that mean I'm not getting my funnel cake cheeseburgers?" Pinball asks with sadness in his voice.

Believe me, I understand why Pinball is disappointed. TechnocRat built the Combat Room 2.0 to be even more realistic than the original Combat Room—and that's saying something! With all of the upgraded sensory technology he added, it's even harder to accept what you're experiencing isn't real, including the smell of deep-fried Oreos.

"It's time for your evaluation," Shadow Hawk says, flipping through papers on his clipboard. "Glory Girl, would you like to go first?"

I respect Shadow Hawk so much I'll be crushed if we let him down—which I'm pretty sure we did. But I take one look at Grace approaching and brace myself. This could get ugly.

"Yeah, I'll go first," she says, throwing her clipboard over her shoulder. "Let me give it to you straight. You guys stunk out there."

"Then I did my job," Skunk Girl says with a smile.

"That wasn't a compliment," Grace says, her face red with anger. "You may have been in a simulation, but stuff like that could happen in the real world. Sure, you took out the villain, but none of you noticed the people on the Ferris wheel. If you're not completely aware of everything around you, then innocent people will get hurt."

Grace's criticism may be sharp but it's accurate. We never should have engaged with Gigantox until we were sure everyone was safe. I feel like a total failure.

"We blew it," Pinball sighs. "Again."

"Look, don't be so hard on yourselves," Shadow Hawk says. "That's why you're practicing in a safe environment. Things don't always go according to plan, but Glory Girl was spot on that you need to be more aware of your surroundings." Then, he looks down at Pinball and adds, "And not get distracted."

"Sorry about that," Pinball mutters sheepishly.

"That being said," Shadow Hawk continues, "once you recognized the danger you reacted well. Epic Zero made a great tactical suggestion for the slingshot maneuver, and Night Owl and Pinball executed it to perfection."

"Gee, thanks," Pinball says, perking up.

"However, no one checked the bathroom stalls for possible civilians," Shadow Hawk says. "So, clearly, there's more work to do. Remember, practice makes progress. The more you work together the more you'll trust each other. Then, before you know it, you'll anticipate what each other will do without even saying a word. And that's when you know you've become a truly harmonious team. Overall, you should be proud of yourselves. That was a very challenging training module."

Even though Shadow Hawk is being encouraging, I still feel like a heel. After all, I'm the team leader, so if I fail I take the team down with me. Plus, I know this mission would be considered a disaster by Freedom Force standards. If we want to be great we'll have to keep practicing.

"Alert! Alert! Alert!" the Meta Monitor blares. "Meta 3 disturbance. Repeat: Meta 3 disturbance. Power signature identified as The Freaks of Nature. Alert! Alert! Alert! Meta 3 disturbance. Meta signature identified as The Freaks of Nature."

"Freedom Force to Mission Room," comes Dad's voice over the intercom system. "Freedom Force to Mission Room."

"Holy smokes!" Pinball says. "Was that a real Meta alert? With real Meta villains? Can we go?"

"I'm afraid not," Shadow Hawk says, pushing a few buttons on his utility belt. "Captain Justice, this is Shadow Hawk. Glory Girl and I have Next Gen in the Combat

Room for training. Give us a few minutes to escort them to the Hangar so they can return to Earth."

"Roger, Shadow Hawk," comes Dad's voice. "But why don't you guys keep training and I'll handle it with the rest of the team. Besides, someone needs to stay behind because it looks like we'll be in deep space and potentially off the grid for a while. Oh, and keep Glory Girl with you. This is good leadership training for her."

"What? Are you kidding me?" Grace exclaims. "Haven't I been tortured enough?"

"Roger, Captain," Shadow Hawk says with a smile. "We're happy to continue here. Well, at least most of us. Good luck."

"Roger," Dad says. "You too." Then, he clicks off.

"Well," Shadow Hawk says, looking at us, "should we try another training module?"

"Absolutely," I say, more determined to get it right than ever. "I want to nail this one. What do you guys say?"

"I'm in," Selfie says.

"Me too," Night Owl says.

"Okey-dokey," Skunk Girl says.

"I suppose," Pinball says, still lying flat on his back. "But can't a guy get a funnel cake cheeseburger around here first?"

Meta Profile
Next Gen
Epic Zero
Dog-Gone
Night Owl
Class: Meta Manipulator
Meta :
Class: Meta-Morph
Meta :
Class: Energy Manipulator
Meta :
Skunk Girl
Selfie
Pinball
Class: Energy Manipulator
Meta :
Class: Magic
Meta :
Class: Meta-Morph
Meta :

TWO

I FILE A MISSING PERSONS REPORT

So, we didn't nail the second run.

In fact, we did even worse. The thing is, I actually thought GISMO 2.0 went easy on us. All we had to do was catch a pair of Meta 2 villains called Fire and Lice who were hiding out in the Keystone City Aquarium. Everything started out okay, but then it all went downhill faster than an elephant on skis.

First, Skunk Girl had to use the bathroom. Then, Night Owl nearly knocked herself unconscious. And finally, not to be outdone, Pinball bounced right past the villains and shattered the shark tank. Seconds later, we were trying not to drown in the deluge of water while the bad guys got away.

So, yeah, not stellar.

After that, everyone went home and I went to bed. Except, I can't sleep. I've been tossing and turning all night, and this time it's not Dog-Gone's fault, even though he's snoring so loud the walls are shaking. I've tried everything to get some shut-eye, from saying the alphabet backward to counting sheep, but no matter what I do I can't stop thinking about our pathetic performance in the Combat Room. That and the look of sheer disappointment on Shadow Hawk's face.

This time, Grace was even more brutal in her critique of our performance and Shadow Hawk didn't say much of anything. Not that he had to, his frown said it all.

According to Shadow Hawk, we'll need to trust each other for our team to work, and if that's the case then maybe we've been doomed from the start. I mean, we haven't had a successful mission yet—so who's responsible for that?

Unfortunately, I know the answer.

Awesome.

Since I'm not sleeping I might as well go for a walk. I carefully peel down the covers so I don't disturb Dog-Gone when I remember I'm still in my costume. I was so bummed out I didn't have the energy to put on my pajamas. Then, I notice the clock which reads 3:13 a.m.

Great. At least the halls should be empty.

As I make my way through the residential wing I

notice my parents' bedroom door is still open, which means they're not back yet. I guess fighting the Freaks of Nature was more challenging than they thought.

I grab a snack from the Galley, loop around the Trophy Room, and saunter past the Medi-wing. That's when I notice that the light in the Monitor Room is on. That's strange. Usually, we let the Meta Monitor do its thing overnight. So, either someone forgot to turn out the light or someone is in there right now.

Since Dog-Gone is unconscious on my bed, there are only two people it could be, and I've never known Grace to skimp on her beauty sleep. I head up the stairs and when I reach the top I find Shadow Hawk sitting in the command chair. What's he doing up so late?

"Hey, kid," he says, not even turning around. "I didn't know you were a sleepwalker."

"I'm not," I say. "I just can't sleep. What about you? Why are you up?"

"I try to get as little sleep as possible," he says, rotating his chair towards me. "Too many nightmares. So, what's keeping you up?"

"Oh, nothing," I say, letting out a deep sigh. "Well, I… I guess I keep thinking about our Combat Room training. We just can't get it together… and it's all my fault."

"How so?" he asks.

"I'm the leader," I say. "So, if we fail it's on me. And I can't seem to get us working as a team."

"I see," Shadow Hawk says, his pointer finger tapping his chiseled chin. "Well, the leader does set the tone for the team. But it's also impossible for a team to function if they don't have a common goal. To be successful as a team everyone has to work together in harmony."

"Yeah," I say. "That makes sense."

"Look, I've been on teams that fell apart because everyone did their own thing," Shadow Hawk says. "But I've also been a part of great teams, like the Freedom Force, where everyone works towards the same goal. And because of that, we trust each other implicitly. Maybe you should see if everyone is on the same page."

Suddenly, a light bulb goes off. Maybe that's where we're going wrong. Maybe we're not all on the same page. I mean, I want us to be the best Meta team ever but do the others want the same thing? Sometimes I think all Pinball wants to do is eat. And Skunk Girl can run hot or cold depending on the minute. Night Owl is still a mystery to me. But Selfie… I know she's with me.

"I… I never thought of it that way," I say. "Thanks."

"No problem, kid," Shadow Hawk says. "I know you'll figure it out. Just don't give up on—"

"Alert! Alert! Alert!" the Meta Monitor blares. "Meta 3 disturbance. Repeat: Meta 3 disturbance. Power signature identified as Warrior Woman. Alert! Alert! Alert! Meta 3 disturbance. Meta signature identified as Warrior Woman."

"Warrior Woman?" Shadow Hawk mutters, his face

turning pale. "But… that's impossible."

For a second, I'm taken aback. I mean, I don't think I've ever seen Shadow Hawk look as white as a ghost before. And as he spins back around in his chair I wrack my brain for where I've heard the name 'Warrior Woman' before. For some reason, it sounds familiar. And then—

"Alert! Alert! Alert!" the Meta Monitor blares. "Meta 3 disturbance. Repeat: Meta 3 disturbance. Identity unknown. Alert! Alert! Alert! Meta 3 disturbance. Identity unknown."

Identity unknown?

"It's coming from the Isle of Alala," Shadow Hawk says, his voice sounding urgent. Then, he pounds his fist on the keyboard and leaps from his chair. "I've got to go."

"The Isle of Alala?" I say. "Isn't that an island in the Pacific Ocean that's home to a group of super-strong Meta women?"

Suddenly, everything clicks.

Holy cow! I know exactly who Warrior Woman is!

"Um, hang on," I say. "Isn't that, like, *the* Warrior Woman? As in, one of the founders of the Protectors of the Planet? As in, the greatest superhero team of the Golden Age of Metas?"

"One and the same," Shadow Hawk says, bounding down the stairs, his black cape billowing behind him. "And she needs my help."

"Not just your help," I say, running down behind

him. "Our help!"

***

As we fly across the Pacific Ocean, I try engaging Shadow Hawk in conversation, but he's lost in thought. Not that I can blame him. I mean, I can't believe I'm actually going to meet Warrior Woman, an original member of the Protectors of the Planet! A few years ago, Shadow Hawk showed me his collection of old newspaper clippings about the team. And Dad is such a Meta history buff he'd flip if he knew where we were going! I kind of feel bad Grace is still sleeping, but hey, you snooze you lose.

But then I realize something.

Warrior Woman has got to be pretty old by now.

I mean, she was a big hero back in the Golden Age, which was, like, forty years ago. The Protectors of the Planet were the premier superhero team of their time before the Freedom Force even existed. The seven original members are legends within the Meta community.

There was Warrior Woman, of course. She came to America as an ambassador for peace but often had to put her formidable fighting skills to use. Then, there was Riptide, Prince of the lost city of Atlantis. He could control water and breathe on both land and sea. And who could forget Will Power, an Earth-born galactic guardian who defended the planet with a magic, alien rock.

An experiment gone wrong gave Goldrush the power of Super-Speed, while the Black Crow was a Meta 0 vigilante who patrolled the night and protected the innocent from evil. His Meta 0 sidekick, Sparrow, was just a boy but his combat skills nearly rivaled his mentor. And last but not least was Meta-Man, the most powerful hero of them all.

Meta-Man came to Earth from an unknown planet. He was called Meta-Man for a reason because he could use different types of Meta powers, but only one at a time. And based on his green costume he earned the nickname 'the Emerald Enforcer.'

As legend has it, all of these heroes came together for the first time to take on a dangerous villain called the Soul Snatcher. After that, they decided to band together to defend the planet from future threats, and that's how the Protectors of the Planet was formed.

Meta-Man was the leader, and over time other heroes joined the team, like Sergeant Stretch, a Meta-morph who could stretch his body into various shapes, and the Marksman, who never missed his target. But according to Dad, Meta-Man left Earth after a mission went horribly wrong and no one has seen him since.

Once Meta-Man took off, the rest of the Protectors went their separate ways. A few of them stayed in the hero game for a little while longer before eventually leaving the scene. I wonder if Shadow Hawk ever met any of the Protectors in person? I'm about to ask him when he says—

"We're here."

I look down to see a lush island sitting in the middle of the ocean. It looks beautiful from up high, and as we get closer I see cobblestone roads and temple-like structures made of white marble. It's impressive, like it was transported here from ancient Greece, but unfortunately, that's not all I see, because there's a giant plume of black smoke coming from the city's center.

"Prepare for landing," Shadow Hawk says gruffly, angling the Freedom Flyer towards the disturbance.

As we head for the smoke, I see marble slabs scattered everywhere. There's no doubt something major happened here. The question is *what*? Shadow Hawk spins us around and touches down in a small clearing near the debris.

But before we exit to investigate, he puts a hand on my arm and says, "Be alert. As far as I'm aware, only Warrior Woman and her husband still live here. No one else has stepped foot on this island in decades. And her husband doesn't have powers."

"Got it," I say, following him out of the Freedom Flyer. I can't help but notice how strange he's acting. I mean, why is he so freaked out?

But as we approach the rubble I realize Shadow Hawk's cause for concern is justified because the broken marble is super thick. Whoever knocked these buildings down must be pretty darn powerful.

"Look at this," Shadow Hawk says, calling me over to a wall that's still standing. Then, he points to a red, smoldering line cut across its face. It's like it was shot with some sort of a laser or something. But as I step around to get a closer look the back of my head SLAMS into something that knocks me to my knees.

"Ouch!" I say, rubbing my noggin which is absolutely throbbing. What was that?

"Are you okay?" Shadow Hawk asks, pulling me up to my feet. Then, I notice the nose of a green, single-flyer airplane behind him. "Warrior Woman's War-Jet," he says.

"Right," I say. I completely forgot that Warrior Woman couldn't fly and used a jet to get around.

"If her War-Jet is still here," Shadow Hawk says, "then it means she didn't get away. So, either she's buried under all of this rubble or—"

"Help!" comes a man's voice.

We spin around to find a very old man hobbling towards us on crutches. His snow-white beard contrasts against his red, sun-burned skin, and his clothes are tattered and torn.

"Mr. Henson?" Shadow Hawk says. "Is that you?"

Mr. Henson? Is that Warrior Woman's husband?

"P-Please," the man says, speaking quickly with sheer panic in his eyes. "Y-You have to save her. H-He took her! He said he… wanted revenge!"

"Mr. Henson, please, slow down," Shadow Hawk

says. "Who took her? Who wanted revenge?"

The old man looks at us but nothing comes out of his mouth. He looks terrified.

"It's okay, Mr. Henson," Shadow Hawk says, putting his hand on the man's shoulder. "Just tell us what you saw."

"H-He looked the same as he did all those years ago," Mr. Henson finally says. "Like he… never aged. Even after all this time. And… he took her."

"Who?" Shadow Hawk asks. "Who didn't age? Who took her?"

"M-Meta-Man," Mr. Henson blurts out. "Meta-Man took my wife. M-Meta-Man is back!"

Meta Profile
The Freedom Force
Captain Justice
Class: Super-Strength
Meta :
Ms. Understood
Class: Psychic
Meta :
Glory Girl
Class: Flight
Meta :
Shadow Hawk
Class: None
Meta :
Epic Zero
Class: Meta Manipulator
Meta :
TechnocRat
Class: Super-Intellect
Meta :
Blue Bolt
Class: Super-Speed
Meta :
Master Mime
Class: Magic
Meta :
Makeshift
Class: Energy Manipulator
Meta :

THREE

I GET A FUNNY FEELING

Meta-Man.

Before he left Earth he was one of the greatest heroes of all time. But now, according to Warrior Woman's husband, he's back—and for some reason, he just ambushed and kidnapped Warrior Woman!

But why?

I mean, Mr. Henson, Warrior Woman's husband said Meta-Man is back for revenge. But for revenge against who? I mean, Warrior Woman was his teammate. What did she ever do to him?

I try picking Shadow Hawk's brain on our trip back to the Waystation 2.0 but he's not very talkative. He's probably as shocked as I am by what happened. After all, he idolizes the Protectors of the Planet.

The only thing he did clear up for me is why the Meta Monitor didn't identify Meta-Man's power signature in the first place. Apparently, Meta-Man left the planet way before TechnocRat built the Meta Monitor, so it never had the chance to register his Meta signature. Meta-Man has a data profile only because Shadow Hawk added it to the database himself.

Even though Mr. Henson gave us an eyewitness account of what happened, Shadow Hawk still wants to make sure it's accurate. That's why we're bringing one of the burned marble slabs back to the Waystation for analysis. Shadow Hawk wants to feed it into the Meta Spectrometer to confirm the type of Meta power that caused the laser marks. And if he can do that, we may be able to track Meta-Man himself.

I sure hope it works, because if what Mr. Henson said is true, Meta-Man clearly didn't come back for a team reunion. There's definitely more to this story, and as soon as we get back to the Waystation I'll see what else I can find out. But as we pull into the Hangar, two familiar figures are waiting for us—one wagging his tail and the other looking like she wants to clobber somebody.

"Um, what's up with Grace?" I ask.

"I don't know," Shadow Hawk says, parking the Freedom Flyer in its usual spot. "But I see the others aren't back yet."

Huh? Then, I notice the empty parking spot next to

us. He's right, the Freedom Flyer my parents took is still gone. Gee, I hope they're okay. But when I look down at Grace's angry face I suspect I'd rather be with them right now, wherever they are.

"I'm going to start the analysis," Shadow Hawk says, popping the hatch and hoisting the marble slab over his shoulder. "Good luck."

"Thanks," I say, swallowing hard. "I think I'm going to need it."

As soon as I step off the ramp, Dog-Gone jumps up and starts licking my face. And then—

"Well, well, nice of you to come back," Grace says with her arms crossed. "Guess who didn't get any sleep last night?"

"You mean, other than Shadow Hawk and me?" I answer. "Because in case you didn't notice, we just got back from a mission that started in the wee hours of the morning."

"Funny you should mention 'wee,'" Grace says. "Because your stupid dog started howling for the bathroom right after you left."

"He did, did he?" I say, kneeling to scratch his neck. "You had to go, didn't you, boy?"

"Yeah, he had to go," Grace says. "And after he woke me up from a dead sleep and I took him, he crawled into my bed and stole all of my covers! So, I'll tell you who didn't get enough sleep. Me!"

"Okay, okay, I'm sorry," I say, heading for the exit.

"But you'll have to excuse me because there's something I've got to look into."

"Elliott Harkness, get back here!" Grace calls out. "I'm not done yelling at you yet!"

"Gosh, that sure sounds like fun," I say, pushing open the Hangar door, "but I've got to run. You see, Meta-Man just kidnapped Warrior Woman so there are a few things I've gotta do."

"Meta-Man kidnapped Warrior Woman?" Grace says. "As in, *the* Meta-Man and Warrior Woman? Hey, hold on!"

I hear Grace's footsteps behind me and when I turn around she's hot on my tail asking for the lowdown on everything that just happened. By the time I fill her in, we've reached the Mission Room. I hop into the command chair and start typing into the keyboard.

"What are you doing?" she asks.

"Finding out more about Meta-Man," I say. "Shadow Hawk told me a little bit about him, but I don't know his whole story."

Suddenly, words start scrolling down the screen:

- *Name: Meta-Man.*
- *History: Very little is known about the origin of Meta-Man. He was born on a distant planet in an unknown galaxy. As a toddler, he was sent to Earth in a spaceship. The reasons for why he was sent to Earth are unknown. His ship landed near Houston where it was discovered by a corrupt oil baron named Maximillian Murdock and his*

wife Sophia. The Murdock family adopted the boy and gave him the name Lucas Murdock. During his youth, the Murdocks discovered that Lucas' skin was impervious to harm, making him invulnerable at all times. As he grew older, Lucas developed many other Meta abilities, including Super-Strength, Super-Speed, Heat Vision, Enhanced Senses, and Flight. However, unlike his invulnerability, he was only able to use one of these newly gained Meta powers at a time. His adopted father tried to get Lucas to use his powers for the benefit of his growing criminal empire, but Lucas rejected his father's wishes and left his home behind. He moved to Keystone City, donned a costume to fight crime, and became the superhero known as Meta-Man.

- *Recent Activity: Meta-Man left Earth and has not been seen for many decades.*

"Wow," Grace says. "I didn't know Meta-Man had a father like that."

"Yeah," I say, "me neither. I mean, imagine being sent as a baby to another planet and then being raised by a criminal. But clearly, Meta-Man was always a hero at heart because he rejected his father's evil ways. Talk about brave. He was a hero through and through."

"Correction," comes a voice from behind us. "He *was* a hero, but not anymore."

We turn to see Shadow Hawk standing in the doorway behind us.

"Then it's true?" I ask. "Meta-Man took Warrior Woman?"

"Yes," Shadow Hawk says. "The Meta Spectrometer confirmed it. Those burn marks on the marble slab came from Heat Vision—just like Meta-Man has. Unfortunately, Warrior Woman was an easy target because everyone knows she makes her home on the Isle of Alala. But the other living members of the Protectors of the Planet will be harder to find."

"Living members?" I repeat. "You mean, some of the Protectors have died?"

"Yes," Shadow Hawk says. "Riptide was killed during a challenge for the throne of Atlantis. And Will Power died of old age. But I believe Goldrush, Sergeant Stretch, the Marksman, and the Black Crow are still alive, and I intend to track them down before Meta-Man finds them."

"So, wait," Grace says. "You think Meta-Man will go after them too?"

"I do," Shadow Hawk says. "If Meta-Man took Warrior Woman, I'm positive the others are next. That is, if he hasn't gotten to them already."

"But how will you find them?" I ask. "Those heroes haven't been active for years."

"I'm going to put my detective skills to work," Shadow Hawk says. "And I won't rest until I find them all."

"We can help," Grace says.

"No," Shadow Hawk says. "It's too dangerous. If Meta-Man is this unstable he could wipe you out in the blink of an eye. It's better if I handle this alone."

"Well, what should we do?" I ask.

"You should stay here where it's safe," he says.

"But I don't get it," Grace says. "Why is Meta-Man even doing this? Why is he looking for revenge against his old teammates?"

But instead of answering, Shadow Hawk simply purses his lips and says, "I'll return later."

And then he's gone.

"Well, that was weird," Grace says.

"Yeah," I say. "He's been acting funny since this whole thing started. I mean, I know he really looked up to Meta-Man and the Protectors. Maybe this is freaking him out or something?"

"Maybe," she says, her eyes narrowing. "Or maybe something else is going on. But the last thing I'm going to do is sit here twiddling my thumbs until we hear from Shadow Hawk. Move over."

"Hey!" I say as Grace nudges me right out of the command chair. "What are you doing?"

"Looking for dirt on the Protectors of the Planet," she says, typing into the keyboard. "Shadow Hawk isn't the only one who's good at detective work. Especially when I combine my big brain with the brain of this super-computer. Let's see who can find them first."

"Well, I hate to break it to you," I say, "but just because you have a big head doesn't mean you have a big brain."

"Go away, neanderthal-boy," she says. "And take

your saber-toothed dog with you. This room is for smart people only."

"Very funny," I say. "C'mon, Dog-Gone, let's give her some space. She'll need it to fill all the emptiness in her big head."

"You'll eat those words when I find them first!" she calls out.

"I won't be holding my breath!" I call back, as Dog-Gone and I head down the hallway.

Honestly, I'm happy to go because I could use a nap. The lack of sleep is really starting to catch up with me. But something is bugging me about our conversation with Shadow Hawk. Unfortunately, my head is so fuzzy I can't put my finger on it.

We make our way back to the residential wing and I enter my room. I just need twenty minutes of sleep and I'll feel like a new superhero. I lay down on my bed and Dog-Gone plops down by my feet.

"Make sure you stay down there," I say, closing my eyes. "This time I need the rest."

Okay, just twenty minutes. That's all I—

BEEP!

My eyes pop open. What's that?

BEEP!

I look at my alarm clock but that's not it.

BEEP!

Just then, I realize it's coming from my Next Gen transmitter watch, which means the team needs me! I pull my wrist close to look at the message, which reads:

<Selfie: Epic Zero, team meeting at Hangout.>

Team meeting?

What do we need a team meeting for? I sit up and rub my eyes. Then, I type:

<Right now?>

<Selfie: Yes. Right now.>

Well, that was clear. Suddenly, I have a bad feeling about this. I type back:

<Ok. Leaving in a few min.>

Well, so much for a nap. I put my feet on the floor and stand up. "C'mon, boy," I say to Dog-Gone. "You can make sure I don't fall asleep while I'm flying."

Dog-Gone and I head back the way we came and poke our heads into the Mission Room. Grace is still at the controls toggling between a bunch of data screens.

"I'm heading to Earth for a meeting at the Hangout," I say.

"Uh-huh," Grace says, not even turning around.

"I'm not sure when I'll be back," I say.

"Uh-huh," she says again.

"There's a giant squid on your head," I say.

"Uh-huh," she repeats.

Right. Well, hopefully, she heard what I said because I'd hate for Mom and Dad to get back and not know where I am. But I figure I shouldn't be gone too long anyway. At least, I hope not.

We head back to the Hangar and hop into a Freedom

Ferry. Dog-Gone shuffles into the passenger seat and I buckle us both in. I enter the coordinates for the Hangout, power up the Freedom Ferry, and we're off.

As soon as we hit outer space, it dawns on me that this little meeting might be about me. I mean, what if the team wants to dump me as their leader? Or maybe they want to dump me altogether!

Ugh. Suddenly, I feel sick to my stomach.

But then again, it could be about anything.

I mean, maybe they're tired of being mentored by the Freedom Force. After all, we promised we wouldn't fight in public without the Freedom Force's supervision. Maybe they don't want to do that anymore. Not that I blame them. I mean, we're kids but we're heroes too.

Wait a second.

Kid. Heroes?

Suddenly, I realize what's been bugging me about our conversation with Shadow Hawk. Strangely, he talked about finding all of the living members of the Protectors of the Planet except for one.

For some reason, he didn't say anything about Sparrow.

Meta Profile
Protectors of the Planet
Riptide
Class: Energy Manipulator
Meta :
Goldrush
Class: Super-Speed
Meta :
Marksman
Class: None
Meta :
Black Crow
Class: None
Meta :
Meta-Man
Class: Multi-Meta Powers
Meta :
Warrior Woman
Class: Super-Strength
Meta :
Sparrow
Class: None
Meta :
Will Power
Class: Magic
Meta :
Sergeant Strech
Class: Meta-morph
Meta :

FOUR

I BRACE MYSELF FOR BAD NEWS

Why didn't Shadow Hawk mention Sparrow?

I know Sparrow was just the Black Crow's sidekick when the Protectors of the Planet were doing their thing, but he was still an original member of the team. With everything going on, did Shadow Hawk forget about him because he was just a kid? The fact that Shadow Hawk didn't even mention him kind of ruffles my feathers.

After all, I'm a kid hero too.

I think I'd be pretty disappointed if people forgot about me. I mean, I've done a few things to save the universe. You know, like getting rid of two Orbs of Oblivion, stopping Ravager from eating the planet, and kicking the Skelton Emperor off of Earth.

You'd think you'd be remembered for stuff like that.

Anyway, before I land at the Hangout, I should probably call Grace to clue her in about Sparrow. I'm sure she's still in the Mission Room because she seemed pretty determined to find the other living Protectors before Shadow Hawk. Maybe she can find Sparrow.

"Freedom Ferry to Waystation," I call into the communicator.

"Roger, Freedom Ferry," comes Grace's exasperated voice. "Why are you bugging me now?"

"I'm not bugging you," I say, rolling my eyes. "I'm letting you know that Shadow Hawk forgot to mention one of the original Protectors."

"Yeah, I know," Grace says. "I'm already looking for Sparrow."

"You are?" I say surprised.

"Of course, I am," she says. "Big brain here, remember?"

Somehow, I manage not to grunt out loud.

"I've already tapped into several databases looking for info on Sparrow," she continues. "Old newspaper articles, police reports, hospital records. He was much younger than the other Protectors so I'm hoping to turn up something. So far I haven't had much luck."

"Okay," I say. "Well, I wasn't sure if you knew so I just thought I'd check."

"Right," she says firmly. "Again, amazing brain here."

"Got it," I say. "And in case you forgot I'm heading

to Earth for a meeting at—"

"Over and out," she says, ending the transmission.

"—the Hangout," I finish meekly. "Over and out," I say, apparently to no one in particular.

Well, she clearly doesn't want to be bothered. And speaking of being bothered, I still don't know what this meeting at the Hangout is about, but something tells me it's not going to be good. In fact, I have a sinking feeling this might be my last appearance as the leader of Next Gen. I find a clearing in the woods behind Selfie's house and land the Freedom Ferry.

"Alright, Dog-Gone," I say, unbuckling my furry companion. "Let's go face the music."

We walk into Selfie's backyard and I look at our treehouse headquarters for quite possibly the very last time. I don't know what I'll do if they want to get rid of me. I mean, these guys are the only friends I've got.

I grab a rung on the ladder when I realize I've got another problem on my hands. Dog-Gone hates climbing ladders. "Oh, come on you big baby," I say. "Get over here."

Dog-Gone backs up quickly, but before he can take off, a shadow wraps around his body like a harness and lifts him off the ground!

"Night Owl?" I say, looking up.

"Don't worry, I've, ugh, got him," she says, struggling to pull him up to the treehouse landing. "But you might want to put him, ugh, on a diet."

"Please, don't say the 'D-word,'" Pinball says as I reach the top of the ladder. "Some of us are simply blessed with more of ourselves than others."

It's great to hear everyone being so cheerful, but as soon as I step onto the landing their faces get serious. Okay, that's not a good sign. I put on a fake smile and say, "So, what's this urgent meeting about anyway?"

"We… need to talk," Selfie says. "As a group. Maybe you should sit down."

"Well, that sounds ominous," I say, taking a seat between Skunk Girl and Night Owl. "So, what do we need to talk about?"

But instead of just coming out with it, Selfie looks down and there's awkward silence. Well, if she can't tell me it can only mean one thing. They're going to fire me as leader.

"Look, boss-man, we need to be honest with you," Skunk Girl says, finally breaking the ice.

Uh-oh, here it comes. I brace myself.

"You're a great hero," she continues. "I mean, you're a member of the Freedom Force for Pete's sake, and… well, we're just a bunch of inexperienced rookies. The truth is, we've realized we probably won't ever reach your level. So, we don't want to hold you back anymore. We think you should dump us."

"What?" I blurt out, totally confused.

They want me to dump them?

But that's crazy!

"Yeah," Selfie says. "We all reached the same conclusion after that second training session. None of us are as fast on our feet as you are, and we certainly can't control our powers like you do. So, why should we make you wait around until we're ready? You could be doing so much more fighting alongside the Freedom Force instead of slumming around with us. We appreciate all the time you've put into trying to make us better, but it's not right for us to drag you down."

"Yeah, you're like, a major Meta," Pinball adds. "You gotta do you, even if that means doing it without us."

I open my mouth to respond but I'm so shocked I can't even find the words. I mean, I appreciate how highly they think of me, but dumping them is the last thing I want to do.

"Sorry we're springing this on you like this," Selfie says, "but we didn't think it was fair to waste any more of your valuable time. Of course, we understand if you don't want to talk to us again."

She looks up at me and I see tears welling in her blue eyes. In fact, the whole team looks sad—even Skunk Girl. I need to put a stop to this.

"Look, guys," I say, "I'm not sure where you're getting this from, but I don't want to leave our team."

"Y-You don't?" Selfie asks.

"No," I say. "I don't. Not even a little bit."

"For real?" Pinball asks. "You're not just saying that because you're a big-time hero and don't want to hurt our feelings?"

"No," I say. "First, I'm no big-time hero. I mean, yeah, I've had some successful missions, but I've messed up plenty too. Second, we're going to get better at this—all of us—but we can't give up. The Freedom Force wasn't perfect on day one and neither are we. We just have to trust each other, and if we do that, I know we'll get there."

Suddenly, their faces perk up.

"Level with us, Epic Zero," Night Owl says. "You've seen true greatness in action. Do you really think we can get there?"

"I do," I say without hesitation. "I really, really do."

Just then, Dog-Gone yawns loudly.

"Well, maybe not all of us," I say, nodding towards Dog-Gone as everyone laughs.

"So, you still want to hang out with us?" Selfie asks.

"Absolutely," I say. "We're a team until the end. The funny thing is, I thought you guys called this meeting to get rid of me."

"What?" Pinball says. "Are you crazy?"

"Maybe," I say. "I just, well, assumed you wanted a different leader. I'm glad I was wrong."

"Totally wrong," Selfie says. "We'd be lost without you. Why would you even think that way?"

"I don't know," I say. "I guess we all feel insecure sometimes. Even a supposed 'big-time hero' like me."

"Well, I'm glad you're sticking around," Selfie says,

wiping her eyes and flashing a big smile.

"Me too," I say, smiling back, my face feeling flush.

Man, I feel such a crazy mix of happiness and relief I don't know whether to jump with joy or kick myself for wasting all that time getting worked up over this meeting.

Sometimes I'm my own worst enemy.

"Okay, boss-man," Skunk Girl says. "Now that we've got that ironed out, your next order of business is to nail down a not-so-lame battle cry for our team. If you yell out, 'Give us liberty or give us death' one more time I'll have to slug you."

"That wasn't even the worst one," Pinball says. "Do you remember when he yelled 'Cowabunga?' I nearly died of embarrassment."

"Okay, okay," I say. "I get it. Don't worry, it'll come to me. Just give me a few more chances."

MEEP! MEEP! MEEP!

"What's that?" Night Owl asks.

"The police monitor!" Selfie says, running over to turn up the volume.

There's some static, and then—SQUAWK!

"—need immediate assistance!" comes a man's panicked voice. "I-I repeat we are under assault! A Meta villain has penetrated our defenses and is tearing this place apart! Our weapons can't seem to stop him and prisoners are escaping! It won't be long until there's an all-out jailbreak! We need immediate assistance, over!"

Prisoners? Jailbreak?

"Roger, Lieutenant," comes a female dispatcher's voice. "We are sending emergency support ASAP. Squadrons four and seven are on their way to your location. Can you confirm the identity of the assailant so I can contact the Freedom Force, over?"

"Never seen him before!" the Lieutenant says. "Hurry!"

"Stay focused, Lieutenant," the dispatcher says. "Can you describe him for me?"

"Y-Yeah, kind of!" the Lieutenant says. "He's super-fast so it's hard to get a good bead on him! But he's wearing a green costume and flying all over the place busting down walls! He keeps demanding we produce someone named 'Max Mayhem,' but we don't have anyone by that name here! Uh-oh! He sees me! Get here as fast as—!"

CLICK! And then there's nothing but static.

"Lieutenant?" comes the dispatcher's voice. "Lieutenant, can you hear me? If you're still there, I'm reaching out to the Freedom Force now. Do whatever you can to fend off the villain. We can't have a jailbreak at Lockdown Penitentiary."

L-Lockdown Penitentiary?

I swallow hard.

"What do we do now?" Pinball asks. "That mission sounds really serious and we promised the Freedom Force we wouldn't go out in public without them."

The Freedom Force?

OMG! Suddenly, I realize that if my parents and the rest of the team aren't back yet, it'll be up to Shadow Hawk, Grace, and, well, me. And who even knows where Shadow Hawk is right now.

"What's the call, boss-man?" Skunk Girl asks. "Do we kick it to the big guns or handle it ourselves?"

I look at the team and see the hunger in their eyes. But Pinball is right, we told the Freedom Force we wouldn't do anything without them. But then again, this is Lockdown we're talking about. It houses hundreds of super dangerous Meta creeps. And if there's a jailbreak there's no way I could get them all back in their cells on my own.

I-I don't know what to do.

"Boss-man?" Skunk Girl says. "You with us?"

"Um, yeah," I say, snapping back to reality.

"What's the call?" she asks.

I know what we promised my parents, but I don't think I have a choice. I take a deep breath and say—

"Let's go mash some Metas."

"Yahoo!" Skunk Girl yells. "Now there's a battle cry!"

Meta Profile

Warrior Woman

Name: Alexandra Noble	Height: 5'11"
Race: Athenian	Weight: 160 lbs
Status: Hero/Inactive	Eyes/Hair: Brown/Black

META 3: Super-Strength

- Extreme Strength
- Extreme Invulnerability
- Wields Javelin of Peace

Observed Characteristics

Combat 100

Durability	95	Leadership	93
Strategy	96	Willpower	98

FIVE

I CAN'T SEEM TO STAY OUT OF JAIL

I have a feeling I'm going to regret this.

I mean, according to what we heard over the police monitor, some Meta is ripping Lockdown apart with his bare hands. And while we didn't learn the identity of the perpetrator, we did learn he's looking for someone named Max Mayhem, whoever that is. But if this villain is powerful enough to withstand Lockdown's substantial defenses, then he's one seriously strong Meta.

But that's not the only problem we'll face. The police lieutenant said Lockdown was close to a jailbreak. If that happens, hundreds of dangerous Metas could be set free. And to add to the drama, I tried contacting my parents from the Freedom Ferry but there was no answer.

So, that pretty much means we're on our own.

Just. Freaking. Wonderful.

Dog-Gone curls up next to me inside the Freedom Ferry as I check on the rest of the team trailing behind us. I offered to give them a lift but they thought it would look more heroic to storm Lockdown under their own powers. I adjust the rearview camera to find Pinball bouncing alongside Night Owl, who is riding a shadow slide with Selfie and Skunk Girl.

Gotta love their enthusiasm.

I just hope I didn't make a big mistake.

I take a deep breath and breathe out. What was I thinking? I got the team pumped up to tackle this mission, but the more I think about it the more I realize we're biting off more than we can chew.

I was so caught up in the excitement of us staying together that I didn't think this through. I truly believe in our potential as a superhero team, but we're just not there yet. I mean, my own experiences with Lockdown have been nothing but nightmares. From losing K'ami to my strange meeting with Tormentus, nothing ever goes right when I step foot in that place.

So, why would this be any different?

What if we get there to find a massive jailbreak? Can Skunk Girl stop a Meta 3 villain like Side-Splitter? Can Pinball take down Deathblow? Deep down I know the answer, which means I also know what I have to do. But before I do that it would be great to set up some legitimate backup other than Dog-Gone.

So, I swallow my pride and flick on the communicator. "Freedom Ferry to Waystation," I say. "Freedom Ferry to Waystation, do you read me?"

"Roger, Freedom Ferry," Grace says. "Didn't I just tell you not to bug me? I'm kind of busy right now."

"Well, so am I," I say, "because it case you didn't know, there's a Meta destroying—"

"—Lockdown?" Grace says, cutting me off yet again. "Yeah, I know. The Meta Monitor is lit up like a Christmas tree over here and I just hung up with the Keystone City Police. The thing is, the Meta Monitor can't identify the bad guy. The Meta signature is coming back as 'identity unknown.' I've been pinging Shadow Hawk but he's not responding. I've already tried him, like, ten times."

Shadow Hawk isn't responding? That's not like him.

"Well, don't worry," I say, "I'm on the case but, um, could use a little help."

"You're on the what?" Grace says confused. "What do you mean you're on the—? Whoa! Hold on there, bucko! You're not heading to Lockdown are you?"

"Well, yeah," I say. "That's exactly where I'm heading."

"Back off," Grace says. "This one is serious. If you die on my watch Mom will take away my phone forever! Stay put, I'm heading for a Freedom Ferry now!"

"Look, I didn't call you for a babysitter," I say. "I called you for backup. And I can't just sit around until you get here. Every second counts."

"Don't you move!" Grace barks into the communicator. "Do you hear me? I'm getting inside the Freedom Ferry right now."

"What? PSSSSSSHHHHHH!" I say, holding the communicator close to my mouth. "Is that static? I couldn't PSSSSSSHHHHHH you!"

"Don't play games with me!" Grace yells.

"Sorry, I PSSSSSSHHHHHH hear you," I say.

And then I flick off the communicator.

Well, that felt good. But despite my bravado, we both know she's right—this mission has all the makings of a major disaster. But what I didn't tell her is that she's got a few minutes to get down here because there's something I have to do first. I've got to send Next Gen home.

I slow the thrusters on my Freedom Ferry when—

"Alert! Alert! Alert!" the Meta Monitor blares. "Meta 3 disturbance. Repeat: Meta 3 disturbance. Power signature identified as Speed Demon. Alert! Alert! Alert! Meta 3 disturbance. Meta signature identified as Speed Demon."

Speed Demon? But how can that be? I mean, Master Mime put Speed Demon in Lockdown years ago.

And that's when it clicks.

Speed Demon just busted out!

Suddenly, I see a small dust cloud in the distance. Except, it's getting bigger and bigger and heading our way at incredible speed! And then I realize that's no ordinary dust cloud, that's Speed Demon!

I switch on the Freedom Ferry's megaphone and yell out to the team, "Look out!" But in the blink of an eye Speed Demon ZOOMS beneath us, kicking up an intense air current that blows the Freedom Ferry sideways!

Dog-Gone YELPS as we're jerked in our seatbelts, but I manage to turn the steering column and hit the thrusters to level us back off. Thank goodness we're okay, but when I look in the rearview camera the rest of the team is gone! I quickly check my radar to find Pinball miles away but there's no sign of the girls.

Where did they go?

Just then, a gigantic shadow parachute floats down, and Night Owl, Selfie, and Skunk Girl land on my hood.

"What was that?" Night Owl asks, forming a giant shadow slide for her, Selfie, and Skunk Girl.

"Speed Demon!" I yell back. "But look out because there might be—"

"Alert! Alert! Alert!" the Meta Monitor blares. "Meta 2 disturbance. Repeat: Meta 2 disturbance. Power signature identified as Talon. Alert! Alert! Alert! Meta 2 disturbance. Meta signature identified as Talon."

Talon? She's a half-human, half-bird creature who loves to terrorize people. She was also at Lockdown. In fact, Blue Bolt just put her there. Then, I see a black dot in the sky. It's coming towards us. Getting larger.

"Get down!" I yell.

Night Owl, Selfie, and Skunk Girl duck right before a

giant, winged woman BUZZES over their heads and BRUSHES past the Freedom Ferry.

An instant later, she's gone.

"Um, thanks," Selfie says, looking off into the distance with dread. "I'm guessing she came from Lockdown."

"Yep," I say, watching Talon's signal disappear off my radar. Well, here we go. Two major villains just got away scot-free and there was nothing I could do. But if I don't act quickly they'll be just the tip of the iceberg. After all, every second I waste is another second a villain might get free. I've got to get to Lockdown fast, but I can't risk my team getting hurt.

So, here comes the first hard part.

"Team, we need to talk," I say.

"Cool," Skunk Girl says, "let's talk strategy."

I see the excitement in her eyes and I feel crummy, but I've got to do what I've got to do.

"Listen," I say, "we're not talking strategy. I know you're not going to like this, but I've got to pull rank and send you guys home."

"What?" Skunk Girl says, her eyes narrowing.

"Look," I say, "Lockdown is filled with deadly villains like Speed Demon and Talon. Plus, there's a Meta 3 we know nothing about breaking them loose. I know it stinks, but this mission is simply too risky for you guys to be here right now. It's my fault. I'm… really sorry."

"Are you kidding me?" Skunk Girl says. "We're not

sitting this one out. You said we're a team."

"I know what I said," I say, "but you've also trusted me to be your leader. So, as your leader, I'm ordering you to go home before someone gets killed."

"Seriously?" Skunk Girl fires back. "Whatever happened to 'let's go mash some Metas?'"

"Skunk Girl, chill," Selfie says, putting her hand on Skunk Girl's shoulder. "That's clear, Epic. You go ahead. We'll find Pinball and head home, just like you asked."

"Phooey," Skunk Girl says, crossing her arms.

"Thank you," I say to Selfie, "and I'm really sorry."

I see the disappointment written all over Night Owl's face but I can't worry about that now. So, I hit the thrusters and Dog-Gone's ears snap back as we take off. I feel lousy but I didn't have a choice. This has already gotten way too dangerous.

Probably even for me.

"Alert! Alert! Alert!" the Meta Monitor suddenly blares. "Meta 3 disturbance. Repeat: Meta 3 disturbance. Power signature identified as Doc Hurricane. Alert! Alert! Alert! Meta 3 disturbance. Meta signature identified as Doc Hurricane."

Followed by, "Alert! Alert! Alert!" the Meta Monitor blares. "Meta 3 disturbance. Repeat: Meta 3 disturbance. Power signature identified as Lady MacDeath. Alert! Alert! Alert! Meta 3 disturbance. Meta signature identified as Lady MacDeath."

Which is then followed by, "Alert! Alert! Alert!" the

Meta Monitor blares. "Meta 2 disturbance. Repeat: Meta 2 disturbance. Power signature identified as Miss Behave. Alert! Alert! Alert! Meta 2 disturbance. Meta signature identified as Miss Behave."

OMG! Villains are getting loose by the truckload!

"Alert! Alert! Alert!" the Meta Monitor blares yet again. I switch it off quickly so I can concentrate. Criminals are pouring out but there's nothing I can do except try to stop it at the source. I put more power into the thrusters and rocket towards Lockdown on overdrive, but as soon as the facility comes into view I wish I was somewhere else.

Thick, black smoke blankets Lockdown, making it difficult to see what's happening on the ground. Unfortunately, what I can see makes me sick to my stomach, because perimeter walls are leveled, guard towers are destroyed, and three of the eight prison wings are missing roofs! And that's not all, dozens of inmates are streaming out of Lockdown on foot, by air, or in stolen vehicles! And as much as I want to catch them I can't because if I don't stop the villain responsible he'll free hundreds more!

But where is he?

"Hang on, Dog-Gone," I say, "we're going down."

I drop the Freedom Ferry through the black smog and touch down hard on a pile of rubble. I look around but the smoke is so heavy you can't see more than a few feet in front of your face. Yet, I do see a melted police cannon, a smashed armored truck, and a flipped-over police car. But that's not all, because inside that flipped police car is a police officer, and he's still buckled in his seat!

"Be careful," I warn Dog-Gone as I remove his seat belt. Then, I pop the hatch and race to the police car.

"Officer, are you okay?" I ask, reaching through the busted window to gently shake his shoulder. His face is beet red and there's a scar across his forehead where he must have hit the steering wheel. "Officer?" I repeat. "Are you okay?"

Suddenly, his eyelids flutter open.

"W-Where am I?" the officer asks, looking around confused. "Who… Who are you?"

"I'm Epic Zero," I say. "I'm a member of the Freedom Force. Let me help you out of here." I reach for the car door when he says—

"N-No." Then, he nods at something over my shoulder. "D-Don't… help me. H-Help… the girl."

The girl? What girl?

Then, I spin around and gasp, because on the other side of my vehicle is another Freedom Ferry! I didn't see it through the smoke but I nearly landed on top of it! But… it's badly damaged. For some reason, it's smashed into the side of the building!

For a split second, I'm confused where it came from.

And then it hits me like a ton of bricks.

"Is she with you?" comes a deep voice from

overhead.

I look up to find a dark-haired man wearing a green costume with an 'M-M' insignia on his chest. As he stares me down with his piercing blue eyes, I notice a thin scar running across his left cheekbone.

At first, I don't recognize him.

And then I realize who I'm staring at.

It's… Meta-Man!

And then I register what he just asked me.

Because in his arms is the body of an unconscious girl with a crimson costume and white cape.

It's… Grace!

Meta Profile

Meta-Man

Name: Lucas Murdock	Height: 6'2"
Race: Unknown	Weight: 232 lbs
Status: Hero/Inactive	Eyes/Hair: Blue/Black

META 3: Multi-Meta Powers
Extreme Invulnerability
Can Only Use One of These Extreme Powers at a Time: Strength, Speed, Heat Vision, Enhanced Senses, or Flight

Observed Characteristics	
Combat 100	
Durability 100	Leadership 100
Strategy 87	Willpower 100

SIX

I COME FACE-TO-FACE WITH A LEGEND

I can't keep my jaw from hanging open.

I'm staring at Meta-Man—the greatest Meta hero of all time! But what's he doing here?

I mean, Meta-Man was known as the Emerald Enforcer, and the police lieutenant said the guy who was destroying Lockdown was wearing a green costume. So, this must be Meta-Man alright. But I have to say, I never expected to meet him like this. Especially since he's holding my unconscious sister in his arms.

However, there's something strange about him. It takes me a second to figure it out, but then I realize he still looks like he's in his prime, just like Mr. Henson said. I mean, for a guy who disappeared forty years ago, you'd think he would have aged—a lot! But instead, other than that scar on his face, he's got perfectly smooth skin, thick, black hair, and rippling muscles. He looks exactly like the picture in his Meta profile. It's like he never aged at all.

How is that possible?

But before I can ask him I hear Shadow Hawk's voice inside my head—*if Meta-Man is this unstable he could wipe you out in the blink of an eye.* Suddenly I'm more concerned about what's going on inside Meta-Man's head than how he looks on the outside. With all of his raw power, instability is the last thing I need.

Unfortunately, the evidence before me is as clear as day. Not only did he kidnap Warrior Woman, but now he's crushed Lockdown and he's holding Grace. So, there's only one logical conclusion.

Meta-Man is totally bonkers.

Now that that's out of the way, how do I stop him without risking Grace's life? I mean, his power levels are off the charts. I could try negating his power but he's still super-strong and Grace could get hurt. I need to proceed with extreme caution.

But how?

Then, it dawns on me. He was a hero once. Maybe I can reason with him. "Um, you're Meta-Man," I say profoundly, my voice cracking.

But instead of answering, he just stares at me with a puzzled expression on his face.

"Meta… Man?" he says finally, his eyebrows

furrowing like the wheels inside his head are spinning. Like he's thinking back to a time long, long ago.

"Um, yeah," I say. "That's your name."

"Y-Yes," he says, his face relaxing. "I-I haven't been called that in… many, many years."

Okay, what's up with him? It's like he forgot who he was or something.

"Well, that was you," I say. "I mean, that *is* you. And maybe you also forgot that you're a hero. You were the leader of the Protectors of the Planet—the greatest superhero team of its time."

"The… Protectors of the Planet," he repeats slowly.

"Exactly," I say, "they were your friends, remember?"

"Friends?" he says, but suddenly, he frowns and there's rage in his eyes. "Friends do not betray friends! And now they will pay the ultimate price for their betrayal!"

Okay, I just hit a nerve. For some reason, mentioning the Protectors of the Planet made him very, very angry, which is the last thing I wanted to do. So, I'm thinking I should avoid asking him about Warrior Woman for now. And why does he think the Protectors betrayed him? I'm dying to know, but my first priority is to rescue Grace. I need to get this conversation back on track.

"Hey, you're clearly upset," I say, extending my open palms toward him. "No one wants to be betrayed. But guess what, we're not them. In fact, I'm a hero, just like you. And so is the girl you're holding. My name is Epic Zero and she's Glory Girl—although between us she's really not that glorious—but we're both members of the Freedom Force, the greatest superhero team of this era. So, how about you put her down gently and we can talk some things through?"

"She fired weapons at me," Meta-Man says. "She tried to harm me."

Darn it, Grace. As usual, you're not exactly making it easy for me to save your life.

"Well, maybe you should look at this from our perspective," I say, trying to sound upbeat. "You didn't exactly tell anyone you were coming back to Earth, did you? And while we're absolutely thrilled to meet a legend like you, even you have to admit it kind of looks like you're trying to free all the prisoners here. So, you can see our conundrum, right?"

"I want Max Mayhem," Meta-Man says. "Bring him to me and I will give you the girl."

"Right," I say. "That sounds fair. I just have one little question. Who the heck is Max Mayhem?"

"Don't play games with me," Meta-Man says.

"I wish I was playing a game," I say. "But the truth is, you've been gone for a really long time and there isn't anybody named Max Mayhem around anymore."

Suddenly, Meta-Man's face turns red.

"I mean, unless he's going by another name now," I

say quickly. "Um, I guess he could have changed his name to Bobby Bedlam or Timmy Turmoil or something catchy like that. Your average villain does it all the time. Sometimes when their big evil plans fall apart, they just trademark a new name, and boom, they're back in business again."

"Max Mayhem is no average villain," Meta-Man says. "He considers himself to be the most intelligent human on Earth. His only goal is world domination and he will stop at nothing until he achieves it. I must find him. He… took something from me."

Wow, did I just hear his voice waver? Whatever this Max Mayhem character took must have meant a lot to Meta-Man. The problem is, there's no Max Mayhem here. In fact, I don't ever remember seeing a profile for Max Mayhem. This guy could be long dead for all I know.

But I don't want to tell Meta-Man that.

"Listen, I'm sorry about what he did to you," I say, "but Glory Girl didn't intend to harm you. As I said earlier, we just didn't know who you were or what you were doing here. So, why don't you let her go, and maybe we can look for this Max Mayhem guy together?"

"Together?" Meta-Man says.

"Yes," I say. "You and me. We'll team up just like heroes should. We'll find him together."

"I… I must find him," Meta-Man says, his eyebrows softening and his lips quivering.

Holy smokes, I think I'm getting through to him.

"So, let's just put her down carefully," I continue, "and we can get started."

Meta-Man hesitates and then lowers himself.

Yes! It's working! It's—

"COW-A-BUNG-A!"

Um, Cowa-what?

Suddenly, a round object comes bouncing out of the smog, heading straight for Meta-Man!

Oh. No.

BOOM!

Before I can react, Pinball SLAMS into Meta-Man, sending Grace flying out of his arms! As Meta-Man hurtles headfirst into a wall, I make like a world-class wide receiver and track Grace's body until it lands limply in my arms, sending us both crashing to the ground.

Needless to say, I take the full brunt of the fall.

"Glory Girl, wake up!" I yell, shaking her shoulder as she lays sprawled on top of me. "It's Meta-Man! We've got to get out of here!"

But Grace only moans.

Well, at least she's not dead. I push her arm off my forehead and roll her onto her back. She's gonna owe me big time after this one. But then again, I wasn't the one who saved her. Although she might regret not being dead when she finds out who did.

"No one messes with my girl!" Pinball yells to Meta-Man, who is buried beneath a pile of rubble.

Yep, she's definitely gonna wish she were dead.

But what's Pinball even doing here? I thought the rest of the team went to find him before going home.

"There you are, Pinball!" Selfie says, suddenly appearing out of the smoke with Night Owl and Skunk Girl in tow. "We've been looking all over for—" Then, she sees me lying next to Grace, waves awkwardly, and says, "Oh, hey there, Epic. How's it going?"

Are. You. Kidding. Me?

Now the whole team is here! And Pinball just ruined all of my work calming Meta-Man down. If these guys don't get out of here fast, it's going to be a blood—

"You will pay for that," comes Meta-Man's voice.

—bath.

I look over my shoulder to find Meta-Man on his feet dusting himself off. We're out of time!

"Run!" I yell to the team. "Get out of—!"

But before I can say another word, there's a green blur and POW! Suddenly, Pinball is rocketing sky-high!

"Well, I'm not looking for him again," Skunk Girl says, watching Pinball's body disappear in the distance.

"Focus on the problem at hand, Skunk Girl," Night Owl says, forming a shadow fist and punching Meta-Man.

But Meta-Man holds his ground, and her shadow fist shatters on contact! That's right! Meta-Man is invulnerable as well! And this time he wasn't taken by surprise like when Pinball attacked him.

"My turn," Selfie says, holding up her magic phone. "Now look over here and smile, creep."

But when Meta-Man turns, his eyes are smoldering with a strange red energy!

"Selfie!" I yell. "Look out for his Heat—!"

But I'm too late, as Meta-Man fires his Heat Vision right at Selfie's phone, knocking it out of her hand!

"AAH!" Selfie yells, pulling her hand away as her smoking phone clatters to the ground.

That's it! We won't last another five seconds if this fight continues. So, I concentrate hard and bathe Meta-Man with my negation powers.

Meta-Man turns my way, his eyes blazing with crackling red energy, but then they suddenly go out. Yes, he's powerless! Now we've still got to reel him in. I take a step towards him when I realize something is very wrong.

Why is he smiling at me?

"Neat trick," he says, his eyes narrowing. "Your power probably lets you turn off the powers of ordinary Metas. But my powers don't work like that. You see, I can reallocate my Meta energy instantaneously. So, as soon as I felt something sapping away my Heat Vision, I just shifted my energy from my eyes to my legs. Which means you've lost this race."

Um, what?

Just then, I realize he's about to mow me down with his Super-Speed! I try to move but it's too late as a green blur heads straight for me! But then, a black line shoots across the ground and Meta-Man goes flying into a wall!

What happened? That's when I notice the shadow

tripwire running along the ground.

"Thanks for the save," I say to Night Owl.

"No worries," she says with a wink. "I'll add it to your bill."

"I'm gonna clock that snake when he gets up," Skunk Girl says, pounding a fist into her other hand.

Okay, we've got to get out of here before someone gets seriously hurt—or worse. But how? It's not like we can outrun Meta-Man. Then, I hear a noise, and when I spin around there's a familiar face poking out of the giant hole in the wall Meta-Man just created.

It's X-Port! He's a Meta 3 Energy Manipulator who can teleport from one place to another! Apparently, Meta-Man just busted into the Energy Manipulator wing. Great, just what we needed, more villains on the loose.

"Thanks," X-Port says, stepping over Meta-Man's body and outside his cell to freedom.

Unfortunately, we don't have time to stop X-Port from getting away. I mean, we've got to get out of here ourselves. Plus, there's no way we'd catch him anyway. After all, he can… he can…

OMG! He can teleport!

I concentrate and duplicate as much of X-Port's power as possible. And just as I feel his Meta energy flood my body, X-Port extends his arms and legs into an 'X' shape and a red void appears. Then, he steps inside and disappears!

Well, there goes my power source. I hope I have

enough juice stored up.

"It's time to end this," Meta-Man says, stepping out of the hole in X-Port's prison wall.

Holy Cow! He's back!

"No," I say, "it's time to exit!"

I spread my limbs into an 'X' shape, activate X-Port's teleportation power, and a small, red void appears. I focus hard and push it out with everything I've got, stretching it to envelop Grace, Selfie, Skunk Girl, Night Owl, and Dog-Gone.

"What are you doing?" Meta-Man asks.

"Leaving," I say.

And then I snap the void closed and we're gone.

Meta Profile

The Black Crow

Name: Unknown	Height: 6'3"
Race: Human	Weight: 230 lbs
Status: Hero/Inactive	Eyes/Hair: Unknown/Unknown

META 0: No Powers
Master Detective
Expert Marksman
Highly-Skilled Martial Artist

Observed Characteristics	
Combat 95	
Durability 58	Leadership 94
Strategy 100	Willpower 100

SEVEN

I CONNECT THE DOTS

A red void opens over my bed.

I hit the mattress first, followed by Grace, then Selfie, Skunk Girl, and Night Owl who all use me as their personal trampoline. My stomach is sore but I'd rather have the wind knocked out of me than fight Meta-Man any day of the week. And thanks to X-Port's teleportation power, it's a miracle we even got out of there alive. I'm just glad we made it.

But as I look at everyone spread out on the floor I realize we're not all here. One of us is missing! I look up to see the void closing fast.

Hold on! What happened to—

AAARRROOOOFFFFF!!!

Just then, a large brown-and-black rump drops out

of the void and SLAMS into my face, knocking me back on to my pillow. Ow! My nose is killing me. Just then, I see three German Shepherds standing over me licking my face. It's only after I blink a few times that they merge into one. Gee, thanks, Dog-Gone.

"Yeah, I'm happy to see you too," I say, scratching his head. "But next time look out for where you're landing."

"Are you okay, Epic?" Selfie asks.

"Just dandy," I say, rubbing my sore nose.

"Where are we?" Skunk Girl asks, looking around. "And why are Batman posters plastered all over the walls? And is that a pair of smiley-face underwear on that chair? Like, totally gross."

"Oh, will you look at that?" I say, springing from the bed and stuffing my underwear into the laundry basket. "We're, um, in my bedroom, back on the Waystation. It was the safest place I could think of to teleport to, but I wasn't exactly expecting company before I left."

"Don't worry about it," Selfie says. "You saved our bacon. That Meta-Man is one major Meta. I barely managed to grab my phone before you got us out of there. Luckily, it still works but it's still smoking from that jerk's eye beams." She holds up her magic phone which has a faint, red haze coming off of it.

"Um, what's going on?" Grace asks, sitting up and rubbing her eyes. "I feel like I missed a few chapters."

"I'm glad you're okay," I say, "but do you seriously

not remember? You tried to take down Meta-Man and he knocked your Freedom Flyer out of the sky. Then, you got taken hostage, which by the way seems to happen way too often. Thankfully, you were saved yet again."

"Oh, wow," Grace says, scratching her head. "I don't remember any of that. Well, I might as well thank you now for saving me so you don't hold it over my head for the rest of my life."

"Oh, no worries," I say with a big smile. "You don't have to thank me because I didn't save you this time."

"You didn't?" Grace says with a puzzled expression on her face. "Then who—"

BEEP! BEEP! BEEP!

Suddenly, my transmitter watch goes off, as do the watches of the rest of Next Gen.

"What's that annoying sound?" Grace says, plugging her ears.

"It's our transmitters," Selfie says, looking at her wrist. "It's a message from Pinball. He says he's in a strange country and people are yelling at him in a foreign language."

"What a surprise," Skunk Girl says, rolling her eyes. "Other countries find him just as annoying as we do."

"Wait, there's more," Night Owl says, looking at her watch. "He says he crashed into some tower that's now leaning at an angle. But he swears he didn't do it."

"At an angle?" Skunk Girl says. "That idiot! He must have smacked into the Leaning Tower of Pisa. That means Meta-Man knocked him all the way to Italy!"

"It's a good thing Pinball is pretty indestructible when he's inflated," Selfie says. "But now we've got to get him back."

"Do we?" Skunk Girl says. "Well, I'm not going."

"You won't have to," I say. "I think Glory Girl should pick him up."

"Me?" Grace says. "Why me?"

"Because Pinball saved your life," I say. "So, I'd say you owe him one."

"What?" Grace says, her eyebrows rising in disbelief. "P-Pinball saved me? Are you kidding me?"

"Nope," I say. "He took on Meta-Man all by himself. He told Meta-Man that no one messes with his girl."

"His. Girl?" Grace says, horrified.

"He's got such a crush on you," Selfie says. "Isn't it cute?"

"I think I just threw-up in my mouth," Grace says.

"Well, you can chew on that while you pick up your boyfriend in Italy," I say. "Remember, you owe him one."

"He's NOT my boyfriend," Grace says, her face turning so red it looks like her head is about to explode. And then she stands up and says, "Fine! I'll pick him up. But then we're even."

"Great," I say. "Oh, by the way, I hear Italy is quite romantic at this time of year."

"Shut it!" Grace snaps before heading for the door. But before she disappears she turns and says, "And I'm bringing earplugs!" Then, she's gone.

"Well, that's gonna be a disaster," Skunk Girl says.

Speaking of disasters, it's not like we can just sit around waiting for the next bad thing to happen. Meta-Man is still out there, and I still don't know anything about Max Mayhem. It's time to see what I can find out.

"Where are you going?" Selfie calls out.

"To the Mission Room," I yell back. "Follow me."

We race through the halls until we reach our destination. I hop into the command chair and pull myself up to the console. That's when I realize my left hand is sitting in something sticky.

"Yuck," Night Owl says. "What's that?"

"Grape jelly," I say, looking at the purple glop on my palm. "I guess Glory Girl was sucking down a jelly doughnut before she got the call from Lockdown. Does anyone see a nap—"

Suddenly, Dog-Gone's head pops up and he licks my hand clean.

"Scratch the napkin," I say, wiping the slobber off on my cape. "Now, let's see what we can find out about Max Mayhem." I punch a few commands into the keyboard and the computer does its thing. Unfortunately, the internet didn't exist when the Protectors of the Planet were fighting crime, so I'm not exactly expecting to find a listing on Wikipedia.

"Do you think you'll find anything?" Skunk Girl asks. "I mean, that guy must be ancient by now."

"I hope so," I say. "I'm tapping into the Keystone City Police Archives. If there's an arrest record for a person named Max Mayhem, it'll show up there."

Reams of data scroll down the screen until it stops suddenly. Okay, here we go. But then the computer spits back: NO RESULTS FOUND.

Ugh. Strike one.

"Well, that's not good," Night Owl says.

"Don't panic," I say. "That was just one database. Let's look at cemetery records next."

"Cemetery records?" Selfie says. "You mean, like, dead people?"

"Yep," I say, typing more commands into the computer. "Skunk Girl said he'd have to be ancient by now. Maybe he's dead. Maybe there's a cemetery plot registered in his name."

The computer goes to work and then flashes: NO RESULTS FOUND.

Strike two. Well, this is frustrating. I tap my fingers on the keyboard. Those were my two best bets and they produced absolutely nothing. Now what?

"Maybe Max Mayhem doesn't really exist," Skunk Girl says. "Did anyone think of that? Maybe he's just some fictional story character Meta-Man made up in his head. He is certifiably crazy, right?"

"Hey, that's a good one," Selfie says.

"See," Skunk Girl says, buffing her nails. "You should listen to me more often. I know crazy when I see crazy. And not just when I look in the mirror."

"No, I mean about stories," Selfie says. "How about old newspaper articles? Back then, that was the way people got their news. Reporters we're always chasing the next big story. Maybe there are articles about Max Mayhem."

"That's a great idea," I say.

"Wait, now she's getting credit for my idea?" Skunk Girl huffs.

"Chill," I say, typing into the keyboard. "We have access to the Keystone City Observer's archives. That newspaper has been around forever. We can enter a keyword and search their whole library of articles. Let's type in 'Max Mayhem' and see if we get anything."

The hourglass icon spirals on the monitor for a few seconds, and then hundreds of hits start popping up! Bingo! But as I scan the list, all of the dates are super old. Apparently, there hasn't been any news about Max Mayhem for decades.

"What about that one?" Selfie says, pointing at the last entry on the screen. "That looks intriguing."

"Protectors of the Planet Disband after Confrontation with Max Mayhem, written by Johnny Oldeson," I say, reading the headline out loud. "Yeah, that does sound interesting. Let's click it."

I select it and an article appears on the screen. Right beneath the headline is a black-and-white picture of a bald guy with a handlebar mustache being led away in handcuffs. Other than his crazy eyes, he doesn't look particularly dangerous. The caption beneath the picture reads: MAX MAYHEM APPREHENDED BY PROTECTORS OF THE PLANET.

"That's Max Mayhem?" Skunk Girl says. "Wow! He looks more like a dentist than a criminal mastermind."

"Totally," I say. "Let's see what happened."

I scroll down to the text, which reads:

Today marks the end of an era. Today, the Protectors of the Planet disbanded after a battle with the evil genius known as Max Mayhem spiraled out of control, resulting in the tragic death of our very own ace reporter, Susan Strong. Details of the confrontation are still coming to light, but what is known is that Meta-Man narrowly saved Century City from being wiped off the map.

According to credible sources, Max Mayhem, the self-proclaimed smartest person in the world, had been baiting Meta-Man, the Emerald Enforcer, for months before unleashing his devious plan. Max Mayhem held Ms. Strong hostage and attacked Century City with a horde of giant-sized robots, resulting in a cataclysmic battle with Meta-Man directly over the bustling city. Using his vast power, Meta-Man was on the cusp of victory until something went wrong and Max Mayhem fired a deadly nuclear missile into the heart of Century City. Meta-Man managed to dispatch the missile seconds before impact, but he was unable to save the life of Ms. Strong, who fell over one thousand feet to her death.

The Protectors of the Planet arrived on the scene soon after and apprehended Max Mayhem, but they were too late to save Ms. Strong. Immediately following the battle, Meta-Man was seen arguing with members of the Protectors of the Planet before flying off into the sky. In a brief statement made to the public, the Black Crow said, "The Protectors of the Planet have decided to go our separate ways. From this point forward, the Protectors of the Planet are no more."

After his shocking statement, the Black Crow did not take questions and the remaining members of the team left the scene. As the Black Crow and Sparrow shepherded Max Mayhem away in handcuffs, this reporter was able to ask Sparrow, also known as the Boy Marvel, for his take on the matter. To which Sparrow replied, "To be successful as a team, everyone has to work together in harmony. And we're no longer harmonious."

It is indeed a sad day. The Protectors of the Planet were the defenders of the innocent. Without their strong arm of justice, what will happen when the next scourge of evil inevitably appears on the scene? Who will rise to protect us?

This reporter would also like to take a moment to honor the life of Susan Strong. Ms. Strong was a seasoned, intrepid reporter who would stop at nothing to bring us the truth, even at her own personal risk. Ms. Strong worked for the Keystone City Observer for over fifteen years and served as a mentor for many young, scrappy reporters, including yours truly. Her insight and skill were a daily gift to us all, and her guts and wit will be sorely missed.

On a final note, no one has seen Meta-Man since.

After we stop reading, there's silence.

"Wow," Selfie says finally. "I mean, I think I read about a nuclear missile almost destroying Century City in my history class, but I never knew what really happened."

"Yeah," I say, "me neither."

But something doesn't feel right.

"Well," Night Owl says, "the article said the Black Crow and Sparrow took that Max Mayhem guy somewhere. Clearly, they didn't take him to Lockdown. So, where did they take him?"

The Black Crow and Sparrow.

I reread the section about the Black Crow and Sparrow.

And then my eyes focus on Sparrow's words: *"To be successful as a team, everyone has to work together in harmony."*

Where have I heard those words before?

Suddenly, a chill runs down my spine. That's when I realize Shadow Hawk just uttered those exact same words to me. But it must be a coincidence, right?

Then, I connect the dots.

Shadow Hawk.

Sparrow.

Two Meta 0 heroes named after birds.

OMG!

No wonder Shadow Hawk didn't mention Sparrow when he was rattling off members of the Protectors he was trying to find.

Shadow Hawk *was* Sparrow!

Meta Profile

Sparrow

Name: Unknown	Height: 5'4"
Race: Human	Weight: 140 lbs
Status: Hero/Unknown	Eyes/Hair: Unknown/Blonde

META 0: No Powers
Skilled Detective
Skilled Marksman
Skilled Martial Artist

Observed Characteristics			
Combat 82			
Durability	32	Leadership	80
Strategy	81	Willpower	90

EIGHT

I HAVE SOME UPS AND DOWNS

I'm kind of stunned right now.

Yet, the more I think about it, the more it makes perfect sense. Shadow Hawk must have been Sparrow when he was a kid. That's why he went off to find all of the living members of the Protectors of the Planet except for Sparrow. I mean, of course, he wouldn't need to find Sparrow—he *was* Sparrow!

And as I run through everything that's happened it all falls into place. First, neither Sparrow nor Shadow Hawk has Meta powers. Second, Shadow Hawk knows a ton of detail about the Protectors of the Planet, including the name of Warrior Woman's husband! And third, I just read an old quote from Sparrow that matches dead on with something he just said to me.

Coincidence? I'm thinking a big fat 'no.'

While Shadow Hawk is one of my all-time favorite heroes, he's also a huge mystery. I mean, even my parents don't know his true identity, and I've never seen him without his mask on. But now I've uncovered a big piece of his secret past. Shadow Hawk was Sparrow, which means he was a member of the Protectors of the Planet long before he joined the Freedom Force.

And according to that article we just read, the Black Crow and Sparrow carted Max Mayhem off in handcuffs after the battle in Century City. Which means Shadow Hawk must know what happened to Max Mayhem! I need to get in touch with Shadow Hawk as soon as possible, but all I have right now is a hunch. It would be great to show him some hard evidence so he can't deny what I'm saying.

But what can I get for evidence?

I tap my fingers on the keyboard when a light bulb goes off! I've got it! I start typing frantically.

"What are you doing?" Selfie asks, looking up at the monitor as I pull up some files.

"Checking something out," I say.

I debate telling them about Shadow Hawk being Sparrow but I want to be sure. So, with a dangerous Meta-Man flying around I'm going to have to look under every possible rock—and inside every possible database.

After a few clicks, I'm in the master network. Every member of the Freedom Force has their own private server, so I'm thinking if I can crack into Shadow Hawk's server I might find something useful. I quickly locate his folder and open it up, only to find the dreaded words: ENTER PASSWORD.

"Are you hacking into someone's account?" Skunk Girl asks. "Cool, this is like a spy movie!"

"Just let me think here," I say. Now, what would Shadow Hawk use as a password?

"Try 'swordfish,'" Skunk Girl says. "That's the password they always use in spy movies."

I try to tune her out so I can focus. Unfortunately, I barely know anything about Shadow Hawk. Caped crusading would be a whole lot easier if everything wasn't password protected.

Wait a second. Protected? Could it be?

I type in 'PROTECTORS' and hit enter. Fortunately, the password field is encrypted so the rest of the team can't see what letters I'm typing. But the screen reads: INCORRECT PASSWORD. PLEASE TRY AGAIN.

This time I type 'PROTECTORSOFTHEPLANET' and hit enter. The screen reads: INCORRECT PASSWORD. PLEASE TRY AGAIN.

Ugh!

"It's 'swordfish,'" Skunk Girl says. "I'm telling you."

"It's not 'swordfish,'" I say. "It's going to be something more specific. Something more personal. Something like—Holy cow, I've got it!"

I type 'SPARROW' and hit enter. The screen reads:

INCORRECT PASSWORD. PLEASE TRY AGAIN.

"Well, this is a bust," Night Owl says. "Let's fly."

Wait, fly? Of course. I type in 'BLACK CROWANDSPARROW' and hit enter. This time the password field disappears and I'm in!

"You did it!" Selfie exclaims.

The desktop opens and there are two file folders on the screen. One is labeled 'FREEDOM FORCE,' and the other is labeled 'PROTECTORS.' Jackpot!

"Now what?" Selfie asks.

"Now we dig further," I say.

I open the PROTECTORS folder, and to my surprise, there's only one file inside. I click it open to find a spreadsheet with only three lines on it:

BLAIR MANOR

LEVEL 13

CODE: MM69244AE7X

"Um, what does all of that mean?" Night Owl asks.

"And what's Blair Manor?" Skunk Girl asks.

"Wait, I think I've heard of Blair Manor," Selfie says. "Isn't Blair Manor that rundown mansion on the outskirts of town? I remember reading about it in the local paper. The city was going to knock it down because the owner hadn't paid taxes on the property in years. But then some anonymous donor stepped in and paid it all up, saving the manor at the last minute. It was a big story for a few weeks."

"Okay," Night Owl says, "but what is that code for?

The front gate?"

"I don't know," I say, "but we're about to find out."

***

It's dark by the time we reach Blair Manor. This time I left Dog-Gone behind and he wasn't happy about it. But even though he has the perfect power for a covert mission like this, stealth isn't exactly his strong suit—especially if he spots a small critter.

At least Grace and Pinball will be back soon to keep an eye on him. That is, unless Grace ejected Pinball from her Freedom Ferry. But as likely as that scenario seems, I can't worry about it now because we've got more important things to figure out. Like, for instance, what's on the thirteenth floor of Blair Manor?

I managed to do a little research on the way over and learned that Blair Manor belongs to someone named Bennett Blair, a billionaire who owned a big corporation before it went bankrupt. I didn't have time to find out what happened to him, but as we approach Blair Manor I figure it can't be good because the place looks like it should be condemned.

Black, twisty vines cling to the home's exterior, threatening to swallow it whole, the over-sized windows are either broken or covered in grime, and the towers bookending the manor are so crumbly they look like they'll fall down if you so much as sneeze. And just to add to the eerie ambiance, there isn't a single light on across the entire estate. So, in short, I'd say the place looks way more 'haunted' than 'house.'

"Well, this is disturbingly spooky," Skunk Girl says.

"Spooky or not," I say, "I've got to get in there."

"*You*?" Selfie says. "What about us?"

"You guys should stay here," I say. "It's too risky for all of us to go inside. We don't want to get caught. I can ride one of Night Owl's shadow slides to that busted window on the top floor and slip right in."

"Now there's a plan I can get behind, boss-man," Skunk Girl says, punching me in the arm. "You're right, there's no need for all of us to go inside that incredibly scary, super-creepy, I'll-have-nightmares-for-days house. We'll just wait out here."

"Well, I'm coming with you," Selfie says, crossing her arms. "It's too dangerous for you to go alone."

"I don't think that's such a good—," I start.

"I'm coming and that's final," Selfie says firmly, ending all debate. "Night Owl, give us a lift."

"Right," I say. Well, maybe it wouldn't be so bad to have some company.

"All aboard," Night Owl says, creating a shadow slide by our feet.

I step on first and then Selfie follows. But as soon as she puts her hands on my shoulders I feel butterflies in my stomach. Okay, get it together, Elliott. You've got to concentrate here.

"Wind us around those tall hedges and then lift us fast so no one sees us," I say to Night Owl.

"Roger," she says. Then, the shadow slide takes off.

"Try not to die!" Skunk Girl offers helpfully.

"Hang on!" I call back to Selfie as we snake our way through the overgrown garden. But the closer we get, the more I realize the window isn't as large as I thought it was. In fact, it looks like it's going to be a tight squeeze.

We're at the base of the manor in no time and then we're suddenly going straight up! Now, I'm no physics expert, but as we hurtle towards the window it dawns on me that when this slide comes to a full stop we're going to go flying like nobody's business. I peer over my shoulder to get Night Owl's attention but I can't even see her anymore. So, this is going to go one of two ways—survival or splat! I can't let Selfie get hurt!

"Get in front of me," I say, spinning Selfie around my body just as we reach the window. "Now jump!"

Just then, the shadow slide stops short and Selfie leaps forward, disappearing through the window. I lift my arms and dive in behind her, amazed that we made it until my feet catch the windowsill and I land hard on my stomach, knocking the wind out of me.

"Are you okay?" Selfie whispers, kneeling over me.

No, but I'm not going to tell her that. So, I force a fake smile and give her a thumbs up.

"Well, thanks for putting me first," she says. "I appreciate it."

"N-No problem," I say, trying to catch my breath. "Just… need a sec. Or… maybe five." Note to self: Talk to Night Owl later about power control.

"I think we're in a library," Selfie whispers.

I finally get to my feet and look around. It's dark in here, but there's enough moonlight coming through the window to make out the rows of bookshelves lining the walls. I take the flashlight out of my utility belt and shine it around. That's when I notice layers of dust on the tables and cobwebs covering the chairs. It's like no one has been in here for years.

"The light switch doesn't work," Selfie whispers, flicking it on and off. "There's no power."

"Interesting," I whisper. "Let's keep moving."

But then I realize something and shine my light at the ceiling.

"What's up?" Selfie whispers.

"How many stories high is this manor?" I ask.

"I counted four," Selfie says.

"Right," I say. "But that file we found said 'Level 13.' So, if we're already on the top floor how can that be?"

"I don't know," Selfie says. "That is odd. Maybe we're in the wrong place?"

"Maybe," I say. "But I don't think so."

We exit the library into a wide hallway with marble floors. We pass by several gigantic paintings and some marble busts of people I don't recognize. Well, this place definitely reeks of old money. As we continue onward, I shine my flashlight into several dark bedrooms and bathrooms but there's nothing out of the ordinary.

Then, something catches my eye.

There's an elevator in the middle of the hallway. Well, that's a convenient thing to have. I randomly push the button, and to my surprise, it lights up. Then, I hear the HUM of the elevator as it makes its way up to our floor.

"If there's no power," Selfie whispers, "then how is the elevator working?"

"Great question," I say, scratching my chin. "Be ready for anything."

DING! But when the elevator doors open, we're staring into an empty, wood-paneled elevator car. That's when I notice something else.

"The lights are operating inside the car," I say, turning off my flashlight. "For some reason, someone is maintaining this elevator service but ignoring the rest of the manor."

I glance at Selfie and then step inside.

"What are you doing?" she says.

"Checking it out," I say. I look around but there's nothing unusual except for the control panel which looks really old. There are buttons for levels 1, 2, 3, and 4, but no button for level 13. I hate to admit it, but maybe Selfie was right. Maybe we are in the wrong place.

"See anything?" Selfie asks.

"Nope," I say, studying the control panel.

"Nothing."

"Well, maybe you should get out of there," Selfie says. "Before something bad happens."

I've got to be missing something. I mean, it's not like Shadow Hawk to write something down that serves no purpose. What am I not seeing here?

"Epic?" Selfie says. "Do you hear me?"

Okay, there's no level 13, but there is a level 1 and a level 3. I wonder if—

"Epic, can you get out of there please?"

Well, I might as well give it a shot.

I put my flashlight back in my belt and then push the buttons for levels 1 and 3 at the same time.

DING!

Suddenly, the elevator jolts, knocking me off balance.

And then the doors start closing!

I look up in time to catch Selfie's alarmed face as the doors SLAM shut between us!

"Epic!" comes Selfie's muffled cry.

"NEXT STOP, THE CROW'S NEST," comes a deep, mechanical voice that echoes inside the car.

And then the elevator drops!

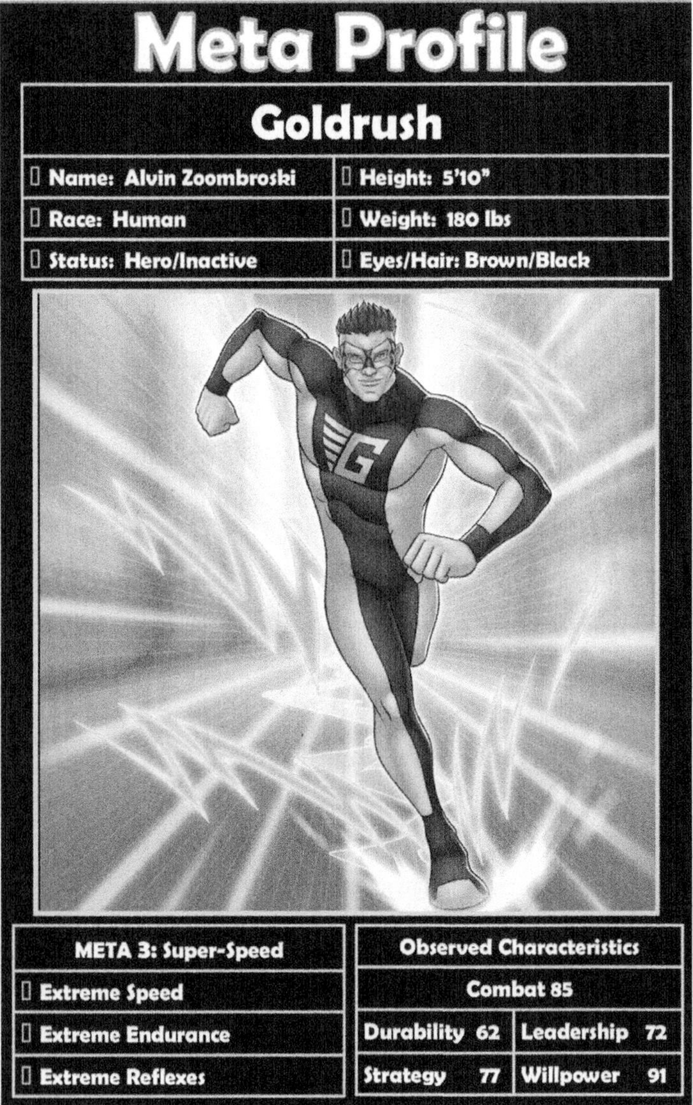

Meta Profile

Goldrush

Name: Alvin Zoombroski	Height: 5'10"
Race: Human	Weight: 180 lbs
Status: Hero/Inactive	Eyes/Hair: Brown/Black

META 3: Super-Speed
Extreme Speed
Extreme Endurance
Extreme Reflexes

Observed Characteristics			
Combat 85			
Durability	62	Leadership	72
Strategy	77	Willpower	91

NINE

I LEARN A FEW THINGS

I'm trapped inside a free-falling elevator.

After my stomach drops and the feeling of sheer panic partially subsides, I think back to how I got here in the first place. I mean, I only found out about Blair Manor and the mysterious 13th level after breaking into Shadow Hawk's server. And now I'm hurtling to my death after cleverly pushing the buttons for levels 1 and 3 at the same time.

When will I learn to stop being so darn clever?

But that's not all. The doors closed so fast I left poor Selfie behind, and according to the mechanical voice that echoed through the chamber, I'm heading straight for something called the Crow's Nest.

Wait a minute! The *Crow's* Nest?

As in, the Black Crow's Nest?

Just then, there's another low HUM and the elevator starts slowing down until it comes to a controlled, gentle stop. I breathe a sigh of relief. Well, I'm not a pancake so that's good, but I have no clue what's waiting for me on the other side of these—

DING!

Before I can even get into a combat stance the doors slide open. But instead of facing a horde of bad guys, I'm staring into a vast, subterranean lair which must be thirteen levels below ground. And plastered high on the ceiling is the insignia of the Black Crow.

Well, there's no doubt about it now. This must be the Black Crow's secret headquarters. Wow, I bet nobody even knows it's down here.

I step off the elevator into the circular room. There's a raised platform in the center holding the biggest supercomputer I've ever seen. All around the perimeter are various stations including a laboratory, a tools workshop, a storage center, and a gymnasium.

I have to admit this place is pretty swanky for an underground lair. And that's when I realize something else. The lights and monitors are on, which means that someone is maintaining this space too. Yet, as my eyes dart around the room I don't see anyone else here.

I head for the platform and climb up the stairs to check out the supercomputer. It's old and looks bigger than my refrigerator. But I guess I shouldn't be too surprised because computer processors were way bigger back then. Today, the Meta Monitor operates on a microprocessor smaller than TechnocRat's little toe!

The supercomputer is certainly an interesting relic, but what's even more interesting is what's happening on its monitor. It seems to be cycling through important world landmarks, from the Washington Monument to the Sphinx. It's like it's hunting for something—or someone.

Since I'm up high, I have a pretty good vantage point of the whole place. But when I turn around my jaw hits the floor, because directly behind me, set deep in the rock wall is… a prison cell!

How did I miss that? But when I glance over to the elevator, I realize my line of sight was blocked by the stairway to the raised platform. And when I look back over at the prison cell my heart skips a beat—because someone is in there!

In fact, I can see the silhouette of a man sitting inside! Except, he's not moving. Suddenly, I feel really uncomfortable. Has he been watching me this whole time?

"Um, h-hello?" I say, my voice echoing through the chamber.

But there's no response.

I squint but can't see the man's features any clearer. My instincts tell me to jump back into that elevator and get out of here, but my curiosity is just too strong. What if it's Shadow Hawk and he's hurt? That would explain why he didn't get back to Grace. Or what if it's one of the other Protectors, like Sergeant Stretch or Goldrush?

Whoever it is, I can't just leave him down here.

But then I get a more disturbing thought. What if it's a dead body? What if it's nothing but a skeleton—the remains of someone who's been trapped down here for decades? I swallow hard. Part of me doesn't want to find out, but I need to know. So, I head down the stairs and slowly make my way over.

I grab my flashlight and aim it at the bars, when—

"It would be quite inhumane to shine that light in my eyes," comes a measured, pretentious-sounding voice.

I freeze in my tracks.

H-He's alive! Well, that's a relief. But I still can't see who it is, so I point my light off to the side and turn it on. Suddenly, I see the face of a bald man with a handlebar mustache. He's sitting in a chair with his legs crossed and his arms folded across his chest, staring back at me with a pair of intense, green eyes.

Instantly, I know who he is.

"Y-You're Max Mayhem," I stammer.

"You are correct," he says, his speech very precise. "Now if you would be so kind as to tell me with whom I am speaking?"

"I-I'm Epic Zero," I say. "I'm… a Meta hero."

"It's a pleasure to make your acquaintance, Mr. Zero," Max Mayhem says. "It's been quite a while since I last spoke with a young person in costume. A long time indeed."

"So, um, exactly how long have you been in there?" I ask. "Approximately."

"Well, as you can see I am presently without a calendar or clock," he says. "But I would estimate it to be forty years, two months, five days, twelve hours, thirty-two minutes, and five seconds. Approximately."

"Oh, wow," I say shocked. "That's a really long time. But at least you're not dead. I-I kind of thought you were dead."

"Really?" he says, his right eyebrow rising. "Well, I am afraid any reports of my death have been greatly exaggerated, for, as you can see, I am very much alive. Although I would much prefer to be alive and free. So, tell me, is that why you are here? To free me? If so, all you need to do is enter the code into the wall-mounted control panel on your left."

I look to my left and see the interface on the wall. Suddenly, I realize what Shadow Hawk's code must be for. It's the code to release Max Mayhem from prison!

"Um, no," I say. "Sorry."

"That is a shame," Max Mayhem says, letting out a sigh. "Although it is refreshing to see a new face. I have been deprived of good conversation for years. The Black Crow and I used to debate for hours until he grew old and feeble. And now his pathetic protege is the only one keeping me alive. Unfortunately, he does not have the gift of gab like his mentor. It's rather sad actually. He was such a curious and gregarious boy before becoming the jaded and sullen man he is today. Nowadays he rarely utters a word."

Jaded and Sullen? Rarely utters a word?

"Wait, are you talking about Shadow Hawk?" I ask.

"The very one," Max Mayhem says. "To tell the truth, I thought his Sparrow costume looked more heroic, but I understand how a grown man in shorts would hardly strike fear in the hearts of his opponents. Oh well, I suppose it's the natural order of things. Everything evolves over time."

Well, there it is. That's all the confirmation I need that Shadow Hawk was once Sparrow. But speaking of evolving, for the first time I realize Max Mayhem looks exactly like he did in that photo taken long ago. But how is that possible? "Um, sorry to ask, but if you've been down here for forty years, why haven't you aged?"

"My, you are an observant one, aren't you?" he says, his lips curling into a sinister smile. "Let's just say I have good genes. But never mind that, why don't we talk about something more interesting, like getting me out of here. I am quite a wealthy man. Just name your price."

"Um, I'll take a raincheck on that," I say. "Besides, if I were you I wouldn't be itching to get out right now. You're probably safer right where you are."

"Whatever do you mean?" he says, his eyes narrowing. "Because if I didn't know better, I would say you're implying that I am in some sort of danger. Tell me,

Mr. Zero, has Meta-Man returned?"

His question catches me off guard.

How do I answer that?

"Well, I… I…," I stammer.

"Then, I am correct," Max Mayhem says, bounding from his seat and wrapping his long fingers around the bars. "You must release me at once. Clearly, you don't understand the danger we're all in. I am the only one who can defeat Meta-Man. I am the only one who can save the human race."

"Whoa! Slow down there," I say. "Meta-Man was a hero, just like me. You're Meta-Man's greatest nemesis. You tried to nuke Century City. I'm not letting you out of here for anything."

"A shame," he says, sitting back down. "But based on how I have been portrayed in the press, it's perfectly reasonable for you to trust him over me. After all, you do not understand why he came here in the first place."

"What are you talking about?" I ask.

"Contrary to popular belief," he says, "the origin of Meta-Man is nothing like the fictional story of 'Superman' from the comic books. Meta-Man was not sent here as the last of his kind from some dying planet. No, his purpose was far more sinister. You see, he wasn't sent here to protect Earth, he was sent here to destroy it."

"What?" I say, totally shocked. "I don't believe you."

"I am sure you don't," Max Mayhem says. "However, it is the truth. Meta-Man comes from a superior race of alien beings—a race whose sole purpose is total domination. To them, we are nothing but fleas on the cosmic skin of life. Meta-Man was programmed to eliminate us, but something went wrong on his long journey to Earth and when he arrived he believed he was a hero. But that was never his true destiny."

Max Mayhem pauses and I'm so dumbfounded I can't even find the words to reply. I mean, does he really think I'm buying this? This is probably a ploy to get me to free him. Well, sorry, I'm not that gullible.

"I think I've heard enough," I say.

"Before you pass judgment," he says, "would you like to know what really happened at Century City?"

I hesitate for a moment. I mean, I am curious about what happened, but I highly doubt his version of the story is the truth. But maybe there's something I can learn to help me find Meta-Man.

"Sure," I say. "Tell me your side of the story."

"Very well," he says, his eyes growing wide. "What happened in Century City was unfortunate, but necessary. You see, after countless years of searching, I finally discovered how to destroy Meta-Man once and for all. But, at that time, it was still only a theory. To confirm that it would work I needed to test it in practice. And to do that, I had to get Meta-Man close to me. Fortunately, I wasn't alone in recognizing the danger Meta-Man posed. By chance, one of Meta-Man's very own teammates reached out to me."

Wait, what?

"We held a meeting in secret," he continues, "where we discussed our mutual concerns about Meta-Man and his potential to dominate the human race. And unlike Superman, unless my theory was correct, there was no Kryptonite to stop him. So, together, we developed a plan to ensure the long-term survival of humanity."

"Hold up," I say. "Are you telling me you teamed up with one of the Protectors of the Planet?"

"Indeed," he says. "And that is how I learned about Meta-Man's girlfriend. A human girlfriend, no less. And once I kidnapped her, it was child's play to get an unsuspecting Meta-Man close to me."

Meta-Man had a girlfriend? But who?

And then that article from the Keystone City Observer comes back to me. Susan Strong, the reporter!

Meta-Man's girlfriend must have been Susan Strong!

"Once Meta-Man learned that I held his one true love captive," Max Mayhem continues, "he predictably came racing headlong to save her. And that is when I struck him with the secret weapon I had fashioned into an armored glove. And do you know what happened next?"

"Um, no," I say.

"He was injured!" Max Mayhem says, his voice sounding almost giddy. "I struck him right in the face, below his left eye. And that's when I knew my theory was correct! But remarkably he did not bleed. Instead, a flash of pure Meta energy left his once impenetrable body. I still remember the surprise on his face when he saw it. The terror in his eyes when he realized he wasn't immortal. And that's when we both knew I could kill him."

Suddenly, I remember seeing that scar beneath Meta-Man's left eye. That must have come from Max Mayhem!

"But… you didn't kill him," I say. "You killed Susan Strong."

"I suppose you could see it that way," Max Mayhem says. "But from my perspective, I would say Meta-Man was responsible for her death. You see, I gave him a choice, he could either save his beloved girlfriend, or he could save the citizens of Century City from my nuclear missile. I thought for sure he would save his true love, but then Ms. Strong begged him to forget about her and save the innocent. She said she would never forgive him if he let them die. So, ultimately it was his decision, wasn't it?"

"You're evil," I say.

"Perhaps," he says. "But I am also practical, and at that point, I needed to escape by whatever means necessary to carry out the rest of my plan. But be careful not to sympathize with that monster. You must remember, despite his heroic façade, Meta-Man was never one of us. It was only a matter of time before he realized his true destiny. And once he did, who would stop him?"

As much as I hate to admit it, he's got a point there.

"So, if Meta-Man has returned you need me," Max

Mayhem continues. "I am the only one who knows how to kill him."

We stare at each other when—

BEEP! BEEP! BEEP!

"What is that infernal noise?" he asks.

"My transmitter," I say, looking at my watch.

<Selfie: Epic r u ok? Where r u? Glory Girl found Shadow Hawk.>

Shadow Hawk?

"I-I've got to go," I say, backing away.

"Wait!" Max Mayhem calls out. "Release me! Don't leave me here! You need me!"

I run around the perimeter and head for the elevator.

"You have no chance!" he yells. "You will die! All of humanity will die!"

I step inside the elevator and push the 'up' button.

"Foolish child! You will—"

And his cries fade behind the closing doors.

Meta Profile

Max Mayhem

Name: Unknown	Height: 5'9"
Race: Human	Weight: 175 lbs
Status: Villain/Unknown	Eyes/Hair: Green/Bald

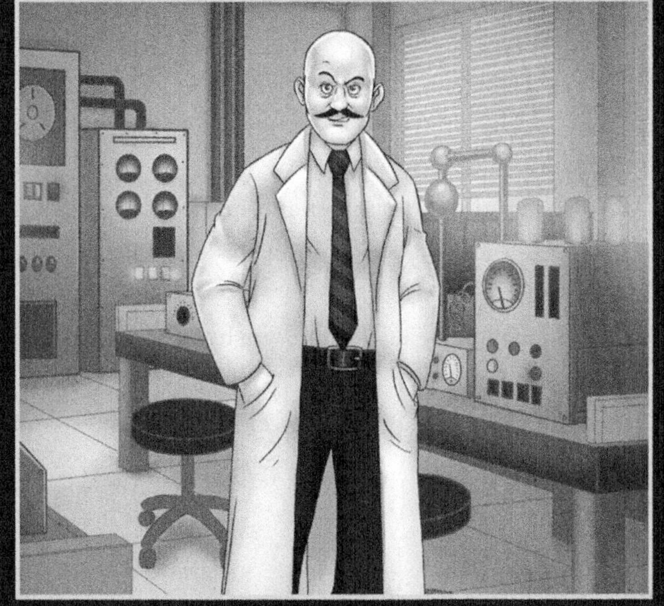

META 0: No Powers	Observed Characteristics			
Brilliant Scientist	Combat 13			
Unparalleled Inventor	Durability	8	Leadership	93
Master Manipulator	Strategy	100	Willpower	100

TEN

I VISIT A NURSING HOME

"I still don't get why we're parked in the woods outside a nursing home," Skunk Girl says.

"Because this is where Glory Girl told us to meet her," Selfie says. Then, she turns to me and asks, "Are you okay, Epic? It sounds like that Max Mayhem guy was pretty demented."

"What?" I say, resting my head on the Freedom Ferry's dashboard. "Oh, yeah, I'm fine thanks."

Selfie smiles so I guess she believes me, but truthfully I'm far from okay.

I mean, I told the team about my encounter with Max Mayhem in the Black Crow's Nest, but I didn't tell them everything. Especially the part about Shadow Hawk being Sparrow. And Max Mayhem dropped so many other bombshells I'm still trying to process it all.

First, he told me Meta-Man wasn't sent to Earth to help humans but to destroy them. Then, he said he partnered with a member of the Protectors to get rid of Meta-Man. And that's how Max Mayhem found out that Susan Strong was Meta-Man's girlfriend, which is how he lured Meta-Man to Century City.

But there's even more to the story. Somehow, Max Mayhem figured out how to kill Meta-Man. I thought Meta-Man was indestructible, but I guess that can't be true because I saw the scar Max Mayhem inflicted on Meta-Man with my very own eyes.

Of course, I wanted to know how he did it, but I knew Max Mayhem wouldn't tell me unless I let him out of his cell. And that wasn't going to happen. So, this mystery just keeps getting more complicated and confusing.

I hear a noise overhead, and when I look into the morning sky, I see Grace's Freedom Ferry coming towards us. I don't know why she wanted to meet us here, but as she touches down I see a frown on her face and Pinball sitting next to her, talking her ears off. Well, at least she didn't eject him over the Atlantic Ocean.

But I don't see Dog-Gone. That means they must have left him on the Waystation. Boy, I sure hope there wasn't any food left out in the Galley because I'd hate to come home to that carnage. That is, if we ever get to go back home.

"Let's go," I say to my team, as Grace pops the hatch and storms out of her Freedom Ferry. "This should be interesting."

"Great to see you, Pinball," Selfie says. "You sure know how to take a licking and keep on ticking."

"Thanks," Pinball says, bouncing out of the Freedom Ferry and landing next to Grace. "I didn't know where I was, but thankfully Glory Girl came to get me. We talked the whole way back. I didn't realize we had so much in common, right Glory Girl?"

But Grace doesn't respond. Instead, she just stands there frowning with her arms crossed.

"Um, Glory Girl?" I say. "Pinball is talking to you."

"What?" she says. And then she reaches up and pulls a pair of earplugs out of her ears. "Sorry, I couldn't hear a thing."

"Well, that's embarrassing," Skunk Girl says as Pinball turns beet red.

"Anyway, we're even," Grace says to Pinball. And then she looks over at the building and says, "Now on to business. I'm pretty sure Shadow Hawk is in there. After I reached out a hundred times, he finally sent me an encrypted message telling me he was fine. So, I booted up TechnocRat's encrypto-tracker app and ran it over and over until it finally located Shadow Hawk's signal. And it came from inside that building."

I look over at the picturesque nursing home sitting atop a hill with a well-manicured lawn and beautiful gardens. A perfectly smooth driveway curves gently towards the red brick building with a sign that reads: Shady View Nursing Home. 3290 Shady View Lane.

It certainly looks like a nice place to ride out your golden years, except Shadow Hawk is way too young to be living there.

"That's a nursing home?" Pinball asks. "It looks more like a college campus."

"Yeah, a college campus full of old people," Skunk Girl says. "Bingo on the quad, anyone?"

"Don't be disrespectful," Selfie says. "They're called seniors, not old people."

"Seniors, old people, whatever," Skunk Girl says. "Why are we chasing Shadow Hawk when that Meta-Man guy is out there?"

"Don't be dense, Skunkers," Grace says, rolling her eyes. "We're here to get to the bottom of whatever is going on, and I think Shadow Hawk knows more than he's letting on."

If only she knew. I mean, I haven't even told her the half of it yet. But I feel like I still need to keep some things to myself until I talk to Shadow Hawk.

"So, what's he doing in there?" Night Owl asks.

Great question. Like Selfie said, nursing homes are for older… Wait a second! Suddenly, Max Mayhem's words pop into my head: *The Black Crow and I used to debate for hours until he grew old and feeble.*

O. M. G!

"Um, I think I know exactly what Shadow Hawk is doing here," I blurt out. "Does Shady View have a list of residents somewhere?"

"We could go inside and ask for one," Pinball says.

"No, you can't, knucklehead," Skunk Girl says. "That information is private."

Just then, I see a postal truck heading down the driveway. "But mailing addresses are usually public," I blurt out. "Hang on. I've got an idea."

I hop back into my Freedom Ferry and turn on the computer. Then, I enter a query to find the names of everyone with a mailing address of 3290 Shady View Lane. Suddenly, a huge list scrolls down my screen. But I'm looking for one name in particular so I sort the list alphabetically.

"Hello?" Night Owl calls out. "You okay up there?"

"Just give me a second," I say, looking for all last names that start with the letter B.

I scroll and scroll and then—there it is!

BLAIR, BENNETT.

That's the Black Crow's real name! The Black Crow lives inside this nursing home. That's got to be why Shadow Hawk is here. Now, I've just got to give the team the good news without revealing that Shadow Hawk was Sparrow. I hop out of the Freedom Ferry.

"Well?" Selfie says.

"Okay, here's the deal," I say. "When I was with Max Mayhem, he confirmed that the Black Crow's secret identity is Bennett Blair, the owner of Blair Manor. And I've just confirmed there's a Bennett Blair inside this nursing home. So, I'm guessing Shadow Hawk is here to take him into hiding before Meta-Man finds him."

"That makes sense," Night Owl says. "But how did Shadow Hawk find out the Black Crow's real identity?"

Uh-oh. How am I going to answer that without tipping my hand?

"Well," I say, "Shadow Hawk is the world's greatest detective, isn't he? Anyway, enough standing around. I bet if we go inside and find Bennett Blair, we'll also find Shadow Hawk."

"And some breakfast," Pinball says, holding his stomach. "I hate skipping breakfast."

We race down the driveway, past a few seniors out for a morning stroll, and into the nursing home. The lobby is nicely decorated, with blue, wall-to-wall carpet, plush sofas, and a giant bulletin board filled with activities. There's a welcome desk in the middle of the room with a friendly-looking woman sitting behind it.

Okay, I should probably take charge.

"I've got this," I tell the team. Then, I walk up confidently and rest my elbows on the desk. There's a small nameplate on top that reads: *Margie Kinford, Administration.* Okay, time to lay on the charm. "Hello, Margie, we're here to see a resident named Bennett Blair. Would you be so kind as to tell us his room number?"

"Visiting hours don't start until nine," Margie says,

looking us up and down. "And aren't you kids a little early for Halloween?"

What? And then I realize she's talking about our costumes. I'm so used to them I sometimes forget I'm even wearing one. "Good one," I say, "but that's the thing, see we're here to, um, surprise him. You see, we're, uh, we're here to deliver a singing telegram. Yes, a singing telegram! Maybe you've heard of us? 1-800-Arm-Strong-Songs?" Then, I flex my right arm and flash a cheesy smile.

"Is this really happening right now?" Skunk Girl says, smacking her palm against her forehead.

"Uh-huh," Margie says, raising her eyebrows. "Come back at nine. And maybe you want to pick up a little deodorant beforehand." Then, she takes a sip of coffee.

I look at the clock on the wall behind her which reads 6:12 a.m. That's like, three hours from now.

"B-But…" I stammer.

"Excuse me, Ms. Kinford," Selfie says, stepping forward with her phone. "Do you mind if I get a picture of you two?" Then, she looks at me with dead eyes and says, "It'll be perfect for our marketing materials."

"Sure, dear," Margie says, fluffing her hair. "Then will you kids leave me alone? This is a nursing home, not a nursery school."

"Of course," Selfie says. "If you two can just squeeze in a little closer. Great, now look at my phone."

I lean in and close my eyes as Selfie's phone flashes,

and when I turn around, Margie's eyes are glazed over.

"Now, Ms. Kinford," Selfie says, "which room was Mr. Blair in again?"

"Sixth floor," Margie says robotically, "room 622."

"Perfect," Selfie says. "You have a nice day. Oh, and by the way, you never saw us, right?"

"I never saw you," Margie repeats.

"Come on," Selfie says, as we follow her through the lobby to the elevator bank.

"Nice job 'handling it,'" Grace says, jabbing me with her elbow.

Okay, that didn't go so well, but we still got through.

One of the elevators opens and we step inside.

"Excuse me," Pinball says, stepping into the elevator last, his girth pushing the rest of us hard against the walls.

"It's… a… good thing… you skipped breakfast," Skunk Girl sputters, nearly out of breath.

"This… is… the last time… I… hang out with you idiots," Grace mutters to me, her left cheek pressed against the wall.

As the elevator climbs, I somehow manage not to pass out. Finally, there's a DING, and when the doors open Pinball gets out relieving all the pressure.

"Well, that was uncomfortable," Night Owl says, straightening her cape. "Now, where's room 622?"

"This way," Selfie says, reading a sign opposite the elevator bank.

We follow her down a large hallway and past an

empty nurse's station. There's a cup of coffee on the counter but fortunately, no one is around. As we head down the hall I look through the door windows at all the elderly people resting in their beds.

"Here we are," Selfie says. "Room 622." Then, she looks through the window and gasps.

"What is it?" I ask.

"Look for yourself," she says, stepping back.

I look inside to find an elderly man lying on his bed—and sitting beside him is a costumed man in a dark cowl. It's Shadow Hawk! So, that man must be Bennett Blair—the Black Crow! I desperately need to talk to Shadow Hawk alone and this might be my only chance.

"I've got this," I tell the team.

"Does that mean we're about to sing?" Pinball asks. "Because I'm not a very good singer."

"Um, no," I say. "Just wait here for a minute. I need to talk to Shadow Hawk."

"No dice," Grace says, pushing forward. "I've got a few choice words for Mr. Shadow Hawk myself."

"Please," I say, looking her straight in the eyes, "just give me a few minutes."

We stare at each other before she finally says, "Two minutes, and then I'm barging in."

"Great," I say. "That's all I need." Then, I open the door, step inside, and close it behind me. Shadow Hawk has his back to me and he's leaning over, his head in his hands. If I didn't know better I'd say he's upset.

"What's up, kid," Shadow Hawk says suddenly, startling me.

"H-How did you know it was me?" I ask.

"You have a certain way of shuffling your feet," he says. "Besides, it was pretty hard not to hear all of you talking outside the door."

"Right," I say, walking over to the foot of the bed and looking at Bennett Blair for the first time. His eyes are closed, his breathing is strained, and his body is hooked up to all sorts of machines. Even though he's an older man now, I can tell by his size that he was once a pretty big guy.

Then, I look over at Shadow Hawk who is just sitting there with his head down. I can't even imagine the pain he's going through seeing his old crime-fighting partner like this. I feel like this isn't exactly the best time to ask him about his days with the Protectors, but we're running out of time. So, I just go for it.

"Why didn't you tell me you were Sparrow?" I ask.

At first, Shadow Hawk doesn't respond. In fact, he doesn't even move. But then he says, "I guess you've become a pretty good detective yourself."

"Maybe," I say, "but I just put all the clues together. That's the Black Crow, isn't it?"

"Yes," Shadow Hawk says.

"Well, I'm sorry he's not in good health," I say.

"Me too," Shadow Hawk says. "You should have seen him when he was in his prime."

"So, if this is the Black Crow," I say, "then what are you doing here? I thought you were going to hide the remaining Protectors from Meta-Man."

"I was," Shadow Hawk says, clenching his teeth. "But Meta-Man got to them first. Believe me, I'd love to take the Black Crow out of here, but these machines are the only thing keeping him alive. So, I have no choice but to stay here until Meta-Man shows up. And when he does I'm going to fight him for our lives."

I smile weakly. I mean, can Shadow Hawk really stop Meta-Man? Shadow Hawk doesn't have any powers.

"But there's something else I found out," I say. "Max Mayhem told me one of the Protectors betrayed Meta-Man."

"You found Max Mayhem, huh?" Shadow Hawk says. "Not bad, kid. I'm impressed."

"Thanks," I say. "But that's not really true, is it?"

Shadow Hawk looks up at me for a few seconds, and then—

CRASH!

The window shatters! I turn away as glass shards fly everywhere, and when I look back over my heart skips a beat because someone is standing in the window frame with his hands on his hips.

It's Meta-Man!

"Yes, Sparrow," Meta-Man says. "Tell us if it's really true. Tell us which one of the Protectors betrayed me."

Meta Profile

Susan Strong

Name: Susan Strong	Height: 5'5"
Race: Human	Weight: 135 lbs
Status: Deceased	Eyes/Hair: Brown/Red

META 0: No Powers	Observed Characteristics			
Investigative Journalist	Combat 11			
Pulitzer Prize Winner	Durability	6	Leadership	90
Strives to Report the Truth	Strategy	74	Willpower	95

ELEVEN

I FEEL DEFEATED

I can't believe it!

Meta-Man just busted into the Black Crow's room at the nursing home! And if we don't do something fast he'll kidnap the Black Crow!

"How did you find him?" Shadow Hawk asks, rising to his feet.

"Oh, that was easy," Meta-Man says. "I simply kept my Super Senses tuned in to that girl from the prison. I believe the boy called her 'Glory Girl.' I had a feeling she would be useful, so I tracked her crossing the ocean and she led me here. But I never expected to find Sparrow, the Boy Marvel, here as well. I see you're still loyal to that old, self-righteous windbag."

"I'm my own man now," Shadow Hawk says.

"We'll see about that," Meta-Man sneers.

Suddenly, the door to the room bursts open, and Grace and the others charge in.

"Ready for round two, creep?" Grace says, clenching her fists as she heads straight for Meta-Man.

"No!" Shadow Hawk barks, blocking her path with an outstretched arm. "He's mine."

"You're a fool if you think you can stop me from taking the Black Crow," Meta-Man says. "I won't rest until I find out who betrayed me to Max Mayhem. And something tells me it was your mentor. After all, he was always jealous of me, wasn't he?"

"You won't be taking anyone anywhere," Shadow Hawk says. "Not while I have this."

Then, Shadow Hawk reaches into the folds of his dark cape and pulls out a shiny, metallic glove! That's funny, I thought I'd seen all of Shadow Hawk's gadgets before, but I don't remember ever seeing that one. And as he shoves his right hand inside, I notice it's covered with strange symbols.

"I'm sure it looks familiar, doesn't it?" Shadow Hawk continues. "The Black Crow held onto it after Century City. He always thought you'd come back."

Century City? What's he talking about? But when I look at Meta-Man, I see a hint of fear flash across his face. And then my eyes land on his scar and everything comes together.

O.M.G! That glove must be the weapon Max

Mayhem used to hurt Meta-Man! And now Shadow Hawk has it!

"I remember it well," Meta-Man says calmly. "But sadly, you're still no match for me. You see, you were always a useless nuisance, weren't you? A lost little boy, following the Black Crow around like a loyal puppy dog. He may have needed your hero-worship, but the rest of us didn't. We simply tolerated you, waiting for the day when you would overstep your bounds and be crushed by some powerful Meta. But somehow, that day never came. Until now."

Then, his eyes flash with red electricity.

"Um, holy cow," Pinball mutters.

"Get out of here!" Shadow Hawk yells.

Grace and Next Gen dive out of the room as Meta-Man unloads a blast of Heat Vision right at Shadow Hawk! But Shadow Hawk stands his ground and parries it aside with the metallic glove! The beams ricochet over the Black Crow's body and slice through the opposite wall!

Wow! What's that glove made of if it can deflect Meta-Man's Heat Vision like that? But I don't exactly have time to figure it out because my skin isn't nearly as impenetrable. Unless…

I've already learned I can't negate Meta-Man's powers, but I haven't tried duplicating them yet. But before I can act, Shadow Hawk charges Meta-Man and tackles him through the window! There's a tangle of capes, and then they drop clear out of sight! I run over to the window when the door flies open again.

"Where did they go?" Grace asks.

"Out the window," I say. "Look, I think you guys should find some doctors to safely move the Black Crow to another location in case we can't take Meta-Man down."

"You guys?" Selfie says. "There you go again! You can't go out there by yourself. He'll kill you!"

Well, she's probably right about that. But I can't just leave Shadow Hawk to fight Meta-Man on his own. I mean, Shadow Hawk doesn't even have powers!

"I'll go too," Grace says. "I owe him one."

"No," I say firmly. "Like it or not, he's too powerful for you too. But I might be able to help with my powers. Look, I know you don't want to hear it, but we both know you need to take control here and get the Black Crow to safety."

"Why am I always the babysitter?" Grace asks.

"Hey!" Skunk Girl objects. "We're not babies!"

"No, you're not," I say. "But imagine if Meta-Man punched you like he punched Pinball back at Lockdown. You aren't as durable as he is."

"Good point," Skunk Girl says.

"That's why I take my meals so seriously," Pinball says, rubbing his round tummy.

I look back at Grace who looks like she's going to explode. I know she's itching for revenge against Meta-Man, but it'll have to wait. "Fine," she mutters. "But as soon as the Black Crow is safe I'm coming back."

"Yeah, I figured," I say with a smile. Then, I reach out to borrow her Flight power and jump out the window.

I hit the air and it takes a few seconds to steady myself, but I don't see Meta-Man or Shadow Hawk anywhere. I climb higher for a more panoramic view but still no luck. Where did they go?

Then, out of the corner of my eye, I see a giant tree being tossed around like a twig in the distance. That's got to be them! Shadow Hawk must have lured Meta-Man away from the nursing home and deep into the woods. I just hope I get there in time.

I turn on the jets and make a beeline towards the action. The thing is, I don't have a plan. And things never go well when I don't have a plan. But it's too late now because I spot them.

They're in a clearing surrounded by trees, and Meta-Man is swinging a large trunk right at Shadow Hawk! Shadow Hawk leaps over it gracefully and hurls a Hawk-a-rang at Meta-Man, but it simply CLANGS off his rock-hard skin. This isn't going to be easy.

"Why are you so far away?" Shadow Hawk asks, raising his gloved fist. "Are you afraid to come closer?"

"I'm not afraid of you," Meta-Man says with a sinister smile. "I'm just seeing what you can do. And in my humble opinion, you're far less skilled than your beloved mentor. But now I've tired of this game."

Uh-oh.

Just then, Meta-Man stomps down with so much force it causes a fissure in the ground, and the cracks are heading straight for Shadow Hawk! But as soon as Shadow Hawk jumps out of the way, Meta-Man swings his tree trunk like a baseball bat and SLAMS Shadow Hawk in mid-air. The glove flies off of Shadow Hawk's hand as his body goes limp, and the hero lands on the ground like a ragdoll.

"Shadow Hawk!" I call out, landing by his side. I kneel to check on him, but he's barely breathing.

"It's finally mine," Meta-Man says.

What? What's his? But when I look over, Meta-Man is holding Max Mayhem's glove! Holy cow! How could I have been so stupid? I was so worried about Shadow Hawk that I forgot to pick up the only weapon capable of stopping Meta-Man! Great going, Elliott.

"Never again," Meta-Man says, tracing his scar with his fingers. "Now, nothing can stop me." And then he rears back and throws the glove so high in the air that it disappears into the blue sky.

"No!" I yell. I've doomed us all.

"You again?" Meta-Man says, now fixing his eyes on me. "You almost tricked me last time. But that won't happen again."

"Look," I say, slowly rising to my feet. "I was trying to help you. I-I thought you were a hero. But you're no hero."

"Perhaps not from your perspective," Meta-Man says. "But I no longer lower myself to human standards. You see, while I lived among you, I tried to blend in with your kind. I believed that if I behaved like a human then maybe I would be accepted by humans. So, I did everything in my power to be like you. I went to school, I took a job, I even… loved. But there were still those who wouldn't accept me because of my alien origin, and over time I started to wonder if they were right. Despite all of the good I did, I still felt like an outsider—like I was fighting against some deeper calling from within. And the more I thought about it, the more I realized I would never be accepted by your kind. But instead, if I embraced my true purpose, then maybe I would be a true hero to those who really mattered. Those who sent me to Earth in the first place."

For a second I'm stunned. I mean, based on what he's saying, Max Mayhem was right! Meta-Man wasn't sent here to help us, he was sent here to destroy us!

"Once my teammates betrayed me," he continues, "it confirmed everything I had been thinking. If the people I fought side-by-side with didn't trust me, then I was truly alone. And that's when I left Earth to find my people. But… I never could. And then, one day in outer space, it dawned on me. Maybe I wasn't supposed to find them. Maybe they would find me once I fulfilled my destiny."

"A-and what's that?" I ask, fearing the answer.

"Why, to destroy mankind," he says matter-of-factly.

"But first, I must settle some unfinished business. I need to know which of my so-called 'friends' betrayed me. Then, I will lay waste to the human race and finally be reunited with my people."

"B-But you don't have to do that," I blurt out. "Sure, there were detractors, but mankind loved you. And you said you were in love yourself. I-I know all about her. I know about Susan Strong, and she loved you."

"Don't say her name!" Meta-Man commands, his eyes crackling with red energy.

"But she was your girlfriend," I say. "You loved her and she was human."

"I warned you!" Meta-Man says.

"NO!" comes a man's voice.

Suddenly, I freeze as red beams erupt from Meta-Man's eyes. But then, someone shoves me hard and my head SMASHES into a nearby tree.

I hear a huge explosion, and then everything…

goes…

dark…

***

"Elliott?"

W-Where am I?

"Elliott, are you okay?"

Someone is talking. Who's talking to me? Boy, my head hurts. I rub my noggin which is sore to the touch.

"Elliott?"

I blink a few times, and as my vision comes back I see a girl with blond hair and blue eyes leaning over me.

"Elliott!" she says, slapping me hard across the face.

I wince. That hurt! How come everybody always slaps me when I'm down? Do I have a slap-me-back-into-consciousness kind of face or something? And then my assailant comes into focus. It's Grace!

"W-What happened?" I ask. That's when I realize I'm lying on my back at the base of a tree.

"Meta-Man got the Black Crow!" she says. "We were loading him into an ambulance when Meta-Man swooped down and took him. We barely had time to react. After he took off, I got worried and came looking for you."

"Is anyone hurt?" I ask, sitting up.

"No, everyone is fine," she says. "Well, Pinball tried to get in the way but he's okay. What happened here? Where's Shadow Hawk?"

Shadow Hawk?

Shadow Hawk! He must have been the one who pushed me out of the way before Meta-Man's Heat Vision nailed me!

"I-I don't know," I say, looking around.

And that's when I see it.

Right where I was standing, wisps of gray smoke are dissipating in the air. That's funny, it looks like one of Shadow Hawk's smoke grenades went off. Then, I see a tree snapped in half behind it, the splintered trunk still smoldering with red energy from Meta-Man's Heat Vision. I swallow hard. That could have been me if Shadow Hawk hadn't saved me. But that's not all I see, because lying next to the fallen trunk is… a utility belt.

No!

I scramble to my feet and race over to it. But when I try to pick it up it singes my glove. That's when I notice the ground beneath my feet is completely scorched.

"Th-That's Shadow Hawk's utility belt!" Grace says, her eyes wide.

"B-But…" I stammer, "Shadow Hawk would never leave his utility belt behind. Like, ever."

What happened? Then, I look around and see scraps of his cape all over the place.

And that's when it hits me.

Suddenly, it feels like there's an anvil stuck inside my chest and I drop to my knees as tears flow from my eyes.

"E-Elliott?" Grace says, wiping her eyes as her voice cracks. "This… this can't be happening, right?"

"I-I wish it didn't happen," I stammer. "B-But Meta-Man vaporized him. Shadow Hawk is dead. And he died… saving me."

Meta Profile

The Marksman

Name: Robin Hoover	Height: 5'11"
Race: Human	Weight: 186 lbs
Status: Hero/Inactive	Eyes/Hair: Brown/Brown

META 0: No Powers
Expert Marksman
Uses a Variety of Weapons
Superior Street Fighter

Observed Characteristics			
Combat 86			
Durability	53	Leadership	84
Strategy	86	Willpower	92

TWELVE

I THINK I'M SEEING DOUBLE

I feel totally hopeless.

It's like someone ripped a giant hole in my heart that won't ever be mended. Shadow Hawk was my idol and now he's dead—and he died saving my life.

I can't stop thinking about all the good times we had together. The hours of one-on-one combat training, the debates over the most dangerous villain of all time, the peanut butter and banana sandwiches he'd make for me.

I-I can't believe he's gone.

And it's all my fault.

Honestly, I just want to curl up and cry, but I know that wouldn't be honoring Shadow Hawk's legacy. If Shadow Hawk were in my cape he'd soldier on. He would do whatever it takes to stop Meta-Man once and for all.

That's why I'm back at Blair Manor. That's why I'm heading down to the Black Crow's Nest to correct the mistake I made before. That's why I'm about to free Max Mayhem from prison. But this time I'm not alone.

"I can't wait to meet this nut job," Grace says.

"Just let me do the talking," I say. "You guys are here if something goes wrong."

"Gee, what could possibly go wrong?" Selfie says sarcastically. "I mean, we're only about to free the greatest evil mastermind of the Golden Age."

"Well, I'm hoping something goes wrong," Grace says, punching her hand, "because I've been itching to pop someone in the kisser."

"Relax," I say, as the elevator slows its descent. "Again, you guys are the brawn, I'm the brains."

"That's debatable," Grace mutters.

DING! The doors slide open and I'm back in the Black Crow's Nest. I think back to my first conversation with Max Mayhem and regret not bringing him along. If I had, then Shadow Hawk might still be alive today.

"Nice digs," Grace says. "It's very, um, retro?"

"This way," I say, leading them around the perimeter until we reach the prison area.

It's dark inside the cell, but I can see Max Mayhem sitting in his chair with his arms crossed.

"Is that him?" Grace whispers as we approach.

I signal for Grace and Selfie to wait off to the side as I continue to the front of his cell. Here, I can see him more clearly, and he doesn't look happy.

"I'm back," I say.

"I can see that, Mr. Zero," Max Mayhem says. "And this time you brought some friends. Am I to be the subject of a class research project?"

"Um, no," I say.

"Then perhaps you are here to provide my rations for the day?" Max Mayhem says. "Apparently, my attendant has decided not to show up for work."

His attendant? He must be referring to Shadow Hawk. Well, I'm not going to tell him what happened.

"I'm not here for that either," I say. "I'm here to offer you a deal. A deal that involves your freedom."

"My freedom?" Max Mayhem says, his left eyebrow rising. "Well, I must say this is the most excitement I've had in decades. Do tell. What is this wonderous proposal you wish to make?"

I open my mouth to speak but hesitate before any words come out. I can't believe I'm offering this, but it's not like I have a choice.

"I'll set you free," I say, "if you help me destroy Meta-Man."

"Hmmm," Max Mayhem says, tapping his pointer finger on his chin. "Let me get this straight. You are offering me my freedom in exchange for destroying Meta-Man? If I didn't know better, it sounds like you need me more than I need you. After all, we both know I am the only one capable of such a feat."

Uh-oh. I can see his wheels spinning. He's going to try pulling a fast one. I've got to stay calm and in control.

"Okay, you don't have to take it," I say quickly. "I mean, we could just leave you here if you want. And who knows when, or even if, your attendant will come back. I guess it's up to you."

"Interesting," Max Mayhem says with a crooked smile. "Are you now suggesting my attendant may never return? Things must be more dire than you had led me to believe."

Darn it! I walked into that one. I said too much and now he knows something happened to Shadow Hawk!

Way to go, Elliott.

"In that case, I propose an amendment to our little arrangement," Max Mayhem says. "I will destroy Meta-Man in exchange for my freedom. But to do so I will first require access to my secret laboratory. Being the hero that you are, I imagine you will not permit me to go there alone, so you, and only you, will accompany me as I prepare for our final battle with Meta-Man. Of course, you will be blindfolded and your friends may not track, trace, or follow us there. How does that sound?"

"Uh-uh," Grace says, stepping forward. "No way."

"Hold on," I say, putting up my hand.

"Epic, no," Selfie says. "It's too dangerous."

She may be right, but I know I can't stop Meta-Man without his help.

"You've got a deal," I say, shaking his hand through

the bars. "I'll enter the code and let you out of here, and you'll help me rid the world of Meta-Man."

***

It seems like we've been traveling for hours, and I'm pretty sure Max Mayhem doubled back a few times to throw me off the trail, but it's hard to know for sure with this blindfold on. And if anything goes wrong I'm essentially on my own because he removed my transmitter watch and insisted on taking the Black Crow's Crow-copter instead of my Freedom Ferry. Not that I blame him, of course, because part of the deal was that we couldn't be followed by Grace and Next Gen.

So, I've basically put my life in his hands.

Just. Freaking. Wonderful.

I know Grace, Selfie, and the others think I'm crazy for doing this but they weren't there when Meta-Man revealed his grand plan. The most powerful hero of all time has gone insane and if I didn't recruit Max Mayhem we'd have no shot at stopping him. I just hope this works.

As I listen to the propellers churn I think about my parents and hope they're okay. I mean, it wouldn't be the first time that wrangling a gang of villains in outer space took longer than they expected, but I sure wish I had their help. Heck, I'd even take Dog-Gone right now.

Just then, the Crow-copter seems to hover in place and I hear a loud BUZZING noise from straight ahead.

The next thing I know, the Crow-copter lurches forward, and based on the change in acoustics it seems like we're flying inside a closed space. Seconds later there's another BUZZ and it sounds like a giant door is sliding closed behind us. Suddenly, we touch down on a hard surface and I hear the propellers powering down.

"Welcome to my humble abode, Mr. Zero," Max Mayhem says, removing my blindfold.

A bright spotlight from overhead blinds me for a few seconds, but when my vision clears I'm staring into a massive hangar filled with all kinds of futuristic-looking vehicles. Then, I notice the sloped ceiling and realize we must be inside a mountain!

"Please, follow me," Max Mayhem says, as he steps out of the Crow-copter and takes a deep breath. "It is so nice to be home again."

I unbuckle myself and exit the Crow-copter. Then, I realize something. Everything in here is shiny and spotless. There isn't a speck of dust on any of the vehicles. So, if Max Mayhem has been in prison for over forty years, who's been taking care of his stuff?

"This way," Max Mayhem says, his footsteps echoing through the chamber.

I follow him through an arched doorway into a glass tube that tunnels through the mountain. After about fifty feet, the tube then connects to a four-way junction that branches off into even more glass tubes. As we walk along I kind of feel like a hamster in a plastic playset, but

I've got to admit it's pretty cool. I wonder how long it took him to build all of this.

We make a few more turns and then enter a tube that's different from the others because this one connects to a series of round, metal doors. Max Mayhem leads me to the last one and says, "This is the entrance to my laboratory. There is something inside I would like you to see."

Um, okay. Why do I have the feeling it's not his baseball card collection? He spins the wheel on the metal door, pushes it open, and then steps to the side. For a second, I hesitate as my alarm bells go off. He's not trying to stick me in a prison, is he?

"Please," he says, extending his arm. "If we are going to work together you will have to trust me."

Well, I wouldn't trust him as far as I could throw him, but he's all I've got so I cautiously step inside. As soon as I enter, my eyes grow wide with astonishment because I'm standing in the largest laboratory I've ever seen. Everywhere I look are well-organized lab stations, from rows of giant microscopes to bays of precision lasers. The walls are covered with monitors tracking experiments in various stages of completion. It's absolutely amazing. I bet TechnocRat would give his entire stash of Camembert for a setup like this.

But then I see something else.

Only a few feet away, a bald man wearing a white lab coat is entering data into a computer. And when he turns around my jaw drops, because he looks like a dead ringer for… Max Mayhem?

"Ah, Number Two," the man says. "I see you have finally returned."

Number Two? Who the heck is Number Two?

"Yes, Number Five," Max Mayhem says suddenly. "And I see you have taken over my laboratory since I've been gone."

Number Two? Number Five? What's going on?

"Pardon me," Max Mayhem says to me. "As you may have realized by now, we are both clones of the original Max Mayhem who died many years ago."

"Although there is no hard evidence of his actual death," Number Five says.

"Wait, what?" I blurt out, looking at Number Five and then back at my Max Mayhem. "You mean, you're not the real Max Mayhem?"

"Oh, no," my Max Mayhem says, "I am not."

"So, is that why you never aged?" I ask. "Because you're a clone?"

"Yes," my Max Mayhem says. "When he created us, the original Max Mayhem was able to tinker with his own cellular biochemistry to delay the aging process. So, we do grow old over time, but at a much slower rate."

"Wow," I say, trying to process everything. But then I realize something else. "Hold on. Does that mean Max Mayhem sent you, a clone, to fight Meta-Man at Century City? Are you saying the real Max Mayhem was never even there?"

"Of course, he wasn't there," my Max Mayhem says. "The original Max Mayhem was obsessed with immortality. He would never put himself at risk."

"So, you've been in prison all these years," I say, "while the real Max Mayhem was free?"

"Oh, yes," Number Five says. "I remember all of us having a great laugh when Number Two was first apprehended. But then we quickly forgot about him. There was just so much to do."

"Well, now I am back," my Max Mayhem says firmly. "And I will also be taking back my lab. Is that clear?"

"No need to pull rank, Number Two," Number Five says, walking towards us. "Per the bylaws, it is within your rights to reclaim your lab. I will simply go do the same to Number Twelve. Now, if you will excuse me."

"Number Twelve?" I say, as Number Five exits. "Wait, are you saying there are twelve Max Mayhem's out there? Are you kidding me?"

"Do not be alarmed," my Max Mayhem says. "One side effect of cloning is that as each duplicate is produced, he holds less and less true to the original copy. Thus, while I possess nearly all of the intellectual capabilities of my originator, copies like Number Five are far inferior. As for Number Twelve, I would be shocked if he even knew his own name. Now, what I wish to show you is back here. Follow me."

My mind is still spinning, but as we move past the

area where Number Five was working, I stop short and gasp. Because on his monitor is an image of something I never thought I'd see again.

It's a picture of a gold ring.

A gold ring with a lightning bolt on its face.

Meta Profile

Will Power

▯ Name: Lawrence Fletcher	▯ Height: 5'10"
▯ Race: Human	▯ Weight: 196 lbs
▯ Status: Hero/Deceased	▯ Eyes/Hair: Brown/Blonde

META 3: Magic
▯ Extreme Energy Manipulation Powered by an Alien Rock
▯ Creates Energy Constructs in Any Shape He Can Imagine

Observed Characteristics			
Combat 82			
Durability	77	Leadership	68
Strategy	69	Willpower	99

THIRTEEN

I DISCOVER THE TRUTH

I can't believe what I'm looking at.

I mean, what is an image of the gold Ring of Suffering doing on Max Mayhem Five's monitor? The Three Rings of Suffering are super dangerous artifacts, and each ring houses a member of the Djinn Three—the three evil genie brothers who have terrorized humanity for centuries. Once upon a time, all three rings were held safe and sound in the trophy room of the Waystation 1.0.

That is, until the Meta-Busters blew it up.

As I stare at the gold ring, I think back to my encounter with Beezle, the evil djinn inside the silver ring. I'll never forget how he intentionally twisted my words around to take Siphon's life energy. Just thinking about it makes me feel nauseous all over again.

Fortunately, I was able to use the last of the three

wishes Beezle granted me to confine him to his ring forever. Now, both the silver and bronze rings are back on the Waystation 2.0, but the gold ring is still out there somewhere. And Terrog, the djinn inside, is supposedly the most powerful of them all. So, why is Max Mayhem's clone looking for Terrog?

"Can I ask you something?" I ask Max Mayhem Two. Well, now that I know he's a clone, I figure I might as well think of him that way.

"Certainly, Mr. Zero," Max Mayhem Two says.

"Great," I say, pointing to the monitor. "Can you tell me why Number Five is looking for this ring?"

"I am not sure," Max Mayhem Two says, leaning over to study the image. "I am personally not familiar with it. However, our originator always had multiple schemes in play and would assign confidential projects to different clones for execution. I suspect he had a good reason for seeking this object, but his purpose is unknown to me. Unfortunately, Number Five is unlikely to reveal why he is seeking the object unless it will significantly advance his goal. And speaking of goals, we have a common one to destroy Meta-Man, so it's time I shared the reason for our visit with you. Now, if you would kindly follow me."

But as we move on, I can't help looking back at the image of the ring. The silver ring was dangerous enough and I couldn't imagine what would happen if the original Max Mayhem got his hands on the gold one. That is, if the original Max Mayhem is even still alive.

Max Mayhem Two leads me past vats of bubbling liquid, vials filled with white, tofu-like globules, and various other stations until we reach the back of the laboratory. That's when I do a double take because we're standing in front of the largest metal door I've ever seen. It spans the entire width of the room and goes from the floor to the ceiling. What's behind that monster?

"Impressive, isn't it?" Max Mayhem Two says proudly as he types into a small keypad mounted on the door. "Let's just say I required a substantial deterrent to keep the others away from my special project."

His special project? What could that be?

Suddenly, there's a loud VOOM that echoes through the lab and the door splits open at its center.

"This way," Max Mayhem Two offers.

I look at his grinning face, step inside, and do a double take.

It's… a spaceship?

Or, more precisely, half a spaceship.

It's about twenty feet high and shaped like a capsule, with three large, curved fins at its base and a cockpit in the center that's big enough to fit a person. Strangely, half of the ship has been stripped away and I can see the understructure that forms its skeleton. And then I notice something else. The ship's metallic panels are covered with familiar-looking shapes and symbols.

Where have I seen markings like that before?

Then, I notice a bunch of lasers stationed around the ship, and several of the ship's metallic panels are splayed out on worktables. For a second I'm confused. What the heck does a spaceship have to do with defeating Meta-Man? I mean, why is he even showing me this? But then it hits me like a ton of bricks.

I know exactly whose ship that is!

"That's Meta-Man's ship!" I blurt out. "That's the ship that brought him here as a baby, isn't it?"

"Very good, Mr. Zero," Max Mayhem Two says. "That is the very ship Meta-Man used to travel to Earth. And that ship is also the key to his destruction."

"What?" I say. "Sorry, but I don't get it."

"That is understandable," Max Mayhem Two says. "At first, I didn't either, but as I mapped out the various methods of potentially defeating Meta-Man, I always suspected the solution was somehow sitting right under my nose. And that is when I remembered his ship, and then everything became clear."

His eyes gleam with confidence but.I'm still lost.

"You see," he continues, "Meta-Man was valuable cargo. If his people put him inside this ship and sent him halfway across the universe, then the material this ship is made from must be incredibly strong. After all, Meta-Man's powers were formidable even as an infant, and the ship must have been built to withstand the full force of his might, not to mention whatever else he would encounter along the way—including changing atmospheric pressure, collisions with space debris, and even possible alien attack. So, if his people designed this ship to protect him, then the material on this ship must be …"

"…stronger than he is," I say, finishing his sentence.

I'm shocked. That's pure genius.

"Precisely," Max Mayhem Two says. "Therefore, if I could break his ship down, then I could use the material to create a weapon I could use against Meta-Man. It took decades of research, decades of testing and tweaking and testing again, but I finally had my breakthrough. I finally identified a way to reshape the material. And once I did, I had to test my theory on my subject."

Test his theory? Suddenly, I realize where I've seen those markings before.

"The glove!" I exclaim. "The glove you used in Century City was made from Meta-Man's ship! That's how you gave him that scar!"

"Yes," he says. "But unfortunately, I was unable to escape from Century City, and thus, my grand plan to destroy Meta-Man never came to fruition. But now I have my second chance."

But there's something still bothering me about his story. Something that still doesn't make sense.

"But wait," I say. "How did you find his ship in the first place? I can't imagine it was still laying where he crash-landed all those years before."

"That is none of your concern," Max Mayhem Two

says dismissively. "The point is that I have it, and now I can exploit it to its maximum potential."

"Um, okay," I say. "But how?"

"With this," he says, pressing a button on a console.

Suddenly, a large box rises out of the floor, and as the front panel slides open I see a shiny suit of armor inside. But then I realize it's no ordinary suit of armor because it's covered head-to-toe with the same strange markings as the glove and ship! At first, I'm confused, but as I look at all the parts lying around I realize the suit is made entirely from the ship's material!

Well, almost the entire suit because it's missing the right glove. And then I notice there's also a matching scabbard and sword.

"You're going to fight Meta-Man with that?" I ask. And then I notice something else. "There's no visor, so how will you see?"

"To defeat Meta-Man, I must be fully encased in the battle armor with no potential openings," he says. "Therefore, I have designed a built-in radar to guide me."

Built-in radar? That sounds cool. I look at his battle armor and realize he might actually have a fighting chance. I mean, if he injured Meta-Man with just a glove, I can only imagine what a whole suit could do. And speaking of gloves, Meta-Man chucked the original glove, so what's Max Mayhem Two going to do?

"What about the right glove?" I ask. "I saw Meta-Man hurl it into outer space."

"No worries," he says, pushing another button. "I am prepared for just such a scenario."

Then, another compartment rises out of the floor with spare parts, including right and left-handed gloves. Max Mayhem Two selects a right-handed glove and says, "I simply need to weld it on."

"Well, that's good," I say. "But what do we do when you're ready? I assume there's no Bat phone to call Meta-Man over."

"No," Max Mayhem says. "If we are going to defeat Meta-Man, we will need to employ the element of surprise. And that is where you come in."

"Me?" I say.

"Yes," he says. "We will need to draw him out in the open. That will be your role."

"So, what exactly does that mean?" I ask.

"It means that you are the bait, and I am the trap," he says. "But do not worry, Mr. Zero. I'll go over everything on our journey north."

"North?" I say. "What's north?"

"Meta-Man's old secret headquarters," Max Mayhem Two says. "We will ambush him there. But first, I must attend to this glove."

***

I hate cold weather.

So, the fact that I'm standing ankle-deep in snow in

the middle of the Arctic isn't exactly what I had in mind when Max Mayhem Two told me we'd be heading north. At least he gave me a parka to wear or I'd really be in trouble. But the longer I'm exposed to the elements, the faster I'll go from being Epic Zero to Epic Sub-Zero.

And since I don't want to turn into a popsicle, I'd better find the entrance to Meta-Man's secret headquarters fast. The thing is, Max Mayhem Two didn't exactly give me directions. He basically dropped me off in the Crow-copter and told me to look for a tunnel entrance somewhere in these snow-capped mountains.

Gee, that was helpful. Not.

Even though my teeth are chattering like crazy, I trudge over to the base of the closest mountain and start searching. But there are so many rocks I could literally be here forever. Especially if I freeze to death.

Why did Meta-Man even have an old secret headquarters in this barren, frozen wasteland? It's isolated and kind of peaceful, but the surroundings are pretty bleak. But suddenly I get it. If Meta-Man never felt human, well, no humans would ever find him here. In fact, I think the only thing alive in these parts is me.

But that probably won't last long, even if I somehow stumble across this magical entrance. After all, Max Mayhem Two's big plan is for me to go inside Meta-Man's headquarters and draw him out in the open. That's when Max Mayhem Two will take him by surprise.

I suppose it's a great plan—if you're not me.

Why did I agree to this?

Well, I'm not finding anything that looks like an opening and my fingers are starting to freeze under my gloves. I consider yelling Meta-Man's name at the top of my lungs, but the wind is whipping so hard there's no way he'd hear me. So, I'll just have to keep searching and pray for a miracle.

That's when I notice something unusual hanging overhead. There's a piece of rock sticking down that looks just like an arrow—and it's pointing at a large boulder sitting on a ledge about ten feet up. It might be nothing but that arrow-shaped rock just seems too odd to be a coincidence. I might as well check it out.

Using all of my strength, I scramble up the slippery mountain until I reach the ledge. That's when I see the boulder which is taller than me. Well, that was all for nothing. I'm about to climb back down when I notice a large hole behind it. That's weird. I lean over the snow-covered boulder for a closer look when I see an opening that leads right into the mountain itself.

That's it! It's the tunnel!

Now that's a great optical illusion because if you were looking from straight on you'd never see the entrance. Well, if I can't get Meta-Man to come out, then I guess I'll have to go in. I take a deep breath and slide down the snowy boulder into the tunnel. My backside is soaked but sometimes you've gotta do what you've gotta do.

I make my way cautiously, the tunnel growing darker with every step. I'd love to use my flashlight but I'm afraid it might give me away. And speaking of giving myself away, my heart is beating so loud it sounds like it's echoing down the tunnel. Every bone in my body tells me to turn back, but I can't let Shadow Hawk down. I need to be brave. I need to do this for him and everyone else.

After about a hundred yards, I hit a fork in the tunnel. Great, which way should I go? I'm about to deploy my fail-safe, decision-making strategy of eeny-meeny-miny-moe when I hear something faint coming from the pathway to the left. Is that… whistling? I lean in and raise my ear. Yep, someone is whistling, which means that someone is down there.

So, I turn left and follow the noise. At first, I'm not sure what tune it is, but as I get closer it kind of sounds like "Taps." I wonder who'd be whistling that?

Then, it dawns on me that it might be coming from one of the Protectors of the Planet. According to Shadow Hawk, Meta-Man had captured all of the living members. I doubt it's the Black Crow based on the state he was in at the nursing home, but it could be one of the others, like Goldrush, the Marksman, Sergeant Stretch, or Warrior Woman. Suddenly, I realize I'm walking a bit faster than I thought. I guess it's second nature now that if someone is in trouble I'll race to the rescue.

The whistling gets louder as I reach the end of the tunnel which opens into a large chamber. I hug the edge of the wall, peer around the corner, and nearly let out a loud gasp. That's because I see five older people with their limbs stretched wide and their hands and feet encased in blocks of ice!

I don't know what I was expecting, but it certainly wasn't this. I recognize the Black Crow which means the others must be his teammates. The three who resemble Goldrush, the Marksman, and Warrior Woman look semi-alert, but Sergeant Stretch and the Black Crow have their heads down.

I've got to help them! But then I realize something.

The whistling has stopped.

Why did the whistling stop?

"Please, do come in," Meta-Man says, his voice echoing through the chamber.

I pull my head back and hold my breath. Darn it! How did he know I was here? I thought I was quiet.

"Don't be shy," he says, his voice booming off the walls. "I know you're out there. I do have Super-Hearing, you know."

I curse myself under my breath. I was hoping to avoid a direct confrontation, but that'll be impossible now. So, I grit my teeth and step into the chamber. And that's when I see Meta-Man sitting on a throne of ice.

"It's about time," he says. "I was getting bored waiting for you."

"Let them go!" I demand, trying not to look scared. "They didn't do anything to you!"

"That's not true," Meta-Man says. "One of them betrayed me, but none of them will tell me who did it. I nearly got it out of Sergeant Stretch, but his weak heart gave out before he could reveal the name."

His heart? I look at Sergeant Stretch and realize he isn't breathing. Then, I see the Black Crow struggling to breathe without his medical equipment.

"You'll kill him!" I yell. "He needs help!"

"And so do you," Meta-Man says. "But you're not alone, are you?"

I keep my mouth shut. I can't let him know about Max Mayhem Two. It would ruin the element of surprise.

"So, where is my lovely father anyway?" he asks.

"Um, sorry?" I say, totally confused. "What?"

"I asked you where my father was," Meta-Man says. "I assume he put you up to this."

"What are you talking about?" I ask. "I don't know your father."

"Oh, but you do," he says. "Because my father is Max Mayhem."

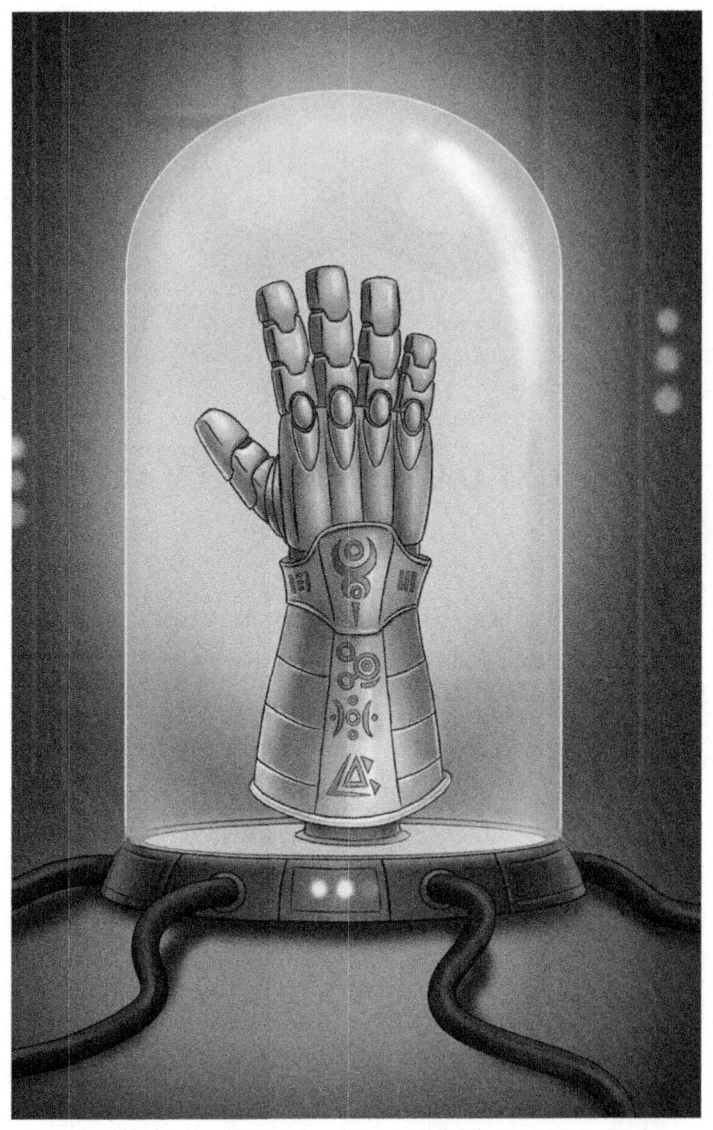

FOURTEEN

I GET MIXED UP IN A FAMILY AFFAIR

Um, what?

Did I just hear what I thought I heard? Did Meta-Man just say that Max Mayhem was his father? But that's impossible because they're arch enemies, right? I mean, the Joker wasn't Batman's father. The Green Goblin wasn't Spider-Man's father. So how could Max Mayhem be Meta-Man's father? Archenemies just aren't supposed to be related like that!

Besides, Max Mayhem couldn't be Meta-Man's father because Max Mayhem is human, while Meta-Man is an alien who adopted Earth as… his… home.

O. M. G.

Adopted?

Just then, I remember Meta-Man's profile, and one particular sentence sticks out in my mind: *His ship landed near Houston where it was discovered by a corrupt oil baron named Maximillian Murdock.*

Wait a second.

Maximillian Murdock?

Max Mayhem?

Maximillian. Max.

Suddenly, everything hits me at once and I feel like such a fool. Max Mayhem is Maximillian Murdock! Which means Max Mayhem is Meta-Man's adopted father! No wonder Max Mayhem had Meta-Man's ship! He simply kept it after he discovered Meta-Man!

And now he's trying to kill his son!

"He's out there, isn't he?" Meta-Man asks. "I can see it on your face. He sent you here to do his dirty work. That's so like him. But you don't have to die for him. If you tell me where he is, I'll spare your life."

I open my mouth to offer a clever retort but no words come out. Honestly, my brain is so scrambled I'm not sure what I should do right now. I mean, why didn't Max Mayhem Two tell me about this? Why didn't he tell me Meta-Man was the original Max Mayhem's son?

"D-Don't listen to him," comes a woman's voice. "He's… lying to you. He'll… kill you."

I turn to see Warrior Woman looking at me, the veins in her neck bulging as she tries to break her hands and feet free of her ice shackles, but she can't.

"Silence!" Meta-Man orders as he rises from his ice throne. "I make the rules here!"

I realize that as much as I want to help Warrior Woman and the Protectors, Meta-Man is way too powerful for me to fight on my own. I might not trust Max Mayhem Two, but he's still the best option I've got.

"So, child," Meta-Man says, stepping down from his ice platform, his eyes glowing red. "What's it going to be? Will you help me, or will you die?"

"Run!" Warrior Woman yells.

Run? Well, that's the best idea I've heard all day. Now, I may not be Blue Bolt, but luckily I'm standing near the next best thing. So, I concentrate hard and reach out to Goldrush, pulling his power into my body. And as his Super-Speed flows through my veins, I realize his Meta energy doesn't feel as strong as I had hoped, but it's way better than what I've got now.

"You make a compelling offer," I say to Meta-Man, "but I'm gonna split." Then, I take off as fast as I can, heading back through the tunnel.

I'm feeling pretty good about my getaway until I realize I'm not alone. I hear footsteps behind me, and when I peer over my shoulder Meta-Man is right on my tail! Great, I forgot he's got Super-Speed too! Even though I'm running so fast sparks are flying from my feet, he's still catching up to me! I hope I remember the way I came in!

I hang my first right and see light in the distance. Yes! This has got to be the way out! I pump my arms and legs with everything I've got until I see the giant boulder up ahead. I bound over it into the daylight and find myself flying through the air! Uh-oh, I forgot the entrance was ten feet off the ground! The next thing I know, I land hard on my stomach, catching a face-full of snow.

Awesome. Just need to… catch my breath.

"Have we reached the end so soon?" Meta-Man asks from behind me, his dark shadow eclipsing my body.

I get up on my knees and realize I'm shivering. Somehow, I've lost my parka and my costume is ripped in various places. But that's not all I notice, because Meta-Man's eyes are glowing! This is it! But then—

"Back off, Lucas!" comes a voice from overhead. Suddenly, there's a CLANG and Meta-Man goes flying backward into the mountainside.

That's when a knight in metallic, shining armor appears before me, except I know there's no noble gentleman inside. It's Max Mayhem Two! And he just clocked Meta-Man with his battle armor!

"Don't you dare call me by that name!" Meta-Man responds, getting to his feet and wiping his mouth with his sleeve. "I'm no longer your son!"

"But I will always be your father," Max Mayhem Two says. "And I will always know what's best for you. It is time we ended this, Lucas. You knew that if you ever came back I would be forced to kill you."

"Just like you killed Susan?" Meta-Man asks. "She was innocent in all of this. And yet, you disposed of her like she was nothing."

"She *was* nothing," Max Mayhem Two says. "You knew it was wrong to start a romantic relationship with a human, yet you did it anyway. You were always different, and if it took her death for you to finally accept the truth, then it was well worth the sacrifice."

"I tried to fit in!" Meta-Man yells. "I wasted my life trying to help humanity!"

"You did try," Max Mayhem Two says. "But we both knew it was all for nothing. You see, from the moment I found you I suspected you were sent here for a reason. It just wasn't apparent what that reason was. But one day, while I was transcribing an ancient text, it came to me. I realized the key to understanding you, the key to understanding everything about you, was always right in front of my eyes. Do you see these strange markings on my armor? These came from your spaceship. But they aren't just random decorations, they're words—they're the words of your people. I realized that they left a communication for you in their own language right on the exterior of your ship. And once I finally cracked the code, their message became all too clear."

"My people left a message for me on my ship?" Meta-Man says, clearly shocked. "Is that why you told me my ship was destroyed when I landed here? Because you never wanted me to see the message? Tell me! Tell me what the message said!"

"You would like that, wouldn't you?" Max Mayhem Two says. "Unfortunately, I cannot do that. But what I can share is that it wasn't so much a message as it was instructions—instructions on how you should contact your people once your mission to annihilate humanity was complete. That is why I ensured you never laid eyes on your ship."

"I can't believe you kept that from me," Meta-Man says, standing tall. "I can't believe you kept me from discovering my true identity. I'll kill you!"

"You can certainly try," Max Mayhem Two says, pulling his gleaming sword out of his scabbard.

Suddenly, there's a blur as Meta-Man uses his Super-Speed to attack Max Mayhem Two, but Max Mayhem Two stands his ground and leans in, repelling the former hero with his shoulder. Undeterred, Meta-Man picks up a huge boulder and hurls it at his father. But this time Max Mayhem Two slices it in half with his sword before it even reaches him.

Next, Meta-Man flies at Max Mayhem Two with tremendous speed but Max Mayhem Two dodges him and lands a roundhouse kick, sending Meta-Man flying into a rock wall. Holy cow! I can't believe it! Max Mayhem Two is matching Meta-Man blow for blow! He might actually do it! He might actually defeat Meta-Man!

"Must we continue?" Max Mayhem Two asks. "Surely, you can see you are no match for me and my battle armor. Why delay the inevitable? You are clearly a lost and tortured soul. As your father, let me be the one to put you out of your misery. And afterward, I promise to finish off the Protectors of the Planet in your honor."

Um, what? Finish the Protectors? Okay, now I know I can't trust that guy. The thing is, how am I supposed to beat him after he destroys Meta-Man?

"Never," Meta-Man says, flying high into the air. But instead of attacking, this time he just hovers overhead, staring down at Max Mayhem Two.

What is he doing?

"Come down and let's get this over with!" Max Mayhem Two commands, like a father berating his spoiled child. "You will not win anything from up there."

"Perhaps not," Meta-Man says with a sly smile. "But from here I can use my Super Senses to scan your battle armor. And while you've done an excellent job overall, I see you've gotten a bit rusty after all of these years."

"What?" Max Mayhem Two says with clear concern in his voice. "What are you talking about?"

"Well, it appears your attention to detail just isn't what it used to be," Meta-Man says. "Because my Super-Hearing is detecting just the slightest difference in sound as the wind blows across parts of your armor."

"No…" Max Mayhem Two says.

"Oh, yes," Meta-Man says with a big smile. "In fact, it 'seems' like there's quite a gap in the 'seam' of your right glove. And I think that's going to be a fatal mistake for you."

But before Max Mayhem Two can react, Meta-Man is a blur. And the next thing I know he's crouching beside

Max Mayhem Two, firing a pinpoint beam of Heat Vision directly into Max Mayhem Two's right wrist! Holy cow! That's where Max Mayhem Two just welded on the new glove!

"NO!" Max Mayhem Two screams, and then there's a giant IMPLOSION inside the battle armor! I shield my eyes from the light, and when I look back Max Mayhem Two's battle armor is lying face down in the snow with a trail of red smoke emanating from his right wrist.

"That was for Susan," Meta-Man says, standing up.

I-I can't believe it! Max Mayhem Two is dead! Fried inside his own suit! But I doubt Meta-Man even knows that Max Mayhem Two was a clone and not his real father.

Now what do I do? I mean, Max Mayhem Two was supposed to take care of Meta-Man. And now Meta-Man is looking at me!

"Hey," I say. "Look, I-I didn't know anything about your whole father-son thing. He never told me. But I'm sorry. It didn't sound like the best childhood a kid could have."

"It wasn't," he says. "But it's over now."

"Great," I say. "So, does that mean you're leaving now? I mean, you did what you came here to do, right? You got revenge on your father. Wasn't that enough?"

"No," Meta-Man says. "That was just the beginning."

"Um, the beginning of what?" I ask.

"The beginning of discovering my true identity," Meta-Man says. "Thanks to my 'father,' all of the pieces have now fallen into place. First, I must destroy the human race. Then, I will decode the instructions of my people and finally learn who I really am."

Meta Profile

Sergeant Stretch

Name: Patrick Johnson	Height: 6'1"
Race: Human	Weight: 202 lbs
Status: Hero/Inactive	Eyes/Hair: Brown/Black

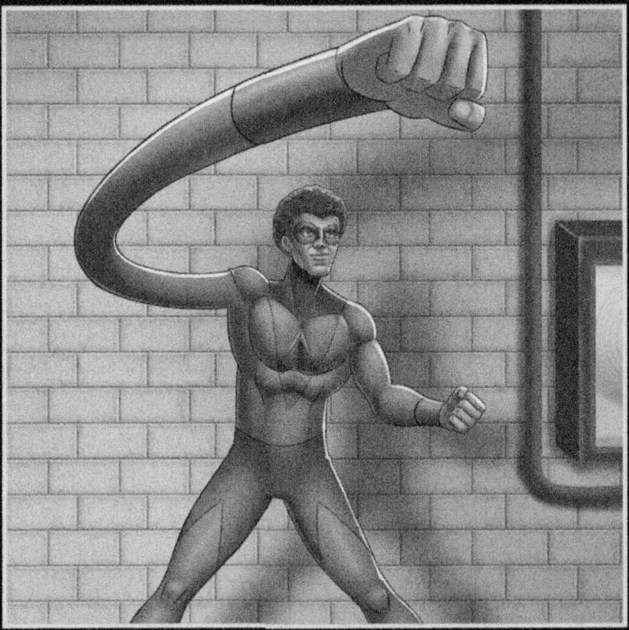

META 3: Meta-morph

- Extreme Body Morphing
- Can Stretch His Body into Various Shapes

Observed Characteristics

Combat 81

Durability	94	Leadership	83
Strategy	72	Willpower	82

FIFTEEN

I FIGHT FOR ALL OF HUMANITY

This is not good.

Meta-Man just destroyed Max Mayhem Two, who was not only the clone of his adopted father but also the only person capable of stopping him. And now that Max Mayhem Two is gone only one person is standing between Meta-Man and the annihilation of the human race—and that's me!

I get to my feet and try to come up with a plan. I don't feel Goldrush's Meta energy inside me anymore, and at this point, Meta-Man is way beyond reasoning with. We both know I can't negate his powers because he can sense it coming, but I haven't tried duplicating them yet.

"You will be the next to die," Meta-Man says, coming towards me, "but you will not be the last."

"Not if I have anything to say about it," I reply, and then I concentrate hard, reaching out for his power, and then pull it back to me. But as his Meta energy flows through me, I realize I don't know what power I've just copied. I mean, Meta-Man has Super-Strength, Super-Speed, Heat Vision, and Flight, but he can only use one power at a time. So, which power did I just grab?

Please, tell me it's Super-Strength!

"Farewell," Meta-Man says, rearing back to punch me into next week.

But then my instincts kick in and I strike first, punching him over a hundred times in the breadbasket with lightning-fast quickness. That's when I realize I didn't get his Super-Strength, but Super-Speed! Except, despite all of my pounding, Meta-Man doesn't budge because I'm only as strong as I am now—which isn't strong at all. Just then, pain shoots from my knuckles up my arms! Ouch! It feels like I just slammed my fist into a steel door a hundred times!

My arms are throbbing, but I still manage to dart out of the way with ease as he swings at me, punching a sizeable hole into the mountain behind me. Okay, Super-Speed is helpful, but it won't be enough to take him down.

I'm gonna have to gamble on another power.

"So, I see you can copy my powers as well," he says, wheeling on me. "Impressive. But I'll figure you out. I always do."

Suddenly, his eyes light up and I bolt just as his Heat Vision scorches the ground beneath me. Well, I'm not going to last long like this. If I can grab his Heat Vision I could try fighting him from long range. So, I concentrate and pull in his powers again.

But as I absorb his new Meta energy, I can feel his old Meta energy slipping away. Meta-Man takes off into the air and I lock my gaze on him. But when I try to activate my Heat Vision nothing happens! That's when Meta-Man circles closer and smiles.

"See, I told you I'd figure you out," he says. "You can copy my powers, but it won't help you much if I'm always one step ahead."

One step ahead? What's he talking about?

Suddenly, I realize I can hear everything around me super well, like the ruffles of his cape fluttering in the wind, the pitter-patter of snowflakes hitting the mountainside, and the drops of sweat falling from my forehead onto the snow. And that's when I realize what he's saying. He felt me using my duplication power and switched his Meta energy to the most useless combat power ever—Super Hearing!

"You might as well surrender," he says, landing in front of me. "Otherwise, I'll just keep shifting my Meta energy around to keep you off balance. You have no chance."

I swallow hard because I know he's right. I can keep trying to grab his current power, but he'll just change it to the next one. I need a different plan. The problem is, I don't know what else to do.

And that's when I hear someone breathing. Someone other than me and Meta-Man!

"Leave the boy alone!" comes a gritty, familiar voice.

I turn to see a dark figure standing on an icy boulder, and I can't believe my eyes. It's… Shadow Hawk!

"Well, well," Meta-Man says, turning to face him. "Look who survived after all. It must be my lucky day because I get to kill you all over again."

Just then, I hear footsteps behind me, and then—

"If you're going to kill him," comes a woman's voice, "then you'll have to kill us too."

I spin around to see three more familiar figures standing beneath the entrance of the tunnel. It's Warrior Woman, the Marksman, and Goldrush! Shadow Hawk must have freed them!

"It's a reunion," Meta-Man says with a sneer. "Unfortunately, I see not all of us could make it. Should I assume the Black Crow died as well? A shame. I was so looking forward to ending his life with my bare hands."

"You can't hold a candle to the Black Crow," Shadow Hawk says. "He's everything you're not. Brave. Honorable. Decent."

"Interestingly, you didn't use the word 'loyal,'" Meta-Man says. "Out of all of you, I always suspected he was the one who sold me out to Max Mayhem. He was always jealous of me. And why wouldn't he be? After all, I had the powers. The headlines. The girl."

"What are you talking about?" Shadow Hawk asks.

"Why, Susan Strong, of course," Meta-Man says. "She told me the Black Crow was interested in her, but she wanted nothing to do with him. No surprise there, of course. After all, he was a rather moody fellow. So, putting two and two together, it wouldn't surprise me in the least if he was the traitor you were protecting. And I was just about to find out when I was interrupted by this child."

"If you're looking for your traitor," Shadow Hawk says, "then look no further."

"Wait, what?" I blurt out.

"You?" Meta-Man says with a chuckle. "Do you expect me to believe that it was you who betrayed me? Nice try, but you were a boy."

"Yes, I was a boy," Shadow Hawk says. "But I was no fool. Not after I found out who you really were that day we battled Hypnotica. Or don't you remember?"

"Hypnotica?" Meta-Man says, his eyebrows rising.

"I'm not surprised you're having trouble recalling that mission," Shadow Hawk says, "so let me refresh your memory. It was our last mission before Century City, and you, me, and the Black Crow were on duty. We received a call at Protector Palace from the police commissioner that Hypnotica, the self-proclaimed Queen of Hypnosis, was robbing the Keystone City Bank. We went to stop her and while you and the Black Crow went inside the bank, I waited around back in case she escaped. But Hypnotica had set a trap, and as soon as you went inside, you were both put under her hypnotic spell. And do you remember what happened next?"

"Let me guess," Meta-Man says. "You saved the day."

"I did," Shadow Hawk says. "But that wasn't all. When I found you, you were still under her hypnotic power. At first, you started babbling gibberish. But then your words became more coherent, and you kept going on and on about your secret destiny, your one true purpose. I didn't know what you were talking about. I thought you were just joking around. So, I figured I'd just play along. But when I asked you what your destiny was, you said it was to destroy the human race."

"You never told me that," Meta-Man says.

"Of course not," Shadow Hawk says. "But do you know who I did tell? The Black Crow. And do you know what he said? He said you were probably just having a bad dream. But he wasn't there. He didn't see the anger and determination in your eyes when you were saying it. I may have been a kid, but I knew you weren't having a bad dream. I had learned all about the power of hypnosis and its ability to surface things from people's pasts they weren't even aware of themselves. I knew you were speaking your truth, and that's when I realized that if you ever decided to carry out your true purpose there wasn't anyone on Earth who could stop you. And that's when I tracked down Max Mayhem."

"So, you *are* responsible," Meta-Man whispers, his eyes narrowing. "You're responsible for Susan's death."

"Her death is my greatest regret," Shadow Hawk says. "Max Mayhem promised me he wouldn't harm her. And… I foolishly believed him."

"Why?" Meta-Man asks sternly. "Why would you trust him? Why would you trust my greatest enemy?"

"I was wrong to trust him with Susan's life," Shadow Hawk says. "But I wasn't wrong that you needed to be stopped."

"This time I'm going to destroy you once and for all," Meta-Man says. "And I'm going to enjoy every second of it."

"No, Meta-Man!" Warrior Woman says. "The Protectors of the Planet stick together. So, you're going to have to get through all of us first. Protectors, attack!"

Meta-Man's eyes go red and he fires a blast at Shadow Hawk who somersaults out of the way. Then, Goldrush is on Meta-Man first, hammering him with a series of high-speed blows, but he's not the hero he used to be and Meta-Man easily slaps him away with the back of his hand. The Marksman is next, unleashing a barrage of throwing stars that EXPLODE upon contact, catching Meta-Man by surprise. But Meta-Man quickly dispatches the former hero with a stomp to the ground, knocking the senior citizen easily off balance.

"Pick on someone your own strength!" Warrior

Woman says, running right at Meta-Man.

They grapple with one another, jostling for position, and to my surprise, Warrior Woman holds her own. But Meta-Man rolls backward, taking Warrior Woman with him, and then he lets go, flinging her into the sky.

"Warrior Woman!" Shadow Hawk yells.

But Meta-Man doesn't wait for a victory trophy, and instead charges at Shadow Hawk like a torpedo, pinning him to the ground.

"I'm going to enjoy this," Meta-Man says, his eyes crackling with bright, red energy.

"Shadow Hawk!" I yell. I've got to act fast, so I grab Goldrush's power and race over to stop Meta-Man. But a microsecond before I get there he raises his fist and I SLAM into it. I feel immense pain in my left side as he knocks the breath out of me and I careen into a rock wall!

He… did it again! Switched from… Heat Vision to… Super Speed to… Super Strength in… the blink of an eye. My left side feels like… it's on fire. I'm… so out of breath. Struggling for air.

But as I look back over, Meta-Man still has Shadow Hawk pinned. He can't get free! I… I don't know what to do. I... can barely stand… after that blow.

Then, Meta-Man's eyes light back up.

N-No! Got to… get up.

He'll… kill him.

But as I pull myself to my feet, I hear—

"Get off of him you monster!"

Out of the corner of my eye, I catch the downstroke of a metallic sword! Suddenly, a flash of red electricity escapes from Meta-Man's back. Meta-Man stands up and spins around, looking down with surprise as a thin line of electricity emanates from the 'MM' insignia on his chest. And then he looks up at me with terror in his eyes as the electricity rapidly expands, completely engulfing him in a giant, crackling ball of red light!

Suddenly, there's a blinding PFOOOM!

The force of the explosion blows me back against the rock and my side feels like it's on fire all over again. For a few seconds, all I see are stars. But as my vision clears, Meta-Man is gone, and Shadow Hawk is leaning over the body of a white-haired man in a hospital gown who is lying face down in the snow.

I-I can't believe it!

It's… the Black Crow!

And in his right hand is Max Mayhem Two's metallic sword. He… he saved Shadow Hawk's life! He destroyed Meta-Man!

BEEP! BEEP! BEEP!

W-What's that?

I look around but can't find the source of the noise. And then I realize it's coming from my utility belt. It's the Freedom Force transmitter Mom had TechnocRat put into my belt! I forgot all about it!

I push the button on the front and say, "H-Hello."

"Epic Z-ro?" comes Grace's broken voice, followed

by static. “Is th-t you?”

“Y-Yeah,” I say.

“I- everyth--g okay?” she asks.

“Yeah,” I say. “Everything… is just… dandy…”

“It -ook us for-ver to find -ou,” she says. “What -re you doing at th- North P-le?”

But I can’t answer.

Because the world goes black.

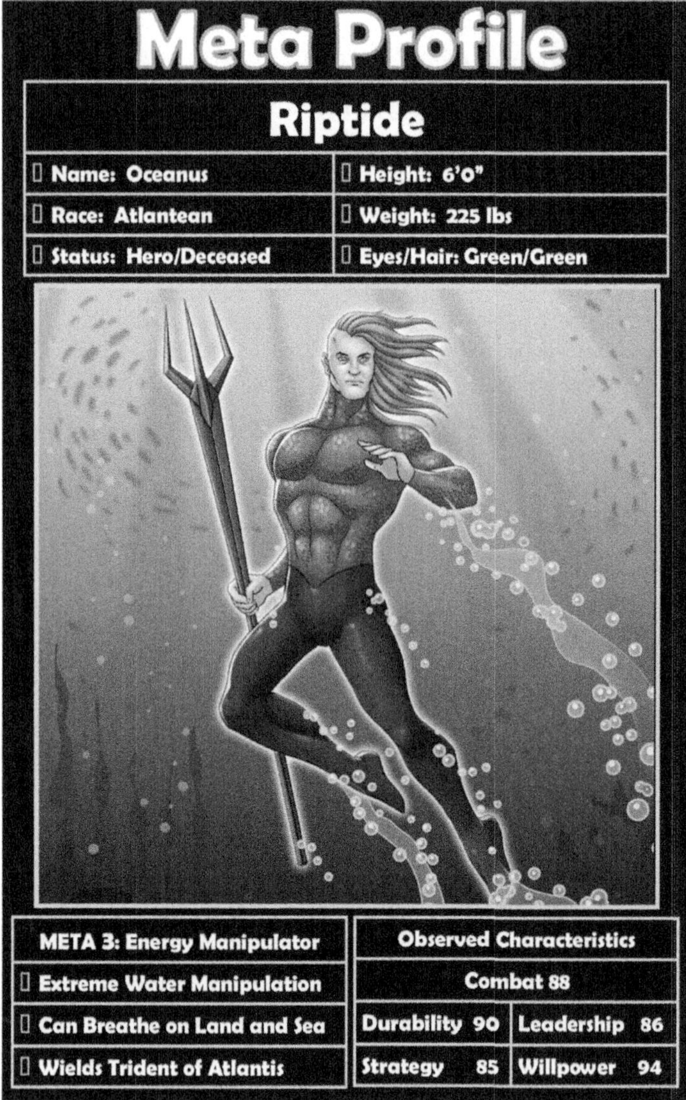
Meta Profile
Riptide
Name: Oceanus
Height: 6'0"
Race: Atlantean
Weight: 225 lbs
Status: Hero/Deceased
Eyes/Hair: Green/Green
META 3: Energy Manipulator
Extreme Water Manipulation
Can Breathe on Land and Sea
Wields Trident of Atlantis
Observed Characteristics
Combat 88
Durability 90
Leadership 86
Strategy 85
Willpower 94

EPILOGUE

I PUT IT ALL TOGETHER

"Elliott?" comes a familiar voice. "Are you okay?"

Who's calling me? I blink my eyes a few times and then open them to see a bunch of concerned faces looking down at me. I see Mom… and then… Dad. They're back! And on the other side is… Shadow Hawk!

"Y-You're okay!" I say, reaching out to him.

"I am," Shadow Hawk says, stepping forward and putting his hand on my shoulder. "And so are you, kid."

Then, I look around and see my all-too-familiar surroundings. "I'm in the Medi-wing again, aren't I?"

"We're thinking of renaming it the Epic-wing," Mom jokes with a smile. "You know, it would be great to come home and not find you here for once."

"Did you catch the Freaks of Nature?" I ask, trying to sit up. But then I feel a dull pain on my left side and look down to find my ribs wrapped in bandages.

"Easy, son," Dad says, helping to lower me back down. "You fractured three ribs. And yes, we caught the Freaks of Nature. It took a lot longer than we expected because they increased their ranks, but we got them all."

"That's great," I say, feeling my left side which is tender to the touch. No wonder I was in so much pain. Although I can't really remember how it happened.

"I filled everyone in while you were recovering," Shadow Hawk says. "I know they're proud of you for taking on Meta-Man."

Meta-Man! Suddenly, everything comes back to me. Meta-Man. Max Mayhem Two. The Protectors of the Planet. "The Black Crow!" I blurt out. "He used Max Mayhem's sword on Meta-Man. He saved us all. But is he…?"

"Yes, unfortunately," Shadow Hawk says, lowering his head. "That was his final act. Somehow, despite his deteriorating condition, he still had the strength to do what needed to be done. We all owe him our lives. I'll never know a greater man… or hero."

"I'm so sorry," I say.

"Thanks," Shadow Hawk says, looking me in the eyes. "But I owe you an apology. I should have told you I was Sparrow. I suppose I was trying to protect you, just like the Black Crow protected me. That's why I faked my own death at the nursing home. I knew if Meta-Man thought I was dead, he would leave you alone to kidnap the Black Crow. But I hurt you in the process and I'm deeply sorry for that."

"Hey, it's okay," I say. "I get it. Sometimes you do what you think is right to protect the people you care about. But I guess being honest is always better in the end. And that's how our team will always stay in harmony."

"You've got that right," Shadow Hawk says. "And you can count on me from here on out."

"What happened to the other Protectors?" I ask.

"The Marksman and Goldrush are okay," Shadow Hawk says. "And I found a very angry Warrior Woman a few miles away. She's the toughest lady I know. Unfortunately, Sergeant Stretch didn't make it. He was a great hero in his own right. I guess the only good to come out of this is that we're planning a real Protectors reunion to honor our friends who are no longer with us."

"Can I come with you?" I ask. "I'd like to thank them for everything they did, and it would be an honor to get to know them better."

"Of course," Shadow Hawk says, "and the honor would be all ours."

"Well, you do have some visitors here who have been waiting to see you," Mom says. "If you feel up for it?"

"My friends?" I ask. "They're here? Yes!"

"They waited all day," Dad says, opening the door. "Come on in, guys. But remember, he's still recovering."

Suddenly, Dog-Gone and my friends come rushing

through the door, followed by Grace. Dog-Gone reaches me first but Dad holds him back so he doesn't jump up on my bed.

"Whoa, boy," Dad says. "Take it easy. He's got ribs to heal."

I reach down to pet Dog-Gone who licks my hand.

"You wouldn't believe what he got into while you were gone," Grace says. "Let's just say we're out of jelly doughnuts… again."

"Oh, no," I say, looking at Dog-Gone.

"Not to mention disinfectant," Grace adds, rolling her eyes. "For the mess."

"I'm glad you're okay, Epic," Selfie says with a smile. "But don't ever run off like that again. Got it?"

I nod in agreement. Believe me, that was the last thing I wanted to do, but it was the only way I could get Max Mayhem Two to help us. I didn't know it would spiral out of control like that. And speaking of spiraling out of control, I still have to tell them that Max Mayhem Two was a clone—and there are at least ten others! But then I remember something else.

Terrog's ring!

It's still out there somewhere. I just hope we find it before Max Mayhem's clone does.

"Well, we'll give you some time to hang out with your friends," Dad says. "Besides, I'm heading to Lockdown to help TechnocRat repair the damage. And you know how irritable he'll get if I'm late."

"And I need to track down the escapees," Mom says.

That's right! Lockdown!

"How many villains got out?" I ask, dreading the answer. I only wish I could have stopped Meta-Man sooner.

"A lot," Mom says, "but don't worry about it now. You need to rest. We'll check in on you later."

Then, my parents exit.

"Are you guys hungry?" Shadow Hawk asks.

"Famished!" Pinball answers. Then, he looks at me and says, "Shadow Hawk promised to make us all cheeseburger funnel cakes. I'm finally gonna cash in!"

"That sounds gross," Skunk Girl says.

"Your loss," Pinball says. "More for me!"

"Would you like one, kid?" Shadow Hawk asks.

"Um, no thank you," I say. But then I get a sudden craving. "Shadow Hawk?"

"What's up?" he asks, stopping at the door.

"Well," I say, "I'd really love one of your peanut butter and banana sandwiches. You know, if that's okay?"

"You got it, kid," Shadow Hawk says with a wink. "I'm on the case."

"So, tell us about the whole Meta-Man mystery," Night Owl says to me. "What really happened out there?"

"Oh, it's a long story," I say, looking over at Shadow Hawk who is still standing at the door. I want to tell them everything, but I'm not really sure how he feels about me telling his story.

But then Shadow Hawk says, "He's right. It is a long story, but it's a good one. And it all started with Epic Zero figuring out that I was Sparrow. Isn't that right, Epic Zero?"

"Yeah," I say with a smile. "That's right."

"Then you should tell them everything," he says. "And don't leave out any of the good parts. I'll be right back with your food." And then he winks again and exits.

As Shadow Hawk leaves I smile.

And then I tell the team everything.

Epic Zero 9: Tales of a Souled-Out Superhero

ONE

I BOWL A GUTTER BALL

It feels great to be in my costume again.

Trust me when I tell you there's only so much TV a kid can watch, especially when the shows keep getting interrupted by Meta Monitor alerts. Thankfully, now that my ribs are fully healed, I'm back in business!

So, look out creeps!

And speaking of creeps, there's plenty of them around after the whole Meta-Man fiasco. That alien psycho demolished Lockdown in his search for Max Mayhem, freeing hundreds of dangerous Meta villains. We finally stopped him with the help of the Protectors of the Planet, but not before he fractured three of my ribs. Honestly, I would have happily fractured *all* of my ribs if it meant getting rid of that monster.

The good news is that the Freedom Force recaptured most of the escapees, but a few of them are still on the loose. That's why Dad and I are here.

We're standing outside a large, rundown warehouse on the outskirts of town. With its boarded-up windows and tinted glass door, you'd think it was empty inside. But we know better because we traced one of the Lockdown fugitives to this exact location. His name is Airstream, a Meta 3 Energy Manipulator who can control air currents.

All we need to do now is reel him in.

The entrance is down a flight of steep, concrete stairs, and there's a tattered sign on the door that reads: *Strike It Rich Bowling. Get Yourself Out of the Gutter. No children allowed.*

Well, that's a first. I don't think I've ever seen a bowling alley that banned kids before. But Dad said I shouldn't be surprised. After all, this is no ordinary bowling alley—it's a secret meeting place for bad guys.

"Put this on," Dad says, handing me a tan trench coat and matching fedora hat. "This place is full of shady characters. If anyone recognizes us there could be trouble. Tuck your cape inside your belt so it doesn't flare out and let me do all the talking. The last thing we need is for someone to notice you're just a kid."

"Got it," I say, putting on the coat and hat. "And mum's the word." I pretend to lock my mouth shut and throw away the key.

"Great," Dad says, putting on his own hat and coat.

"Now let's go in there and grab Airstream."

I nod in agreement, but as soon as I take my first step down the steep stairs, I hesitate. For some reason, I feel uneasy. I mean, I know I'm rusty and all, but I don't think that's it. It's only when I see Dad standing by the door that it hits me.

The entrance is way below ground.

Suddenly, I flash back to all of my other underground missions. Like the time I chased Alligazer into the sewer system. Or when I dropped into the 13th Dimension with Aries to rescue Wind Walker. I don't know why, but underground missions and I just don't mix.

"Are you okay?" Dad asks. "Do you want to wait here outside?"

"N-No," I say, my voice cracking. "I'm good."

I take a deep breath and head down the stairs.

As soon as Dad opens the door my senses go on overload. Between the dim lighting, the CRASH of bowling balls against pins, and the putrid, antiseptic smell, I feel a little disoriented. But I shake it off and follow Dad across the dingy, blue carpet to the front desk where a short, bald man with a long, black beard works the cash register. Behind him are dozens of bowling lanes occupied by rough-looking customers in street clothes.

"Excuse me, sir," Dad says, "we're looking for someone who—"

"Yeah, ain't we all?" the man interjects gruffly. Then, he looks us up and down and says, "You fellas gonna bowl in those getups?"

"Um, no," Dad says. "We're not here to bowl. We're looking for—"

"Look, I don't want no trouble," the man interrupts again, pointing at us with a stubby finger. "I'm not gonna have my joint busted up by masked hooligans like you. If you're here to bowl then bowl. If not, take a hike."

Well, this is going swimmingly.

I take a step back to the exit but Dad just stands there and says, "Give us a lane."

"Good choice," the man says, pushing buttons on his console. "Lane thirteen. Pay when you're done. The wings are half off when you buy a large pitcher of beer."

"Great," Dad says, starting to walk off.

"Hey, hold on there, Superman," the man says, looking down at Dad's feet. "No way you're scuffing up my lanes with those boots. You gotta rent bowling shoes."

"Right," Dad says, removing his red boots and putting them on the counter. "Give me a size fourteen." And then he puts his hand on my shoulder before I can speak and says, "And my partner here needs a size seven. An adult size seven."

"Comin' up," the man says, and then he reaches down and places two pairs of hideous brown-and-green bowling shoes on the counter.

What is it with bowling shoes anyway? Are they made this ugly on purpose so no one steals them? I turn in my boots and take my pair, but as we walk towards our lane I whisper, "Are we really bowling right now?"

"No," Dad whispers back, "but now isn't the time to make a scene. Even though no one's in costume, I already recognize two Meta villains in here. Slime-Wave is on lane four and Cat's Paw is on lane twenty."

I take a seat in our lane and lean back to get a clear view of lane four. That's when I spot a skinny man with greasy, blond hair picking up a neon-green ball. Yep, even without his costume, I recognize Slime-Wave. He's a Meta 1 Energy Manipulator who projects slime from his nose. Then, I lean forward and see a woman to our right with red, spikey hair and super-long fingernails bowling with cat-like quickness. Well, there's no doubt about it, that's Cat's Paw. She's a Meta 2 with Super-Speed.

"Where's Airstream?" I ask.

"I don't know," Dad says, tying his bowling shoes. "Let's split up and do some reconnaissance. I'll go left and you go right. But if you spot him don't do anything without me. Remember, Airstream is extremely dangerous."

"Got it," I say, tightening the way-too-long laces on my bowling shoes. But as soon as I stand up my feet slide on the carpet and I nearly topple over. Awesome. Gotta love the slippery soles of these ridiculous clown shoes.

I head over to the ball rack and pretend to examine some balls while studying the bowlers. Slime-Wave was easy to pick out of a crowd, but Airstream isn't as distinctive. From what I remember from his profile, he has brown hair, brown eyes, and a medium build. But that could describe a million people.

I kneel to look at a purple ball with orange flames when I think I spot him. He's on lane six just about to bowl. I watch him closely, looking for any sign that I've got my man. Then, he releases the ball and it veers sharply left, rolling straight for the gutter. Except, the next thing I know, the man waves his hand and the ball suddenly changes direction landing a perfect strike!

Bingo! That's got to be Airstream!

Wow. I guess villains cheat at everything—including bowling.

I try to get Dad's attention, but he's on the other side of the alley and I don't want to make a scene. I look back at Airstream who is now standing at the ball return looking my way! Uh oh, does he recognize me?

I know Dad told me not to do anything without him, but I'm pretty sure he wouldn't want Airstream to get away. And if I wave or yell to call Dad over it'll definitely tip Airstream off. So, it looks like I need to go solo.

I stand up and head over to his lane.

"Hey, nice strike," I say, stopping on the platform. "But does it really count if you had to use your Meta powers to get it?"

"Who are you?" Airstream asks, looking at me funny.

I couldn't have asked for a better segue. So, I throw off my hat and trench coat and say, "I'm—"

"—Epic Zebra!" comes a deep voice from behind.

Huh? I spin around to find a very large, muscular man staring down at me with a big, goofy smile on his face. And in his giant mitts are three pitchers of beer and three platters of chicken wings.

"You're Epic Zebra," he repeats. "You were on the news a while back."

"Well, yeah, I was," I say, thinking back to my nightmare of an interview on the CNC Morning Newsflash. "But my name isn't really—"

"Didn't you read the sign?" the large man interjects. "No children allowed. This is an adult establishment."

"Well, yes," I say. "But—"

"Hang on," the large man adds, his brow furrowing. "Aren't you a member of the Freedom Force?"

"Well, yes again," I say, standing up a little taller. "As a matter of fact, I am. And I'm here to—"

"Wait, *he's* on the Freedom Force?" Airstream says, cutting me off. "You're kidding, right?"

"Well, no," I say. "And I don't know why you find that so surprising. I might be a kid, but—"

"Scram, kid," the large man says brushing past me and handing Airstream the wings. "Let us bowl in peace. Besides, we've got plans to make."

"The only things you'll be making," comes a voice from behind me, "are your prison beds when we return you to Lockdown."

"Captain Justice!" Airstream says, his eyes bugging

out of his head.

"The one and only," Dad says. "And I see you've met my colleague, Epic Zero." Then, Dad glares at me and whispers, "Who should have stuck to our agreement."

"Sorry," I say sheepishly.

"We'll talk later," Dad whispers. Then, he says to the crooks, "But it's our lucky day because we have our very own two for one special. Not only did we find Airstream, but we've also found another Lockdown escapee. Isn't that right, Pulverizer?"

Pulverizer? That big guy is Pulverizer? No wonder his biceps are bigger than his head. And he's got Meta 2 Super-Strength!

"That's right, Captain," Pulverizer says. "Except, we're not going back to Lockdown. So, let's celebrate. This round is on you!"

The next thing I know, Pulverizer throws the pitchers of beer right in Dad's face. But that's not all, because Airstream flicks his wrists, lifts several bowling balls into the air, and then sends them straight at me!

I duck and they fly over my head, CRASHING through the wall behind me. But when I look back, I see one more! And it's coming so fast I can't avoid it!

UGH! I grunt as it nails me in the left thigh! Ouch, that really hurt! I'm lucky it didn't hit me in the ribs. But as soon as I step towards Airstream my whole leg feels numb and I topple to the ground.

"Epic Zero!" Dad calls out.

"Look out!" I yell as Pulverizer rears back his giant fist. He's gonna pummel Dad!

I focus fast and bathe Pulverizer with my negation power right as his fist connects with Dad's jaw.

CRACK!

"My hand!" Pulverizer screams as he bends over in pain. "Your face broke my hand!"

"Sorry, Pulverizer," Dad says with a wink. "I guess that was a real jaw breaker." And then Dad slugs Pulverizer so hard the villain flies down the lane and SMASHES into the pins, leaving only the two far ones standing.

"I hate those 7-10 splits," Dad says. Then, he turns to Airstream and says, "Care to help me pick up a spare?"

"I'm out of here!" Airstream says, raising his arms and taking off into the air.

"Hey, you didn't pay!" the owner yells as Airstream flies over his head.

I try standing but my leg still feels dead. So, I focus my concentration again and send my negation powers in Airstream's direction. Suddenly, Airstream loses altitude and SMASHES headfirst through the tinted glass door.

He doesn't get back up.

"I knew you guys were trouble!" the owner yells. "You're gonna pay for this!"

Dad collects Pulverizer and when he returns I realize we're surrounded by dozens of other bad guys, including

Slime-Wave and Cat's Paw! I swallow hard. This is about to get ugly—real ugly.

"Our apologies," Dad says, hoisting an unconscious Pulverizer over his shoulder, "but these men are escaped criminals. Now, I'll happily pay for the repairs, but if you're referring to some other kind of payment then I advise everyone to back up before you all end up joining these two at Lockdown."

"Okay, relax, boy scout," the owner says, his hands in the air. "Give them some space!" he yells to the crowd.

"Let's go, Epic Zero," Dad says.

He helps me up and I hobble along behind him when I remember something. I limp over to the front desk, grab our boots, and head for the exit.

"Hey, keep the shoes," the owner says graciously.

"Gee, thanks," I say. "We'll cherish them."

Then, Dad scoops up Airstream with his other arm and we head out in our brand-new bowling shoes.

Meta Profile
The Freedom Force
Captain Justice
Class: Super-Strength
Meta :
Ms. Understood
Class: Psychic
Meta :
Glory Girl
Class: Flight
Meta :
Shadow Hawk
Class: None
Meta :
Epic Zero
Class: Meta Manipulator
Meta :
TechnocRat
Class: Super-Intellect
Meta :
Blue Bolt
Class: Super-Speed
Meta :
Master Mime
Class: Magic
Meta :
Makeshift
Class: Energy Manipulator
Meta :

TWO

I HATE SCARY MOVIES

After we dropped Airstream and Pulverizer at Lockdown, I received my *own* form of punishment.

Dad lectured me the whole ride home about how I should have waited for him before approaching Airstream. I didn't want to hear it, but I knew he was right. And now I'm so sore I can hardly move.

Not only is my left thigh still smarting after getting nailed with that bowling ball, but my ribs are also a little tender. Fortunately, TechnocRat checked me out in the Medi-wing and nothing is broken. But I do have an impressive bowling-ball-sized welt on my thigh to commemorate the occasion, complete with the outlines of three finger holes.

Awesome.

Since we finished late and missed dinner, I decided to raid the Galley cupboard for a bowl of Frosted Letter-Bites cereal. They're shaped like letters of the alphabet and topped with frosting. I know they aren't the healthiest snack in the world, but hey, after a hard day's work sometimes you've gotta treat yourself.

I pour the milk and sit down when I feel something brush my leg under the table. Great, an invisible Dog-Gone is lurking down there, just waiting to strike. I hate it when he's in stealth mode like this. Sometimes I'll forget he's even there, which is exactly what he wants. And if I get up to get something he'll pounce on my food and the beast will feast.

But not this time. This bowl of Frosted Letter-Bites is all mine and I'm gonna savor each bite. I load up my spoon when—

"Does Mom know you're eating that?" comes a snarky, all-too-familiar voice.

"No," I say, lowering my spoon, "she doesn't."

"Well, I don't think she'd approve," Grace says, entering the Galley and leaning against the counter. "In case you forgot, she doesn't like us eating junk like that, especially for dinner. Besides, that's Makeshift's cereal. Did you ask him if you could have some?"

"Well, no," I say, super-annoyed. "But he eats our stuff all the time. I'm sure he won't care."

"There you go again," Grace says, shaking her head.

"Not thinking about the needs or feelings of other people. No wonder your picture is in the dictionary next to the word 'selfish.'"

"*My* picture?" I say, now outraged. "What are you talking about? Unlike you, I think about other people all the time. Weren't you the one who forgot to return TechnocRat's Future Vision goggles?"

"I gave them back," Grace says, buffing her nails. "I just wanted to see what I'd look like in twenty years."

"Well, I'm shocked the goggles didn't break," I say.

"That's it," Grace says, standing up. "I'm telling Mom what you're eating."

"Go for it," I say, lifting my spoon. I just want to take a freaking bite.

"Don't worry," Grace says. "I will."

"You'll what?" Mom asks, rounding the corner with several bags of groceries floating in the air behind her. She lines them up with her mind and places them gently on the counter. Then, she sees me and says, "Elliott, what in the world are you eating?"

"Holy cow!" I say, dropping my spoon. "Can't a kid eat a bowl of cereal around here?"

"Didn't you have dinner?" Mom asks. "I left you a plate of meatloaf in the refrigerator."

"How was I supposed to know that?" I say.

"I always make you a plate if you miss dinner," Mom says, opening the refrigerator. "You know that."

"Well, I forgot, okay?" I say, frustrated. "It's been a

while since I went on a mission, remember?"

"I hear you," Mom says, warming up my plate in the microwave. "But that's not a healthy choice for a growing superhero like you."

Are you kidding me? I'm just trying to eat some cereal, is that so bad? Then, I look down to see a group of Frosted Letter-Bites floating together in the milk spelling the word: N-E-V-E-R.

Well, that's ironic since I'm clearly N-E-V-E-R going to eat this bowl of cereal. Then, the microwave BEEPS and Mom opens it with her mind. Before I can react she mind-lifts my cereal bowl off the table and replaces it with the plate of meatloaf. As my bowl floats away, I see Grace wearing the biggest I-told-you-so smile in the history of humankind.

"Enjoy your meatloaf," Grace says smugly.

"Oh, I will," I say. "Just look out for leftovers in your boots."

"You wouldn't dare!" Grace says.

"I wouldn't be so sure of that," I say.

"Enough bickering, you two," Mom says. "Elliott, you still have homework to do. Please take care of it after dinner."

"C'mon, Mom," I say, "I was out with Dad all afternoon. Can I just do it tomorrow?"

"What's that old saying?" Grace pipes in. "Don't put off until tomorrow what you can do today."

"Really?" I say. "I thought it was 'don't stick your

nose in other people's business.'"

"I said *enough*," Mom says. "But your sister is right, we don't know what might come up tomorrow, so you should do it tonight."

I look at Grace who sticks out her tongue.

Well, it's been a great night. First I'm down a bowl of cereal and now I'm stuck doing algebra problems.

BEEP! BEEP! BEEP!

Speaking of problems.

"What is that noise?" Mom says, looking around.

"It's my Next Gen transmitter watch," I say, looking at my wrist.

<Selfie: Epic, we're watching a scary movie 2-night. Wanna come?>

Yes! Talk about great timing. This might be the get-out-of-jail-free card I was hoping for. Plus, I haven't seen my friends for a while because of my rib injury.

"What's going on?" Grace asks.

But as she tries looking at my watch, I cover the screen. I'd love to tell them I have a mission to go on, but that won't work since Next Gen is still under the watchful eye of the Freedom Force. Plus, Mom's a Psychic so I might as well tell the truth.

"The gang is watching a movie tonight," I say. "Can I go?"

"What kind of a movie?" Grace asks.

"What's the difference?" I say. "And I'm asking Mom, not you."

"Okay, I'll ask then," Mom says. "What kind of a movie is it?"

Drat. "According to Selfie," I say, "it's, um, a scary movie."

"A scary movie?" Grace repeats with a chuckle. "You can't handle scary movies. You'll have nightmares for weeks."

"I will not!" I say. "That was years ago."

"Says the kid who ran out of the room five minutes into Night of the Living Bread," Grace says. "And that was an animated movie!"

"Look, that sourdough was pure evil and you know it!" I say. Then, I turn to Mom and plead, "Can I see my friends, Mom? Please? I mean, I've been stuck here for weeks waiting for my ribs to heal."

Mom stares at me with her I'm-about-to-say-no face, but then she relaxes her expression. "What time will you be back?"

"Seriously?" Grace says. "Are you really letting him go? What about his homework?"

"No later than nine," I say. "I promise."

"Alright," Mom says. "But please finish your meatloaf first. Deal?"

"Deal!" I say.

I text Selfie I'm coming and then stuff my face. When I'm finished, I clear my dish, hug Mom, and then blow Grace a kiss as I skip off to the Hangar.

***

I take a Freedom Ferry to the Hangout and park in the woods behind Selfie's house. I feel kind of bad leaving Dog-Gone behind, but he's pretty much the worst movie companion of all time. He'll settle in nice and quiet, and by the time the previews end, you'll realize he's eaten all of your popcorn. So, tonight I'm going Dog-Gone-free.

Although I didn't want to admit it, Grace is right, I really do hate scary movies. I know they're fake and all, but they completely freak me out. Maybe it's the dumb decisions the characters make, like 'hey, what's that strange noise outside my window at 4 am? I should investigate.' Or maybe it's the creepy background music that always ratchets up right when something bad is going to happen. Whatever it is, scary movies make me anxious.

And don't I have enough anxiety in my life already?

But I'm willing to put myself through this to see my friends. I mean, I haven't seen the team in weeks, so it'll be nice to hang out together—especially with Selfie.

As I approach the treehouse, I hear—

"Hey, Epic! I'm glad you made it."

"Same here," I say, looking up at Selfie who is leaning over the railing. It's really great to see her again, even though my stomach gets butterflies every time I do. I smile and start climbing the ladder.

"Are you okay?" she asks. "It looked like you were

limping across the lawn. Are you sure you're totally healed?"

"Oh, yeah," I say, reaching the platform. "I just got hit in the leg with a bowling ball, that's all. You know, the usual stuff."

"Right," she says. "Well, I guess that answers my second question." Then, she looks down at my feet.

As I follow her gaze, my eyes land on my feet and I feel my face go flush. I can't believe it! I'm still wearing those stupid bowling shoes! Well, that's embarrassing.

"You're making quite the fashion statement," Night Owl says.

"Hey," Skunk Girl says. "I bet if you bowled Pinball, you couldn't miss. You'd get a strike every time."

"Well, aren't you just hilarious," Pinball says, absently rubbing his round tummy. "Can we just watch the movie already? I've got to be home by nine. I have an orthodontist appointment in the morning."

"Okay, everyone chill," Selfie says, rolling over a cart with a TV on it. "Take a seat by the snacks and I'll get this started."

Snacks? I look over and see a table with boxes of popcorn on it. Yep, good thing I didn't bring Dog-Gone.

"Um, what movie are we watching anyway?" I ask as I take a seat on the floor.

"It's called Zombie Buffet," Skunk Girl says enthusiastically. "It's got an awesome tagline."

"Oh, cool," I say. "What is it?"

"You'll never want to eat again," she says dramatically.

"Well, that's appetizing," I say, my voice cracking. "I assume it's animated, right?"

"Animated?" Skunk Girl says, looking at me funny. "No, it's not… Wait a minute, you're not scared, are you?"

"What, me? No way," I say with a way-too-nervous-sounding laugh. "Are you kidding? Me? Scared?"

"Let me squeeze in here," Selfie says, sitting down between me and Skunk Girl.

Great, just what I need. I was hoping to close my eyes through the terrifying parts, but now I'll have to watch the whole thing. The last thing I want is for Selfie to think I'm a complete goober.

"Did everyone get a snack?" Selfie asks, holding up her box of popcorn. "Epic, where's yours?"

I look at the table but all of the boxes are gone. What happened to mine? Then, I hear CRUNCHING behind me, and when I turn I see Pinball stuffing his hands into two boxes at once.

"Hey, you stole my popcorn!" I say.

"I did?" Pinball says. "Oh, sorry. Here." Then, he licks his fingers and offers me one of the boxes.

"Um, no, you keep it," I say.

"Gee, thanks!" Pinball says, munching away.

Just. Freaking. Wonderful.

Now, I not only have to watch the movie, but I get

to hear Pinball scarfing down my popcorn.

Maybe I should have stayed on the Waystation.

"Here, you can share with me," Selfie says, offering me her box.

But then again, maybe not.

"Now, let's get scared out of our minds," Selfie says, clicking the remote control.

Okay, here we go. I take a deep breath and exhale as the title, Zombie Buffet, pops onto the screen. Then comes the creepy background music. I reach into the popcorn box when my hand bumps into Selfie's hand.

"Sorry," I whisper, looking at Selfie.

"It's okay," she whispers back with a smile.

OOOOOOOOOOOOOOOOOO!

Wow, the volume is really loud. But when I look back at the screen the camera is focused on two people having a peaceful meal in a restaurant. There's not a zombie in sight.

OOOOOOOOOOOOOOOOOO!

Okay, that was even louder. But this time I was watching the movie and it didn't seem to come from there. I look at the others who are totally engrossed in the movie.

That's weird. Am I the only one who—

Suddenly, the treehouse SHAKES!

"Whoa!" Pinball says. "I didn't know this movie was 3D. Do you have 3D glasses?"

"That's not the movie, you dufus," Night Owl says,

looking around. "Something just shook the Hangout."

"Um, something like what?" Pinball asks.

"Don't be ridiculous," Skunk Girl says, standing up and walking to the edge of the platform. Then, she looks over the edge and says, "You guys are just being—AHHHH!"

"What?" Night Owl asks. "What is it?"

Skunk Girl turns and her face is as white as a ghost.

"What's going on?" Selfie asks.

"Th-There's a… a…," Skunk Girl stammers.

"A what?" Pinball asks. "What is it?"

"A-A monster!" Skunk Girl blurts out. "There's a monster climbing up the ladder!"

Meta Profile
Next Gen
Epic Zero
Dog-Gone
Night Owl
Class: Meta Manipulator
Meta :
Class: Meta-Morph
Meta :
Class: Energy Manipulator
Meta :
Skunk Girl
Selfie
Pinball
Class: Energy Manipulator
Meta :
Class: Magic
Meta :
Class: Meta-Morph
Meta :

THREE

I MAKE A BIG MISTAKE

That Skunk Girl has quite the sense of humor.

I mean, just a few seconds ago we were watching a horror movie called Zombie Buffet when we heard strange noises coming from outside. Then, something shook the Hangout pretty hard. And now, after going to investigate, Skunk Girl claims there's a real-life monster climbing up the treehouse ladder.

I'll tell you, that Skunk Girl is a real prankster. I'm not sure how she made those noises and shook the Hangout, but I'm not falling for it. Nope, not this time.

Except, either she's a really good actor or that look of sheer terror on her face is real.

"Didn't you hear me?" Skunk Girl yells. "Run!"

Suddenly, a purple, hairy hand lands on the platform and everyone SCREAMS.

"Quick!" Night Owl yells. "Knock over the ladder!"

"Too late!" Pinball cries, as his popcorn goes flying.

Then, a gigantic figure leaps onto the platform with a THUD, bouncing us off the floor. As I scramble to my feet, I take in the monstrosity before us. Whoever he is, he's absolutely huge—with thick, rounded shoulders and a purple, fur-covered body. He almost looks like a massive gorilla, except when I look into his purple eyes, I notice his vacant expression, like he's not all there.

Yet, for some reason, he looks vaguely familiar. I feel like I should know him, but I can't figure out why. And then I notice a strange, orange glow coming off his body.

What's that about?

But instead of attacking, the monolith stands at the edge of the platform, looking at each of us in turn until his intense gaze lands on me! It's like he's evaluating me.

Then, it hits me where I've seen him before. But… that's impossible. Of course, I didn't recognize him because he's not supposed to be here.

He's supposed to be… dead!

"You okay, Epic Zero?" Night Owl asks.

Not really. But right now, I'm so stunned I can't even find the words to respond. I mean, the last time I saw the villain standing before me, he was vaporized at Lockdown in the battle between Meta-Taker and the Skelton High Commander!

So, how is he here?

"Well, I'll take charge then," Night Owl says, stepping forward. "And I think it's time we returned this grape ape to the zoo."

"W-Wait!" I blurt out. "I mean, don't get too close. I don't know what's going on here, but that's no zoo animal. Th-That's the Berserker. And he was a Meta 3 Strong-man with incredible strength."

"Um, why are you speaking in the past tense?" Selfie asks. "He's standing right here, you know?"

"Because you don't understand," I say. "He died!"

"Died?" Pinball says. "Well, if he's dead then I'm a delicate flower."

I look back at the Berserker, who furrows his brow and bellows, "MMEETTAA PPOOWWEERR!"

Um, what? Meta power?

And then he steps towards me in an abrupt, herky-jerky manner. What's wrong with him? The way he's moving, it's almost like he's a… a… zombie?

"Okay, let's call this a wrap!" Night Owl says, stepping in front of me. Then, she grabs a shadow from the floor and wraps the Berserker from head-to-toe in a shadow-net.

But clearly, it's not going to be that easy because the Berserker flexes and the shadow-net shatters like it was nothing! Then, the Berserker backhands Night Owl who SMASHES into the wall and lands on the floor.

"Night Owl!" I call out, but she doesn't answer.

And when I look back, the Berserker is still lumbering towards me!

"Hey, back off!" I yell.

"I've got it," Skunk Girl says, stepping in front of me to face the Berserker. "Okay, slow poke, get ready to be sick to your stomach!" Then, she unleashes a barrage of stink fumes right in the Berserker's face.

But the Berserker lumbers through it and screeches, "MMEETTAA PPOOWWEERR!"

Even though I'm standing behind her, Skunk Girl's putrid odor reaches my nostrils and I gag, but it's having no effect on the Berserker at all. And then, with shocking speed, he reaches out and grabs Skunk Girl by the wrist. She screams as her body suddenly lights up with the same orange glow that's surrounding the Berserker!

"Skunk Girl!" Pinball yells.

The next thing I know, Skunk Girl's orange glow fades as the Berserker's orange glow intensifies. And when he releases her, she drops to her knees. What just happened? I mean, as far as I'm aware, the only Meta power the Berserker had was Super-Strength.

"M-My powers," Skunk Girl mutters. "I-I can't feel my powers."

"Time to exit!" Pinball says, and then he bounds across the platform, scoops up Skunk Girl, and bounces out of the Hangout.

"MMOORREE MMEETTAA PPOOWWEERR!" the Berserker cries.

More Meta power? Holy cow! I think I know what's going on. Somehow, the Berserker absorbed Skunk Girl's Meta power. But how?

And then I realize something else. I have the most Meta power out of all of us. Is that why he's so focused on me? Am I letting out some kind of a Meta signal he can read? If so, I've got to draw him away from here before someone else gets hurt. But before I can move—

"My turn," Selfie says, stepping in front of me and raising her magic phone. "How about a big smile?"

"Selfie, no!" I call out.

But it's too late! All I can do is turn away as Selfie pushes the button on her phone which emits a bright, hypnotic flash. It takes a few seconds for my vision to come back, but when it does my worst nightmare is realized, because the Berserker is far from hypnotized—and he's holding both of Selfie's arms!

"Aaaah!" Selfie cries. "Epic! Help!"

"MMEETTAA PPOOWWEERR!"

"Selfie!" I yell. "Let her go!"

I've got to act fast before he does to Selfie whatever it was he did to Skunk Girl—or worse! So, I concentrate hard and throw all of my negation power at the Berserker. There, that ought to do the trick. But instead of simply making his Meta powers disappear, to my surprise, the Berserker himself disappears—taking Selfie with him!

Then, I hear CLATTERING at my feet, and when I look down, I see Selfie's phone spinning on the floor.

OMG! She's… gone!

"Selfie?" I call out at the top of my lungs. "Selfie, where are you? Selfie?"

But there's no answer.

I look at my hands in disbelief. What did I just do? I mean, my powers have never done that before. They only duplicate or negate powers, they don't make people disappear.

Suddenly, a wave of nausea comes over me and it feels like I was punched in the gut. If something bad happened to her because of me, I'll never forgive myself.

But what if it wasn't me?

I mean, could the Berserker have teleported? But if he did, how? He didn't have that kind of power before. But then again, he didn't have the ability to wipe out Skunk Girl's powers before either.

I spot Selfie's phone out of the corner of my eye and pick it up when—

"Epic Zero?" comes Night Owl's weak voice from behind me. "I-I blacked out. What happened?"

I wish I knew, but I can only look at her helplessly and say, "I have no idea."

***

All I feel is a crushing sense of guilt.

Needless to say, I barely managed to fly us back to the Waystation 2.0 without having a total breakdown. I barely talked the whole flight because all I could think about was Selfie. We looked everywhere and still couldn't find her. Where did she go? What did I do?

And poor Skunk Girl. We're hoping what happened to her is temporary, but she still hasn't gotten her powers back. Probably for the first time ever, she didn't say much either.

The only good news was finding Mom waiting for us in the Hangar. I don't know if it was mother's intuition or her Psychic powers, but whatever it was, I sure was glad to see her. I didn't even have to say anything. She just put her arm around my shoulder and led us to the Galley where she had some hot cocoa waiting for us.

When the rest of the Freedom Force arrived, I explained everything that happened—including my big mistake. Unfortunately, no one had any ideas about how the Berserker came back to life or what happened to Selfie. So, basically, we're still at square one.

Just then, I feel a warm tongue licking my fingers.

"No, Dog-Gone," I say, pulling my hand away. "No cocoa for you."

Dog-Gone whimpers and slinks away.

Okay, maybe I was a little harsh, but I have a lot on my mind. I can't believe Selfie is gone. I mean, everything felt normal when I used my powers on the Berserker, so why did it produce such a different result? I look at Selfie's phone sitting on the table and crumple inside.

"Well, I checked the Meta Monitor," Dad says,

returning to the Galley after going upstairs. "There weren't any signals from the Berserker at all. Are you sure that's who it was?"

"I'm positive," I say. "And it wasn't just me. We all saw him. He was like a zombie. A Meta zombie."

"That's for sure," Pinball says, sucking down his hot cocoa which leaves a chocolate mustache. "And I'll never forget him. Can I get a refill?"

"Of course," Mom says, pouring him another mugful. Then, she picks up Skunk Girl's mug and gently puts a hand on her shoulder. "Skunk Girl, are you sure you don't want any?"

"No thanks," Skunk Girl says, forcing a smile. "I mean, I still don't know what happened to my powers, but I'd give them up just to have Selfie back again."

"This has been a big shock for you all," Mom says, rubbing Skunk Girl's back, "but you're safe now. And we'll do everything we can to find Selfie."

I hear the optimism in Mom's voice, but what if we can't find Selfie? What if she's gone forever? I take a deep breath and exhale. Ugh, this is the lowest point of my entire life.

"I realize this may not be the best time for this," TechnocRat says, scampering up Skunk Girl's chair, "but the other big mystery is how the Berserker was able to cancel your powers and whether the effect is temporary or permanent. If you're willing, I'd love to run some analysis on you to see if there is any trace of that strange, orange glow you described. It might reveal some important information that will help us get to the bottom of this mystery."

"Yeah, sure," Skunk Girl says. "I'll do whatever it takes, especially if it helps get our friend back."

"Night Owl and I will come too," Pinball says. "We're a team and teams stick together."

"Thanks, Pinball," Skunk Girl says. "You know, sometimes you're alright."

"Wow, are you actually being nice?" Pinball asks, reaching out his hand to help Skunk Girl to her feet.

"Don't get used to it," Skunk Girl says. "You caught me in a weak moment."

"I would never dream of such a thing," Pinball says. "Hey, Epic Zero, do you want to tag along?"

"Um, I'll catch up with you guys in a bit," I say. "I've… got some things to check out first."

I wait until the team exits before turning to my parents and saying, "I feel like this is all my fault." Suddenly, it's like a dam of emotion bursts inside of me and I start bawling uncontrollably.

"Oh, Elliott," Mom says, hugging me tightly. "It's not your fault. I didn't want to pry, but I knew you had something weighing heavily on your mind."

"Y-Yeah," I say, as tears stream down my face. "I-I'm the one who used my powers on the Berserker and he disappeared with Selfie. Of course, it's my fault."

"Well, you don't know that for sure, son," Dad says.

"It could just be a coincidence."

"That was no coincidence," I say, wiping my eyes.

"Listen, little bro," Grace says, "I know you're upset but whether it was your fault or not, sitting around wallowing in self-pity isn't going to get Selfie back. Instead, why don't you put your energy into finding her?"

I look into Grace's blue eyes and realize she's right. I'm not the victim here and crying about it isn't going to solve anything. It's time to stop feeling sorry for myself and go find her.

I leap out of my chair.

"Where are you going?" Mom asks.

"To find Selfie!" I say.

But first I need to change out of these bowling shoes. Dog-Gone trails behind as I stop in my room for my real boots, and then I make my way down the hall and up the twenty-three steps to the Monitor Room.

"Sorry about earlier, bud," I say.

Dog-Gone yips, accepting my apology.

I hop into the command chair and pull up the Berserker's information. It's weird that Dad couldn't find any Meta signals from the Berserker. I mean, we all saw him use some kind of Meta power on Skunk Girl, so it should be traceable.

But when the Meta Monitor finally updates, I'm not looking at the Berserker's Meta Profile, but rather a very large word that's flashing on the screen over and over again. It reads: SHOW.

SHOW?

What's that supposed to mean?

Did TechnocRat update the operating system or something? Then, the word finally fades away and up pops the Berserker's profile. That's him alright—big, hairy, and downright scary. But his status still says DECEASED. So, what's going on here?

Epic Zero!

I jump out of my chair at the sound of my name and look behind me, but no one's there.

That's weird? Who called my name?

Epic Zero, we need your help!

Okay, there it is again. But this time it sounded like it came from inside my head!

That's it. I've officially gone crazy.

Epic Zero, it's Zen! We're being attacked by Meta zombies! Come quickly! Help us! Hurry!

Meta Profile

Airstream

Name: George Mitchell	Height: 5'10"
Race: Human	Weight: 190 lbs
Status: Villain/Active	Eyes/Hair: Brown/Brown

META 3: Energy Manipulator
Extreme Air Current Generation
Can Use Air Currents to Fly

Observed Characteristics			
Combat 67			
Durability	34	Leadership	45
Strategy	76	Willpower	66

FOUR

I GET SWARMED

Japan was the last place I expected to be right now.

But even with everything going on, there was no way I would ignore Zen's mental plea for help. Zen is a good friend and a member of the Rising Suns, the premier superhero team of the East. The last time I saw her, the Rising Suns were the Skelton Emperor's prisoners during his quest to take over the planet. Even though we won that fight, the consequences were awful since Tsunami, her teammate, lost his life in the process.

We can't repeat that again.

Zen's voice sounded desperate when she reached out to me, but her actual message was even more concerning. After all, she said the words 'Meta zombies,' which was just like the Berserker, except plural. He was a handful all by his lonesome, so I can't even imagine what it'll be like to face more than one.

That's why the big guns are going on this mission. Dad, Blue Bolt, Makeshift, and Master Mime are here, while Mom, Grace, Shadow Hawk, and TechnocRat stay behind to keep an eye on things and help Next Gen. And there was no way I was letting Dog-Gone in on this one.

Besides, I had to fight to get on this mission myself. Mom wanted me to rest but I finally convinced her to let me go since I was the one who Zen reached out to. Mom wasn't happy but she had no choice. Of course, who knows what she mentally told Dad.

Anyway, what counts is that I'm here. My primary goal is to help Zen and the Rising Suns, but I'm also hoping to get some answers along the way. Like, what happened to Selfie? It can't be a coincidence that Meta zombies are popping up in both the United States and Japan. The question is why?

Dad guides the Freedom Flyer beneath a bank of clouds and we get our first look at Tokyo below. It's a dense city, packed with buildings of all shapes and sizes. But what really stands out is the Tokyo Skytree, the tallest tower in the world rising over two thousand feet high. Believe me, I wish we were here for sightseeing, but unfortunately, we have far more pressing business on our hands.

"Multiple Meta signals at eight o'clock," Dad says,

reading the dashboard. "Strangely, I only see Meta signatures from the Rising Suns. Get ready team, we should have visuals in twenty seconds."

I lean forward and realize I won't have to wait twenty seconds, because I already see plumes of black smoke billowing up from the city center, along with leveled buildings, overturned cars, and cracked roadways.

But that's not all.

In the middle of the chaos, it looks like there's a small band of ants fending off hundreds of other ants. Except, I know they aren't ants—they must be Meta zombies—and they're closing in on the Rising Suns! I try counting them all but there are just so many of them I can't keep track. If I didn't know better, I'd say there's at least a hundred.

"Prepare for landing," Dad says.

Dad lowers the landing gear, and before I know it, we've touched down behind a demolished parking garage, completely hidden from view. I hear seat belts unclicking behind me and Dad says—

"Listen, this is a simple rescue mission. Our objective is to get the Rising Suns out of here as quickly as possible. If these zombies are anything like Elliott described, they may be able to take away our powers. Don't waste time duking it out with them and don't get yourself cornered. Is that clear?"

"Clear," Blue Bolt and Makeshift say in unison while Master Mime gives a thumbs up.

Then, Dad turns to me and says, "Elliott, when Zen reaches out please let her know we're on our way. But I agreed with your mother that you need to stay here in the Freedom Flyer where it's safe."

"Wait, what?" I say. "I knew she mentally said something to you! That's not fair!"

"Listen, son, you've been through enough recently," Dad says. "Promise me you'll stay here."

I stare into his eyes and I can see he's not going to budge. "Fine," I say, crossing my arms and slumping down in my seat. "I promise."

"Thank you," Dad says, popping the hatch. "Freedom Force—It's Fight Time! Oh, and Elliott, lock up until we get back."

Then, the heroes leap out and they're gone. I close the hatch and press the lock button. Then, I focus my mind, hoping to hear Zen reaching out but there's nothing. I hope she's okay.

Unfortunately, Dad parked behind this wreck of a parking garage so I can't see a thing. I push a few buttons on the dashboard and get five Meta signals on the radar. There's Dad, Blue Bolt, Makeshift, Master Mime… and Zen! Great, she must be okay. But what happened to the rest of the Rising Suns? I don't see anything for the Green Dragon, Fight Master, or Silent Samurai?

Does that mean they're knocked out? Or maybe the Meta zombies stole their powers just like the Berserker did to Skunk Girl? And why don't these Meta zombies show a Meta signal? I mean, I know they're out there. I saw them with my own eyes. This is so weird.

I know I promised Dad I'd stay in the Freedom Flyer, but now I'm worried. I mean, if those Meta zombies got a powerful hero like the Green Dragon, then Dad and the Freedom Force might be in more trouble than they realize. I can't just sit here and let something bad happen to them.

Just as I unclick my seatbelt, a big chunk of rubble slides down the parking garage heap and THUNKS against the hood of the Freedom Flyer, making me jump. Boy, that surprised me. It's so quiet here I guess I'm a little skittish.

But as soon as I stand up, a hunk of cement comes hurtling off the pile and SMACKS against the windshield, startling me. Um, how did that happen? There's no one around but me.

Suddenly, I see something moving in the middle of the rubble. And when I lean forward to see what it is, an object pops through! Except, it's not an object, it's… a hand?

BOOM!

My ears ring and I turn away as debris suddenly rains down on the Freedom Flyer! And when I turn back I see something moving. Coming my way.

It's… a man!

He's broken through, lumbering awkwardly towards me! His skin is pale and he's wearing a ripped red-and-orange costume with a flame insignia on it. And when I stare into his empty, yellow eyes a chill runs down my spine!

It's Flameout—the Meta 3 villain who can turn into pure fire! But… he also died at Lockdown, along with the Berserker! But now he's back!

And he's not alone! Suddenly, more dead Meta villains appear behind him, climbing over the rubble. I see Black Cloud, and Ripcord, and Amphibia! And that's when it dawns on me. They're not here by accident. They're coming for me, just like the Berserker did!

How did they even know I was here?

Well, I can't worry about that now because I've got to scram. Fortunately, I'm in the Freedom Flyer so I should be out of here in no time. I jump into the pilot's chair, flip on the controls, and get ready for lift-off. Except, when I hit the ignition, I don't lift off! In fact, the Freedom Flyer feels like it's being dragged backward!

I call up the rearview camera and get the shock of my life! Dozens of other zombies are holding the Freedom Flyer down! Where did they come from?

"WARNING: THRUSTER JETS CRITICALLY DAMAGED," the Freedom Flyer reports.

What? I look out the window and find Meta zombies tearing my left-wing thruster to pieces. And when I turn right it's the same thing! Then, I'm rocked hard as the zombies start shaking the Freedom Flyer.

SCREEECH! SCREEEEEEEECH!

Holy cow! They're pulling the Freedom Flyer apart to get to me! I'm trapped!

I feel myself hyperventilating but I've got to stay calm. Okay, I need to get out of this ship. I can't take off, but I can… That's it! I snap in my seatbelt, flip open the armrest, and smash the eject button.

FWOOM!

The next thing I know, the hatch pops off and my stomach goes topsy-turvy as I'm catapulted hundreds of feet into the air. I look down and see the blank faces of my adversaries shrinking away, and then I'm long gone.

Unfortunately, so is the Freedom Flyer.

As my momentum slows, I work the touchpad to activate the propulsion jets mounted to the bottom of my chair. Fortunately, they engage, and I steer myself north toward the action and the Freedom Force.

It doesn't take long to find them.

Down below, I see Dad and the others, but they're surrounded by Meta zombies! But that's not all! Dad is the only one moving. And the mindless monsters are pushing up against some kind of invisible force field encircling the heroes.

But how's that possible? Dad can't do that.

And that's when I see Zen. She's standing dead center with her arms outstretched. She must be using her telekinesis to keep those zombies at bay. Now I know why she didn't get back to me.

SPUTTER! PUTT! PUTT!

Uh-oh, I'm going down! I forgot the pilot's chair doesn't hold much fuel. I've got to find somewhere to touch down, but this place is crawling with zombies!

That's when I realize something. When I used my negation powers on the Berserker he disappeared. So, if I use my powers on a lot of these zombies then maybe I can clear my own landing zone. The thing is, I'm gonna have to be precise so I don't make Dad and the other heroes disappear like I did Selfie.

I may be about to make another big mistake, but if I don't try something I'm a goner. So, at around fifty feet, I take a deep breath and hyper-focus my negation power on an area just to the right of the force field. And then, just like that, all of the zombies in that area suddenly disappear!

"Epic Zero?" Dad says, clearly shocked to see me.

"Oh, hey there, Captain Justice," I say, waving weakly as my chair sputters to the ground. "Sorry to drop in like this."

But as soon as I touch down, all of the zombies suddenly turn my way! Then, they come for me!

"Epic Zero!" Dad calls out.

I unclick my seatbelt and stand up, but before I can tell Dad that I'll take care of the rest, he says—

"Zen, open the bubble! We've got to save him!"

"No!" I yell back.

But as soon as I try to move, I can't!

In fact, I can't move a muscle! It's like I'm… frozen?

"Stay there!" Dad calls out. "I'm coming!"

I want to shout 'no,' but I can't even move my mouth. I'm literally locked in place, except for my eyes. I-I don't understand. What's going on?

I see Dad running towards me when all of the Meta zombies suddenly close ranks around him. Dad skids to a stop and tries to jump out of the fray, but the zombies swarm him.

'Dad!' I try calling out, but there's no sound. I dig deep to push out my negation power but nothing happens. The zombies are piling on top of him!

'Someone, help him!' I think, but when I look at the other heroes all I see are more zombies!

"Epic Zero!" Dad yells.

And then he's gone—buried beneath a pile of zombies who are glowing with that bright, orange light!

'Stop!' I try calling out.

I need to help him, but I can't!

Why can't I move? What's happening?

Suddenly, my vision gets blurry.

Dad's cries echo in my ears but I can't see him.

And then everything goes black.

Meta Profile

The Berserker

Name: Unknown	Height: 7'2"
Race: Unknown	Weight: 613 lbs
Status: Villain/Deceased	Eyes/Hair: Purple/Purple

META 3: Super-Strength
Extreme Strength
Extreme Invulnerability
Extreme Agility

Observed Characteristics			
Combat 90			
Durability	95	Leadership	12
Strategy	29	Willpower	84

FIVE

I TAKE A MEETING

"Dad!" I call out.

This time, to my surprise, my voice echoes loud and clear all around me. And that's not all! I can move again! I try opening my eyes but my lashes are stuck together. After a little effort, I manage to pry them open, only to find myself engulfed in complete darkness.

I reach into my utility belt and pull out my flare. But once it's lit, I realize I'm standing inside a narrow, underground tunnel. How on earth did I get down here?

I extend the flare from side to side but all I see is dirt and rock. Where am I? Then, I hear water trickling overhead, which means I'm not just underground but deep underground.

Suddenly, my entire body feels clammy.

I hate being underground!

What am I doing here? This makes no sense.

Just a few seconds ago, I was in the middle of Tokyo helplessly watching Dad get overrun by Meta zombies. And now… well, I've got no clue where I am. But I can't stay here. Dad, Zen, and the others need my help!

Maybe I'm just having a nightmare. Maybe I'll wake up safe and sound next to Dog-Gone slobbering all over my pillow. Boy, it'll be great to see him again—bad breath and all.

But when I reach out and touch the wall it feels too realistic to be a dream. In fact, the rocks are bone-chillingly cold and their edges are super sharp. So, there's no way this is a dream.

Maybe I'll be trapped down here forever!

Right as I'm about to go into full-throttle panic mode, I see something move out of the corner of my eye and gasp. It's a shadow—of a man! I freeze. But just as quickly as it appeared, it's gone!

Okay, am I seeing things? My head tells me to call out to see if he's real, but my gut tells me that's probably not a good idea. So, I stand stock-still and wait for him to come back.

Except, he doesn't. I stay perfectly still for a few minutes but there's no movement and no sounds other than the trickling water overhead and the pounding of my own beating heart.

I don't think he's coming back so I guess the next

move is mine. Either I risk heading his way to see if I'm imagining things, or I play it safe and go the other way. I debate the merits of each option in my mind, and finally conclude that if someone else is down here, he might know the way out.

So, I raise my flare and move forward.

After walking several cautious feet, I reach a bend in the tunnel and peek around, only to hear—

"Please, Elliott Harkness," comes a warm, familiar voice, "join me in my office."

Instantly, the hairs on the back of my neck stand on end. I-I know who it is.

But it can't be. Can it?

I swallow hard and step around the bend into a small, rocky chamber. And sitting in its center, leaning back in his chair with his feet propped up on his desk, is the purple-skinned fiend I hoped I'd never see again.

Tormentus!

"Oh, don't be shy," he says, his yellow eyes narrowing. "Have a seat." Then, he waves his purple hand and a chair magically appears out of nowhere.

Trust me, sitting down with him is the last thing I want to do, but suddenly my legs start moving against my will and don't stop until they plant me firmly in the seat across from him.

"There you go," Tormentus says. "Isn't that more comfortable? Let's put out that flare. We have plenty of light." Then, he waves his hand again and my flare snuffs out as the room gets mysteriously brighter.

That's when it hits me.

"You made me freeze," I say. "You're the one who prevented me from helping Captain Justice and the others."

"Guilty as charged," Tormentus says with an ear-to-ear grin. "But you don't have to call him by his formal name. I know he's your father, remember?"

That's right! I first met Tormentus when I was searching for Beezle. Tormentus told me it was his business to know things, including the secret identities of my parents and me. I thought I was done with him after he took Siphon's soul, but clearly, I was wrong. I don't know what he's up to, but something tells me I'm not going to like the answer.

"What do you want?" I ask firmly.

"Please, relax," Tormentus says. "It's been a while since we've seen one another and I thought it would be good to catch up. Besides, my Meta zombie army has things well under control, so we have plenty of time to get reacquainted."

Suddenly, I feel like I've been hit by a truck.

"*Your* Meta zombie army?" I say, totally shocked. "You mean, you're responsible for all of this? You're the one who brought those villains back from the…"

Then, everything hits me at once.

How could I have been so stupid? Of course, it's Tormentus! After all, Tormentus makes deals in exchange for people's souls. So, he must have made bargains with those dead Metas and is somehow bringing them back to life as zombies! But how? And… why?

"I see the gears turning," Tormentus says, putting his hands behind his head, "but you still look puzzled. Would you like me to explain?"

Drat. I didn't want to give him the edge by seeming clueless but I guess it's written all over my face. "Um, yeah," I say, "if you don't mind."

"It would be my pleasure," Tormentus says. "You see, I realized I didn't properly introduce myself the first time we met. So, let's start with the basics. You may not realize it, but you are sitting with royalty. For I rule over one of the seven kingdoms of the Underworld."

Um, can we rewind that?

Did he just say 'Underworld?'

"My kingdom is known by many names," he continues. "Some call it 'Purgatory,' others call it 'the In Between,' but you can think of my realm as the first stop in your soul's journey between the Overworld—which is your current plane of existence—and its final destination, wherever fate shall determine that to be."

I'm trying to follow him, but if what he's saying is true, then who is this guy? And why does the 'In Between' sound so familiar?

"I hold many titles, including Soul Snatcher of the Underworld and the Supreme Ruler of the In Between. But while my realm is vast and my responsibilities great, I have grown bored of doing the same thing over and over again. Torturing souls and defending my borders simply doesn't hold my interest like it used to. Sure, I could crush my enemies and dominate the seven kingdoms, but why bother? In the end, it is an empty prize."

I nod my head like I'm understanding, but the way he's talking, he's making it sound like he's some kind of a… a… demon lord?

"However, things are different on your plane," he says, flashing a disturbing smile. "After all, humans in the Overworld possess something that's been extinguished by the time they reach my kingdom. Do you know what that is?"

"Um, no," I say. "Not really."

"Free will," Tormentus says. "Humans in the Overworld operate according to free will. Unlike in the Underworld, on your plane I can utilize my superior talents of persuasion and intellect to their full potential. I can literally strike billions of bargains. I can feel… alive!"

His smile sends a chill down my spine.

"Thus, my revelation," Tormentus continues. "Why settle for ruling over a dismal, dead empire when I could rule over an entire realm of living, thinking beings? The choice is obvious. I will rule the Overworld. I will break the free will of every man, woman, and child. The Overworld will be my playground and shaping humanity's future will be my game."

I swallow hard. Is that what this is all about? He

wants to rule the Overworld?

"My army will not fail me," Tormentus says, cracking his knuckles. "But there is one detail in the fine print that may prevent me from completing my plan. And that's where you come in."

Me? I knew he brought me here for a reason.

"And, um, what's that?" I ask, fearing the answer.

Tormentus stares directly into my eyes and says, "Meta energy."

"M-Meta energy?" I repeat.

"That's right," he says, pulling his feet off the desk and sitting up in his chair. "Unfortunately, based on the infernal laws of the Underworld, I'm unable to remain in the Overworld without a constant supply of Meta energy. So, to remain in the Overworld, I need a reliable solution."

Okay, where is he going with this?

"Fortunately, I struck a bargain with a new business partner," Tormentus continues. "With his help, we turned my collection of lost souls into a Meta-draining army capable of stripping Metas of their Meta energy for my personal use. But once that Meta energy has run out there will be nothing left to sustain me, and I will be forced back to the Underworld. However, if I had a constant, uninterrupted supply of Meta energy, well, then I could stay in the Overworld forever."

Suddenly, I get a bad feeling. By the way he's looking at me, he either thinks I'm a juicy steak or the source of this uninterrupted supply of Meta energy! I don't know what he's got planned, but something tells me I don't want to find out!

"Wow," I say, trying to stand up. "That's quite a conundrum you've got there, but I don't think I'm the right guy for the job."

My limbs aren't moving. Why can't I stand up?

"I think I can change your mind about that," Tormentus says. "After all, I have something you want."

Then, he SNAPS his fingers and a masked girl with bright, blue eyes appears beside him.

"Selfie!" I call out.

"Epic!" she cries out as soon as she sees me. She looks scared out of her mind.

Then, Tormentus SNAPS again, and just like that, she's gone.

"Selfie!" I shout. "Bring her back!"

"Are you sure you want her back?" Tormentus asks. "After all, you're the one who sent her to the Underworld in the first place. Truthfully, I wouldn't mind keeping her. I could use the company. It's rare we get a living person in our realm, although it does seem to be happening with greater regularity. Anyway, it's up to you. It does look like she's having a terrible time down there."

"Yes, I'm sure!" I yell. "I'll do anything!"

"That's great news," Tormentus says, "because I have a deal for you. It may seem harsh at first, but I think it's more than fair. Would you like to hear it?"

I nod, bracing myself.

"Perfect," he says. "So, here it is. If you agree to willingly come to the Underworld and do my bidding forever, I'll release your friend back to the land of the living."

"Um, what?" I say, in shock.

"Now, don't answer before you think about it," he says, "because it's literally a once in a lifetime offer."

I'm stunned. I mean, I'd put Selfie's life before mine every time. But if I do, he'll use me to stay on Earth and rule over humanity forever. This is bad.

Really bad.

"So, Elliott Harkness," Tormentus says, "what's it going to be?"

I-I wish I could answer.

But I don't know what to do.

SIX

I GET AN OFFER I CAN'T REFUSE

He's got me and he knows it.

Tormentus just made me an offer I don't think I can refuse. He said he'll return Selfie to the Overworld if I agree to do his bidding in the Underworld—forever! I don't exactly know what his 'bidding' entails, but it sure doesn't sound good. But then again, I don't know of any other way to get Selfie back on my own.

And right now, I'm haunted by how terrified Selfie looked when Tormentus showed her to me. I've never seen her so scared. And it's all my fault.

None of this would have happened if I didn't use my powers on the Berserker zombie. Selfie would be here by my side instead of being held prisoner in Tormentus' Underworld kingdom. And that's the other problem.

It's not like Selfie is in the next town over. I've got no clue how to get to the Underworld to save her, so this might be my only option.

But if I do go with him, he'll use my powers somehow to stay on Earth forever. Then, he'll rule 'the Overworld,' as he calls it—which basically means all of humanity. I'm no odds-maker, but I'd call this a lose-lose situation.

I don't want to sacrifice the planet, but if I don't agree to his bargain Selfie may never get out of the Underworld again. I've got to decide but my brain is so scrambled I can't think straight.

"Well?" Tormentus asks, smiling from ear to ear.

I wish I could slap that grin off his smug, purple face but I still can't stand up. He's holding me down until he gets what he wants. My instincts tell me to reject his offer outright, but maybe that's the wrong decision.

I mean, could I really live with myself if I just skipped out of here without guaranteeing Selfie's safe return? After all, she's, well, kind of special to me. I can't just leave her in the Underworld to rot.

Of course, if I agree to his bargain all of humanity will be doomed. But then again, isn't something bound to doom humanity eventually? I mean, it's only a matter of time before some bad guy destroys the world, right? I stare into Tormentus' eyes and his smile widens.

Okay, I know what I need to do.

I need to right the wrong I caused.

I open my mouth to agree to his terms when—

'STOP!' comes a girl's voice from inside my head.

Huh?

"Whatever you are, get out!" the voice calls out.

Wait a minute. I know that voice.

Just then, it feels like something lifts from my head, like I was wearing a helmet I didn't even know about, and suddenly my mind feels clearer. What happened?

"Epic Zero, can you hear me?" comes the voice again, but this time I know exactly who it is.

"Yes, Zen," I say, touching my fingers to my temples.

"No!" Tormentus yells as he stands up.

Then, everything goes wavy, and Tormentus, the rocky tunnel, the desk, and the chairs disappear! The next thing I know, I'm staring into Zen's eyes.

"Epic Zero, can you see me?" Zen asks, waving a hand in front of my face. "Do you hear me?"

"Y-Yeah," I say, shaking off the cobwebs and squinting in the bright sun. "Where am I?"

"T-Tokyo," Zen says, her voice suddenly sounding strained. "I don't know what happened but you froze. And when I entered your head I sensed a dangerous presence lurking inside your mind."

Lurking inside my mind?

Tormentus! He must have been using his Psychic powers to influence my thinking, just like he did when I first met him. And he almost had me. But then I feel heartbroken, because if I'm here, then Selfie is still—

"Epic Zero, I-I need your help," Zen says, and then I notice she's wincing. "I… nearly let down my guard to help you. W-We've got to get everyone out of here. I-I can't hold them off much longer."

Them? Them who?

Then, as my eyes adjust to the light, my jaw drops because we're surrounded by Meta zombies! There are hundreds of them encircling us, stacked five deep, and pounding against some kind of an invisible wall! And that's when I realize what's happening.

Zen must have absorbed me inside her psychic force field, and she's holding the zombies off single-handedly! But there are so many she's straining to maintain her defense. Just then, my foot brushes against something and when I look down I see Dad!

He's lying on his back and he's not looking so good. His eyes are closed, his costume is shredded, and his breathing is shallow. And the rest of the team are lying all around us, in equally bad shape!

I've got to help Zen! She's down on one knee, giving it all she's got. But if she breaks down we're zombie meat! And it's not like we've got an escape plan. After all, those zombies demolished the Freedom Flyer. So, I guess that leaves us with only one option.

"Get ready to drop the force field," I say.

"Wh-What?" Zen says. "Are you crazy?"

"Probably," I answer, looking at all of the threatening faces surrounding us. "But you'll just have to trust me on this one, okay? So, when I say 'go,' drop the force field."

Zen glances up at me and I dig deep, summoning every iota of negation power in my body. I feel a massive surge through my veins as the Meta energy rushes inside of me. I collect it, bundle it, shape it into a tight ball, but I can feel it pushing back, waiting to explode. I… can't… hold it.

Then, I grit my teeth and yell, "Go!"

Zen relaxes her posture, and suddenly, the first wave of zombies topples over as the force field resisting them dissolves. Then, just as the second and third waves trample over the first, I release my negation power in every direction at once. The energy floods out of my body and washes over the Meta zombies. And then, just like that, they're gone.

"Y-You did it!" Zen says amazed.

I did, but more waves are coming. I want to fight back but I feel dizzy, like I'm out of energy. "N-Need to rest a sec," I say, taking a seat on a giant chunk of rubble. I feel like I'm gonna barf.

"What's that?" Zen says, pointing to the sky.

I squint and see something blurry flying towards us—something big with wings. I try focusing on it, but I can't. And then my eyelids flutter and all I see is black.

***

I wake up to BEEPING, and when I open my eyes

there's a rat with a clipboard standing on my chest. Then, I notice an IV in my left arm.

"Medi-wing?" I ask, rubbing my eyes.

"Yep, your favorite spot," TechnocRat says, scribbling down some notes. "I just finished my examination. Do you want the good news or the bad news?"

"I'll take the good news," I say, stretching my back. Then, I realize my brain is so fuzzy I don't even know what I'm doing here. What was the last thing I did again?

"The good news is your vitals look surprisingly normal," TechnocRat says. "Your blood pressure was low when you first arrived but it's stabilized now." Then, he gestures to the IV and says, "Once we get all of these fluids into your body you'll be good to go."

Well, that is good news. But instead of giving me the bad news, TechnocRat just stands there blinking at me.

"And what about the bad news?" I ask, getting up on my elbows. "Didn't you say there's bad news?"

"Oh, yeah," TechnocRat says, stooping to look up my nostrils. "You've got major bats in the cave. You may want to clear those out before I get the others."

Seriously? I'm gonna kill that rat. I roll my eyes, reach for a tissue, and blow my nose.

"Why don't you hold onto that," TechnocRat says as he scrambles down the bedrail. "I'll grab the rest of the team so we can update you on the zombie situation."

The zombie situation? Suddenly, it all comes racing

back. The Meta zombies! Zen! Dad!

Just then, the door opens and Mom, Skunk Girl, Pinball, Night Owl, and Shadow Hawk walk in. But I don't see Grace, Zen, Dad, or the rest of the team. Where are they?

Just then, Dog-Gone pops up and gives me a big, wet slobber.

"Hey, boy," I say, rubbing his muzzle.

"How do you feel?" Mom asks, gently placing her hand on my arm.

"Still a little woozy," I say. But I honestly don't care about myself right now. "Where's Captain Justice, and Zen, and everyone else? Are they okay? Tell me they're okay."

Mom opens her mouth but hesitates.

"Well?" I ask, my voice rising an octave.

"Glory Girl is helping Zen recover in the Galley," Mom says. "But Captain Justice and the others were impacted by the Meta zombies." Then, she looks down and says, "Like Skunk Girl, they've… lost their powers. There are so many of them we set them up in the Combat Room to get some rest until we can figure out what's going on."

"What?" I say, in total disbelief. "That can't be. There's got to be a way to get their powers back, right, TechnocRat?"

"I'm sorry, kid," TechnocRat says, his whiskers drooping. "I've tried everything I can think of, but this is a mystery even *my* super-intellect can't solve. Plus, while you were off on your mission, I ran a full battery of tests on Skunk Girl, and not only are her powers gone but there's also no trace of Meta energy from the zombie who took them. In fact, none of the Meta zombies seem to generate a Meta signature. And just like Skunk Girl, Captain Justice and the others are now, well, Zeroes."

Zeroes?

Just hearing the word makes me feel like I was punched in the gut. I mean, Dad—a Zero? I can't believe it. Suddenly, my mind flashes back to Tokyo and Dad being overwhelmed by Meta zombies. I wanted to help, but there was nothing I could do about it. And it's all because of—

"Tormentus!" I blurt out.

"Tormentus?" Shadow Hawk repeats with a quizzical look on his face. "Isn't that the villain from Safari Park? The one who took Siphon's soul? What does he have to do with this?"

"He's the one responsible for this," I say. "He told me he's tired of being the Soul Snatcher of the Underworld. He said he's declared war against the Overworld, and his army of Meta zombies are going to drain the power of every Meta on the planet."

"Um, did you just say Underworld?" Pinball asks, pointing down. "As in, *that* Underworld?"

"It doesn't matter where he's from," Skunk Girl says. "When I get a hold of him I'll show him who's boss."

"I think getting a hold of him is the problem," Shadow Hawk says. "This character seems pretty shifty. Did you say he called himself the Soul Snatcher?"

"Yeah," I say. "Why?"

"Because I never put two and two together until now," Shadow Hawk says, scratching his chin. "The Soul Snatcher was the reason we formed the Protectors of the Planet in the first place. We banded together to stop him. So, if Tormentus and the Soul Snatcher are the same person, then he's been toying with humans for decades."

"Wait a minute," Night Owl says. "If you faced him before then how did you beat him?"

"We didn't," Shadow Hawk says. "His powers were too immense, even for us. He was on the verge of victory when he suddenly vanished. I still remember the surprised look on his face when it happened. It didn't seem like it was part of his plan and we never saw him again after that."

"Interesting," TechnocRat says, twitching his nose. "I wonder if he was summoned back to the Underworld."

"No," I say, remembering my conversation with Tormentus. "He said he needs Meta energy to stay on our plane. Maybe he ran out?"

"Well, that's even more interesting then," TechnocRat says, "because it can't be a coincidence that he's using his Meta zombies to steal Meta energy. He must be storing it somewhere for his personal use—to keep him here in the 'Overworld,' as you said he calls it.

But where is he storing it? You'd think the Meta Monitor would detect such a large quantity of Meta energy."

"Unless it's not on Earth," Shadow Hawk suggests. "Maybe he's storing it in the Underworld."

BREEP! BREEP! BREEP!

"What's that?" Skunk Girl asks.

"I know that frequency," Mom says, her eyebrows rising. "That's a direct call coming in from Lockdown. To the Mission Room!"

"Hey!" I yell as they all exit the room. "What about… me?"

But they're long gone and I'm stuck here attached to this IV. Fortunately, it's on wheels, so I throw my legs over the bed and roll the IV unit along as I head to the Mission Room. I don't know why Lockdown is calling, but I'm betting it isn't good. Unfortunately, I can't hear the information firsthand, because by the time I reach the Mission Room, Mom is finishing the call.

"We'll send a team right away!" Mom says, and then hangs up as the monitor switches to static. Then, she turns and sees me standing in the doorway. "Epic Zero, what are you doing out of the Medi-wing?"

"Helping," I say. Then, I nod at the IV unit and say, "despite my obstacles. What's the story?"

"That was Lockdown," Mom says. "They've spotted a battalion of Meta zombies approaching in the distance."

"Meta zombies at Lockdown?" I say.

Then, a lightbulb goes off. Of course, Tormentus

would go after Lockdown. After all, where else could he find such a large supply of Meta energy all in one place?

"We've got to stop them!" I say. "Those Meta prisoners are sitting ducks!"

"Yes," Mom says. "But there's no 'we,' here. You need to get back to the Medi-wing to rest while—"

"I'm sorry, but there's no time for rest," I say.

"Excuse me?" Mom says, crossing her arms.

"I appreciate your concern," I say, "but let's face it, I'm the only one here capable of sending those monsters back to where they came from. So, if someone can unhook me from this contraption we can get going already."

Meta Profile
The Rising Suns
Green Dragon
Class: Super Strength
Meta :
Zen
Class: Psychic
Meta :
Fight Master
Class: Meta-Morph
Meta :
Silent Samurai
Class: Magic
Meta :

SEVEN

I FACE AN ONSLAUGHT

Why do all roads lead back to Lockdown?

I mean, I was here only a few weeks ago trying to stop an insane Meta-Man from busting the place wide open. Of course, that didn't go so well, which was how Meta creeps like Airstream and Pulverizer got free in the first place. And speaking of Airstream and Pulverizer, it feels like Dad and I hauled them in a million years ago instead of just yesterday.

So much has changed since then.

Thinking about Dad crushes me. I wish I could have seen him before we left but there just wasn't time. I know things could have been different if Tormentus didn't freeze me. But unfortunately, that's not what happened.

I look out the window as Grace pilots our Freedom

Flyer through the clouds. We'll be at Lockdown soon enough, and if we don't stop those zombies before they reach the prisoners then Tormentus will get his grubby little hands on a huge amount of Meta energy.

Unfortunately, we'll be fighting short-handed. With most of the team out of action, it's basically up to Grace, Pinball, Night Owl, Shadow Hawk, TechnocRat, and me. Honestly, I didn't even want to bring Pinball and Night Owl but Shadow Hawk thought they could be useful. I wish Mom was here, but we all agreed it was better to have her on the Waystation in case things went sideways.

I just hope we can complete this mission quickly. TechnocRat said he has a big plan to keep Lockdown out of reach. I asked him what he meant by that, but he said it's a surprise. Believe me, I trust TechnocRat, but sometimes his 'surprises' worry me. You know, like that time I was almost eaten by a T-Rex while he fiddled with his Time Warper device.

"Look alive, people," Grace says, flicking some buttons on the dashboard. "Lockdown at five o'clock."

I feel a knot in the pit in my stomach as the prison comes into view—and it's far from a sight for sore eyes. I have to say, Dad and TechnocRat did a great job on the repairs because it looks like new. But based on what I'm seeing it's not gonna last long.

Not by a longshot.

"Um, are all of those dots down there what I think they are?" Pinball asks, swallowing hard. "Because if they're zombies, then it kind of looks like there's thousands of them."

He's right about that. There are more Meta zombies lumbering toward Lockdown than were swarming us in Tokyo. The prison guards are doing their best to hold them off but their weapons are useless. The zombies just keep on coming.

I hope I can pull this off, because if I can't…

"I know this might sound weird," Grace says, "but are we thinking about this the right way? I mean, maybe we should just save the guards and let the zombies go to town on the prisoners. After all, if they take away the prisoners' Meta energy aren't they doing us a big favor? There'd be, like, no more bad guys."

"It might seem that way," TechnocRat says, "but if all of that Meta energy is transferred to Tormentus, I fear we'll have an even bigger problem on our hands." Then, he looks out the window and says, "Land near the front entrance. I need to get inside the control room to execute my plan. Everyone should be prepared to take off as soon as you get my signal."

"Roger that," Grace says, adjusting our flight path to land inside the compound.

"How do you feel, kid?" Shadow Hawk asks, patting my shoulder from the seat behind me.

"Good to go," I say, lying through my teeth.

Truthfully, I feel lousy but now isn't the time to shake the team's confidence. They're depending on me.

"Great," Shadow Hawk says. Then, he turns to the others and says, "Remember what we're facing here. This isn't the time for unnecessary heroics. Is that clear?"

"Oh, you won't have to worry about that with me," Pinball says.

"Perfect," Shadow Hawk says. "But just in case, I'd like you and Night Owl to accompany TechnocRat inside Lockdown. If those zombies get past our defenses, he'll need all the help he can get. Glory Girl and I will run interference for Epic Zero while he disposes of the enemy."

Well, he made that sound easy. Not.

I have to say, it's great having Shadow Hawk and his strategic brain with us this time. Besides, he's already a Zero, so he can fight those zombies without worrying about losing his powers.

Of course, if I screw up he could lose more than that—like his life! No pressure.

"Prepare for landing," Grace says.

I clutch my armrests as we touch down smoothly next to the front door. Then, we unhook our seatbelts and Grace pops the hatch. Ready or not, here we go.

"Let's rock, kiddos," TechnocRat says to Pinball and Night Owl as he turns on his jet pack and flies out of the vehicle. "And try to keep up!"

"You've got this," Night Owl says to me before exiting via a shadow slide.

"Don't do anything I wouldn't do," Pinball adds.

"Um, dude, I've got to do something," I say.

"Right, scratch that," Pinball says. Then, he bounces out of the Freedom Flyer.

"You've got some weird friends," Grace says.

"Tell me about it," I say.

"Are you ready?" Shadow Hawk asks.

Grace and I look at each other and nod.

"Alright then," he says with a wink. "Freedom Force—it's Fight Time!"

Grace takes off into the air as Shadow Hawk and I leap out of the Freedom Flyer. It was nice to hear Shadow Hawk use Dad's battle cry, but at the same time, it makes me sad. I wish Dad was here to say it himself, but I'll do my best to make him proud.

Unfortunately, that's gonna take more than I thought, because as soon as we run through the front gates I gasp. Zombies are everywhere—marching our way like an unstoppable, undead army, stretching as far as my eyes can see. And as I assess the monumental task before me, Shadow Hawk's words about Tormentus echo in my brain: *he's been toying with humans for decades*. Well, that must be true, because it must have taken years to bargain with all of these souls!

Suddenly, panic sets in. There are so many of them. I-I'm not sure I can do this.

"Steel yourself, kid," Shadow Hawk says as he pulls out his Hawk-a-rang. "Because we've got less than a minute before they're on top of us."

"Yeah, I've got this," I say, unconvincingly.

"Shouldn't you get started already?" Grace calls out, flying overhead. "There's no time like the present."

"Glory Girl, stay as high as you can," Shadow Hawk says. "Everything should be fine, but if we're about to be overrun, forget about me and get Epic Zero out of here. Got it?"

"Yep," she says, climbing higher, "but let's not let it get to that point. So, you better get cracking."

"Okay, okay!" I say, closing my eyes I've got to focus. I've got to start negating their Meta energy.

GGGGRRRRRRRR!

The proximity of the sound surprises me and I open my eyes to find a gray Meta zombie only four feet away—and he's coming right at me! He's wearing a ripped black and gray costume with the insignia of a cloud on his chest.

Is that Black Cloud?

"Wake up, kid!" Shadow Hawk says, as his Hawk-a-Rang CLANGS against the zombie's skull before circling expertly back into his hand. "It's go time!"

He's right. It's now or never.

I concentrate and pull as much negation power as I can muster, but I can tell it already feels like less than what I had in Tokyo. What gives? I mean, I've never felt a limit to my powers like this.

"Epic Zero?" Shadow Hawk says, knocking Black Cloud back with a kick to the gut.

I take in the massive number of villains before us and feel nervous. But what did Shadow Hawk say? Steel myself? Well, here goes nothing.

I spread my arms and unleash my negation energy, pushing it as far and wide as I can. Suddenly, Black Cloud and hundreds of other zombies disappear at once.

"That's it!" Shadow Hawk says.

Thank goodness. But that only took care of the first wave. There's more coming—lots more.

The problem is, I'm not sure I have anything left in the tank. I probably should have let more of those fluids get into my body before I came down here, but it's too late now.

"Get ready," Shadow Hawk says.

I look in the distance at the next wave coming, and the waves after that. The funny thing is, they seem to be reorganizing themselves, spreading out into a wider circle around us. That's weird. Why are they doing that?

"Guys, look out!" Grace yells. She's pointing at something close. "Look down! Right in front of you!"

Right in front of us? What's she talking about?

But then I look down and do a double take, because coming out of the ground, in the same area where I just negated the zombies, are even more zombies! They're coming back—resurfacing out of the ground!

But how can that be?

"Epic Zero!" Shadow Hawk calls out. "Use your powers!"

Holy smokes! I reach inside to pull up what I can, but I'm just so exhausted it feels like there's nothing left. The next thing I know, Black Cloud emerges again and cuts me off from Shadow Hawk. And now I'm completely surrounded!

RUUUUMMMMBBBBLLLEEE!!!

Suddenly, the ground shakes beneath my feet, and I hear an ear-splitting SCREECH. Just then, a giant shadow blankets us as if something huge is hovering overhead. And when I look up my eyes go wide because Lockdown is rising into the air! But how? And that's when I see eight massive rocket jets firing beneath Lockdown, lifting the entire structure skyward!

For a second, I'm confused, and then I realize this must have been TechnocRat's plan all along! When he said he'd keep Lockdown out of reach, I never would have guessed he meant *this*!

"Surprise!" TechnocRat yells from a window.

Man, that rat is annoying, but I've got to hand it to him, he's a genius.

OOOOOOORRRRRRGGGGG!

I feel hot breath on the back of my neck, and when I spin around, I find a Meta zombie right behind me! I stare into her vacant, yellow eyes and recognize her costume. It's Death Nell! She was a Meta 3 Energy Manipulator who died a long time ago!

I-I want to fight back, but I'm so tired I can't do anything. Is this how it's going to end?

Death Nell reaches for me when I feel someone grab me beneath my armpits and lift me into the air!

"Time to get out of here," Grace says.

"But what about Shadow Hawk?" I ask, looking down. "I don't see him anywhere."

"Don't worry," she says. "He's coming."

FWOOP!

Just then, I see a grappling hook hurtling through the air. The metal claw wraps itself around one of Lockdown's jets and pulls the cable taut. Then, it retracts, pulling Shadow Hawk out from beneath a pile of zombies.

I can't believe it! He made it!

And as we climb into the sky, I'm relieved we accomplished our mission, but terrified by Tormentus' awesome power.

Meta Profile

Black Cloud

Name: Boris Dutreich	Height: 6’0”
Race: Human	Weight: 200 lbs
Status: Villain/Deceased	Eyes/Hair: Blue/Blonde

META 3: Meta-morph
Extreme Gas Manipulation
Can Disperse Body into Toxic Gas Molecules

Observed Characteristics			
Combat 84			
Durability	90	Leadership	62
Strategy	83	Willpower	88

EIGHT

I PUT A RING ON IT

We almost didn't get out of there alive.

Thankfully, we're safe and sound back on the Waystation, but, for a few seconds there, I thought I was a goner. Those Meta zombies were a heartbeat away from capturing me, and then, well, I don't want to think about what might have happened next. Fortunately, Grace rescued me just in time. I definitely owe her one, and I'm sure she won't let me forget it.

As for Lockdown, I had no idea TechnocRat built the facility with massive, emergency rocket jets in case something catastrophic happened. He certainly didn't tell me, and apparently, he failed to mention this enormous detail to anyone else. The way that rat thinks continues to amaze and confound me.

I look through the Galley porthole at the Meta prison orbiting peacefully next to us. TechnocRat is over there now, helping the guards adjust to their new environment while ensuring the facility holds up to the extreme atmospheric pressures of space. Boy, I hope everything is okay because the last thing anyone needs is for that thing to implode on us.

I can't take any more problems right now.

"So, what else do you guys have to eat?" Pinball asks, rummaging through the pantry.

Pinball was starving when we got back, so I brought the gang into the Galley for a snack. Of course, I feel sick to my stomach and can't eat a thing.

"I don't know," I say, absent-mindedly spinning Selfie's phone on the table. "What you see is what we've got."

"Ooooh!" Pinball exclaims as he pulls out the box of Frosted Letter-Bites. "I love these but my parents won't let me have them. Is it okay if I have a bowl?"

"Knock yourself out," I say, realizing there's no one here to object. "Spoons are in the drawer, bowls are in that upper cabinet, and milk is in the fridge."

"Thanks," he says, pouring the dry cereal into a bowl and putting it on the table while he goes for the milk.

"So, what do we do now?" Night Owl asks.

I wish I knew, but I don't have a clue. Tormentus is way more powerful than I imagined, Dad and most of the heroes are powerless, and Selfie is still trapped in the

Underworld. I don't think I've ever felt so hopeless.

CRUNCH! CRUNCH!

"Hey! Stop that!" Pinball yells, and when I look over Dog-Gone's snout is buried deep in Pinball's cereal bowl.

"Eat your own food!" Pinball says, pulling the bowl away as Dog-Gone licks his lips and turns invisible.

I guess no matter how dire the circumstances, nothing can stop the furry mercenary from striking.

I spin Selfie's phone again. I wish she was here right now. I bet she'd know what to do.

Then, I notice something. Her screen looks different. Instead of all the apps, there's just a big, single word flashing on her display screen. It reads: WEAKNESS.

Huh? That's weird.

"Listen, boss-man," Skunk Girl says, "I know you're feeling guilty about Selfie and all, but now is not the time to fold like a chair. She needs our help. Well, given the current state of my powers, I guess she needs *your* help. And you're not going to help her by sulking in this booth. We need some fresh thinking here."

I look into Skunk Girl's eyes and realize she's right. I'm not going to save Selfie if I'm down on myself like this. We need fresh thinking. Fresh thinking and action.

The problem is, I don't even know where to start.

But then again, I know someone who might.

"Where are you going?" Skunk Girl asks.

"I'll be right back," I say, grabbing Selfie's phone and standing up. "You guys finish your snack. C'mon, Dog-

Gone, let them eat in peace."

I leave the Galley and Dog-Gone appears beside me.

"Follow me," I say, taking the stairway down to the Combat Room. I wanted to do this earlier but I couldn't. So, now is my chance to see Dad and get his advice on things. After all, he's led the Freedom Force through more challenging missions than I can count. He'll know what we should do next.

But when we reach the Combat Room my stomach sinks, because the large, white room has been converted into a temporary hospital ward. Beds and medical equipment are organized into neat rows, and the beds are occupied by once-great heroes like Blue Bolt, Master Mime, the Green Dragon, and… Dad.

I see him lying at the end with his eyes closed. He's still in his ripped costume, but he's wearing an oxygen mask and hooked up to various monitoring devices. I want to go over but hesitate.

"Hey," comes a familiar voice from behind.

I turn to see Mom who flashes a weak smile.

"Hey," I say. "I'll… come back later."

"Don't be scared," Mom says. "He's just resting. Go over and sit with him. He'll know you're there and it will mean a lot to him. I'll keep Dog-Gone here with me."

"O-Okay," I say nervously and start walking slowly towards Dad. As I pass the other beds only Blue Bolt is awake and she winks at me. I wave back awkwardly and smile, but I feel so bad for her, so bad for all of them.

When I reach Dad, I hear a low BEEPING noise from the monitor. He's breathing much better than the last time I saw him but it hurts to see him like this. I mean, he was the strongest hero I knew.

And now…

I sit on the edge of the bed.

"H-Hey, Dad," I say, as a tear rolls down my cheek. "I-I just wanted to let you know how sorry I am for what happened. I-I wish I could have helped you. I wish I could have stopped Tormentus from freezing me. I-I wish… I wasn't so weak."

I tap Selfie's phone against my palm and out of the corner of my eye I see that word again. WEAKNESS.

Then, it dawns on me that I've seen a lot of random words lately. There was that one flashing on the Meta Monitor. SHOW. Then, there was that one in my bowl of cereal. What was that one again? NEVER?

WEAKNESS. SHOW. NEVER.

Why does that seem so—

Suddenly, a shockwave runs through my body.

WEAKNESS. SHOW. NEVER.

NEVER. SHOW. WEAKNESS.

OMG! I-I know those words. But that can't be a coincidence, can it? And then two things hit me at once.

One, the last time I saw K'ami, she said she was in a place called 'the In Between.' And two, that's the same name Tormentus used for his kingdom!

So, why am I seeing these words—K'ami's words—

now? Is it just a coincidence, or is she sending me a message from beyond?

And then I realize something else. Selfie is Tormentus' prisoner in the Underworld. Could K'ami be with Selfie?

I jump off Dad's bed and start pacing. I mean, this is just too specific to be a coincidence. K'ami must be reaching out to me. She must be trying to tell me something—but what? Then, a lightbulb goes off.

Suddenly, I know exactly what I need to do.

I need to go to the Underworld.

Yes, it sounds nuts, but if I'm gonna stop Tormentus and save Selfie, I'm not going do it up here in 'the Overworld,' as Tormentus calls it. I'm going to have to do it down there—where he may be storing his Meta energy. It's a gamble, but it's a risk I've got to take.

But how will I get there? I mean, as far as I know, there aren't any flights heading to the Underworld. And I definitely don't want to go there the traditional way, if you know what I mean.

"Are you okay?" Mom asks, nearly making me jump out of my skin. "I don't want to pry but it looks like you have a lot on your mind."

"Oh, yeah," I say, stopping my pacing. "I'm good."

"Is there anything I can do to help?" Mom asks.

I wish I could tell Mom what's going on, but if I do she'll never let me go. I wish I could tell her. I wish…

Wait a minute? Wish? That's it!

"Elliott?" Mom asks. "Do you need anything?"

"Um, no," I say, trying to stay calm so she'll think everything is okay and will stay out of my thoughts. "Now that I've visited Dad, I-I think I'll go back upstairs to hang out with my friends."

"Okay," she says with a suspicious look on her face. "I know this is hard. Remember, I'm always here if you need me."

"Thanks," I say, hugging her. "C'mon Dog-Gone." I exit the Combat Room calmly and then, as soon as I'm out of sight, I book up the stairs as fast as possible. I hate not being truthful with Mom, but I have no intention of seeing my friends.

I've got other plans.

I exit the stairwell, but instead of turning toward the Galley, I head the other way.

WOOF!

Uh-oh. I forgot about Dog-Gone. His body is pointed toward the Galley but he's looking back at me.

"You go ahead," I say. "I'll, um, be there soon."

But Dog-Gone doesn't move and I get the sense he knows I'm not telling him everything.

"Go on," I say. "Tell you what, you can eat all the cereal you can get your muzzle on until I get back. Deal?"

Dog-Gone's tail wags and he takes off, turning invisible right before he enters the Galley. I feel bad doing that to Pinball, but I've got to get moving.

I race through the halls until I reach my destination—

the Trophy Room. The Trophy Room is an area that's filled with display cases holding all sorts of strange and assorted souvenirs from the Freedom Force's various missions. Some of the items are simply fun, like Mr. Mint's giant quarter or the Mad Popper's Bubble Gum Gun, while others are more, well, dangerous.

I ignore everything else and make a beeline for a display case sitting in the corner. The plaque on the stand reads: *The Three Rings of Suffering. Extremely Dangerous. Do not remove from glass. DO NOT WEAR UNDER ANY CIRCUMSTANCES.*

I take a deep breath.

And then I remove the glass cover.

I stare at the two rings sitting innocently on the stand. One is bronze and the other is silver, but both have lightning bolt symbols carved into their faces. Just looking at them sends a shiver down my spine.

After all, each Ring of Suffering contains one of the Djinn Three, evil genie brothers who have plagued mankind for centuries. Beezle won't be useful since I trapped him in his silver ring for all of eternity. And I have no clue where Terrog and his gold ring are. So, that leaves me with one ticket to the Underworld.

Rasp.

I pick up his bronze ring and exhale.

I mean, am I really going to do this?

But then I think of Selfie and K'ami and slip the ring on my finger.

NINE

I GO DOWN UNDER

I shield my face as the bronze ring sparks with electricity.

And then, the next thing I know, out swirls a gray, spirit-like creature who swells up to ten feet tall. He's just as ugly as Beezle, and by the look of sheer disgust on his face, I can tell there's no need for introductions.

"Um, hey there, Rasp," I offer.

"YOU!" Rasp practically spits. "*You* dared to summon *me*?"

Suddenly, it dawns on me that this was probably a huge mistake. After all, when I was Beezle's master I used my last wish to trap him inside his own ring for all of eternity. And right before he obeyed my command, Beezle told me his brothers would avenge him.

So, like the genius I am, I've now given Rasp his

opportunity to get me back.

Just. Freaking. Wonderful.

"Yes, I summoned you," I say as confidently as I can. "I need your help."

"Well, I refuse," Rasp says, crossing his arms and turning his back on me. "I refuse to help the sworn enemy of my brother. So, I suggest you simply remove the ring and I will return to my home."

"Um, that's not how this works," I say, holding out my ring finger. "I'm wearing the bronze ring, see? Which means I'm your master now and you know it."

Rasp scrunches his gray face in anger, and if he could turn red I'm pretty sure he'd look like a flaming tomato right now.

"Indeed," he says after a long pause, looking at me from over his shoulder. "That is correct. As you are now the bearer of the bronze Ring of Suffering, you are my master and I am at your service. But I do not have to like it."

"Works for me," I say with a shrug.

"As you undoubtedly know by now," Rasp says matter-of-factly, "I am here to fulfill your utmost desires. I can grant you three wishes. However, there are limitations. I am not able to bring the dead back to life and I am not permitted to grant you unlimited wishes. You have three wishes at your disposal. So, let's get this over with if we must. Now tell me, what do you desire… master?"

Well, it definitely took him a lot of effort to get that last word out. Believe me, I'm not thrilled about partnering with an evil genie with attitude problems either, but I need him to get me to the Underworld and back again.

Unfortunately, traveling to the Underworld is going to use two of my three available wishes. I mean, I don't know what I'm going to run into when I actually get down there, but I'm pretty sure it's not going to be rainbows and unicorns. Frankly, this whole situation terrifies me, but this is my only shot so I've got to take it.

But that's not my only concern.

Based on my experience with Beezle, I need to make sure my wishes are as specific as possible. Beezle tricked me by intentionally twisting my words and I can't let that happen again. I'll also need to keep close tabs on my mental state. Especially since each Djinn can warp minds, and while Rasp is less powerful than Beezle he could still try to influence my thinking.

"Rasp," I say, "I'd like to make my first wish."

"Oooh, how exciting, tiny master," Rasp says dryly.

I roll my eyes, but before I share my wish I realize I need to think this through. I need to get into the Underworld, but where exactly should I go? According to Tormentus, there are seven kingdoms down there so the Underworld must be huge. I guess I could ask Rasp to drop me in Tormentus' kingdom, but I'm sure he'd happily dump me in the middle of some hot mess.

That just seems too risky.

I could ask him to take me to K'ami. I'd love to see her again, but what if I read those clues wrong? Even though that message seemed to come from her, I can't be sure. So, the only thing I know for certain is that Selfie is down there and saving her is my number one priority.

"Rasp," I say, "here's my first wish and I want you to listen closely. I want you to take me into the Underworld and make sure I appear right next to Selfie. Is that clear?"

"Your wish left no room for misinterpretation, my insignificant master," Rasp says. "However, if you do wish to travel to the Underworld, I must remind you that I am unable to bring the dead back to life. So, if that is the purpose of this journey, then I am afraid I will not be of service."

K'ami's face flashes through my mind. The last time I saw her she told me she was dead, so there's no chance of me bringing her back.

"That's not why I'm going," I say. "But thank you."

"Very well, my cowardly master," Rasp says. "Now hold on to your cape, because your wish…" Then, he waves his hand, "… is fulfilled."

Suddenly, I'm no longer standing in the Trophy Room, but on a sooty, black surface in a very strange place. Everywhere I look are twisted pathways, some going straight up and others going diagonal or straight down. It's like the laws of gravity don't exist! And the sky above—if you can even call it that—is a mass of dreary, brownish-yellow clouds. Suddenly, my whole body feels really warm and I pull on my neck collar to get some relief.

Is-Is this it? Am I really in the Underworld?

But where is Selfie?

I look up at Rasp who is scratching his chin with a puzzled expression on his face.

"Hey!" I call out. "I told you to make me appear next to Selfie. Where is she?"

"I was just wondering the same thing myself," Rasp says. "I feel like I was properly attuned to her location, but it does seem like there is no one here but us, doesn't it?"

"Don't play dumb with me," I say. "I know you did this on purpose. You're trying to get revenge on me for what I did to your brother. But I'm your master now so you've got to obey me."

"Yes, of course, my shallow master," Rasp says. "But please, believe me, I did not try to sabotage you. At least, not yet. While your friend is not here, I do believe she passed through here recently. It just may be that there are different rules at play when one uses Magic in the Underworld. After all, I can already sense this place has some unusual characteristics, which you no doubt see with your very own eyes. Thus, the use of Magic here may be… unpredictable, to say the least."

Great. I look into Rasp's eyes but I don't know if I can trust what he's saying or not. He has it in for me for sure, but it's also clear this is a very strange place.

"If you would allow me a suggestion, oh lowly master," Rasp adds. "If you would like, you could use another wish and we could simply try again? Perhaps my Magic will be far more accurate since we are now in the Underworld itself. I am certain I could find your friend if you give me a second chance."

I look at Rasp suspiciously. He's trying to bait me into burning my second wish. If I did that, it would leave me with only one wish left and that doesn't seem like a good idea. Especially since I don't know what I'm going to find. And I need to hang on to my final wish to get Selfie and me out of here.

"You know, I'm gonna pass on that," I say. "You said she was here recently so maybe I'll do a little looking around first."

"As you wish, my unconfident master," Rasp says.

"And can you please stop with the insults?" I ask.

"Of course, my less-than-adequate master," he says.

I roll my eyes. Well, this is going to be fun. Now the big question is, where am I supposed to look? All I see are these crazy pathways going in all directions. Some end abruptly while others disappear in the distance.

"Do you know which path she took?" I ask.

"Well, I am a Djinn and not a detective," Rasp says, looking down by my feet. "But if I were you, I might consider following those footprints."

Footprints?

I look down, and to my surprise, there's a set of footprints in the sooty material. I kneel to investigate and realize they're boot prints, about the same size as Selfie's feet! Could they be her footprints?

"Let's go," I say.

I follow the footprints until the pathway suddenly goes straight up at a ninety-degree angle. Yet, somehow, the footprints continue. But how can that be?

I lift my right foot and plant it on the vertical surface. Then, I step up, and to my surprise, the surface holds my weight! I lift my other foot and realize I'm now standing parallel to the pathway I was just on. Okay, this is pretty wild, but I'll have to debate the physics at play here later. Right now, I need to keep following these footsteps.

As I walk straight up, I realize everything feels completely normal, like gravity has adjusted to me instead of me adjusting to it. After I've gone a hundred yards or so the pathway levels off again and widens considerably, connecting to a much larger landmass. But unlike the pathway, the terrain here is much more diverse, with rocky hills, tall stalagmites, and towering mountains.

I continue into a dirt ravine when the footprints suddenly stop. That's strange. It's like the person who made them vanished into thin air.

"What happened?" I ask.

"It appears you have reached the end of the trail, my not-so-observant master," Rasp says. "I do hope your friend did not meet a tragic end."

I'm about to tell him to shut his trap when I notice a towering rock castle in the distance. And then I hear—

"Stop lollygagging and keep moving!"

Someone is coming!

I look for the closest hiding spot and dive behind a rock pillar.

"Get back into your ring," I whisper firmly to Rasp, whose body is floating in plain sight. "They'll see you!"

"Is that a wish?" Rasp asks, raising an eyebrow.

"No, it's an order," I snap. "Now do it!"

"Very well," Rasp says, as he shrinks back into the bronze ring.

I peer around the corner and see a group of people heading our way. But as they get closer, I realize their bodies are transparent like ghosts, and they aren't walking but floating along the surface. Holy cow! Are those… souls?

And that's not all. Behind them, shepherding them along with pronged spears, are two gargantuan figures that set off my alarm bells. They have muscular, human-like bodies, but the heads of bulls! If I didn't know better, I'd say they looked like… Minotaurs? And unlike the ghost people, the Minotaurs look completely solid.

"Keep it moving," a Minotaur says. "We don't have all day to process you sorry bunch."

Process? Hmmm. Isn't that what Tormentus told me. Didn't he say his kingdom was the first stop for souls on their journey?

As they pass by, one of the Minotaurs suddenly turns his head in my direction and I duck out of sight. I hold my breath and stay perfectly still. Hopefully, he didn't see me. As their voices fade away, I wait a long time before braving another look. And when I do I'm relieved to see they're gone.

Whew! That was close.

I wipe the sweat off my brow and step back into the open when I'm suddenly lifted into the air by my cape!

"Well, what do we have here?" comes a deep voice.

I'm shocked as my body swivels around and I suddenly find myself staring into the hair-filled nostrils of a Minotaur! H-How did he get there? I mean, I didn't even hear him.

"You nearly avoided me," he says, as his hot breath hits me square in the face. "I probably wouldn't even have noticed you if it weren't for that. You see, nothing shines in the Underworld."

Shines? What's he talking about?

And when I look down, I see something rectangular emitting a bright light from inside my utility belt.

What the heck is that?

And then I realize what gave me away.

It's Selfie's phone!

And it's lit up like a Christmas tree!

TEN

I STEP INTO A STICKY SITUATION

Well, this is quite a pickle.

I hoped to grab Selfie and get out of the Underworld undetected, but I guess that's not going to happen now. Especially since I'm currently in the clutches of a burly Minotaur who is holding me in the air by my own cape!

Ironically, I wouldn't even be in this compromising position if it wasn't for Selfie's phone. For some reason, it decided to light up in my utility belt, giving my position away. If that didn't happen, well, I'd still be free.

But how I got into this situation doesn't matter right now. Instead, I need to focus on getting out of this mess. And my options for that aren't looking particularly good at the moment.

"It must be my lucky day," the Minotaur says, his

voice deep and gravelly. "I'll surely be rewarded when I deliver you to the Supreme Ruler. You're the third living Overworlder to enter the realm."

Wait, what?

Did he just say I'm the *third* living Overworlder to come down here? So, if Selfie is one and I'm another, then who is the third?

"But first, tell me," he continues. "Why are the living so interested in visiting the land of the dead?"

That's a great question. I mean, I know why I'm here, and Selfie never wanted to be here in the first place. But I don't know the motivations of any third person. However, that gives me an idea. Maybe I can use that information to bluff my way out of here.

"I-I'll tell you," I say, struggling to speak as I try to pull my cape free from his iron grip. "But… you've got to let me… go." The neckline of my costume is tightening around my throat, making it hard to breathe.

"I don't think so," he says. "You are in no position to negotiate. Besides, it's a long way from here to the royal castle. If you fail to tell me now, you may run out of air before we arrive."

He's… right about that. If I don't do something, he'll hang me out to die. Well, he'll never see this coming.

I concentrate and try duplicating his power, but quickly realize there's no Meta energy there. So, that means he's not a Meta at all! Ugh, he's just naturally super strong! I feel deflated but I can't give up. Need to…

remove my cape. I reach into my Utility belt and pull out my pocketknife when he slaps it clean out of my hand.

Ow! That hurt!

Okay, I've had enough of this guy! I rear back with my right fist and swing, but I miss and my body twists around and around.

"You are quite the little warrior," he says. "Now, stop this senseless struggling and tell me why you are here? What is your purpose?"

"N-No!" I shout.

My… vision is getting blurry so I guess that leaves me with only one option. I didn't want to use my second wish this early, but clearly, I don't have a choice. I try saying Rasp's name, but it's hard to get enough air in my lungs to say anything!

"R… Ra…," I sputter.

I-I need to catch my breath. I bet Rasp knows what's going on. He's probably watching this from inside his cozy ring, enjoying every second. And why not? He's getting his revenge for what I did to Beezle without even lifting a finger.

Just then, my eyes start watering and I gag. Costume… too tight. This isn't how I imagined things ending. And the worst part is, I… couldn't save Selfie.

I close my eyes and wait for the inevitable, when—

"Release him!" comes a girl's voice.

"Huh?" the Minotaur says, turning his head.

And then—

POW!

The Minotaur's head snaps back and I'm suddenly dropped to the ground. My cape flies over my head as I land hard on my hands and knees. I throw my cape off and inhale huge gulps of air. And that's when I see my savior.

She's wearing a brown cowl and moves faster than lighting. The Minotaur twirls his two-pronged spear and jabs, but the girl easily kicks the weapon out of his hands. The Minotaur looks momentarily shocked, but then tries to pummel her with his gigantic fists. But the girl simply sidesteps him and lands a right hook followed by a left. And then she executes a silky-smooth, jumping roundhouse kick, nailing the brute square in the chest.

The Minotaur CRASHES into the rock pillar, splitting it in half. And then the upper portion topples over and CRACKS on the Minotaur's cranium. Surprisingly, the Minotaur doesn't go down. He merely shakes his head and steps forward, only to fall face-first to the ground.

He doesn't get back up.

Satisfied, the girl brushes off her hands, turns to me, and removes her cowl. And as I stare into her familiar, neon green eyes, my knees go weak.

"K-K'ami?"

"Yes, Elliott Harkness," she says coolly. "It is me."

I-I can't believe it. And other than the cowl, she looks exactly the same as the last time I saw her, with pale, yellow skin, dark, curly hair that cascades down her shoulders in ringlets, and a white outfit with gold trim.

For the first time, I feel a sense of… hope?

"It is good to see you again," she says.

"I-I'm so happy to see you," I stammer, still in a state of disbelief. "I-I can't believe you're actually here."

I try standing up but I feel weak. Then, K'ami reaches out her hand and I take it. For some reason, something seems weird but I can't place it. And as she pulls me to my feet I look at her pretty face and realize I have so much I want to tell her, but I'm tongue-tied.

There's a moment of awkward silence, and then K'ami looks down at the prone Minotaur and says—

"We should leave this place quickly."

"Right," I finally manage to say. "Great idea."

"Follow me," she says, and then takes off, running toward a dark forest I don't remember seeing before.

As I follow her, I'm confused at how I could have missed such a notable landmark. I mean, there must be thousands of trees in here, each stretching hundreds of feet high. So, why didn't I see this forest before?

I don't know the answer, but I do know my lungs are burning. It feels like we've been running forever and I still need to catch my breath. Finally, we reach a clearing, and K'ami stops.

"We should be safer here," K'ami says.

"Thank you," I say, leaning against a tree. "Where are we anyway?"

"We are in a place called the Forgotten Forest," she

says. "It is forgotten unless you remember it."

"Um, what's that supposed to mean?" I ask.

"It means the forest is always here," she says, "but only if you consciously desire to see it. Otherwise, it does not exist. It is like all things in the 'In Between.' Nothing is as it seems."

"Wow, I see that," I say. "Anyway, thanks for saving me back there. I guess I owe you twice now. Once when I was facing Krule and now this."

"If it is within my power," K'ami says, "I will never let you suffer."

"I-I know," I say, suddenly feeling guilty. She's always been there for me, but I couldn't prevent her from dying at Lockdown.

"Elliott Harkness, you cannot change the past," she says, almost like she's reading my mind. "It is impossible to undo what has already been done. The only thing you can change is the future."

"Yeah," I say. "I-I guess so. You know, after the last time I didn't think I'd ever see you again. But then I realized you were sending me messages and I figured you might still be, well, alive."

"I would not call this living," K'ami says, lowering her head. "But yes, I reached out to you because I knew you were searching for your friend, the one who owns that device." Then, I notice she's pointing at my utility belt.

Device? That's right. I reach into my belt for Selfie's phone, but when I pull it out it's no longer shining.

"That's funny," I say. "It lost its light. That's what gave me away to that Minotaur."

"Interesting," K'ami says. "We have moved further away from the castle. Perhaps that device has a homing instinct. Maybe it comes alive the closer it gets to your friend. I heard a rumor that a living Overworlder was inside the castle. Perhaps it is your friend?"

The castle? Suddenly, I remember seeing that rock castle in the distance. The Minotaur was going to take me there. He called it the 'royal castle,' which means it must be home to one of the seven rulers of the Underworld.

"Who's castle is it?" I ask.

"It is the Castle of the Soul Snatcher," K'ami says. "The Supreme Ruler of the In Between."

The Soul Snatcher?

"Tormentus!" I say. "If that's his castle then that's great news! Selfie must be in there!"

"The castle will be difficult to enter," K'ami says. "There are guards posted everywhere. If we get caught, I may not be able to protect you, and the consequences will be… dire."

"I don't care," I say. "I-I have to try. I understand it's high risk, but would you be willing to help me?"

"Of course," K'ami says. "We will go at once."

"Thank you," I say relieved. "You know, I'm lucky to have you as a friend."

"As we said once upon a time," K'ami says, "we are BFFs, are we not?"

"Yes, we are," I say. "Always."

"Then, let us find your friend," she says. "But first, I must warn you. The road will be difficult and you must be mentally prepared. Just like the Forgotten Forest, we will encounter things that will not appear as they truly are. Therefore, if I ask you to do something that seems dangerous, you will need to trust me completely."

"Are you kidding?" I say with a chuckle. "Of course, I trust you. In fact, other than my parents and Selfie, you're probably the person I trust the most."

"I am glad to hear that," she says, smiling for the first time. "We should go. But I recommend we travel in silence as you never know who, or what may be listening."

"Got it," I say, and then I follow her back through the forest.

This time, I keep Selfie's phone handy. After all, if it is acting like a homing device, then it might tell us when we're getting closer to Selfie. I just hope we're not too late.

As I look up at the twisty trees I think about my parents. I sure hope Dad is doing okay, and I bet Mom has figured out I'm no longer on the Waystation. I feel bad not being honest with her, but the last thing I wanted is for her, or anyone else, to follow me into the Underworld. I mean, as far as I know, I punched the only ticket here with Rasp's ring, but I wouldn't put it past TechnocRat to figure out some other way to get down here. So, I'd better figure this out fast.

And while rescuing Selfie is my number one priority, something tells me the secret to beating Tormentus in the Overworld is here in the Underworld. Tormentus said he needs Meta energy to stay in the Overworld. And if the Meta Monitor couldn't find where he's storing it on Earth then maybe Shadow Hawk's theory is correct.

Maybe Tormentus is storing his stolen Meta energy here—in the Underworld.

And if so, it's up to me to stop him.

I watch K'ami put her hand on a fallen tree and leap over it with ease. Now there's a real warrior. What she did to that Minotaur was more than impressive. It's like she's become an even better fighter since she's been stuck here.

But for some reason, something still isn't sitting right. The previous time we saw each other, K'ami told me it was only possible because she asked the Orb of Oblivion for the power to save me one last time. So, if that was the last time, how are we meeting now?

And that's not all. The last time I was in the In Between, K'ami touched my temple but I didn't feel a thing. It was like she was a ghost or a spirit or something.

But now she seems, well, almost real.

I mean, she clocked that Minotaur and then helped me get back on my feet. I don't think a ghost or a spirit could do that, could they? I reach out and touch the fallen tree she just touched. Yep, that feels solid to me.

So, am I imagining things? But then, something else

strikes me funny. She said she reached out to me because she knew I was searching for my friend.

How did K'ami know that if she's been down here?

So, either I'm getting paranoid or I need to get to the bottom of this.

"Um, K'ami?" I whisper.

"Shhh," K'ami says, putting her finger to her lips. "First, let us cross. We can talk safely on the other side."

Cross? Cross what?

I look up and realize we've exited the Forgotten Forest and are now standing at the edge of a huge chasm. There's more land on the other side, but to get there we'll have to cross over a decrepit, wooden bridge hanging in between.

"Seriously?" I ask. "We have to walk across that?"

"Seriously," she says. "We have no choice. The castle is on the other side."

Of course, it is.

I peer over the edge and the bottom seems rather, well, bottomless. I guess we can talk once we get to the other side.

SNAP!

"Did you hear that?" K'ami says, her eyes darting all over the place. "Quickly, you go first and I will follow."

"Are you sure?" I ask.

"I told you to trust me," K'ami says.

"Right," I say, stepping onto the bridge. But for some reason, the wood planks are really sticky and I can't lift my feet. It's like I've stepped in super glue or something.

"I-I'm stuck!" I shout.

"Yes, you are, aren't you?" K'ami says, her voice turning ice cold.

"K'ami?"

When I look back, K'ami is still standing at the edge of the chasm, but her eyes are crackling with orange electricity.

ELEVEN

I RUN INTO AN OLD FRIEND

"K'ami?"

What's happening right now? Just a few seconds ago, K'ami and I were racing to Tormentus' castle to save Selfie. And now my feet are stuck to this wooden bridge while a strange orange energy is pouring out of K'ami's eyes. Something tells me this is trouble.

Big trouble.

"Um, K'ami, are you okay?" I ask. "Because some weird stuff is happening to your eyes."

"I am fine, Elliott Harkness," she says, breaking into a mischievous smile. "But at this moment, you should be more concerned about yourself."

Okay, what's that supposed to mean?

Then, she waves her hand, and suddenly, the chasm

and wooden bridge disappear and I'm standing on top of a huge spider web that stretches from one end of the chasm to the other. I look down and notice the webbing is thicker than a crowbar. So, if this web is strong enough to hold my weight, then I'm guessing whatever spider spun this sucker must be absolutely huge.

Suddenly, the web tilts forward, and when I look across the chasm I see something big, red, and hairy climbing onto the web itself. Now, normally, one would want to stay calm in a situation like this.

So, naturally, I panic.

"K'ami, help!" I call out, helplessly trying to lift my feet off the web. "I-I can't get unstuck!"

"Nor will you," K'ami says, crossing her arms. "After all, the web of a Demon Spider is a notoriously fatal trap."

D-Demon Spider? Did I ever mention that I hate spiders? And I'm pretty sure that includes the Demon variety!

Then, the web pulls again, and when I look up the Demon Spider has reached the center! Now that it's closer I have a better appreciation of its true size, which appears to be larger than a minivan! It fixes its six eyes on me and I suddenly feel like a plate of french fries sitting between Dog-Gone and Pinball.

But as tragic as this is about to become, there's something even more tragic that doesn't make any sense. Why isn't K'ami helping me? When I look back at her joyful face, I remember her words: *We will encounter things that will not appear as they truly are.*

And that's when it hits me.

K'ami would never let something bad happen to me.

Which means…

"Y-You're not K'ami," I say.

"No," she says. "Not anymore."

"Then, who are you?" I ask.

"Are you sure you don't know?" she asks, as the corners of her mouth curl into a sly smile. "I would think it was obvious."

Obvious? What's she talking about? But as I look deep into the orange energy sparking from her eyes, my knees buckle with realization.

No. It-It can't be. It's not possible.

I mean, I destroyed it. Twice!

But as much as my head wants to deny it, in my heart I know it must be true.

It's… the Orb.

The Orb of Oblivion.

The cosmic parasite that feeds off your darkest desires so it can make itself stronger. But how?

My mind starts spinning. I mean, the last time I saw K'ami, she used the power of the Orb to save me from Krule. The Orb agreed to her request when she was holding it, when she was dying in my arms. I remember her telling me she thought the Orb agreed for its own selfish purposes in case something happened to me.

But maybe it wanted something else.

After all, the Orb was a sentient being. I remember K'ami telling me the story of how her people first discovered it. How it had orchestrated its own freedom when it was abandoned on a distant moon.

"What did you do with K'ami?" I demand.

"Oh, she is still here," the Orb says, talking with her voice, speaking through her mouth. "You see, ever since I wrested control of this form, we have been anxiously awaiting your arrival."

"B-But why?" I ask. "I don't get it. Why are you using her? Why are you waiting for me?"

"It's a shame that, despite all of the experiences you have gained, you are still so naive," the Orb says.

"What are you talking about?" I say.

"When we first met," the Orb says, "it was apparent that you, and you alone, had the potential to be an all-powerful host. That if you so desired, you could use me to rule the multiverse with an iron fist. But while you had near-limitless power, you also had an incorruptible heart. Thus, I fully expected that you would ultimately reject my advances—and that if I fell into your hands my fate was sealed."

"I destroyed you!" I shout. "And I'll do it again when I get out of this mess!" I try lifting my feet but I'm still stuck. Then, I remember the Demon Spider and turn back around, but it's still sitting there, staring at me with its multiple beady eyes.

"Yes, you destroyed me," the Orb says. "Or, at least, most of me. You see, when your friend, K'ami Sollarr foolishly took possession of me, I knew that was my one chance to ensure my survival. So, while I was in her grasp, I carved out a fragment of my being and planted it deep inside her mind."

Wait, what?

The Orb put a piece of itself inside K'ami's mind? It really is the ultimate parasite! I mean, how many lives does this thing have? Is there no end?

"This provided me with a means of escape," the Orb continues. "And while I did not expect to travel to this forsaken place, I managed to survive—and then thrive. And the stronger I grew, the more I was able to use her desires to restore her body."

"You don't deserve to be in her body!" I yell. "She's too good for you! Leave her alone!"

"Your compassion for the well-being of your friend is touching," the Orb says, placing the palm of K'ami's hand over her heart. "The good news is that I agree with you. After all, I'm desperate to leave here as quickly as possible. However, there is some form of magic here that is preventing me from leaving on my own. But you are able to come and go as you please. As long as you are wearing the Ring of Suffering."

The Ring of Suffering?

I look down at the bronze ring on my finger.

"How did you know about that?" I ask.

"I know far more than you imagine," the Orb says. "After all, you were connected with me, as was your friend K'ami. And thus, we are connected with each other, which is how you became a useful pawn in my master plan."

Master plan? What's it talking about?

"Allow me to explain," the Orb says. "Let's just say I only recently learned of the Rings of Suffering and the powerful magic they hold inside. Conveniently, I also learned that you, Elliott Harkness, held two of those rings on your space headquarters. As fate would have it, I also recently discovered that your friend, Selfie, was being held inside Tormentus' castle. Therefore, through considerable effort, I was able to exploit our mutual connection to send you direct messages from K'ami Sollarr guiding you to the Underworld. I hoped that you would deliver my means of escape, and that is precisely what you have done."

O.M.G. I'm beyond stunned right now. Based on what the Orb is telling me, this whole thing was a setup! The Orb used those messages from K'ami to lure me down here! But what did it mean when it said I would deliver its means of escape?

"I'll never help you escape," I say.

"Ah, but you already have," it says, "merely by what you're wearing on your finger."

My finger? I look down and see the bronze Ring of Suffering and my stomach sinks. So, is that what it wants?

Does it want to use the ring to get out of here?

"Now we have reached the final stages of my plan," the Orb says. "As I mentioned previously, I am unable to leave this realm on my own. But if you allow me to enter your mind, I will release the soul of your friend, K'ami Sollarr. Then, you will use the Ring of Suffering to return us both to your dimension. Once we are there, I promise to leave your mind for another host. And then I will leave your planet entirely."

"No way!" I yell.

"Think about it," the Orb says. "You failed to save your friend, K'ami Sollarr, once before. But this is your chance for redemption. This is your chance to correct your mistakes of the past. This is your chance to end her suffering once and for all."

I-I can't believe it. The Orb of Oblivion wants to use me to escape the Underworld! But there's no way I can do that. I mean, I want to help Selfie and K'ami more than anything, but I can't knowingly unleash the most powerful weapon of all time back into the universe. Plus, I know K'ami wouldn't want me to do that either.

"Sorry, but no dice," I say.

"That is unfortunate," the Orb says. "I was so hoping you would participate willingly. Now, I will need to take your mind over by force."

Then, it waves K'ami's hand.

SCREEEEE!

Scree? I twist to the source of the noise and the

Demon Spider is on the move again! It's heading straight for me, and this time it doesn't look like it's going to stop!

"Ahh!" I scream. Suddenly, I feel a familiar pressure inside my head. The Orb may only be a fraction of itself, but it still possesses incredible power!

"Yield!" the Orb commands.

"N-Never," I reply through gritted teeth.

I've got to push back, but then, out of the corner of my eye, I spot the Demon Spider! It's even bigger up close, and it's really close—like, nearly on top of me! Then, it extends its front, spindly legs!

"Ahhh!" I yell as the Orb hammers down on my brain. It's… hard to focus with the Demon Spider so close, but I guess that's the Orb's plan! It's trying to distract me so it can grab hold of my mind. So, I've got two choices. Either I can get eaten by a Demon Spider or mind-controlled by the Orb of Oblivion.

If only I… could call for help.

Call? Wait, that's it!

I just need a little space. I concentrate and push back on the Orb with all the mental energy I can muster.

"Ugh!" the Orb yells, as K'ami's body blows back.

Now I've got to time this right. As the spider grabs me around the waist and lifts me clean out of my boots, I focus on Selfie's phone. Then, I quickly duplicate its Magic and send it back through the phone itself.

"Hypnotize the spider!" I command, turning the phone's display towards the hairy beast.

I close my eyes as the phone emits a blinding white flash. And when I open them again the Demon Spider is standing stock still! I-I did it! I used Selfie's phone to hypnotize the spider!

"Now, put me down on dry land," I command, and the spider lowers me back onto solid ground. "Good boy, now wait here."

The spider stays put as I square off with K'ami, or should I say, the Orb inside of K'ami, who has now gotten back to her feet.

"If you destroy me, you'll destroy her," the Orb says, "and I know you don't want that to happen. But if we work together, we can both get what we want."

What it's saying is tempting, but I know right from wrong. And while Selfie's phone is useful, it's not going to get rid of the Orb of Oblivion. Fortunately, I have another solution for that.

"Rasp!" I command. "Come out! Now!"

"Ooh, so commanding, my repulsive master," Rasp says, flowing out of his ring and wrapping around my body like a snake.

"Rasp, I'm making my second wish," I say. "I want you to remove all traces of the Orb of Oblivion from this girl and extinguish its life energy. Now!"

"No!" the Orb yells from K'ami's mouth.

"Aaah!" I scream, dropping to my knees as the Orb sends another wave of pressure through my brain.

"Yes, my suffering master," Rasp says. "Would you

like me to do that now? Or should I wait?"

"N-Now!" I yell.

"Of course," Rasp says, waving both hands.

Suddenly, the pressure in my brain stops as the crackling orange energy streams out of K'ami's eyes and forms a ball over her head. And then Rasp waves his hands once more and the ball is gone!

"Wh-Where am I?" K'ami says. Then, she opens her eyes and they're neon green again. "E-Elliott? Is that really you?"

"Yes," I say, running over to her. But when I put my hand on her shoulder it falls through her entire body! "W-What happened?"

"You have freed me from the Orb," K'ami says. "I have reverted to my soul form. I am sorry for my role in deceiving you."

"K'ami, are you kidding?" I say. "It's not your fault. You were being controlled by the most powerful cosmic parasite in the universe."

"Yes," she says. "But no longer, thanks to you."

"Well, me and Rasp," I say, pointing over my shoulder.

"Thank you, Rasp," K'ami says to the Djinn.

"Oh, it was nothing," Rasp says, waving dismissively and looking embarrassed. "Just some old genie magic."

K'ami smiles, but then I realize her whole body is… fading away?

"What's happening to you?" I ask.

"It is time," K'ami says. "Now that the Orb is no longer holding me here against my will, my soul can finally go to where it belongs. In peace."

"Wait, what do you mean?" I ask, my voice cracking.

"You will understand when it is your time," she says, closing her eyes and extending her arms out to her sides. "Take care, Elliott Harkness. You are an amazing hero. Always remember, never… show… weakness…"

And then she's gone.

TWELVE

I SEE TROUBLE IN TRIPLICATE

K'ami is gone.

And this time, I don't think she's ever coming back.

So much has happened I just want to sit down to process it all, but I can't. I've got to keep moving, and now I've used my second wish to get rid of the Orb of Oblivion—again.

It was a big sacrifice, but I'd do it all over again if it finally gives K'ami the peace she deserves. Besides, it's not like I could let the Orb escape from here. Hopefully, it's gone for good, but I've mistakenly thought that before. I guess the only thing that could have possibly gone wrong is if Rasp didn't do exactly as I asked.

Which, come to think of it, is highly possible.

"Rasp," I say, looking up at my evil genie. "You

fulfilled my wish exactly as I stated it, right? You didn't pull any funny business, did you?"

"Funny business?" Rasp responds, looking offended. "Do you take me for a court jester, my feeble master? I am obligated to obey your wishes and that is precisely what I have done. There is no need to worry your anti-heroic little head."

Great. That's exactly the response I was worried about. But I guess there's nothing I can do about it now. That whole episode was a crazy detour, but it's time I got back to my original mission, which is all about saving Selfie and stopping Tormentus. I just need another minute to catch my breath.

I wiggle my toes in the dirt and look down at Selfie's phone. At least I was able to use it to hypnotize that Demon Spider. I peer over my shoulder and the creature is still standing at attention, waiting for my command.

"Hey, Mr. Demon Spider," I order, "can you please unstick my boots from your web and bring them over?"

As the spider dutifully follows my instructions, I think back to my encounter with the Orb. During its monologue, it said a few things that piqued my interest. Like, how did it learn about the Rings of Suffering down here in the Underworld? I guess it could have used the mental bond between itself, K'ami, and me. But at the same time, it said it could barely get those messages to me in the Overworld. So, that theory doesn't hold much water.

And the more I think about it, the more I realize the Orb had nothing to do with Selfie's disappearance. The Orb said it had been trapped inside K'ami's body for a long time. It merely used my desire to rescue Selfie as a means to get me and the bronze Ring of Suffering into the Underworld so it could escape.

Talk about a bizarre coincidence.

But at least it confirmed one thing I needed to know. It told me Selfie was inside Tormentus' castle. So, now that I know that for sure, I need to go there as soon as possible. I just need to get across that chasm. But how?

Just then, a spindly leg drops my boots in front of me.

Bingo, I think I just found my ride!

I scrape the soles of my boots on the ground to remove any leftover sticky residue and put them back on my feet. Then, I stand up, face the Demon Spider, and say, "Okay buddy, put me on your back and carry me to the other side. And no eating me, got it?"

The Demon Spider stares at me with its multiple, unblinking eyes, and then picks me up with its front legs and places me gently between its thorax and abdomen. Somehow, I resist the urge to barf my brains out as I grip its hairy back. Then, once I'm settled, the giant spider turns around and crawls across its web.

I look down into the bottomless abyss and count my lucky stars. Without my eight-legged taxi, there's no way I could have cleared this gorge without using my third wish. And I'm saving that one to go home again.

Speaking of home, I sure hope the team has held on without me. After all, I was the only one who was somewhat effective against those Meta zombies. But I was nearly out of gas when the zombies I negated suddenly reappeared. That showed me the awesome power of Tormentus.

But something tells me the secret to defeating him is here in the Underworld. I just don't know what it is or where to find it.

Just then, the Demon Spider steps onto land and I realize we've made it to the other side. Well, that was fast. I slide off its back and face the hairy beast. That's when I realize I don't know how long Selfie's hypnosis power lasts, so I better not tempt fate.

"Well, thank you," I say. "I appreciate your help, but now I'm leaving so don't even think about following me. Oh, and it was great taking you out for a spin."

Then, I make a quick getaway. After walking a good distance, I peer over my shoulder to confirm that the spider stayed put. I'll tell you, Selfie's phone is a useful tool. If we ever get out of this mess, I'll have to borrow it to make Grace do my chores.

But before anything like that can happen, I've got to find Tormentus' castle. According to K'ami, it was on this side of the chasm. Fortunately, it doesn't take long to find it, because as soon as I climb over the next ridge, I spot a large structure protruding from a mountaintop.

It's the castle!

It's absolutely ginormous, and as I take it all in, I realize that it's shaped like a massive skull. Two large circles are carved into the face of the rock that look like eye sockets, and there's a smaller, triangular hole in the center that looks like a nose. The entrance is a large, jagged 'jaw-bridge' forming the lower part of its mouth. And at the top are two huge, curved spires that look like horns.

Well, I'm no architect but whoever designed this place did a great job making it look as unwelcoming as possible. Before I go rushing inside, I realize I should probably double check if this is the right place. After all, there's nothing more embarrassing than busting into the wrong evil castle.

Now, I don't have a GPS, but I do have the next best thing. So, I pull out Selfie's phone which greets me with a big, blinking arrow pointing directly at the castle. Well, that's pretty clear, but just in case, I rotate the phone and the arrow rotates with it, so it's always pointing back to the castle. Well, I guess that confirms it. This is the place.

Just. Freaking. Wonderful.

I swallow hard, tuck the phone back into my belt, and head for the castle. As I cross the rugged terrain, I try to stay low and behind rock cover at all times. After all, the castle is situated perfectly for a panoramic view of the land below. So, if I want to stay undetected, I need to operate in full stealth mode.

"I can get you there faster if you wish, my less-than-conspicuous master," Rasp says, the sudden sound of his voice making me jump out of my skin.

I look behind me and smack my palm against my forehead. Rasp! How could I forget about Rasp? And he's just floating along behind me—in plain sight!

"Get back in your ring!" I whisper firmly.

"I don't understand why you are bothering with all of this sneaking around," Rasp says, shrugging his shoulders. "With one simple wish, I can transport you right inside the castle. It will save you hours of effort."

"Nice try," I say. "But I'm not wasting my last wish on that. Now, please get inside your ring before you give us away."

"Is that a wish?" Rasp asks.

"No," I say. "It's an order."

"Very well," Rasp says, "but in the future, I would be very appreciative if you would knock before calling upon my services again. I plan to indulge in a long nap, which is far more exciting than the boring wishes you have requested thus far."

Then, he smiles and flows back into his ring.

Well, there's one crisis averted. I continue for what seems like hours until I finally reach the base of the castle. Looking up, I see several Minotaurs patrolling the drawbridge and realize the hard part is just beginning.

Now, how do I get inside?

I have to admit, Rasp's offer is appealing. I mean, sure, I could use my last wish to magically appear inside the castle, but then what? Plus, who knows where he'd drop me anyway? I'm sure he'd love nothing more than to dump me in the middle of a Minotaur birthday party or a pit of lava. And then there's that small problem of never getting Selfie home again.

No thanks. I'll take my chances and do it the hard way. So, I guess it's time to use some of those tricks Shadow Hawk taught me.

I reach into my utility belt and pull out a handful of smoke pellets. Then, I chuck them onto the drawbridge, as far away from the entrance as possible.

PFOOM!

A huge cloud of black smoke erupts.

"What's that?" a Minotaur calls out.

As the guards race towards the smoke cloud, I spring into action. I pull out my grappling gun, set it to silent, and fire at the entranceway. The claw-end hooks the side of the drawbridge and the line goes taut. Then, I release the trigger and it pulls me skyward.

Using my upward momentum, I swing my legs over the drawbridge, roll onto the surface, and run inside. Seconds later I'm standing inside a huge foyer, but it's so dark I don't know where to go next.

Then, I hear footsteps!

I duck behind a wide column as a squad of Minotaurs rushes past to join the investigation outside. I'm breathing hard but I can't just stay here. It's not going to take them long to figure out it was a diversion. I've got to keep moving, but to where?

Then, I look down and see a rectangular light shining from my belt. Duh! Selfie's phone! It'll tell me exactly where to go!

I pull it out and this time the arrow on the display screen is pointing to my left, away from the foyer. I take off, covering the bright light with my glove. Now and then I peek beneath my hand to make sure I'm on track. First, the arrow points right, and then left, and then right again as it leads me through a maze of corridors until we come to a dead end. I'm now standing in front of an arched doorway and when I look at the arrow it's now pointing straight down.

Down?

That's when I realize I'm standing in front of a pitch-black stairway. I shine the phone inside and see a set of narrow, stone stairs winding downward. Seriously? Is an underground mission in the Underworld really fair?

Maybe the phone has it wrong? Except, when I look at the screen again the arrow is still pointing down, but now it's blinking aggressively like it's yelling at me. Well, I guess there's no mistaking it. It's telling me Selfie is down there.

"This way!" comes a surprisingly close voice.

Uh-oh! Gotta move so I step inside. As I race down the dark stairs, I consider pulling out my flare, but it's so bright it might give me away. Instead, I turn Selfie's phone outward and let the display light guide me.

By the time I reach the bottom I'm out of breath, but when I flash the phone around, I gasp because I'm standing in some sort of a… dungeon? The ceiling is low and the space is narrow. The center is filled with wooden tables, iron shackles, and branding irons, but the prison cells lining the walls are empty.

Where's Selfie?

I check the phone again and this time the arrow is pointing straight ahead. I follow it through the dungeon when the space suddenly opens up into a larger, airier chamber. The ceiling is high and there's a row of small windows letting in light. Strangely, there's a circular, stone structure sitting in the center of the room, and as I walk towards it, I pass a heaping pile of bones.

The arrow on Selfie's phone is now blinking on overdrive, and as I walk around the stone structure it gives way to an opening blocked by metal bars. It's another prison! And when I look inside, I see a brown-haired girl in a white costume huddled in the corner.

"Selfie?" I call out.

As the girl slowly raises her head, her blue eyes go wide. "E-Epic?" she says weakly. "Is that really you?"

Suddenly, my heart soars and tears of joy flow freely from my eyes. I-I can't believe it! It's her! I did it! I found her!

"Yes!" I say, grabbing the bars. "It's me! Now let's get you out of here!"

"E-Epic!" Selfie says, her voice cracking.

"It's okay," I say, pulling on the bars but they don't budge. "I'll get you out of here. Just give me a minute."

"N-No!" Selfie stammers.

"No?" I say confused. "Are you saying you don't want to get out of here?"

I step back and look into her eyes. Maybe she's mad at me. I mean, I couldn't blame her after what I put her through.

"N-No, stop!" Selfie says again, this time pointing over my head. "I-I mean, look out!"

Look. Out?

Suddenly, I hear heavy panting behind me—lots of heavy panting—like Dog-Gone in stereo. What could be making all that racket?

Then, I remember the heaping pile of bones.

I swallow hard and turn around slowly, only to find six eyes staring down at me. And that's when I realize I'm in trouble times three, because I'm not just looking at the razor-sharp teeth of a giant dog, but a giant dog with three angry-looking heads.

THIRTEEN

I MIGHT BE A CHEW TOY

You know when they tell you life's not fair?

Well, I don't know who 'they' are, but I'm guessing *they* were probably referring to a mission like this. I mean, after all I've been through—which includes traveling to the Underworld, arguing with an evil Djinn, destroying another Orb of Oblivion, almost being a spider snack, watching the soul of my best friend vanish into thin air, and finding my long-lost teammate—now I'm destined to be dog kibble?

Yep, life's definitely not fair.

Especially when it's about to end in the messiest way possible. That's because, at the moment, I'm standing face-to-snout, or should I say 'snouts,' with a giant, three-headed dog who looks hungrier than Dog-Gone at an all-you-can-eat chicken buffet.

And to make matters worse, this particular dog looks like a cross between a Rottweiler and a pack of Timber Wolves—in triplicate! It has jet-black fur, six orange eyes, and lots of really, really sharp teeth. As I look from vicious head to vicious head, two thoughts come to mind. One, they must go through a ton of chew toys around here. And two, I think it's planning to add me to its bone collection!

Just then, the center head positions itself above me and a dollop of wet slobber rolls off its oversized tongue and drenches my feet. Well, that's disgusting.

"ROWLFF!" the left head barks, jarring my ears.

"Hey, easy there, big guy," I say, backing up against the cold bars of Selfie's jail cell. "I'm not here to hurt you. I'm friendly. I love dogs. Except when they steal my popcorn, of course, but I'm sure you wouldn't do that."

"GRRR!" the right head growls, its nostrils flaring.

Great, now everybody is in on the act.

"Epic, be careful!" Selfie warns.

I'd love to, but right now I'm not sure that's an option. I've had some pretty intense wrestling matches with Dog-Gone before but that was for fun. This is an entirely different dog show! I really don't want to tangle with a rabid three-headed dog, and then I realize I may not have to.

I reach into my utility belt and grab Selfie's phone. This little doohickey has been a real lifesaver so far, so let's hope it's got one more trick up its microchip.

"How about a group picture?" I ask. "Why don't you get those heads together and show those pearly whites?"

"My phone!" Selfie exclaims. "You brought it with you!"

"Yep," I say, flashing her a cheesy smile. "Now check it out as I—"

But before I can even finish my sentence, the three-headed hound lashes out with its oversized paw and bats the phone clear out of my hand! I watch in horror as Selfie's phone flies through the air and CLATTERS onto the hard, stone floor. Well, that's what I get for being overconfident.

Then, the dog narrows its eyes—as in, all of them.

Uh-oh.

"Get back!" I yell, diving out of the way as the center head lunges forward and CRUNCHES through the metal bars of Selfie's cell!

I hit the ground hard and my right knee flares in pain, but I can't worry about that now. I need to make sure Selfie is okay. Unfortunately, I can't see anything behind the massive body of the three-headed dog, including Selfie's prison.

"Selfie?" I call out, but there's no answer. "Selfie, are you okay?"

Why isn't she answering?

As the center head spits out metal bars, the other heads bare their teeth and SNAP! I scramble to my feet, barely avoiding a chomping. Okay, I've had enough. It's time to go on the offensive!

I don't want to use my last wish, so I reach back into my belt and activate my flare. I wave it threateningly and the dog backs up. I knew it would work! "That's right pup," I say. "I'm the one in charge h—"

CHOMP! GULP!

Holy smokes! The right head just swallowed the flare whole! That's ridiculous! I mean, what are Underworld dogs made of these days?

"GGGRAARRL," the heads snarl as the dog pushes me into a corner.

"Um, bad dog!" I yell. "Sit!"

But it doesn't listen. As my back presses against the rock wall, I realize I'm out of options except for one. I look down at the ring on my finger. Well, I may never get home, but at least I won't be dog food.

I'm about to call Rasp when—

"Hey, look this way you overgrown flea bag!"

As the dog turns its heads there's a bright, white flash. I shield my eyes, and when the light subsides, I find the three-headed nightmare standing motionless.

Which means—

"Epic!" Selfie says, running towards me, and the next thing I know she throws her arms around my shoulders.

I feel my face go flush as I hug her back and her body shudders as she cries in my arms. I'm so happy she's okay that tears flow down my own cheeks. And then she suddenly lets go and pulls back, her face bright red.

"Sorry about that," she says, looking embarrassed and wiping her eyes. "I'm just so happy to see you. I-I can't believe you came for me. I knew you'd try to help me. I just didn't know if you could."

"Believe me," I say, dabbing my eyes with my cape, "I'm happy to see you too. I-I couldn't live with myself if I left you down here. I mean, it's my fault you're even here in the first place." Then, I look down at my feet and say, "If I didn't negate the Berserker's Meta energy, then none of this would have happened. It's okay if you're mad at me. You can sock me if you want to."

"What?" she says, her eyebrows rising. "I'm not going to sock you. And I'm not mad at you either. Look, what happened wasn't your fault. It was just… unexpected. It's not like you did it intentionally."

"A-Are you sure you're not mad at me?" I ask.

"Of course, I'm not," she says. "Now stop being ridiculous."

"Okay," I say, feeling relieved.

"By the way," she says, "how did you get down here anyway?"

"With this," I say, showing her the ring.

"Epic, are you crazy?" she asks. "That's the bronze Ring of Suffering! You barely managed to control Beezle!"

"Yep," I say, "and trust me when I tell you the Djinn inside this one is a real peach. But he's also our only ticket home. I've got one wish left."

"Well, you'll have to hold onto it," she says, "because as much as I want to go home, we can't go yet. I think Tormentus' power source is down here."

"Wait, what?" I say. "How do you know that?"

"Because when I first got here," she says, "I escaped from the Berserker and took off. All of these giant Minotaur goons were chasing me, but I managed to hide from them, at least for a little while. But while I was on the run, I ducked inside a massive chamber that was unlike all the others. I mean, practically the whole room was a pool, but it wasn't holding water. Instead, it was holding a massive reservoir of orange energy."

Did she just say orange energy?

As in, orange Meta energy?

"But that's not all," she continues. "Floating above the pool was a man, but he looked kind of out of it. At first, I couldn't figure out what he was doing, but as I watched the flow of orange energy it became clear. It was like he was acting as a conduit. Like he was drawing the energy out of the pool, through his body, and up to the surface."

A conduit?

Suddenly, Tormentus' words come back to me: *If I had a constant, uninterrupted supply of Meta energy, well, then I could stay in the Overworld forever."*

So, is this man that Selfie saw providing Tormentus with his supply of Meta energy? I don't know for sure, but I do know one thing, we've got to get to that chamber as quickly as possible. If this is where Tormentus is storing his stolen Meta energy, then this is how we can stop him!

"Do you remember how to get there?" I ask.

"I think so," Selfie says. "I think it was close to here."

"Great, then let's go," I say. But then I see the three-headed dog sitting at attention. "What about Fido?"

"He'll stay," Selfie says. "Isn't that right, good boy?"

As the three-headed monster wags his tail, I realize Selfie's phone might also be a useful training tool for other pooches suffering from obedience issues, like a certain invisible German Shepherd I know. But that'll have to wait. Right now, we've got a world to save!

"Okay, then," I say. "After you."

I follow Selfie back through the dungeon to the stairwell. I have to say, it feels great having her by my side again. She's amazing. In fact, sometimes I think she's even braver than Shadow Hawk. I mean, after being trapped in the Underworld she could have begged to go home, but instead she's leading the charge to stop Tormentus. Now that's a real hero! But now that I've got her back, I need to make sure I get her out of here alive.

"Follow me," she says, entering the stairwell.

"Just be careful," I whisper. "I heard voices when I was at the top of the stairs."

Selfie gives me a thumbs up and ducks into the stairwell. I stay close behind and when we reach the top, she gives me the 'wait' signal. She presses her back against the wall and listens intently. After a few seconds, she gives me the 'all-clear' sign and we start moving again.

I try to keep up as she leads me through a series of corridors. Eventually, we return to the main hall, and suddenly, Selfie pulls me behind a pillar as a battalion of Minotaurs runs past. I'm guessing they figured out my smoke pellet diversion by now. Once they're gone, Selfie nods, and I follow her across to another stairwell. Then, she goes down the stairs.

Great, here we go again.

I take a deep breath and follow. This stairwell has more steps than the last one, and as we descend, I suddenly feel a strange sensation coursing through my body, like my blood is… electric? When we finally reach the bottom, Selfie stops me on the last stair. That's when I notice a strange, orange glow illuminating the stairwell.

"This is it," she whispers. "It's in there."

I nod but based on how my body feels I could already tell. I mean, that orange glow isn't coming from some orange light bulb, it's coming from pure, unfiltered Meta energy!

"Check it out," she says. And then she slips inside.

I follow her lead, but as soon as I step inside I do a double take, because the vision I had of what she described doesn't do this place justice.

Not by a longshot.

First, the pool of orange Meta energy is way bigger than any pool I've seen. In fact, it looks more like a lake!

And the surface of the pool isn't smooth and calm, but choppy and volatile, emitting random orange sparks. Then, I realize Dad's Meta energy, Skunk Girl's Meta energy, the whole team's Meta energy are all contained in this bubbly, churning mass.

And second, just like Selfie said, a man is floating above the pool, covered in swirling orange energy. Except, the more I stare at him, the more I realize he isn't a man at all. In fact, he looks… familiar?

Then, my stomach drops.

O. M. G!

"Um, Epic?" Selfie says. "Are you okay?"

No. Not really.

Because that's no man.

That's… Siphon?

FOURTEEN

I GET A SUPREME SURPRISE

I can't believe what I'm seeing.

That's definitely Siphon, and he's hovering over this giant pool of Meta energy, funneling it through his body to the Overworld! When Tormentus told me he wanted a constant, uninterrupted supply of Meta energy to keep him in the Overworld, I never imagined he meant something like this!

But how is this even possible? I mean, the last time I saw Siphon, Beezle intentionally twisted my wish around and removed all of Siphon's life energy. Then, to pour salt in the wound, Tormentus showed up out of nowhere and took Siphon's soul. So, I guess that explains what Siphon is doing here. But does that also mean…

I lean forward for a closer look when I realize I can see right through Siphon's body, just like I could with

K'ami. So, that means Siphon is just a soul!

Somehow, Tormentus is using Siphon's Meta Manipulation power to funnel Meta energy to the Overworld. That's got to be how Tormentus is staying up there!

But if Tormentus has Siphon, why does he need me? I mean, Siphon and I are both Meta Manipulators. But then I remember something else. Tormentus said if I came to the Underworld willingly, he'd release Selfie back to the Overworld. I didn't catch it at the time, but he never said anything about just taking my soul. Nope, instead he wanted all of me—body *and* soul!

Which means he wanted me down here alive, not dead. But… why?

Then, I notice something. The Meta energy flowing from Siphon isn't a constant stream. It's sporadic, coming in spurts. And that's when the lightbulb goes off.

Because Siphon is just a soul, maybe he can't generate a consistent flow of Meta energy. And if that's the case, now I understand why Tormentus needed me. Since I'm alive, my Meta Manipulation power would generate a stronger flow of energy to him in the Overworld.

Well, sorry Tormentus, but I'm about to foil your plan. In fact, I'm about to cut off your Meta supply!

But before I can act—

"Um, Epic," Selfie says, tapping me on the shoulder. "We're not alone."

What? The next thing I know, Minotaurs appear

behind us!

"Epic!" Selfie yells, as two Minotaurs grab her arms.

"Let her go!" I order.

But the Minotaurs don't listen, and then the brutes step aside as a larger Minotaur wearing a red cape strides into the chamber.

"Your presence is requested by the Supreme Ruler," he says to me with a booming voice. "Come or the girl will pay the price."

Everything inside of me wants to clobber this guy but Selfie is in danger. I can't risk anything happening to her.

"Okay," I say quickly. "I'll come but don't hurt her."

"A wise choice," the caped Minotaur says. "This way." And then he turns sharply and enters the stairwell.

The Minotaurs close ranks behind me and we go back up the stairwell. I can't believe it. We were about to stop Tormentus and now this.

As we reach the top something strikes me as odd. Wasn't Tormentus the Supreme Ruler? So, if he's still in the Overworld, then how could he request our presence?

We move through a labyrinth of corridors until we reach a large chamber that's different from the others. As our footsteps echo on the black marble floor I notice large, blood-red banners hanging from the ceiling and dozens of stained-glass windows lining the walls, each depicting innocent souls in various states of torture.

Lovely.

I wish I could see in front of me but the Minotaurs

are so huge all I see are their bulging back muscles. Then, they suddenly stop and kneel, and I find myself staring at a throne made of human skulls! But that's not all, because sitting on the throne is a man wearing a suit of intimidating black armor. And he's staring at me with a pair of intense, green eyes through a slit running across his helmet.

I swallow hard.

Well, there's no mistaking it. This must be the Supreme Ruler—whoever he is. There's a moment of awkward silence, and then—

"Welcome, Mr. Zero," he says finally breaking the silence with a surprisingly pretentious, nasally sounding voice. "I have waited a long time to meet you."

For some reason, I feel like I know that voice, but I can't figure out why.

"I see you're not alone," he says. "And I am not referring to your teammate."

Huh? What's he talking about? And then I realize he's looking down at my right hand. But why? And that's when I remember I'm wearing the bronze ring!

How does he know about that?

But then he raises his right hand and I see something gleaming on his ring finger. Suddenly, a chill runs down my spine. H-He's wearing a gold ring—and carved into the face is the symbol of a lightning bolt!

"Th-That's the gold Ring of Suffering!" I blurt out.

"Ah, so you have noticed," he says, spinning it

around his finger with his other hand. "Indeed, it is."

I'm shocked. I thought the gold Ring of Suffering was lost for good, but now it's here, right in front of my eyes, sitting on the finger of the Supreme Ruler of the Underworld! Well, this isn't good, because the gold ring supposedly holds Terrog inside, the most dangerous of the Djinn Three!

"Now, Mr. Zero, please hand me your ring," the Supreme Ruler says. "I would love to add it to my collection."

Wait. Did he call me 'Mr. Zero?'

Suddenly, everything clicks. Mr. Zero. That nasally voice. The gold Ring of Suffering. The last time I saw the gold Ring of Suffering, it was an image on a certain someone's laboratory screen. Which means I know who the Supreme Ruler is.

"Y-You're Max Mayhem!" I exclaim.

At first, the Supreme Ruler doesn't respond, but then he reaches up and removes his helmet, revealing his bald head and handlebar mustache.

Th-That's him! I was right! But then again, is it the original Max Mayhem or just another clone?

"Very good, Mr. Zero," Max Mayhem says as a smirk creeps across his creepy face. "I am impressed."

"But what are you doing here?" I ask. "What do you want?"

"You have an inquisitive mind," Max Mayhem says. "I like that. I will be more than happy to answer all of your questions—after you hand over the bronze Ring of Suffering."

"No!" I say, instinctively covering the ring with my other hand. My gut tells me to call Rasp and use my last wish to get Selfie and me out of here, but in my head, I know I can't do that. I'm not sure what Max Mayhem is doing here, but something tells me he's involved with Tormentus. But how?

Then, I remember what Tormentus said.

He told me he struck a bargain with a new business partner. And with his partner's help, they turned his collection of lost souls into a Meta-draining army.

Then, I remember something else. That Minotaur who nearly killed me told me I was the third living Overworlder to come into the realm. So, if Selfie and I are two of the three, then Max Mayhem must be the third!

"You're helping Tormentus, aren't you?" I ask. "You're helping him conquer our world! But why?"

"For a good cause," Max Mayhem says. "Actually, the greatest cause of all. My immortality."

"What?" I say confused. "What are you talking about?"

"I will explain," he says. "But first, the ring."

"I-I won't give it to you," I say.

"I understand," Max Mayhem says. "Gentlemen, please remove the girl's arms."

"Epic!" Selfie screams.

"Wait!" I say quickly. "Okay, okay. Here." I slip the ring off my finger and hand it to the caped Minotaur who brings it to Max Mayhem.

"There, that was easy, wasn't it?" Max Mayhem says, closing his fist around the bronze ring. "Now I will answer your questions. Why am I here? It is quite simple. As you have probably realized by now, the laws of physics behave differently in the Underworld. But what you may not have realized is that the laws of time are equally distorted. And while I am the world's smartest man, not even I could stop what was happening to my body in the Overworld."

"Your body?" I say. "What was happening to your body in the Overworld?"

"I was dying," Max Mayhem says rather matter-of-factly. "After working tirelessly on behalf of humanity to rid the world of that alien scourge known as Meta-Man, I failed to realize that, all the while, he was slowly getting rid of *me*. You see, although I didn't know it at the time, the chief object of my study—Meta-Man's alien spacecraft—was destroying me. As I labored for decades over Meta-Man's ship, studying its symbols, breaking down its exterior, in turn *it* was breaking *me* down. That's because Meta-Man's ship was slowly releasing deadly, undetectable waves of radiation that were ravaging my body. When I first got sick, I thought it was just the natural effects of aging, but I quickly realized I had contracted an irreversible alien cancer for which there was no manmade cure."

An alien cancer?

I'm stunned. I mean, one of Max Mayhem's clones showed me Meta-Man's ship but never said anything about cancer.

"I was not going to let Meta-Man get me before I got him," Max Mayhem continues, his eyes narrowing. "So, I tasked my clones with secret missions. Each mission had two key objectives. The first was to find a solution to fully restore my health. The second was to uncover the path to true immortality. Many clones perished during their experiments, but then, one day, my strategy paid off."

You know, by the way he's talking I think he's definitely the original Max Mayhem!

"One of my clones discovered the location of this gold ring," Max Mayhem says. "And once we recovered it, I became Terrog's master. When I first summoned him, I thought he could heal me with a simple wish, but I was mistaken. Due to its alien origin, Terrog was not able to use his Magic to reverse the cancer that was mutating my cells. But he had another idea. He told me about the Underworld, where time moved much more slowly. He convinced me that if I came here, I could live forever. Ironic, isn't it? After all, this is where souls come once you die. Yet, if you come here while you're living, you can avoid death for all of eternity."

Okay, this guy is even crazier than his clones!

"So, I used my first wish," Max Mayhem says. "I commanded Terrog to bring me to the Underworld. Here, I met Tormentus, the famed Snatcher of Souls. We quickly realized we had common goals. We both wanted to rule, but while he desired to rule the Overworld, I told him my goal was to rule the Underworld. From there everything fell into place. We devised a bargain, and in exchange for his seat of power ruling the In Between, I used my second wish to equip him for success in the Overworld. I gave Tormentus an army of Meta-draining zombies and repurposed Siphon's soul as a Meta energy funnel to keep him in the Overworld. We both got what we wanted. Or so he thought."

Hold on. Is he saying he lied to Tormentus?

"I withheld a small detail," Max Mayhem says. "For while I desired to rule the Underworld, I never lost my desire to also rule the Overworld. And now that you are here, I will be able to do both."

"Now that I'm here?" I say. "What does that mean?"

"Quite a lot, actually," he continues. "I have been watching you. In fact, ever since you put on the bronze Ring of Suffering, I have been tracking you quite closely."

Wait, what? What's that supposed to mean?

And then it hits me.

"Rasp!" I blurt out.

"Yes, Rasp," Max Mayhem says. "You see, the Djinn Three are in constant communication with one another inside their rings."

Inside their rings?

OMG. I'm such an idiot. I mean, how many times did I order Rasp back inside his ring? No wonder he didn't put up a fight about it. Every time he went inside, he was talking with his brothers! He was updating them on everything I did!

"Through Rasp, I learned of your exploits in great detail," Max Mayhem says. "From how you destroyed the Orb of Oblivion fragment to how you escaped my three-headed pet. But most important of all, I learned about your immense Meta power. And according to Terrog, you are exactly the one I seek."

"Seek?" I say nervously. "For what?"

"For my reign of power to begin," Max Mayhem says. "You see, Terrog believes he can irradicate my alien cancer if his Magic is boosted with a substantial load of Meta energy. And despite our significant stores of Meta energy, we still do not have enough. But that has all changed now. According to Terrog, your level of Meta energy is substantial. And once I use my final wish to transfer all of your Meta energy to Terrog, he can finally restore me to full health. And then I will destroy Tormentus and fulfill my destiny as ruler of both the Overworld *and* Underworld."

FIFTEEN

I WISH I WAS SOMEWHERE ELSE

I've got major problems.

Max Mayhem just told me he's going to give all of my Meta energy to Terrog who will heal him from his alien cancer. Then, he's planning to destroy Tormentus and take over both the Overworld and Underworld! I need to stop him, but he took the bronze Ring of Suffering so I can't call Rasp for help. And Selfie is still being restrained by Max Mayhem's Minotaur henchman.

So, this is not good.

I've got to think of a way out of this, but Max Mayhem is leading us back down to the Meta energy pool so I'm running out of time!

"Watch it!" I say to the Minotaur behind me as he prods me with his two-pronged spear.

Boy, I sure wish Mom was here. I regret not telling

her what I was doing. Maybe I was wrong thinking she'd try to stop me. Maybe she would've come with me. Then, I probably wouldn't be in this mess right now.

Suddenly, we reach a familiar stairwell and I swallow hard. The Meta pool is only a few steps away. I need a plan to stop Max Mayhem, but I don't know what to do.

"Keep moving!" bellows the caped Minotaur.

As my boots echo down the winding stairs, I try to come up with some brilliant plan to turn this situation around. Unfortunately, my brain is empty. But then, as we near the bottom, I feel the rushing sensation of Meta energy again. That's it!

When we reach the bottom, someone shoves me hard and I stumble into the chamber. That's okay, I'll take my lumps now because as I look at that pool of beautiful orange Meta energy, I realize everything I need is right here. I'll just have to pick my moment carefully because Selfie is still in enemy hands.

I glance over and she looks scared out of her gourd. I sure wish I could tell her what I'm thinking but I can't. Then, I notice the phone holster on her belt is snapped shut and I wonder if her phone is in there.

Suddenly, the caped Minotaur grabs my collar and pulls me to the edge of the Meta pool. I peer over my shoulder at the bubbling mass behind me and it dawns on me that I've never duplicated straight Meta energy before. With everyone's powers all mixed up, I'm not sure what will happen when I duplicate its energy—or if my body can even handle it.

"Do you take me for a fool, Mr. Zero?" Max Mayhem asks.

"Um, was that a rhetorical question?" I ask.

"I know what you are thinking," he says, "and I advise you not to do anything foolish. Unless you would like to watch your friend being torn limb by limb."

"Epic?" Selfie says, her face terrified.

"Relax," I say to Max Mayhem, raising my hands. "I'm not going to do anything stupid."

Darn it, he's on to me. I don't want Selfie to get hurt, but I've got to do something. Otherwise, it's lights out for the world.

"Excellent," he says. "I have waited a long time for this moment, and it would be a shame if we had to stop for any… unnecessary delays."

Then, he raises his right fist and my eyes go wide because he's not only wearing the gold Ring of Suffering but the bronze one too! Which means he's now the master of both Terrog and Rasp!

"Before we begin," Max Mayhem says, as a broad smile stretches across his face, "I must thank you for all of your gifts. Not only will you be the catalyst to restoring my health, but you also brought me three extra wishes. And while you will not survive to see them in use, I can assure you they will be used wisely."

Not. Survive?

"Now we have some pressing business to attend to,"

he continues. "Terrog, I summon you!"

Suddenly, the gold ring sparks, and a trail of red smoke swirls around Max Mayhem twice before stopping over his head in the form of a giant, hideous creature. Similar to Rasp and Beezle, he's spirit-like and resembles a troll, except with red skin, bulging red eyes, long pointy ears, and a shock of black hair that reminds me of a shark's fin.

"Yes, master," he says, his screechy voice like nails running down a chalkboard. "How may I serve you?"

A chill runs down my spine. I-I can't believe it. I mean, after all of this time wondering about Terrog, here he is! And he's not only the most powerful of the Djinn Three but the most terrifying. I suddenly have the sinking feeling things are about to get much, much worse.

"Terrog, it is time," Max Mayhem says, his voice jubilant. "I am ready to follow your guidance."

"Yes, master," Terrog says, eyeing me up and down. "He appears unimpressive on the outside, yet he is most certainly the one. If I combine his substantial Meta energy with the energy collected in this pool, I will be able to boost my power and relieve you of your illness. All you need to do is wish it to be so."

Wait, what? Everything is moving too fast! I look back at Selfie and the Minotaurs have her arms stretched wide, ready to pull if necessary. I-I've got to do something!

"With pleasure," Max Mayhem says. "Terrog, I am

using my third and final wish to do exactly as you say! I wish for you to combine the Meta energy of this child with the Meta energy collected in this pool to boost your Magic and relieve me of this wretched alien cancer!"

"Yes, master," Terrog says, his eyes glowing red. "Your wish is my command."

Uh-oh.

Terrog lifts his arms, throws back his head, and chaos ensues. First, all of the pool's Meta energy redirects away from Siphon and starts funneling into Terrog's body! Then, Terrog looks down at me and I feel sharp, intense pain all over!

"Aaahhh!" I scream, doubling over and dropping to my knees. It… feels like he's ripping my skeleton right out of my body! But I know it's not my skeleton, it's my Meta energy. And when I look up, I see it for the first time, flowing between us like thick, orange strands! I try pulling it back, but… he's just so powerful. It's like we're playing tug-of-war with my Meta essence!

"Epic!" Selfie cries out.

"Yes!" Max Mayhem shouts. "Yes!"

I-I've never felt pain like this before. It's… soul-wrenching. I-I'm fighting with everything I've got, but he's too strong. I can feel it… slipping away! And then it releases—and the orange strands leave my body and flow into his.

No!

Suddenly, I feel faint. And when I look up, orange

energy is circling around Terrog like he's the nucleus of a giant atom!

"Now, Terrog!" Max Mayhem commands. "Relieve me of this cursed cancer now!"

"Yes, master," Terrog says, his eyes flickering orange. "I shall relieve you of your illness. But first, I must attend to my own pressing business."

"What?" Max Mayhem says, clearly confused. "Terrog, what are you talking about?"

"I am talking about this!" Terrog says, and then he points a finger at Max Mayhem and fires a powerful orange beam right at Max Mayhem's hand.

"Arrghh!" Max Mayhem yells, and then I hear TINGING, like fragments of metal hitting rock. "What are you doing?" Max Mayhem says, shaking his smoking hand. Then, he looks at his finger and his eyes go wide. "Th-The gold ring! Where is the gold ring?"

That's when I notice Terrog looks different. He's no longer transparent, but… solid?

"The ring—my prison—is destroyed!" Terrog says, his eyes wide with glee. "You may be the smartest human in the world, but you are also the most naïve. Did you really think I needed all of this Meta energy to heal you? You fool! I needed this Meta energy for one reason and one reason only—to sever my bond to my ring!"

"No!" Max Mayhem yells. "I-I am your master! You must obey me! You must heal me!"

"Oh, do not worry," Terrog says. "I still plan to

honor our contract. I promised to relieve you of your illness once and for all and relieve you I will!"

Then, Terrog fires another energy beam at Max Mayhem's chest that tears right through his armor.

"Ugh!" Max Mayhem grunts, grabbing his chest.

Then, he falls to the ground face first.

"Y-You killed him!" Selfie shouts.

"Correction," Terrog says, "I granted his wish with my new Meta powers. He did not specify how he wanted to be relieved of his ailment, so instant death seemed like an adequate solution. Now, who is next?"

The Minotaurs look at one another and take off, dumping Selfie to the ground. Now, it's the three of us.

"So," Terrog says, looking into my eyes, "you are the one who trapped my brother inside his own ring?"

"Yeah," I say, "and I'd do the same to you if I had the chance."

I try standing up, but I'm a little dizzy and my legs wobble. But I've got to get my act together or Terrog will destroy us.

"Unfortunately, that chance has passed," Terrog says. "Now that I am free from my ring, imprisonment is no longer possible. The only master I serve now is myself. And with all of this power, I can shape the universe as I see fit, which starts by destroying you."

"Not on my watch, bucko!" comes Selfie's voice.

And then she steps between us holding her phone.

"Selfie, no!" I shout, but it's too late.

Her phone flashes and I turn away as the bright, white flash fills the room. And that's when my eyes land on someone I completely forgot about.

Siphon!

He's still floating over the now-empty Meta pool, yet I can still see Meta energy flowing out of his body to the Overworld. But how? Then, it hits me. When Terrog absorbed all of the Meta energy from the pool, he must have forgotten to grab the Meta energy Siphon had already collected! Which means Siphon still has power!

But the question is, do I?

"That was a mistake, child," Terrog says to Selfie. "A tragic mistake."

I've got to act fast, so I dig deep and reach out to duplicate Siphon's power! C'mon, there's got to be something left inside of me! A spark. An ember. But at first, I feel nothing. And then, suddenly, I feel a small warmth inside my chest, and then it expands, spreading outwards, coursing through my veins. Yes!

But strangely, I don't have the feel of any specific power. It's kind of like a mash-up of powers—kind of like… Meta-Man!

Well, here goes nothing.

"Hey, ugly!" I call out. "Eyes on me!" And then I channel the Meta energy behind my eyes and release a concentrated force of Heat Vision right at Terrog's chest.

FWOOM!

The blast catches Terrog full-on, sending him flying

across the chamber until he SMASHES into the wall.

I-I did it!

But he'll be back, so I grab Selfie's shoulder.

"You've got to get out of here!" I say. "I don't know how long I can hold him off!"

"No way," she says, shaking her head. "You came back for me and I'm not leaving you. We're sticking together to the end. You stopped Beezle and we can stop him too."

Beezle. For some reason, her mentioning Beezle's name triggers something. When I first researched Beezle, I remember the Meta Monitor saying something about Beezle only being able to use his powers if he has a human guide to steer it. So, that must mean…

"I've got it!" I blurt out.

"Got what?" she says.

"Terrog destroyed his ring," I say quickly, "which is the source of all of his Magic. So, with his ring destroyed he might be free, but he can't have a human master anymore, which means he's no longer able to use his Magic. So, if we can strip him of the Meta energy he's got now, he just might be powerless. I don't know, it's a theory, but it's all I've got."

"It's not bad," she says, "In fact, it might just work."

"And you know what else?" I say. "His ring may be destroyed, but someone else's isn't."

"Rasp's ring," Selfie says. And then she points over my head and yells, "Incoming!"

"Enough!" Terrog shouts, flying towards us. "You are holding me back from my destiny!"

Then, he rears back and unleashes a powerful bolt of orange lightning, but I borrow a trick from Zen and block it with a Meta forcefield. Except he's so powerful I can barely hold it back! He's... pushing hard! Gonna... break my shield!

Then, out of the corner of my eye, I see Selfie sneak away and bend over Max Mayhem's body. She's exposed! Is she crazy? I try extending my shield to cover her, but she's too far out. What is she doing? And then—

"I've got it!" she says suddenly, holding up the bronze ring! "Epic, catch!"

"Unhand my brother!" Terrog commands, and then he blasts Selfie with an energy beam just as she tosses the ring!

"Auuugghh!" she screams, falling to the ground.

"Selfie!" I call out, but it's too late. Then, I hear something PING by my feet. It's Rasp's ring!

Every fiber of my being wants to help Selfie, but I can't do it without dealing with Terrog first. So, I scoop up the bronze ring and jam it onto my finger.

"Rasp!" I command. "I summon you immediately!"

Just then, the gray Djinn swirls out of his ring, looking none too pleased.

"I thought you were going to knock?" Rasp remarks, yawning and stretching his arms. And then he sees his brother. "Ah, Terrog, failing at world domination I see."

"Do not help him, brother," Terrog says. "I can free you from your prison just as I have freed myself."

"Don't listen to him!" I say. "I'm your master!"

"Look at him ordering you around," Terrog says. "Wouldn't you rather be your own master? Like me?"

"Of course," Rasp says, furrowing his brow. "Except you had already promised to free me at the same time you freed yourself. Yet, it appears one of us is free and the other is not."

"I was getting to that, dear brother," Terrog says quickly. "But as you can see, I had to deal with this inconvenience first."

"It seems that you are not dealing with it well," Rasp says, crossing his arms. "I sense you are all out of Magic. Funny, I never thought you, the powerful Terrog, would be stymied by a mere human child?"

Okay, clearly, they don't get along as well as I thought. And based on what Rasp is saying, it looks like Terrog went back on his word to free Rasp from his bronze ring. This might be my chance.

But then I realize something. If I play this right, I may be able to kill two birds with one stone. I may be able to get rid of Terrog's Meta energy *and* stop Tormentus all at the same time!

"Rasp!" I command. "I am your master and I'm making my third and final wish. I want you to remove all of Terrog's Meta energy and send it back to its rightful owners in the Overworld. All of it, every last iota! Now!"

"Oh, my brave master," Rasp says, sneering at Terrog, "nothing would give me more pleasure."

"Brother, please!" Terrog says in desperation. "You do not have to do this! You do not have to be a slave!"

"I would rather be a slave, brother," Rasp says, "than a magicless traitor. My heroic master, your wish… is fulfilled!"

Then, Rasp waves his arms.

"No!" Terrog screams as his body starts to shimmer. First, his eyes shine bright orange, and then Meta energy starts pouring out of his mouth and ears, engulfing him in a huge ball of orange energy. The ball grows and pulsates, slowly at first, and then faster and faster, like a ticking time bomb.

Holy cow! I throw up a shield around Selfie and me when—

KABOOM!

FLOOOSHH!

There's a huge explosion and nearly all of the Meta energy vanishes through the ceiling except for a concentrated burst that hits my body. I feel it coursing through my veins again, and when I look to where Terrog was floating, he's gone!

"I-Is he…," I stammer.

"I hope so," Rasp says, buffing his nails. "And good riddance. I grew tired of his empty promises. And speaking of endings, I have now granted all three of your wishes, which means our contract has come to an end."

"Wait, what?" I say, realizing I've just used my final wish so we can't go home. "Um, can't you grant me an extra wish? You know, for being a loyal customer?"

"I am afraid not," Rasp says. "Three is all you get."

Maybe for me, but I look down at Selfie. She's still down for the count but if I give the ring to her…

"I know what you are thinking," Rasp says. "But I will be long gone before she is conscious."

"Long gone?" I say. "Where are you going?"

"Out," he says. "Remember when I told you Magic reacts differently in the Underworld? While inside my ring, Beezle discovered a way for me to exit this infernal place. He also wishes you a long and excruciating life here. Oh, and I suggest you prepare for your next visitor. I imagine he will not be as happy to see you as I am to leave you."

My… next visitor?

"Take care, little master," Rasp says. And then he disappears in a puff of gray smoke, along with the bronze ring on my finger!

Darn it! How did he do that?

But then—

"You!" comes a booming voice from behind, making me jump out of my skin.

And when I turn around, I'm staring at Tormentus!

Just. Freaking. Wonderful.

"You're responsible for this?" he asks, his face furious. "You drained my pool of Meta energy? You brought me back here?"

Holy cow. If he's here, then I did it! I eliminated Tormentus' Meta energy supply! That's when I notice Siphon is gone! He must have faded away, just like K'ami!

"Um, yeah," I say. "It was me, but I also saved you from your business partner. Max Mayhem was going to pull one over on you. He said he was going to destroy you and rule over both the Overworld and Underworld. So, I guess I kind of did you a favor."

"Is that so?" Tormentus says, poking Max Mayhem's body with his foot. "I am not surprised. I never trusted his intentions. You may have foiled my plan, but as you are now trapped here, that is at least a small consolation. I'm looking forward to our time together. Your eternal torture will provide me with endless joy."

Eternal torture? I swallow hard.

Clearly, this isn't good for me, but I need to get Selfie home—no matter the cost.

"Look," I say. "I'll do anything if you send her home."

"Anything?" Tormentus says, raising an eyebrow. "Of your own free will?"

"You heard me," I say firmly, standing tall.

"No way!" comes a voice.

And when we turn, Selfie is standing there.

"I can't let you do that," she says. And then she raises her phone and there's a bright flash.

EPILOGUE

I LEARN MY LESSON

"Epic?"

That voice. It's… a girl's voice. Familiar. Soothing.

"Epic, can you hear me?"

I blink my eyes open and see Selfie leaning over me, frantically waving her hand in front of my face.

"Am I dead?" I ask.

"No," she says, "you're in the Combat Room."

"Oh," I say. "Well, that's good."

As Selfie leans back, my vision clears, and I see people gathered around me. There's Mom, Grace, Shadow Hawk, Pinball, and Night Owl. And then something warm and wet brushes my cheek and I turn to see Dog-Gone's big head over the side of my bed.

"Hey, boy," I say, scratching him between the ears. "It's great to see you." Then, I realize something and sit up. "Wait a minute! If we're here, then we're—"

"—no longer in the Underworld," Selfie says with a smile. "Thanks to this." Then, she holds up her magic phone.

"But… how?" I ask, feeling a little foggy. I don't remember much, except, that purple face! "Tormentus!"

"Oh, I took care of him," Selfie says.

"You did what?" I say.

"Yep," she says. "I hypnotized Tormentus into returning us home. I'm sorry you got hypnotized too, but I wasn't about to let you do something stupid just to get me home, although I appreciate the thought."

That's right! I was just about to trade anything—including my eternal soul—to get Selfie home. Boy, I'm glad that didn't happen. But I guess that explains why I'm feeling so woozy.

"Gee, thanks for saving me," I say to her.

"Well," she says with a smile, "I couldn't live with myself if I just left you down there. You're kind of, well, important to me."

Suddenly, my cheeks feel warm when—

"Speaking of doing something stupid…," Mom says, crossing her arms.

Uh oh. She doesn't look so happy with me. And I'm not surprised because I didn't exactly tell her the truth.

"Why on Earth did you take the bronze Ring of Suffering and go into the Underworld without us?" she asks. "You told me you were going upstairs to be with your friends. And then, minutes later, you and Selfie suddenly appeared right here in the Combat Room having had this crazy adventure."

Wait, what?

Only minutes later? How is that possible?

But then I remember what Max Mayhem told me. He said that time moves much slower in the Underworld. So, even though it felt like I was down there forever, to Mom it probably seemed like I was gone for a few minutes!

"I'm really sorry about that," I say. "I made a big mistake. And by the time I realized it, it was too late."

"I'm just glad you're okay," Mom says.

"And saved the day!" Pinball says. "We were about to have a final showdown with Tormentus and his army when suddenly, they all vanished into thin air! If you didn't do what you did when you did it, I think we'd all be goners by now."

"Well," I say, looking at Selfie. "I didn't do it alone. I had a great partner."

"Aw, shucks," Selfie says, turning red. "We make a great team."

A great team? Wait a minute! I quickly scan the room and realize all of the other beds are empty.

"Where's Dad?" I ask. "What happened to him?"

"I'm right here," Dad says from the doorway.

And when I turn, I see Dad, Blue Bolt, Master Mime, Makeshift, Skunk Girl, Zen, and the rest of the Rising

Suns walking towards us. Then, TechnocRat comes flying through on his jetpack and lands on my bedrail.

"Well, I have some very good news," TechnocRat says. "Whatever you did worked like a charm. I ran a bunch of tests and it's confirmed. Everyone has their Meta powers back."

"Seriously?" I ask, my voice rising with excitement.

"Seriously," Dad says, putting his arm around Mom. "I'll be able to lift the kitchen table while mopping again."

"Very funny," Mom says. "Instead, why don't you help TechnocRat put Lockdown back on Earth?"

"Oh, yuck!" Grace says suddenly, pinching her nose. "What's that smell?"

"It's glorious me!" Skunk Girl says, throwing her arms wide. "I'm back, baby!"

"Fabulous," Grace says with a frown.

"On behalf of the team, we want to thank you," Dad says, putting his hand on my shoulder. "What you did was truly heroic and brave. Hopefully, the threat is over."

I smile back and wonder if it really is over. I mean, so much happened down there it's hard to process it all. I never expected to see K'ami or face the Orb of Oblivion again. And who knows where Rasp went? Not to mention Tormentus. He's still down there, and when Selfie's hypnosis wears off there's no telling what he'll do next.

I guess that's the drawback of being a superhero, nothing ever really ends, does it?

"Well, at least there's one good thing to come out of

this mess," Grace says.

"Yeah, what's that?" I ask.

"Well," Grace says, "when you came back hypnotized, I took the opportunity to plant a secret trigger word inside your brain that'll make you cluck like a chicken on command."

"What?" I say. "You didn't!"

"Didn't I?" Grace says with a shrug and a smile. "Well, I guess we'll find out soon enough, won't we?"

My blood starts to boil, and when I look over at Mom she says—

"She's just kidding. And don't worry, I checked."

"Busted!" Grace says, giving me a big hug. "I'm just glad you're back. Now don't go running off like that again, you lunkhead."

"Believe me, I learned my lesson this time," I say, hugging her back.

"I've got an idea," Mom says.

"What's that?" I ask.

"How about we all celebrate with some Frosted Letter-Bites cereal?"

"That sounds perfect!" I say.

And as I look at all of the smiling faces around me and think about everything I almost gave up to Tormentus, I realize there's nowhere else I'd rather be.

Epic Zero 9

EPIC ZERO 10 IS AVAILABLE NOW!

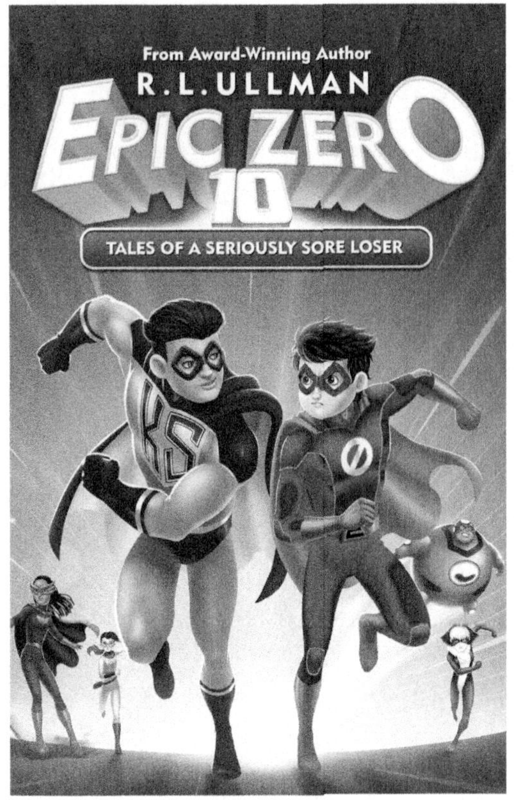

Elliott isn't the most powerful Meta kid around! First, he meets Kid Supreme, a hero whose power is exceeded only by his ego. Then, Harmony bursts onto the scene. She'll do whatever it takes to bring world peace—including exterminating villains! Everyone loves Harmony, but when Elliott investigates her mysterious past he realizes the world is in grave danger! But will anyone listen?

Get EPIC ZERO 10:

Tales of a Seriously Sore Loser today!

YOU CAN MAKE A BIG DIFFERENCE

Calling all heroes! I need your help to get Epic Zero Books 7-9 in front of more readers.

Reviews are extremely helpful in getting attention for my books. I wish I had the marketing muscle of the major publishers, but instead, I have something far more valuable, loyal readers, just like you! Your generosity in providing an honest review will help bring this book to the attention of more readers.

So, if you've enjoyed this book, I would be very grateful if you could spare a minute to leave a review on the book's Amazon page. Thanks for your support!

Stay Epic!

R.L. Ullman

META POWERS GLOSSARY

FROM THE META MONITOR:

There are nine known Meta power classifications. These classifications have been established to simplify Meta identification and provide a quick framework to understand a Meta's potential powers and capabilities. **Note:** Metas can possess powers in more than one classification. In addition, Metas can evolve over time in both the powers they express, as well as the effectiveness of their powers.

Due to the wide range of Meta abilities, superpowers have been further segmented into power levels. Power levels differ across Meta power classifications. In general, the following power levels have been established:

- Meta 0: Displays no Meta power.
- Meta 1: Displays limited Meta power.
- Meta 2: Displays considerable Meta power.
- Meta 3: Displays extreme Meta power.

The following is a brief overview of the nine Meta power classifications.

ENERGY MANIPULATION:

Energy Manipulation is the ability to generate, shape, or act as a conduit, for various forms of energy. Energy Manipulators can control energy by focusing or redirecting energy towards a specific target or shaping/reshaping energy for a specific task. Energy Manipulators are often impervious to the forms of energy they can manipulate.

Examples of the types of energies utilized by Energy Manipulators include, but are not limited to:

- Atomic
- Chemical
- Cosmic
- Electricity
- Gravity
- Heat
- Light
- Magnetic
- Sound
- Space
- Time

Note: the fundamental difference between an Energy Manipulator and a Meta-morph with Energy Manipulation capability is that an Energy Manipulator does not change their physical, molecular state to either generate or transfer energy (see META-MORPH).

FLIGHT:
Flight is the ability to fly, glide, or levitate above the Earth's surface without the use of an external source (e.g. jetpack). Flight can be accomplished through a variety of methods, these include, but are not limited to:

- Reversing the forces of gravity
- Riding air currents
- Using planetary magnetic fields
- Wings

Metas exhibiting Flight can range from barely sustaining flight a few feet off the ground to reaching the far limits of outer space.

Often, Metas with Flight ability also display the complementary ability of Super-Speed. However, it can be difficult to decipher if Super-Speed is a Meta power in its own right or is simply a function of combining the Meta's Flight ability with the Earth's natural gravitational force.

MAGIC:
Magic is the ability to display a wide variety of Meta abilities by channeling the powers of a secondary magical or mystical source. Known secondary sources of Magic powers include, but are not limited to:

- Alien lifeforms
- Dark arts
- Demonic forces
- Departed souls
- Mystical spirits

Typically, the forces of Magic are channeled through an enchanted object. Known magical, enchanted objects include:

- Amulets
- Books
- Cloaks
- Gemstones
- Wands

- Weapons

Some Magicians can transport themselves into the mystical realm of their magical source. They may also have the ability to transport others into and out of these realms as well.

Note: the fundamental difference between a Magician and an Energy Manipulator is that a Magician typically channels their powers from a mystical source that likely requires the use of an enchanted object to express these powers (see ENERGY MANIPULATOR).

META MANIPULATION:
Meta Manipulation is the ability to duplicate or negate the Meta powers of others. Meta Manipulation is a rare Meta power and can be extremely dangerous if the Meta Manipulator is capable of manipulating the powers of multiple Metas at one time. Meta Manipulators who can manipulate the powers of several Metas at once have been observed to reach Meta 4 power levels.

Based on the unique powers of the Meta Manipulator, it is hypothesized that other abilities could include altering or controlling the powers of others. Despite their tremendous abilities, Meta Manipulators are often unable to generate powers of their own and are limited to manipulating the powers of others. When not utilizing their abilities, Meta Manipulators may be vulnerable to attack.

Note: It has been observed that a Meta Manipulator requires close physical proximity to a Meta target to fully manipulate their power. When fighting a Meta

Manipulator, it is advised to stay at a reasonable distance and to attack from long range. Meta Manipulators have been observed manipulating the powers of others up to 100 yards away.

META-MORPH:

Meta-morph is the ability to display a wide variety of Meta abilities by "morphing" all, or part, of one's physical form from one state into another. There are two sub-types of Meta-morphs:

- Physical
- Molecular

Physical morphing occurs when a Meta-morph transforms their physical state to express their powers. Physical Meta-morphs typically maintain their human physiology while exhibiting their powers (with the exception of Shapeshifters). Types of Physical morphing include, but are not limited to:

- Invisibility
- Malleability (elasticity/plasticity)
- Physical by-products (silk, toxins, etc…)
- Shapeshifting
- Size changes (larger or smaller)

Molecular morphing occurs when a Meta-morph transforms their molecular state from a normal physical state to a non-physical state to express their powers. Types of Molecular morphing include, but are not limited to:

- Fire
- Ice
- Rock
- Sand
- Steel
- Water

Note: Because Meta-morphs can display abilities that mimic all other Meta power classifications, it can be difficult to properly identify a Meta-morph upon the first encounter. However, it is critical to carefully observe how their powers manifest, and, if it is through Physical or Molecular morphing, you can be certain you are dealing with a Meta-morph.

PSYCHIC:

Psychic is the ability to use one's mind as a weapon. There are two sub-types of Psychics:

- Telepaths
- Telekinetics

Telepathy is the ability to read and influence the thoughts of others. While Telepaths often do not appear to be physically intimidating, their power to penetrate minds can often result in more devastating damage than a physical assault.

Telekinesis is the ability to manipulate physical objects with one's mind. Telekinetics can often move objects with their mind that are much heavier than they could move physically. Many Telekinetics can also make objects move at very high speeds.

Note: Psychics are known to strike from long distance, and, in a fight, it is advised to incapacitate them as quickly as possible. Psychics often become physically drained from the extended use of their powers.

SUPER-INTELLIGENCE:

Super-Intelligence is the ability to display levels of intelligence above standard genius intellect. Super-Intelligence can manifest in many forms, including, but not limited to:

- Superior analytical ability
- Superior information synthesizing
- Superior learning capacity
- Superior reasoning skills

Note: Super-Intellects continuously push the envelope in the fields of technology, engineering, and weapons development. Super-Intellects are known to invent new approaches to accomplish previously impossible tasks. When dealing with a Super-Intellect, you should be mentally prepared to face challenges that have never been encountered before. In addition, Super-Intellects can come in all shapes and sizes. The most advanced Super-Intellects have originated from non-human creatures.

SUPER-SPEED:

Super-Speed is the ability to display movement at remarkable physical speeds above standard levels of speed. Metas with Super-Speed often exhibit complementary abilities to movement that include, but are not limited to:

- Enhanced endurance
- Phasing through solid objects
- Super-fast reflexes
- Time travel

Note: Metas with Super-Speed often have an equally super metabolism, burning thousands of calories per minute, and requiring them to eat many extra meals a day to maintain consistent energy levels. It has been observed that Metas exhibiting Super-Speed are quick thinkers, making it difficult to keep up with their thought process.

SUPER-STRENGTH:

Super-Strength is the ability to utilize muscles to display remarkable levels of physical strength above expected levels of strength. Metas with Super-Strength can lift or push objects that are well beyond the capability of an average member of their species. Metas exhibiting Super-Strength can range from lifting objects twice their weight to incalculable levels of strength allowing for the movement of planets.

Metas with Super-Strength often exhibit complementary abilities to strength that include, but are not limited to:

- Earthquake generation through stomping
- Enhanced jumping
- Invulnerability
- Shockwave generation through clapping

Note: Metas with Super-Strength may not always possess this strength evenly. Metas with Super-Strength have been observed to demonstrate powers in only one arm or leg.

META PROFILE CHARACTERISTICS

FROM THE META MONITOR:
In addition to having a strong working knowledge of a Meta's powers and capabilities, it is also imperative to understand the key characteristics that form the core of their character. When facing or teaming up with Metas, understanding their key characteristics will help you gain deeper insight into their mentality and strategic potential.

What follows is a brief explanation of the five key characteristics you should become familiar with. **Note**: the data that appears in each Meta profile has been compiled from live field activity.

COMBAT:
The ability to defeat a foe in hand-to-hand combat.

DURABILITY:
The ability to withstand significant wear, pressure, or damage.

LEADERSHIP:
The ability to lead a team of disparate personalities and powers to victory.

STRATEGY:
The ability to find, and successfully exploit, a foe's weakness.

WILLPOWER:
The ability to persevere despite seemingly insurmountable odds.

GET THE EPIC ZERO CHARACTER GUIDE!

VISIT rlullman.com

FOR EVEN MORE EPIC FUN!

Get a FREE copy of EPIC ZERO Extra!

Check Out EPIC ZERO Merchandise!

T-shirts & More!

Get FREE EPIC ZERO Printables!

Create Meta Profiles & More!

Meta Profile

Name: Height:
Race: Weight:
Status: Eyes/Hair:

META

Observed Characteristics
Combat
Durability Leadership
Strategy Willpower

OTHER SERIES BY R.L. ULLMAN

UNLEGENDARY DRAGON SERIES

MONSTER PROBLEMS SERIES

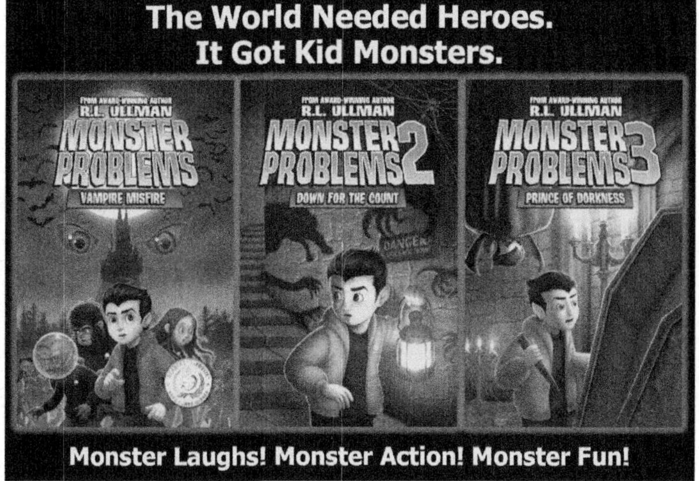

ABOUT THE AUTHOR

R.L. Ullman is the bestselling, award-winning author of books for young readers, including the EPIC ZERO® series, the UNLEGENDARY DRAGON™ series, the MONSTER PROBLEMS series, and the PETUNIA THE UNICORN™ series. He writes the kinds of books he loved reading as a kid, featuring fast-paced action, laugh-out-loud humor, and lots of heart. R.L. lives in Connecticut with his laptop and family. Visit rlullman.com for signed books, special editions, book merchandise, and more!

CONNECT WITH R.L.

Join R.L.'s mailing list at rlullman.com for discounts, exclusive offers, free content, and notifications about new releases! See what R.L. is working on at r.l.ullman_author on Instagram and @authorRLUllman on Facebook.

ACKNOWLEDGMENTS

I couldn't have written these books without the support of my own team of Meta heroes. I would like to thank my wife, Lynn (a.k.a. Mrs. Marvelous); my son Matthew (a.k.a. Captain Creativity); and my daughter Olivia (a.k.a. Ms. Positivity). Also, a huge thanks to the many readers who have connected with Elliott and his epic universe!

Printed in Great Britain
by Amazon